ALL THE DEAD GIRLS

GRAVEYARD FALLS

ALL THE DEAD GIRLS

GRAVEYARD FALLS

RITA HERRON

Montlake
Romance

Published by Montlake Romance, Seattle

www.apub.com

Amazon, the Amazon logo, and Montlake Romance are trademarks of Amazon.com, Inc., or its affiliates.

ISBN-13: 9781503939134
ISBN-10: 1503939138

Cover design by Marc J. Cohen

Printed in the United States of America

To my amazing son, Dr. Harrison Adam Herron—
congratulations on making it through med school.
You made Mom proud!

PROLOGUE

She had to run away.

JJ Jones had been planning it ever since she'd learned what would happen on her fifteenth birthday.

She would become a substitute for her foster father's wife.

Her birthday was tomorrow.

Her stomach roiled at the thought, and she slipped from bed, retrieved her backpack, and then tiptoed over to Sunny's bed.

Sunny was two months younger than JJ, but she was small for her age, frail, and terrified of her own shadow.

She gently shook her foster sister. "Wake up, Sunny, it's time."

Sunny groaned and rolled to her side.

"Come on, we have to go now," she whispered.

If Herman caught them, she'd be punished.

He liked to punish.

Sunny's eyes slowly opened, confusion clouding them. "What? I was dreaming."

Probably of a better place to live. Clean clothes. A real family.

JJ had given up on those things a long time ago.

"It was Christmas, and we got to go to a party," Sunny said.

She pressed her finger to Sunny's lips. Sunny was always dreaming about parties or going to Disney World or to a beach.

JJ had her own dreams—or she used to, anyway. Dreams of a family, a nice house. Friends. Someone to love her.

Maybe she could save Sunny from becoming as jaded as she was. "Remember, I told you about my birthday. I won't let that man touch me. We have to go *now*."

Fear flickered across Sunny's face, but she nodded, threw her covers aside, and dropped to the floor. They'd packed their backpacks before they'd gone to bed and slept in their clothes. Not that they had many clothes. Herman Otter and his wife, Frances, used the money the state gave them to support their booze habit.

JJ grabbed her jacket and shrugged it on, then tossed Sunny hers.

The wind howled outside, thunder rumbling. JJ's adrenaline kicked in. They had to get to the bus station before the storm hit.

She jammed her feet into her boots, and Sunny did the same. They threw their backpacks over their shoulders, crept to the window, shoved it open, and crawled outside. The air was refreshing compared to the stench of the dirty house and the smell of liquor.

JJ had repeatedly phoned the social worker for help, but the woman had such a big caseload that she ignored JJ's calls. JJ didn't know what else to do but run.

Sunny's legs buckled as she hit the ground, and JJ steadied her. A noise echoed from inside. JJ froze, terrified he'd woken up.

She motioned toward the woods in back, then mimed the word "Go." Sunny nodded, and they ran toward the woods. JJ had stolen a flashlight from the house, and once they were far enough away not to be seen, she flicked it on and used it to light their path.

The coach's son had promised to meet them at eleven. She hurried Sunny along, wincing as the bitter wind ripped through her and raindrops began to pelt them. The pennies in the jar in Sunny's back-pack jingled as she walked.

Sunny's father had told her that the pennies were lucky, so Sunny collected every one she could find. So far they hadn't brought her any luck, though.

She and Sunny yanked their jacket hoods over their heads, then picked up their pace, slogging through the woods as fast as they could.

A half mile from the house, she cut to the right toward the street, and they jogged toward the Dairy Mart where she was supposed to meet the boy. The lights were off inside the ice-cream shop, and the parking lot was empty.

JJ ushered Sunny beneath the awning to the side of the building, and they huddled in the rain, waiting.

Seconds dragged into minutes. Minutes bled into an hour. Disappointment and despair tugged at JJ.

"He's not coming," Sunny said, shivering.

JJ rubbed Sunny's arms to warm her. A chill had wormed its way through JJ, too, and her teeth were chattering. She hated to admit it, but Sunny was right.

Lightning zigzagged across the sky, crackling as if it had struck a tree. Rain turned to hail, the icy pellets pounding the concrete.

They couldn't stay here all night. Sooner or later the local cops might show, or someone would see them.

Then they'd take them back to *him*.

No way would JJ let that happen.

She grabbed Sunny's hand. "We're not giving up. We'll walk."

Sunny dug her heels in. "But it's miles. I'm tired and cold."

"Then let's hurry." Sunny balked, but JJ shook her by the shoulders. "Listen to me, you'll be fifteen in two months. Then he won't count you as a kid anymore either, and he'll want you."

Sunny's face paled, ghostly white against the dark, gloomy night. "Where are we going?" Sunny whispered.

"My grandmother's. She lives in Nashville."

"I thought she didn't want you," Sunny said in a choked voice.

JJ's heart clenched in pain. Sunny was right. Her grandmother hadn't wanted her as a baby. But JJ refused to let that stop her from finding a better place to live. A safe one.

"She was sick when I was born," JJ said. "When she hears what Herman planned to do to me, she'll let us stay." At least she hoped she would. Otherwise, she had nowhere to turn.

"What if she lets you stay but won't keep me?" Sunny cried.

The fear in Sunny's voice tore at JJ. She had no idea how her grandmother would react. Fifteen years ago, she'd told social services she couldn't raise an infant. Would she feel the same about a teenager?

No, JJ would convince her she could take care of herself. All she and Sunny needed was a roof over their heads and for people to leave them alone.

"Don't worry." She gave Sunny a reassuring look. "I promised to take care of you, and I will."

Sunny wiped at a tear, then gripped JJ's hand, and they headed down the street together. The country road had no streetlights, and the clouds shrouded the moon. Sunny stumbled, and JJ flicked on the flashlight again.

She guessed it was about ten miles to the bus station. Thunder rumbled and the rain beat down, pounding the ground and soaking them to the core. Mud and water seeped into JJ's shoes, adding to the chill.

A half hour later, Sunny complained that her legs were hurting. Occasionally a car passed, but JJ would quickly turn off the flashlight, and they'd duck behind some trees to hide.

Another mile and despair threatened. Sunny tripped over a tree stump, collapsed to the ground, and cried out in pain. "I hurt my ankle."

JJ wiped rain from her face, willing herself not to cry, too. They had a long way to go. She shined her light on Sunny's foot. It was turning red and swelling.

Panic streaked through her. What were they going to do?

The sound of an engine made her pause, and she pivoted. A truck was coming toward them. The headlights nearly blinded her, and she slid an arm around Sunny's waist to help her stand.

"I can't put weight on it," Sunny whined.

Brakes screeched. The driver must have seen them. He slowed, gears grinding as he veered to the side of the road. The passenger door opened with a groan. JJ squinted through the bright lights.

"You girls need help?"

She couldn't make out the man's features, but a girl sat beside him. And there was someone else . . .

JJ's lungs squeezed. Surprise filled her at the familiar face.

Thunder rumbled, startling Sunny. JJ helped her up, pushed Sunny into the cab first, and then hauled herself onto the seat.

As she closed the door, JJ turned to see who the man was, but it was so dark inside his face was shadowed. His clothes smelled, though, like some kind of men's cologne. A cologne she'd smelled before . . .

"I'm sorry," the girl said in a low voice.

JJ frowned. What was she sorry for?

A second later, the man shoved a rag over JJ's mouth and nose, and the world swirled to black.

CHAPTER ONE

Fifteen years later—Graveyard Falls, Tennessee

No one in Graveyard Falls knew the real reason Sheriff Ian Kimball had moved from Sweetwater to this town. Hopefully, no one ever would.

None of that mattered, though.

He had a real mess on his hands.

Just a year ago, a serial killer had stalked the town. A sadist, nicknamed the Butcher, who'd carved women's faces up and marked them with claw marks that resembled talons.

That case had been spawned by the movie being made about the previous Bride Killer and Thorn Ripper murders—a story based on a true-crime book written by Josie DuKane, the daughter of a local resident.

With those cases solved, some locals had moved away as soon as they could find jobs and other homes. But others who'd grown up in these foothills believed that good existed here. They'd fought the gossip and rumors that evil was bred in these mountains, that you could hear the whisper of it in the wind.

But as he drove toward the trailer park to meet one of his deputies, a sick feeling seized his gut. Dammit.

Their strength and fortitude had given him hope that the town would survive. Seeing people work together to help each other and overcome obstacles raised his admiration for the human spirit. It made him want to protect them.

No one had ever needed him before. His family . . . well, he wouldn't go there. They'd let him down, and he'd let them down.

The people in Graveyard Falls and the surrounding county depended on him. He wouldn't make them regret it.

His gaze swept the terrain as he turned on the mountain road. The F-3 tornado that had hit thirty-six hours ago was just too damn much. It was almost like the town was cursed.

The nearly two-hundred-mile-per-hour winds and flooding had swept over the Southeast, striking three counties, including Graveyard Falls—and Sweetwater, where he'd grown up—with a funnel cloud that had ripped up trees by their roots and flung houses and cars as if they were ping-pong balls. The devastating damage had left the town picking up the broken pieces of their homes and shattered lives.

His tires churned over gravel, and he swung left to dodge broken branches, then parked at the edge of the trailer park.

One of his deputies, Clint Whitehorse, paced the edge of what had once been a mobile home but now looked like a mountain of twisted metal and aluminum.

Whitehorse had been with him over a year now. Although sometimes Ian felt like he didn't know the man. He was quiet and intense, but he'd grown up in these mountains and knew them inside and out.

"Shit, I can't believe this." Deputy Whitehorse removed his hat and rubbed sweat from his forehead. "Just when the dust settled from that Butcher case, now this storm."

Ian's boots dug into the muddy earth as he assessed the damage.

Metal, glass, household items, clothing, underwear, lamps, kitchen utensils, dishes, linens, broken furniture, and children's toys were scattered across miles of soggy soil. Ancient oaks and pines were split in two, ripped from the ground, and branches and limbs that had once been large and sturdy lay in piles like kindling.

Ian had already walked the town square. Most of the businesses and residents in the city limits had fared better than those in the outskirts, but the Falls Inn had lost its roof, a live oak had fallen through the kitchen at Cocoa's Café, and numerous homes had flooded.

Ian had caught a couple of scam artists trying to rip people off with repairs, but he'd turned folks on to a couple of reputable renovation experts, and the neighbors had given him a deluge of casseroles for it.

The women's club from the Methodist church had designated one of their basements as a lost-and-found where items retrieved in the debris could be recovered. The Baptist church had donated blankets, quilts, housewares, and clothing.

"How many casualties?" Ian asked.

"Three so far," the deputy said grimly. "A woman trying to get home to her kids was struck by a tree when it crashed into her VW."

Sympathy welled inside Ian. "Jesus, poor family." Now those kids would grow up without a mama.

Deputy Whitehorse pushed his ponytail over his shoulder. "Ninety-year-old Marvin Trullet tried to save his chickens and got thrown against his tractor on the way to the barn. He died instantly."

"If only people had heeded the warnings we issued," Ian said, hating to hear about the old man. "Who else?"

"Edna Mae, elderly woman in the trailer on the end. Neighbor, Rudy Pillings, said Edna Mae lost her hearing and was confined to a wheelchair. He tried to convince her to let him take her to a safe place to wait out the storm, but she refused to leave her home. Rescue workers found her dead beneath the kitchen table. She was holding a Bible, a picture of her husband, and a tin of snuff."

He pointed to where the trailer had once stood, but all Ian could make out were a few pieces of metal, broken china, a needlepoint family tree, and a damp photo album that probably held precious memories of the woman's life.

Sorrow for the families struck him, but he didn't have time to dwell on it. There was too much to do.

The Red Cross had rushed in with emergency supplies, including a blood bank collection unit to help restock the hospital, and utility companies were working around the clock to restore power.

Rescue crews had worked nonstop to help residents escape their flooded and demolished homes and uncover victims who might be trapped. The community center that had been used to stage auditions for production of the movie was now ironically being used to house the homeless.

Ian's phone buzzed. He snatched it from his hip, dread balling in his gut when he saw the name. His other deputy, a new hire, Ladd Markum. The last thirty-six hours had been nothing but bad news. "Sheriff Kimball."

"Sheriff, you need to come to Hemlock Holler."

Hemlock Holler was a desolate stretch of land by the river surrounded by hemlock trees. Rumors claimed nothing would grow on the stretch because the land was haunted.

A prison had stood on the grounds, but it had been destroyed in another flood five years ago. Seventy prisoners had died in the flood, leading locals to claim that their ghosts haunted the hills and the holler. "What's going on?"

"We've got a problem. A *big* problem." The deputy's voice cracked a notch. "The pilot from that search and rescue team called. They spotted something suspicious, so I drove over to check it out."

"And?"

"You have to see it for yourself."

"I'll be right there." Wiping sweat from his forehead, Ian disconnected, then addressed Deputy Whitehorse. "I have to go. Let me know if there are any other casualties."

Whitehorse nodded grimly. "I'll keep you posted."

Ian rushed to his police SUV, jumped in, hit the siren and lights, and sped toward the holler. Debris and tree limbs in the road slowed him, and he had to drive around a utility truck working on downed power lines, but finally he made it.

Early morning sunlight fought to find its way through the aftermath of the dark storm clouds and lost the battle, an oppressive gray clouding the sky. The deputy's vehicle was parked at an overlook on the mountain where tourists often stopped to enjoy the scenic view—or hear the so-called ghosts of the dead prisoners.

Ian swung his SUV in beside the deputy's, dragged his jacket up to ward off the chill, and hiked down the hill. Wet dirt, gravel, and rocks created a slippery path. Ian latched on to trees and broken limbs to keep from falling and careening down the embankment.

His deputy waved him toward where he stood by a patch of mangled trees that created a V shape.

A hissing sound filled the air. Ian drew his gun and searched for rattlesnakes. But the tangled weeds and brush were so thick, he couldn't see.

Deputy Markum tilted his hat to acknowledge Ian, but the man's face looked colorless, almost sickly.

Ian rubbed his hand over his bleary eyes. He was going on forty-eight hours with no sleep himself. "What is it?"

"The storm was nothing. Just look." The deputy shined his flashlight across the ground.

Ian followed the path of the light, cold engulfing him like nothing he'd ever felt before. A sea of white that resembled ghosts bobbed up and down on the surface of the flooded valley. He narrowed his eyes, trying to discern what he was seeing. The prison ghosts the locals gossiped about?

No. The white—Jesus, it was a river of thin, white, gauzy fabric. Well, at least it used to be white.

On further scrutiny, he realized the fabric was nightgowns. Gowns mired in mud, dirt, and leaves.

"What the hell?" He moved his flashlight across the murky water with a grimace. More sticks and twigs, broken branches?

No.

The truth hit him like a fist in the gut.

Bones.

The ground was covered in bones. *Human* bones. They floated in the water, protruded from the earth, clung to the white fabric, and lay scattered over the ground where the water had receded.

He swallowed back bile. Good God.

His deputy coughed. "Someone was buried here."

Ian ground his teeth. "Not someone. There are hundreds and hundreds of bones." He removed his hat and scrubbed a clammy hand through his hair. "This is a damn graveyard."

♦ ♦ ♦

Knoxville, Tennessee

Terror seized Beth Fields.

He hadn't died in the prison flood after all. He'd escaped. He was hiding out in the mountains.

She'd moved to Knoxville in a secure building to be safe, but he'd found her.

He was watching her through her bedroom window. The man who'd destroyed her life fifteen years ago. The man who'd killed her best friend.

The man who'd held her for three days and then dumped her like she was nothing but roadkill.

His face was pressed against the glass, shadowed by the darkness. She strained to see his eyes. His mouth. Something to help her identify him.

Only she couldn't distinguish his features.

A noise sounded. Loud. A car horn. Then a fire truck.

Beth jerked awake and clenched the bed covers, barely stifling a scream. God help her. She'd done everything possible to escape him and the nightmares. But nothing worked.

Every time she closed her eyes, she saw that blank face again. Felt his breath on her cheek as he pressed a knife to her throat.

His eyes pierced her through the darkness. The evil eyes of a predator. Wild and sinister—they were hollow black holes, ghostly looking.

Chest heaving for a breath, she slipped from bed and crept to the window to look out. But the face was gone.

Trembling, she ran to the living room and peeked out the windows overlooking downtown Knoxville. Nothing but the first hints of sunlight streaking the dark.

A self-deprecating chuckle rumbled in her throat. How could he be outside her window? She'd intentionally chosen an apartment on a higher floor and a building with top-notch security so no one could get in.

Especially *him*.

Shortly after the trial where her high school soccer coach who also served as the school counselor, Coach Gleason, was convicted of kidnapping her, she'd been placed in a group home. There she'd received counseling. To overcome the stigma and rumors dogging her, her therapist had encouraged her to change her name. Jane Jones had died, and she'd been reborn as Beth Fields.

Five years ago, when she'd heard Coach Gleason had escaped prison, she'd been grateful for the name change.

Hiram Vance, the executive assistant director of the criminal investigations division of the FBI, had assured her that he'd erased any paper trail to JJ, but she wore her nerves on her sleeves and saw Gleason everywhere she went. Although she'd questioned his guilt over the years, she still panicked at the thought of him hunting her down.

She blinked to clear away the nightmarish images that bombarded her. She was safe. Dammit.

She'd taken self-defense classes, learned to shoot, and joined the bureau in order to protect other girls from suffering as she had. Her specialty had become abductions, especially nonfamilial ones, and she'd honed profiling skills on the job. Immersing herself into the mindset of a killer helped her understand his motivation, his criteria for choosing his victims, and aided her in pinpointing his hunting ground.

But nothing could change the fact that she'd been a victim. That her foster sister, Sunny, had never been found.

And that the man accused of kidnapping her might want revenge for his imprisonment. That he could be searching for her.

Snippets of the past taunted her—whether they were real or figments of her imagination triggered by fear, she couldn't be certain.

She and Sunny were trapped, locked in some dark place, their hands and feet bound. They huddled together, cold and crying . . . Sunny was afraid of the dark . . . Another girl screamed from somewhere deep in the cave . . . yes, it was a cave. Water dripped, a monotonous sound that made her want to pull out her hair. Another scream. Footsteps. A knife glinted against the dark.

She called out for help but no sound came out. Then everything went blank.

When she woke up, a deadly quiet surrounded her. No water dripping. No footsteps. No crying Sunny.

Machines beeped instead . . . low voices, carts clanging . . . a sea of white coats . . . a hospital . . .

Shivering, she shut out the images. Determined to fight her demons, she yanked on running clothes, strapped her weapon in the holster, unlocked and opened the door, and stepped into the hallway.

Old fears and training kicked in as she entered the elevator, and she kept her gaze focused on the door as it opened to the lobby.

He saw the beautiful graves in his mind just as he'd dug them for the angels. He'd left each girl with a candle to chase away her fear of the dark and to light her way to heaven. He'd also given them a cross to cling to, a symbol that they'd been saved.

But the tornado and flood had destroyed the peaceful bed where they'd lain together, linking hands as they sang the praises.

A wave of sadness washed over him that their peace had been destroyed.

The sheriff had found the graveyard. He was here now.

He and his deputies would scour the floodwaters and excavate the bones. Then his people would pick them apart and analyze them with their tools and tests as if they were nothing but a science experiment.

No longer would the sweetlings lie saintly in their white gowns as he'd left them. So young and innocent. So in need of prayer and guidance.

He'd given them both.

Until the storm ravaged the area, they'd had each other.

Now a hand floated freely, a skull, a femur, the rib cage of another. They were scattered around randomly, disconnected, like a puzzle with missing pieces that needed to be put back together.

He clutched the edge of the tree where he stood, clawing at the bark so hard that blood dripped from his hand. Mesmerized as he had been when the blood had flowed from the girls, freeing them of their pain, he watched his own blood spatter the ground.

The droplets fell randomly like tears, creating a pattern on the soil. He always found a pattern in the blood spatters. This time the image looked like a face, features distorted . . .

Voices dragged him from the image, and he glanced back at the graveyard. The sheriff snapped a picture, then another and another, then knelt to examine the skull of one of the angels.

He bit down hard on his tongue to stop from shouting for the sheriff not to desecrate the girls' remains.

Tears for the lost souls slipped down his face and fell, mingling with the blood at his feet.

His work wasn't done.

Only he'd have to find a new burial ground for the others.

CHAPTER TWO

Ian cursed. The wind kicked up, swirling leaves across the terrain, and bringing the scent of damp earth and death. Graveyard Falls had earned notoriety for its ghost legends and the bizarre number of serial killers drawn to the area.

Not the kind of publicity the town wanted or needed to bring in new businesses.

Parishioners from the Holy Waters Church, the fundamentalist church his own mother belonged to, touted that the tornado was God's way of dealing with the evil as God had done with the floods in the Bible.

Gravel, sticks, and debris crunched beneath his boots as he slid down the hill. The cold floodwater seeped into his shoes, mud squishing. There were at least a dozen corpses here, maybe more.

When he'd first heard about the prison flooding five years ago, he'd been sick to his stomach. His stepfather, Coach Gleason, the man he'd known as Dad, had been locked in that prison. Most of the inmates had been trapped inside and had drowned in their cells.

The bodies of the ones with families had been sent home to be buried. The unclaimed ones were buried where the prison had stood, not far from the holler.

But two bodies hadn't been recovered from the flood—the men had escaped. A month later, one of the inmates had been caught. He'd admitted that Ian's father had made it out, but they'd parted ways quickly.

Five years had passed, and Ian had heard nothing. He had no idea if his father was dead or alive.

He hadn't given up, though. Every year he'd conducted searches of different parts of the mountain looking for him.

Memories launched him back to the horror that had ripped his family apart.

His senior year of high school, he had a nice life with his mother and stepfather in Sweetwater, Tennessee, a couple of hours from Knoxville. He was popular, athletic, and the girls liked him.

But midyear a freshman female, Kelly Cousins, a student his father counseled, committed suicide.

Rumors spread that his dad had an inappropriate relationship with her.

The gossip and accusations had destroyed the family. His mother divorced his stepfather, left Sweetwater, and moved to a neighborhood close to Graveyard Falls to escape the stigma.

Ian had defended his father and insisted on staying with him so he could graduate with his class. But those months had been hell. His dad had become sullen and depressed. Kelly's parents claimed they'd found notes Kelly had written about being in love with Ian's father. She'd also implied he'd lead her on and broken her heart.

They accused the coach of seducing her.

The kids at school had turned on Ian. Their parents didn't want their teens hanging out with him and refused to let them come to his house. His grades slipped. The girls stopped flirting with him. Instead, they acted as if they were afraid of him.

Three months later, just when he thought his dad was cleared, two girls from school disappeared. JJ Jones and Sunny Smith.

With his father already under police scrutiny over Kelly's suicide, and the fact that he'd known all the girls, the sheriff automatically focused on Coach Gleason as the key person of interest. Because he was also the school counselor, the girls would have trusted his dad and gotten in the car with him.

Ian couldn't believe the man who'd raised him like his own son would hurt anyone. His dad volunteered at school functions, donated to charities, took Ian fishing and camping, and taught him how to play soccer. He'd also instilled in Ian a respect for girls.

But Ian's opinion of his father hadn't mattered to the sheriff.

Sunny Smith had never been found. The other girl, JJ Jones, had turned up alive but traumatized and suffering from amnesia.

Judging from the bruises and cigarette burns on her arms, JJ had been abused. He'd felt sorry for her and had stepped in to defend her when some of the "it" girls had teased her about her raggedy clothes.

After that day, she'd looked at him like he was some kind of hero.

But he was nobody's hero.

He'd let her down in the worst way.

On the morning before she disappeared, she'd told him she was going to her grandmother's. Ian had agreed to give her and Sunny a lift to the bus station that night. But at the last minute his father had refused to let him have the car.

That fact had worked against his father at trial and intensified Ian's guilt over the kidnapping.

If only his father had allowed him to visit while he was in prison. If he'd just talked to Ian, maybe Ian could have helped him.

But the moment the verdict had been read, he'd completely shut Ian from his life.

The wind screeched, the water churning and washing more bones onto the bank, drawing him back to the skeletal remains at his feet.

"What do we do now?" Deputy Markum asked.

Ian surveyed the sea of bones with a grimace. "This is too big for us," he said through gritted teeth. "We need help." A rescue team to excavate the bones, investigators, the medical examiner. They'd also need a forensic anthropologist.

Knowing how the Feds operated, they'd swoop in, take over, and treat him like he was a moron.

Only, he *had* worked with two agents who were decent, Special Agents Dane Hamrick and Cal Coulter. He'd call them for help. At least they knew he was competent and respected his position in the town.

A human skull drifted through the water and landed at his feet, the hollow eyes staring up at him in horror.

This one had begun to deteriorate but not as severely as the others, as if it was a recent kill.

Anger shot through him.

Was *another* serial killer hiding out in these mountains?

Five days later—Knoxville

More nightmares.

Another morning run.

Beth was always running. Always on guard.

She quickly surveyed the street as she left her apartment. A handsome gentleman in a three-piece suit smiled at her as he emerged from the building's coffee shop.

She barely gave him a nod.

Flirting was not part of her life. Finding and tracking down criminals was what she lived for.

She specialized in abduction cases and had instigated plans to change the foster care programs to prevent other kids from getting lost or abused in the system. Better safeguards for following up on placements, more home visits, and hiring additional staff to handle the workload were part of her proposal.

Maybe one day she'd catch enough bad guys to make up for the one who'd stolen Sunny.

Through the front window of the shop, a face appeared. Dark brown hair. Scruffy beard. Wide jaw.

It was *him*.

Coach Gleason.

Fear momentarily paralyzed her as she recalled the trial. The rage in his eyes, anger aimed at her, when she'd sat silently and let the jury convict him. The bitterness in his son Ian's expression.

Ian—the only boy she'd ever had a crush on. The high school soccer star. The boy everyone had liked.

Until his father had been accused of sleeping with one student, then kidnapping Sunny and herself.

The brisk wind assaulted her as she stepped onto the sidewalk. A few pedestrians crossed the walkway to the left. A car pulled from the parking space beside the building.

No, not him.

A woman was driving.

She scanned the area, checking across the street. A man in a gray coat walked up the steps to the church.

Coach Gleason?

She started to cross at the intersection, but tires screeched, and she jolted to a stop just before a cabbie slammed into her. He rolled down the window and shook his finger at her. "Watch out, lady!"

She muttered that she was sorry and searched the street again, but the coach had disappeared, and she had no idea which direction he'd gone. Damn.

Had she imagined seeing him, or had he tracked her down?

Images of the photographs from her file taunted her. Some truck driver had found her lying in the bushes at a rest stop. Her clothes had been torn and muddy, her hair dirty, her face gaunt.

In the hospital photos, her eyes had been vacant, and she'd looked thin and lost.

Because she had been—lost in her own dark world where Sunny's cries echoed constantly.

Why she continued to torture herself by studying the file she didn't know.

Yes, you do. You want to find Sunny.

Only logic told her that her friend was dead.

She plugged her earbuds in, flipped her music to shuffle, then broke into a jog. Need to Breathe's soulful mix of country/gospel/rock music filled her ears and rejuvenated her.

Her feet pounded the sidewalk as she headed toward the river. She passed the park where mothers pushed their babies in strollers and children played, and then she jogged by the river, her gaze taking in the dreary fog over the water.

God, she envied the mothers and kids. She wanted that family, that home.

But she'd given up on it a long time ago. Not only had her past created trust issues, but her job wasn't conducive to a family life. Too many long hours. Traveling. And the danger.

She veered to the right and then ran up the hill toward Market Square. Joggers, commuters, and locals dotted the sidewalks, and the coffee shop was beginning to fill up.

Beth's cell phone buzzed on her hip. She had an hour until it was time to report to the office, but crime knew no boundaries or clock.

She quickly connected the call. "Special Agent Fields."

"Beth, it's Vance."

Beth tensed at his clipped tone. She could always tell when he was calling on a case. He didn't waste time on small talk. "What's wrong?"

"It's about you." He paused, making her stomach knot. "*Your* case."

The truth hit her like an ice bath. When she'd first joined the FBI, she'd been upfront about her past. Vance had assured her that her identity was safe. That he would alter records to keep her former name from leaking to coworkers.

"You found Coach Gleason? He's alive?"

"No." Tension vibrated over the line. "It's Sunny," he said in a low voice. "They found *her*."

Beth instinctively stroked the penny she'd made into a necklace because it reminded her of Sunny's lucky pennies. She never took it off.

"Beth?"

She steeled herself. "I'm here."

She didn't have to wait for him to tell her the news. She knew it in her heart.

Sunny was dead.

CHAPTER THREE

Beth dropped onto a park bench, leaned over, elbows on knees, and inhaled a deep breath.

"Beth?"

"I'm here," she managed to say. "You're sure it's Sunny?"

"The ME identified her body based on dental records, and the forensic anthropologist confirmed after examining the bones and comparing them to her medical records."

Beth took a moment to absorb that information. "Where was she found?"

"That's the interesting part. Graveyard Falls."

"Graveyard Falls? The town where all those serial killers were exposed?" Jesus. The town was close to the prison where Coach Gleason had been incarcerated. During the recent murders in town, she'd expected his name to pop up as a suspect.

But the deaths had indicated psychopathic behavior, which didn't fit Coach Gleason's profile.

"That's it. Apparently Sunny was buried in an area they call Hemlock Holler. The tornado that ripped through last week led to flooding and uprooted the grave. Search and rescue spotted the bones from the air."

Beth massaged her temple, desperate to make the pieces fit. How had Sunny gotten to Graveyard Falls? It was at least an hour from the rest stop where Beth had been found unconscious. That rest stop had also been a good forty-five miles from Sweetwater.

Of course, the killer could be moving around. Hell, he could have driven out of his way to leave Sunny in Graveyard Falls in order to throw police off his scent.

Around her the street grew crowded. More joggers and locals headed to work. Someone laughed. The sun had the nerve to break through the dark clouds.

How could the sun shine and people laugh when her world was falling apart?

Instead of sensing her distress, people flitted by as if nothing was wrong.

Everything was wrong. She'd always suspected Sunny hadn't survived, although in the back of her mind she had held on to hope that she'd escaped.

But Sunny was dead.

It was Beth's fault.

Vance cleared his throat. "There's something else."

The somber note to his voice reminded her that her boss was on the phone. He'd understood her need for answers but made sure she walked a tight line on the job. Fearing Coach Gleason would look for her, he'd alerted her and local police after the prison flood.

He called her name again. "Are you there?"

For fifteen years she'd wondered what had happened to Sunny, had imagined horrific torture and rape. "Yes."

"Are you okay?" he asked quietly.

She'd been asked that a thousand times during Coach's trial. No, she hadn't been okay, but she'd put on such a solemn face that some reporters had painted her as callous.

Vance had worked with her on enough cases that he saw through her tough façade and understood.

She swallowed back her emotions. She was a professional. She could handle this. "Yes. You just took me off guard. Tell me everything."

Vance sighed. "All right. According to the ME, Sunny sustained serious cuts to her wrists. They were so deep they cut to the bone, leading him to believe that she bled out." He heaved a breath. "There's more, Beth. Sunny wasn't alone."

Beth's chest clenched. "What do you mean, she wasn't alone?" The quivering voice of the other girl in the truck that night echoed in her head. She couldn't remember her face either but wondered what had happened to her.

"Hers wasn't the only body they found," he said in disgust. "There were over a dozen. The ME and forensic anthropologists are trying to piece them together and determine identities."

Beth's pulse hammered. "The bodies were all young females?"

"Yes." He paused. "The local sheriff called us for help, so Agents Coulter and Hamrick went to the scene. It took a couple of days for the crime team to do its work and for them to recover all the bones. They transported the remains to the morgue at Graveyard Falls Hospital for analysis and identification."

Beth shot to her feet, adrenaline kicking in. "I want on the case."

A heartbeat passed. "I don't think that's such a good idea. This case is too personal to you."

Damn right it was personal. "All the more reason I need to work it." Beth scanned the area, her skin prickling as more questions assailed her.

The fact that the location of the burial ground was near the prison was too coincidental not to take notice.

She needed to know the dates the girls went missing, an estimated time of death, COD, and if the victims were related.

Beth broke into a sprint, anxious to reach her apartment and get on the road. "Is there a task force in place?"

"Not yet, but we're organizing one. We're supposed to meet in Graveyard Falls day after tomorrow."

"I'll be there," Beth said.

"Beth—"

"Please, I can help. If these victims were all adolescents and killed by the same man, you need someone who specializes in missing and exploited children. You know that's my area of expertise." She'd proven herself last year when she'd tracked down a killer who targeted teenage boys for sexual trafficking.

Vance mumbled a sound of frustration. "All right, but I don't like it. Promise me that if the case gets too difficult, you'll step away."

"Of course," Beth agreed. Although there was no way in hell she'd walk away until she learned the truth about who killed Sunny. In spite of the conviction, the profiling skills she'd learned had made her question Coach Gleason's guilt.

He hadn't fit the profile. Gleason was confident, educated, socially adept, and had grown up in a loving, normal home. No signs of abuse. No record of hurting animals, violence, or drug or alcohol abuse.

Her friend deserved justice—Beth owed her that.

And if the unsub was actively abducting girls, she'd track him down and make sure he never hurt another young girl again.

Graveyard Falls

Tension knotted Ian's shoulders. It had been seven days since they'd found the bodies.

The panic was rising. The phone had been ringing off the hook with terrified locals and false leads.

And that damned reporter Corbin Michaels—the same bastard who'd covered the other serial cases in Graveyard Falls—had pounced on the news of the graveyard of bones and had already dubbed the case the Boneyard Killer.

Some hack who believed the town was cursed had started a damn blog post about weird cities in the Southeast, featuring Graveyard Falls and the legends of ghosts. The blog was gaining followers fast, intensifying the hysteria.

The number for the Holy Waters Church appeared on his caller ID. Ian answered, determined to keep the conversation short. He didn't like the preacher, Reverend Jim Benton. "Sheriff Kimball."

"Hello, Sheriff. I've organized a prayer vigil at the Holy Waters tonight to honor the victims found in that graveyard."

Ian reigned in a crude comment. That church reminded him more of a cult than a place of peace. His mother's husband, Bernard, together with Reverend Benton, had alienated her from Ian.

"Thanks for letting me know. I'll pass the word."

Benton started to say something else, but another call was coming through. "I have to go." He clicked to take the call. "Sheriff Kimball."

"This is Executive Assistant Director Vance with the criminal division of the FBI," the man said curtly. "I've organized a task force. We're meeting at a room at the morgue in half an hour. The ME and forensic anthropologist will fill us in on what they've learned so far. I thought you might like to be present."

Ian could barely contain his agitation. Just as he'd expected, Vance was swooping in to take over.

"Of course I'll be there. This is my town."

"All right. I just spoke with the ME, Dr. Wheeland. So far we've identified three of the dead: Sunny Smith, Retha Allen, and a third, Hilary Trenton."

That meant several more to go.

"A specialist in facial reconstruction is re-creating images of what the victims might have looked like," Vance continued. "The FBI are running those pictures through facial recognition software, focusing on the database for the National Center for Missing and Exploited Children."

"What about the most recent victim?"

"No ID yet, but hopefully soon. Special Agent Cal Coulter and Special Agent Dane Hamrick are in charge of questioning the families and friends of the victims to get a picture of what happened."

So what was his role? He didn't intend to sit back and twiddle his thumbs.

"I'll see you at the meeting," Vance said.

Ian holstered his gun, grabbed his jacket and keys, strode outside, and then drove through town. Traffic was minimal, very few people on the streets. Residents seemed to think if they holed up in their houses, the killer couldn't touch them.

A few locals had even moved away. They wanted to raise their families in a safer place, one that hadn't become famous for its serial killers.

The wind swirled dead leaves across the street as Ian parked at the hospital.

The past few days had been hell.

How much bad news and horror could one town suffer?

Dread knotted his gut as he walked down the steps to the morgue and entered. He was reeling from learning that Sunny's body was among the deceased in Hemlock Holler. When he pictured her in his mind, she was a shy, frail adolescent, just the type his father tried to help.

Ian removed his father's picture from his wallet and studied it. Coach Gleason was tall and muscular, but he'd had gentle hands, and he'd never laid one on Ian in anger. His father couldn't have killed Sunny or any of those girls. He'd gone out of his way to supervise after-school functions and ensure the teens' safety. Twice he'd paid for medical care for families who couldn't afford their doctor bills.

He'd also been an animal lover. Together they'd volunteered at the rescue shelter. More than once Coach had brought home a sick dog and nursed it back to health.

How could a kind man like that possibly kill a young girl?

He tucked the picture back inside his pocket. Where had he been the last five years? How had he survived? What did he live off of? Did he have a job? If so, it would have to be something under the radar, a job that didn't require references or a background check.

A job beneath his education and skills.

His father had loved counseling and teaching and coaching. It must have torn him up inside to be deprived of doing that.

The scent of death and cleaning chemicals jerked Ian from his memories. He glanced through the glass window on the door, but Dr. Wheeland, the ME, wasn't inside, so he walked next door to the room they'd dubbed "the bone room," where the team had spread the skeletal remains across several tables.

If one or more had died while his father was incarcerated, Ian could clear his name and give his father back his life.

Finding the real killer would also help assuage his guilt over Sunny's death, and the trauma JJ had suffered, too.

During the trial, she'd been quiet, sullen, had avoided looking at him. He'd stared holes at her, hoping she'd remember something to clear his father.

But she'd barely spoken or shown any emotion.

The trauma nurses said JJ had repeatedly called his father's name when they'd brought her in. The police assumed she was trying to relay the name of her kidnapper.

Did she know about Sunny?

◆ ◆ ◆

By 10 o'clock in the morning, Beth arrived at Graveyard Falls Hospital. The task force was meeting at the morgue in the basement.

Nerves clawed at her stomach.

Ever since that phone call, snippets of memories had tapped at her subconscious. Sunny crying and clinging to her hand the night they'd run away. The relentless rain. The smell on that rag—a smell she now knew had been chloroform.

After that, everything went blank.

The driver's face. Where he'd taken them.

What had happened while she'd been held captive.

She clenched her briefcase with a white-knuckled grip.

Occasionally an image of a hand or shadow floated to her, and she sensed she was on the verge of remembering her attacker's face. Then she'd reach for the image and fall off a cliff into a vat of darkness.

She inhaled a deep breath, giving her legs time to steady.

Holding her head up high to feign an air of confidence, she stepped into the conference room down the hall from the autopsy room. Chairs surrounded a long table. A whiteboard and screen for displaying photographs and information had been hung on one wall, and a coffee bar had been created in the corner, stocked with coffee, bottled water, and pastries.

Director Vance met her at the door, his expression grim. "I don't like you being here."

Beth jutted her chin up. There was no way she'd allow him to dismiss her. "I know, but I need to do this."

His hard gaze locked with hers for a heartbeat, and she held her breath.

Finally he gave a brief nod. "I'm warning you, Beth, if I see you're in trouble or taking unnecessary risks, you're off the case."

She pasted on her best tough-girl look. "Understood."

The door opened, and several people filed in—the ME, Dr. Wheeland; Special Agent Cal Coulter; and Special Agent Dane Hamrick. Cal had uncovered the connection between the Thorn Ripper and Bride Killer cases, which led to the arrest of a mother and son.

Dane had spearheaded the investigation into the Butcher, who'd carved women's faces with claw marks.

Doctors and crime techs, two deputies she hadn't yet met, and a cluster of others she didn't recognize gathered inside the room.

Peyton, the agency's best analyst and a computer whiz, gave her a warm smile. Beth had bonded with the thirtysomething slender woman with dark brown hair and glasses over the child trafficking case.

Vance rapped his knuckles on the podium. "Thank you all for coming. I realize you've been working diligently since the graveyard was discovered." He paused. "Grab some coffee or water and have a seat."

A Native American man with shoulder-length hair tied back with a leather strip approached her, two cups of coffee in hand. "I'm Deputy Whitehorse."

Beth identified herself and accepted the coffee, grateful for his friendly demeanor. Small-town law enforcement often resented the Feds' presence. "Thanks for the welcome. I assume the sheriff will be here."

He nodded just as the door opened. Out of the periphery of her eye, she caught sight of a tall, broad-shouldered uniformed man entering the room. Thick, wavy dirty-blond hair, five o'clock shadow, dark Ray-Bans.

Handsome and tough was her first impression.

Brooding and sullen came next. That from his grim expression and tight jaw.

Deputy Whitehorse cleared his throat. "There's our fearless leader now."

The sheriff's boots pounded as he strode to the coffee station and poured himself a cup. He didn't look happy, but he accepted Vance's proffered hand.

Something about the man rattled Beth's nerves. He looked rough around the edges, not at all welcoming. A hat pulled low on his head shielded his face, and those dark glasses hid his eyes.

Vance called the meeting to order and introduced himself. "I'm Executive Assistant Director Vance from the bureau, but for ease you can just call me Director Vance. Thanks to your hard work, we have identified three victims." He crooked his thumb toward Beth. "This is Special Agent Beth Fields who works with NCMEC. Her experience with missing children and their families and her profiling skills should be invaluable to the investigation."

She raised her chin, irritated that the sheriff hadn't acknowledged her. "I'm honored to be part of this task force."

Director Vance gestured toward the table where everyone was seated. He quickly introduced everyone and their positions, ending with Sheriff Kimball.

From her research on the town, Sheriff Kimball had proven helpful on the previous cases because he knew the area and the locals, but surely he realized this case was over his head.

Special Agent Cal Coulter began. "We're investigating two of the victims, Retha Allen and Hilary Trenton. Unfortunately we haven't found a connection between them."

"Hopefully the families of the girls can shed some light on their activities prior to the dates they went missing," Agent Hamrick said. "We were told the FBI has information on the third girl, Sunny Smith."

Emotions crowded Beth's throat, but she gave a brief nod.

"We'll get to that shortly," Director Vance said.

Dr. Wheeland introduced himself and the two forensic anthropologists, Dr. Emma Wright and Dr. Harris Lee, who specialized in facial reconstruction.

Next came the CSU team led by a tall man named Lieutenant Ward, then two deputies.

She'd met Deputy Whitehorse. The other deputy, Ladd Markum, was handsome in a rugged-cowboy kind of way.

The sheriff pushed to his feet. With one broad hand, he removed his hat, then lifted his head to meet her gaze.

A tremor rippled through Beth.

Dear God, it couldn't be.

His deep-set dark eyes narrowed on her face. "Sheriff Ian Kimball."

She barely stifled a gasp.

The man facing her was her high school crush. But his last name hadn't been Kimball—it was Gleason.

God . . . she'd forgotten that his mother divorced the coach during the trial. She must have taken back her maiden name and so had Ian.

He was older, had bulked up, gained muscle, and grown at least three inches. Gone was the young, flirty soccer star. Instead, a bitterness shadowed his eyes that hadn't been there fifteen years ago.

In fact, everything about him was intimidating.

Her own anger surfaced. He was supposed to give her and Sunny a ride to the bus station the night they'd been abducted.

Only he'd left them stranded and alone.

If he'd shown up, Sunny might be alive.

CHAPTER FOUR

An image of the girl he'd known fifteen years ago flashed behind Ian's eyes. Heart-shaped face. Long auburn hair. Big pale-blue eyes. A faint sprinkling of freckles across her nose.

Except the freckles were not as distinct now—or she'd covered them in makeup. This woman's hair was black and pulled back at the nape of her neck into a low bun, too, almost severe, not loose like JJ had worn hers.

Besides, Beth was her name.

Except those pale-blue eyes were the same haunting color and shape, the same pain-filled ones that tormented him when he slept.

She glanced at her notepad as if stalling. The movement caused her jacket sleeve to ride up, exposing her left arm.

And three scars—cigarette burns. Distinctive in that they formed a triangle.

Damn.

She *was* JJ.

He'd been disgusted when he'd seen the burns fifteen years ago. Even as a teen, he'd recognized them for what they were.

Abuse.

The smile she'd given everyone else in the meeting faded. She opened her mouth to speak, then paused, her breath rasping out. "Sheriff."

Ian extended his hand. "JJ?"

She paused, then gave a quick shake of her head. "It's Beth Fields, *Agent* Fields."

The moment he closed his fingers around her palm, an almost electrical tingle ripped through him. Her eyes widened as if she felt it, too, and she quickly stepped back.

Chairs shifted and voices rumbled slightly, jarring him back to the fact that the room was filled with professionals who had no idea what was going on in his head. Shit. Agents Hamrick and Coulter knew he could do the job, but no one else in the room did. Director Vance had only included him as a courtesy and to serve as a bridge to calm residents.

"Sheriff," Director Vance said, "tell us more about the town and what your deputies have learned so far."

"Of course." Ian directed their attention toward the whiteboards. "These are shots of Hemlock Holler when we first discovered the bodies." He'd viewed the pictures a dozen times, but the sea of white gowns and skeletons remained powerful. Bones had decayed, teeth had come loose from jaws, bugs and insects had gnawed away at any fleshy remains.

"As you know, the tornado and flooding ripped up trees, destroyed homes and a trailer park nearby. In the aftermath, rescue workers spotted this ravine where we discovered the remains of over a dozen adolescent girls. My deputies secured the area. They've also been working to keep the residents calm."

"Any suspects or idea if the killer is from Graveyard Falls?" Agent Coulter asked.

"Nothing so far, although we've been busy weeding out false leads from panicked locals." He pointed to the photograph of the most recent victim. "Judging from the state of the bodies and the sheer number of victims, he's been killing for years, and he has no plans to stop."

♦ ♦ ♦

Nausea flooded Beth. The photographs were gruesome.

"Thank you, Sheriff," Vance said as Ian finished and took a seat.

"Our priority is to identify the latest victim," Vance continued. "If the unsub is close by, maybe we'll get a lead and prevent another murder."

That would be great. But this killer hadn't managed to stack up this many bodies by making mistakes.

Having a recent victim meant the killer could be nearby, though. He might be hiding in the town in plain sight.

She'd thought she'd prepared herself for the situation, but the picture of the uprooted makeshift graveyard reminded her of a scene from a horror movie.

Bones and skeletons floated in the water and protruded from the mud, a grisly sight that taunted her with the realization that she could have been one of those skeletons.

She ripped her eyes from the photographs to glance at the second board, which held sketches of the three victims they'd identified.

The drawing of Sunny was so accurate that tears burned the backs of Beth's eyelids.

She blinked hard, desperate to keep them at bay. Although she wanted to know who'd killed Sunny, she had to be objective.

A memory tickled her conscience, one of Coach Gleason bringing an abandoned puppy to school to see if any of the teachers or students wanted to adopt it.

Could that man have murdered all these girls?

It didn't seem likely.

"Agent *Fields*, did you have something to say?" the sheriff asked.

Beth stiffened at his sarcastic tone.

He knew who she was.

She gave him a chilly look, daring him to reveal her identity. If he told the others, they might insist she be pulled from the investigation. She didn't want their pitying stares either.

And if the killer found out her real name, he might come after her. She had to focus.

"I was thinking about the MO of the Bride Killer, the fact that he dressed his victims in wedding gowns." She'd read Josie DuKane's tell-all book and had seen the movie. "What is the white in the photograph of the floodwater? Are they wedding dresses?"

"Actually, they're nightgowns. The material is cotton." Peyton flipped open a sketch. "This is a drawing of what one of the gowns looked like when it was intact. With this more recent victim, we might be able to trace where it was bought. Although much of the fabric disintegrated from the elements, it resembles a christening gown."

Beth began to mentally create a profile of the unsub.

Why would this unsub dress his victims in christening gowns or nightgowns as if he were baptizing them or putting them to bed?

When she glanced at the sheriff, he was focused on her, his eyes cold, hard.

She needed to talk to him after the meeting. Find out how he'd ended up in Graveyard Falls overseeing the case where her friend's body had been discovered.

Had he moved to town to be close to his father because Ian knew he was alive? Had Ian kept in contact with Coach during his incarceration? Or since his escape?

Peyton tapped another sketch. "We also discovered pieces of candles buried with the bodies. Although many were broken and crumpled, mired in mud and water, they were plain white taper candles."

Sheriff Kimball addressed Peyton. "Can you trace where the killer purchased the candles?"

"The candles are common and can be bought in any drugstore, discount store, department store, online," Peyton said with a shrug.

Agent Hamrick pointed to a photo of several gold necklaces that had been recovered from the graveyard. "What about those?"

"They're inexpensive plain gold crosses," Peyton continued. "Nothing outstanding about them, so they'll be hard to track down as well."

Beth jotted another note. Crosses, white candles, christening gowns—religious symbols. An angle to explore and one that obviously held significance to the killer.

"Thanks, keep us posted." Vance turned to the medical examiner. "What can you tell us about cause and time of death?"

Dr. Wheeland adjusted his bifocals and rubbed at his eyes as if the photos were getting to him, too. Beth had consulted with him on two missing child cases. He was detail-oriented, smart, insightful, and compassionate.

"The most recent victim was killed roughly two weeks ago. I'm working on time of death for the other victims. Our forensic anthropologists are making progress on identifying the remains, although it'll take time. The three victims we *have* identified are between the ages of twelve and fourteen. Judging from the deep cuts into the bone, their wrists were cut."

"And the most recent victim?" Beth asked.

"She has the same wounds—deep cuts to the wrist. COD is exsanguination."

"Cuts to the wrists sound like suicide," Agent Coulter commented.

Beth's heart beat like a drum. "Are you suggesting the girls killed themselves?"

Dr. Wheeland twisted his mouth in thought. "I can't say at this point. Once we learn more about the victims, we can make that determination."

"You think they made a suicide pact?" Deputy Whitehorse asked.

"Since the three deaths occurred at different times and in different states, I doubt it," Dr. Wheeland replied. "There are numerous factors to consider regarding suicide. The victim's frame of mind. Right-handedness versus left-handedness. The presence or lack of defensive wounds."

"Perhaps the unsub forced the girls to slit their own wrists," Deputy Markum suggested.

Dr. Wheeland shrugged. "It's possible, although I would expect hesitation marks if that was the case. There were no hesitation marks on the most recent victim. The wounds appear to be clean and direct, as in one swift, harsh cut."

Beth lifted her hand to speak. "These girls were buried in that holler with a candle and a cross. He also dressed them in gowns. That suggests a serial killer. His ritual is significant." A theory started to take shape in her mind. "Sheriff, maybe your deputies can begin by exploring the local churches."

"We're in the South," the sheriff said. "Do you know how many churches there are?"

Beth nodded. "Yes, but it could be important. It would help if your people screened the pastors, church leaders, and gathered a list of parishioners."

"Yes, ma'am," he said tightly.

Dr. Wheeland pointed toward one photo on the board. "This girl is Retha Allen. She was twelve, suffered from anorexia, and sustained a broken leg when she was younger." He moved to the second victim. "Hilary Trenton was fourteen, had injuries that are consistent with child abuse. She suffered several broken bones."

"Have you found any connection between the two girls?" Sheriff Kimball asked.

Agent Coulter's hand shot up. "Not yet. Retha was from Lexington, Kentucky. She disappeared four years ago from a temporary foster home. Her mother was in rehab."

"You're going to Lexington to speak to the police?" Ian asked.

"Yes, I'm driving there after the meeting."

"Hilary lived in Chattanooga," Agent Hamrick interjected. "I'll notify her father. According to reports, she went missing three years ago after a teenage pool party. I pulled police reports and reviewed their investigation. The father admitted that he and Hilary argued earlier that day. She wanted to leave school, join a band, and be a country music star. Police questioned him, but he had an alibi the night she disappeared."

Beth jotted down a note. These murders were fairly recent.

Coach Gleason could be a suspect. Although the MO included a religious angle—she didn't recall that he'd been a super religious man.

Vance gestured toward the entire group. "Report everything to our analyst, Peyton. She'll run comparisons and search for common denominators. Special Agent Fields has information regarding the third victim we've identified, Sunny Smith." He arched a brow. "Agent Fields?"

Ian folded his arms, a challenge in his eyes. Was he going to reveal who she was now?

All eyes settled on Agent Beth Fields. Tension crackled in the room as Ian's mind launched him back to his teenage years.

Those cigarette burns on JJ's arm had infuriated him. Worse, he'd seen the way she'd tried to hide them. Detected the shame in her eyes.

Aware JJ was in foster care, he'd cornered her outside the school one day to ask if she was okay. She'd refused to talk about her home life or the burns.

But the next week, she'd asked him for a ride. Had told him she and Sunny were going to her grandmother's. That her grandmother was expecting her.

Three days later, when she and Sunny hadn't been found, the police were ready to write them off as runaways when suspicions turned toward his father.

"I do have information on Sunny Smith," Beth said. "She was living in a foster home with a couple named Herman and Frances Otter. Sunny and another foster child—fourteen-year-old Jane Jones, who went by JJ—ran away one cold night in late February. A few hours later, the girls were picked up by someone in a truck near a Dairy Mart not far from Sweetwater, Tennessee, a small town about an hour from Graveyard Falls. The driver was never identified. Police investigated and arrested the counselor/soccer coach at the girls' school."

"Was JJ able to identify her abductor?" Dane asked.

Beth shook her head. "No. She was found three days after the abduction at a rest area off I-75 near Chattanooga. She was traumatized, dehydrated, and suffered from amnesia. In her agitated state, she repeatedly murmured the coach's name."

"That statement led to the police focusing on Coach Gleason as a suspect, didn't it?" Ian asked.

Beth's mouth tightened. She obviously recognized him, too, and didn't like the fact that he was hiding his relationship to Coach Gleason.

"Actually, the coach was already under suspicion because one of his students, Kelly Cousins, had allegedly committed suicide," Beth said.

"What would a suicide have to do with a kidnapping?" Agent Coulter asked.

"There were allegations that Coach Gleason pressured Kelly for sex," Beth said.

Ian's chest clenched. Had Beth—JJ—really believed his father was guilty of sexual misconduct with a student? She hadn't said so at the trial.

Then again, she hadn't said much. She'd looked stunned and confused. "But there was no evidence of rape or sexual assault on JJ when she was found, was there?" he asked.

Beth shifted, biting on her lower lip. "No."

"If sexual assault was part of his MO and the coach was guilty, why didn't he molest JJ?" Ian asked.

"I don't know," Beth said. "There are numerous questions about what happened to her when she was being held. However, it's possible that he molested Sunny."

Ian turned to the ME. "Can you confirm or deny that?"

"It's impossible to tell with the condition of the remains. Although I completed the autopsy of the recent victim, and there is no sign of sexual activity."

"Didn't JJ say a man in a small truck picked her and her friend up?" Ian asked.

Beth nodded. "Yes."

"Coach Gleason didn't own a truck," he said bluntly.

Low voices rumbled, then a sudden hush.

"Actually, a stolen truck was discovered not too far from Sweetwater where the crime occurred," Director Vance said. "There were hairs from JJ and Sunny inside along with a partial print on the steering wheel that belonged to the coach."

Ian cursed, surprised Vance knew so much about the case. That damn partial was the one piece of evidence his father couldn't explain.

Director Vance continued. "Also, Coach Gleason had no alibi the night of the abduction, and he was the only connection they discovered between Kelly, JJ, and Sunny. He was convicted of kidnapping and spent ten years in the Graveyard Falls prison. That prison flooded five years ago. One prisoner who escaped confirmed that the coach got away."

Director Vance gestured toward Peyton. "Make sure each member of the task force receives a photo of what he might look like today." He angled his head toward the ME. "Dr. Wheeland, let's identify that latest victim. She could be the key to finding this unsub."

Beth jotted a note. "Send me her photo and info, and I'll check with NCMEC."

Peyton nodded. "That would speed things along."

Emotions churned through Ian. If the police hadn't spent all their time on his father, they might have determined another suspect. "It's been fifteen years since Sunny and JJ went missing," Ian pointed out. "It's possible that since that time, some of JJ's memories have returned. I'll talk to her after the meeting."

Beth's gaze met his, a wariness settling in her eyes. He didn't care if she was uncomfortable.

He needed to know if Beth Fields—JJ—had recovered any details from the past about the true culprit.

He hung the latest blood spatter pattern on the wall and studied the way the particles had dispersed. Just like a snowflake, every pattern was different. Unique. This one reminded him of a tree branch. Not a maple or magnolia, but it mimicked the spiny ridges and sharp needles of a pine.

He'd been collecting the blood spatters since he was a child.

The first time he was five. He'd thrown a rock at a squirrel and knocked it from a tree. While it lay dying, he'd been mesmerized by the blood flowing from the creature.

He'd sat for hours, studying how the dark-brownish insides stained the grass with a murky color and the way bits of the exterior clung to the blood.

He'd snuck his daddy's old Polaroid camera, snapped a picture, then taped the photo on the inside of his closet door.

Every chance he'd gotten, he'd sneak open the door and admire his handiwork.

Studying blood spatters had become a hobby. Almost an obsession.

He'd gone on to killing mice, snakes, frogs, and other animals.

Each time his infatuation with the blood had grown. One night his father caught him smashing a bird with a hammer and drawing his finger through the blood. He'd been terrified his father would punish him.

That night his father had told him about the Calling. That it was his job to save the sinners just as his father had and his father before him.

The thrill had intensified when he'd watched the blood spatter from the girls' wrists.

He made the sign of the cross as he hung the picture he'd snapped of the graveyard on the wall in his private room. The room where he kept his trophies.

The girls had been beautiful alive, but more so in death. They resembled angels floating in the water.

But they hadn't been angels. Not until he saved them.

To do that, they'd had to die.

CHAPTER FIVE

Dread balled in Ian's stomach. He wasn't looking forward to his conversation with Agent Fields, but he had to talk to her. Any detail she remembered could be useful.

Director Vance stood. "Now we'll hear from Peyton."

Peyton stood. "I've set up a central site where I'll post spreadsheets, a timeline, and information as we gather it. We need all eyes searching for connections to the victims and their families. Establishing a timeline for the deaths and locations where the girls were abducted should give us insight into where and how the killer chooses his victims."

"Since the killer buried the girls near Graveyard Falls, have you looked at those cabins on the river where the film crew and my agents stayed before?" Director Vance asked Ian. "Maybe he's staying out there."

Irritation gnawed at Ian. "Of course we checked them. But I don't think the killer would stay so close to town. These mountains are full of old houses and shanties, places off the grid."

"Then have your deputies search the town and mountains for abandoned cabins, old homesteads, anyplace where our unsub might be hiding out," Director Vance said. "If Gleason is our unsub, he's had plenty of time to get to know the area."

Ian folded his arms. Dammit, Vance had to bring the suspicion back to his father.

Beth tapped her fingernails on the table. "With at least one of the victims from Kentucky, we can't assume the unsub lives close by. He could have killed the girls in different locations and then dumped them in Graveyard Falls to throw off suspicion in case the bodies were discovered."

Ian followed her train of thought. Sweetwater, Lexington, Chattanooga—all were in close proximity to I-75, a major interstate that ran all the way from Georgia to Tennessee to Kentucky.

"True. He could be traveling up and down the highway," Peyton pointed out. "That's another reason we need to ID the victims as quickly as possible, find their families and their hometowns." She indicated the photo of the latest victim. "Since her kill is fresher, maybe someone saw something."

"Talking to the girl who survived is imperative," Agent Hamrick said.

The director spoke. "Agent Fields has already established contact with Jane Jones and will follow up on that lead."

Gratitude flickered in Beth's eyes as she and the director exchanged a look. Ian stiffened. The director knew her real identity.

Odd that he'd allowed her to come here and work the case anyway.

Ian gestured to Beth. "I'd like to talk to Agent Fields in the hall, please."

Beth stood. "Certainly."

Without waiting for him, she strode into the hall. Before he proceeded he had to find out Beth's agenda.

If she knew more than she was saying, it was time she filled him in.

◆ ◆ ◆

Through the glass window, Beth spotted the bones spread on the tables in the bone room.

Sunny was in there.

A soul-deep ache throbbed inside Beth. She could see Sunny's pretty blonde hair blowing in the wind when they'd walked to school. See her collecting pennies and rubbing them as she made a wish.

She could hear Sunny's soft giggles when they daydreamed about places they wanted to visit. Sunny had wanted to ride the Ferris wheel at the carnival and have a princess dress at her wedding one day.

Now there was nothing left but bones.

She could have been lying on that table, too.

The question that had tormented her for years nagged at her again. *Why had the killer let her go?*

Footsteps echoed behind her. She whirled around, braced for a confrontation. He closed the door and gestured toward a small office across the hall. Arms crossed, she lifted her chin and stepped inside.

"You are JJ, aren't you, Beth?" he asked as he released the handle.

Her breath quickened. For so long, she'd tried to create a new identity. Seeing Ian and hearing that name resurrected old fears.

"Where have you been?" he asked as if her silence had confirmed what he already knew. "Why did you change your name?"

Beth held up a warning hand. "I don't intend to be interrogated, Sheriff Kimball."

A muscle ticked in Ian's jaw. "This is not an interrogation. But you came to my town with a false name and are deceiving everyone in that room. I deserve an explanation."

"You *deserve* it?" Beth bit out. "You blamed me for your father's arrest."

Ian sucked in a sharp breath. "I didn't blame you for anything," he said. "I just believed my father was innocent. Maybe if the police hadn't been so quick to throw the book at my father, they would have found another suspect."

Beth twisted her hands together. "I wish I could tell you what you want to hear, but I don't remember any more today than I did fifteen years ago."

Ian raised a brow as if suspicious. "Nothing?"

The image of a man's hand flashed back. Then dark eyes.

"No." The image blurred. "I saw a therapist to help me recover the memories, but it didn't work. She suggested I change my name to protect myself." After all, her name and picture had been plastered all over the TV and in the papers.

"You changed your hair color to disguise yourself, too," he said matter-of-factly.

Beth nodded. "You have no idea what it was like to have everyone, especially other teenagers, staring at me and whispering behind my back. They treated me like I was a freak. I didn't want their questions or skepticism or pity." She squared her shoulders. "I don't want it now."

"That's not what this is about," Ian said. "And I do know what it was like to have others stare at you. You're forgetting that my family was ripped apart because of Kelly Cousins's suicide, then because of your abduction and the trial."

Beth swallowed hard. "I'm sorry. I . . . that wasn't fair of me."

Tension stretched between them for a long minute. Finally Ian broke the silence. "We can't work together if you're not honest."

Anger seized Beth. "Like you're being honest?" She folded her arms. "Are you going to tell the other agents that you knew me? That you were supposed to pick me up the night I was abducted? That your stepfather was convicted of my abduction?"

Ian's lips compressed into a thin line. She hadn't meant to say that, but the words just slipped out. Now they stood between them like a giant boulder that couldn't be crossed.

It was the truth in all its ugliness.

Just like the ugliness Beth had lived with all her life.

♦ ♦ ♦

Ian's chest ached with the effort to breathe. He'd expected JJ—Beth—to hate him. Hell, he'd blamed himself for what had happened to her.

But the bitterness in her voice cut through him like a knife.

"I'm sorry," he said, his voice gravelly with regret. She had no idea how tormented he'd been those three days she'd been missing. How nightmares of her shock-glazed face had dogged him.

He'd imagined the worst kind of torture.

Then the sheriff had hauled his father in for kidnapping.

His mother had been so caught up in her grief and shame, she'd fallen apart. Ian had tried to convince the authorities that they were wasting precious time by not searching for other suspects.

But more than one authority figure suggested that he'd lied for his father.

With the crime happening in a small town and pressure from locals, the DA had moved quickly to prosecute his father. Ten months later, he'd been convicted. The judge had made an example of him and given him the maximum sentence.

Ian tried to visit, but his father refused to see him. He'd told Ian to get on with his life.

What life? His friends had turned against him.

He went to live with his mother, but their differing opinions over his father's guilt had caused a chasm between them. Then she'd joined that cult-like church, and the distance became greater. As soon as he was eighteen, he'd moved out.

Driven to clear his father, he'd signed up for the police academy. After the prison flooding, he'd moved to Graveyard Falls to search for his father.

No wonder his father had run after the flood. If he hadn't, he'd have spent the rest of his life in jail.

"So do you know where your father is?"

"No. I moved to Graveyard Falls to look for him."

"Have you found evidence to exonerate him?"

"Not yet, but I've studied the case files. Except for his partial print on that truck, which could have been planted, there was no concrete evidence that my father did anything but prevent me from driving his car that night. Think of all the students he helped over the years. He's not a killer." He pounded his chest. "He treated me like a son when I wasn't even his kid."

Beth ran a shaky hand over her hair. "I'm sorry, Ian. I *never* said that your father was the driver. I . . . honestly don't know who was behind the wheel."

Ian jammed his hands in his pockets. "If my father is innocent, then another man took you and Sunny." He swallowed hard. "Another man who's been free all this time to hunt and kill."

"Don't you think I know that?" she hissed. "I'm well aware that if I'd remembered what happened, I could have ensured that the right man went to jail. Every time I walk out the door, I wonder if my kidnapper is hunting me down. I look at men on the street and wonder if it was one of them instead of Coach."

The agony in her tone tore at him. But it was a relief to hear that she wasn't convinced of his father's guilt. "Not a day has passed that I haven't kicked myself for not picking up you and Sunny."

Silence stood between them, thick with the pain of their admissions.

Finally Beth heaved a breath. "Look, Ian, we both want the same thing." Her voice became a hushed whisper. "We both want the truth."

He gave a clipped nod. "That's the reason I became a cop."

"And the reason I became an agent." Beth straightened.

The door to the room squeaked open, and Director Vance appeared, Peyton behind him holding a laptop.

"We have to talk," the director said.

Peyton set the computer on the desk and angled it toward them. "I ran a search on Jane Jones. She went to live in a group home near

Knoxville after Coach Gleason's trial, but six months later, it's as if she disappeared. There's no paper trail, no driver's license, address, education, or job."

Ian tensed. He and Beth couldn't possibly lie to the people they worked with and expect the team to trust them.

Dammit—he hadn't wanted anyone in town to know the reason he'd come here. But soon everyone would know.

◆ ◆ ◆

Beth had seen Peyton working on her computer during their meeting but hadn't realized what she'd been doing.

A photograph of JJ the day she'd been found on the side of the road was displayed on Peyton's screen along with news articles and photos of her hospital stay.

Just as Peyton had used age-progression software on the victims, she'd done so on JJ, and a sketch appeared.

The resemblance was so accurate it was eerie. Her glasses were gone, but the heart-shaped face, slightly button nose, and deep-set eyes remained the same.

Beth forced herself to face the truth. She was foolish if she thought she could keep her identity from these trained experts. Finding missing people and murderers was their job.

Peyton's voice softened. "Am I wrong, Special Agent Fields, or is this you?"

Beth had tried so hard to create a new identity. But finding Sunny's body had thrust her back in time to when she was a confused teenager.

"Yes, it's me," she said, relieved that her voice held out. "I changed my name after the abduction."

"I can understand that," Peyton said sympathetically. "But the members of the team—they're going to figure it out."

Beth nodded. "I know. We were just discussing the situation." In spite of her bravado, she gripped the desk edge.

The image of those bones flashed behind her eyes, then Sunny's face the first time she'd met her when Sunny was ten and had come to live with the Otters.

She'd been so thin, so sickly. Beth had taken her under her wing, protected her.

Grief threatened to make her ill. If only she hadn't gotten into that truck. She'd literally pushed Sunny into the cab with a killer.

She owed it to Sunny to find the bastard and make him pay.

Old man Croney, the algebra teacher with the big ears and buckteeth, droned on about x's and y's, but Priscilla Carson ignored him. She had other things on her mind.

Her argument this morning with her mama, for one. Prissy was almost fifteen now, and she wanted to go and do what she wanted to go and do.

Not be smothered by her mama's questions and lectures about being a good girl.

Good girls didn't get the hot guys or the breaks.

Besides, it wasn't like her mama had been a good girl. Hell, she'd gotten knocked up at sixteen.

Prissy didn't intend to shack up in a trailer with a loser like her mama. She wanted Blaine Emerson, and she would damn well have him. Blaine was smart and popular. He'd been voted Most Likely to Succeed. He was going places in life.

And she was going with him.

She giggled at the thought of finally giving her virginity to him. She'd been so excited when she told him that she nearly peed her pants.

When she gave herself to him, he'd be tied to her forever.

"Don't forget your homework tonight," the teacher said.

She had no intention of wasting time on boring homework.

She checked her watch. This day was dragging by.

It was hours till school was out. She'd packed her backpack with extra clothes this morning. After school she and Blaine planned to sneak off to one of the empty cabins in the woods by the creek. With all the flooding causing chaos and tearing up her mama's trailer, she'd left a note saying she was going to spend the night with her friend Vanessa.

After all, Mama couldn't expect her to sleep in the room with the tree sticking through the roof and the toilet backed up.

Her teacher kept yakking about the square root of something, and Prissy drew a big heart on her notebook paper and scribbled her initials and Blaine's.

Prissy Emerson sounded good, so she wrote that name, then tried out variations. Mrs. Blaine Emerson. Mrs. Prissy Emerson. Blaine and Prissy Emerson.

Finally the lunch bell rang, and she hurried out to the tree by the breezeway, giddy. Blaine would be waiting on her.

Her hair flew around her face in the wind as she rushed to the big oak tree. The football players gathered on the steps and were huddled together discussing spring practice. The smokers hid behind the awning in the rear and acted cool as they passed a joint around. The cheerleaders were laughing and primping, talking about prom. A few nerds were playing with some robot one of them had made in science class.

A girl's singsongy voice echoed nearby. She glanced over her shoulder and spotted Sari Hinkerton.

Prissy's heart dropped to her knees.

Sari had her arms wrapped around Blaine's neck, and he had his arms wrapped around her. Sari laughed, and then they fused their mouths in a lip lock. Blaine's hand slid down to grope Sari's butt. The two of them pulled apart just long enough for them to clasp hands.

Blaine tossed Prissy a grin. Then he and Sari raced toward his Camaro.

Disappointment and anger choked her, and tears blurred her eyes.

A chorus of "Poor Pissy Prissy" broke out as three of the popular girls chanted her name. Other kids snickered and laughed.

"Did you really think Blaine would go out with you?" one of the girls said as she passed Prissy.

More tears burned Prissy's eyes. She was such an idiot.

"Poor Pissy Prissy, Poor Pissy Prissy . . ." The chanting grew louder.

"Gonna piss your pants?" someone else said.

Humiliated, she clutched her backpack and ran toward the parking lot. She didn't have a car, but she had to get out of here.

No way could she face the girls in PE, or Vanessa.

Vanessa had warned her that Blaine used girls. That he wasn't interested in a geek like her.

But Prissy had loved him so much.

Swiping at her tears, she jogged toward the woods behind the school, diving deeper into the thicket of trees so no one would see her.

She sure as hell couldn't go back to her mama and that drunken asshole she lived with.

Her calves ached as she ran, but rage drove her forward, and she jumped over tree stumps and broken limbs. She had to get as far away as she could. She hated this school and her family. Most of all she hated Blaine.

She broke through a clearing about two miles down the road and was huffing and puffing. Two cars passed by, but she ducked behind a tree to hide. Another two miles and she reached the city border. The sign welcomed folks to Graveyard Falls.

Stupid sign. Stupid people in this dumb-ass town.

A sedan raced by, and she cursed it. Lucky driver. He had a way out of this hellhole.

She made up her mind then and there. She was getting out.

Another two miles and she got a stitch in her side. She slowed, pressing her hand to her abdomen, and trudged on.

She tried to remember how far it was to the next town. About twenty miles, maybe.

The pain wouldn't let up.

More tears threatened. She was getting a dad-gum blister.

A truck passed, then another.

She turned toward the road and stuck out her thumb. A black pickup barreled toward her. She jumped back as dirt and gravel pelted her. She yelled at the truck driver, and then he surprised her by slowing.

He screeched to a stop. Prissy hesitated.

Don't be a scaredy-cat. This is your way out of Loserville and your screwed-up life.

She ran toward the truck, yanked open the door, and climbed inside.

CHAPTER SIX

Ian rubbed his jaw, the sound of his beard stubble bristling a reminder that he needed sleep and a shower.

Both would have to wait.

"I might as well give full disclosure myself." His gaze latched with Beth's. "Beth—JJ—and I went to school together. Coach Gleason, the man who was convicted of JJ Jones's abduction, was my father. Actually, my stepfather."

Director Vance's eyes widened. "That's the reason you came to Graveyard Falls? To find him?"

Ian nodded. "I've been searching for him on my own."

"You wanted to prove his innocence," Beth said.

Ian nodded. "Coach Gleason insisted he never touched Kelly Cousins, and that he didn't abduct Sunny or JJ. I believed him. I think someone planted that evidence in the truck."

"Have you found any proof?" Beth asked.

Ian shook his head.

"Would you tell us if you did?" Vance asked.

Ian wiped sweat from the back of his neck. "Yes. But I haven't heard from him. I don't even know if he's still alive."

"Perhaps you should excuse yourself from this case," Director Vance suggested.

Ian squared his shoulders. "You may have jurisdiction here, sir, but I know the people in town. They'll be more likely to trust me than an outsider."

"What if your stepfather *is* the killer?" Peyton asked.

A vein pulsed in Vance's neck. "Yes, Sheriff. How will you handle that?"

Ian swung his gaze toward the bone room. "Then I'll bring him in myself. But you have to be questioning his guilt. My father was connected to Kelly Cousins, to Sunny and JJ, but he had no connection to these other girls." Ian took a breath. "Think about it. How would he have had access to girls in different states?"

"He's right. That would have been difficult," Beth agreed. "I've worked with profiling. Serial killers often have a history of child abuse or a mental disorder which doesn't fit Coach Gleason. As we learn more about these victims, I can narrow that profile down."

Vance turned to Beth. "Then you're in charge. Sheriff Kimball, you'll answer to Agent Fields."

Anger at the idea of working under Beth heated Ian's blood. He opened his mouth to protest, but Vance cut him off. "I'm giving you both fair warning. If I see signs that you aren't handling the case objectively or if you aren't sharing information, I'll pull you both from the case."

Anxiety knotted Beth's shoulders as she, Ian, Peyton, and Director Vance crossed the hall to the meeting room.

She was surprised Ian had confessed to his past. But he obviously realized Peyton and the others on the team were savvy and that holding back might work against him later.

When they entered, the director walked to the front of the room, and the rest of the team took their seats. Director Vance tapped the podium, and voices quieted.

"Thank you for your patience," Director Vance said. "Before we broke, we were about to hear from Special Agent Fields regarding what she knows about Sunny Smith and the girl who was abducted with her, Jane Jones." He waved to Beth. "Special Agent Fields?"

Beth rose on shaky legs, mentally chastising herself for letting Ian affect her. She had survived fifteen years ago. She was trained in self-defense, interrogation tactics, tracking and hunting down criminals, reading behavior cues, and compartmentalizing her emotions. She'd also undergone therapy to understand her amnesia, and she'd taken classes on child and adolescent behavior.

Early in her career, she'd worked as a forensic interviewer for abused children, an eye-opening experience about predators and their manipulative ploys to lure young girls and boys into a trap. From there, she'd studied profiling.

"Thank you, Director Vance. I'm glad to be part of this team." She adopted her most professional mask, pushing her feelings to the side. "I chose to work with NCMEC for personal reasons. Although the hunt for Sunny Smith went cold years ago, I've been searching for Sunny ever since."

Special Agent Hamrick raised a hand. "Have you interviewed Jane Jones?"

Nerves gathered along Beth's spine. "I know a lot about her because I am Jane Jones."

Shocked looks and murmurs floated through the room.

She lifted a hand to signal for them to listen. "Let me start from the beginning. Sunny and I were living in the same foster home when conditions became unbearable. Our foster father, Herman Otter, had molested another foster child named May, who ran away. Fifteen was the age Herman Otter liked. He thought twelve-, thirteen-, and fourteen-year-olds were children, but at fifteen girls were women, so he could justify taking them to bed." An awkward silence fell across the room. Gathering her courage, she continued. "The night before my fifteenth birthday, we ran away to escape him. That night it was storming . . ." Her voice cracked, but she didn't dare look at Ian.

Seconds passed while the team waited, the air thick with the somber reality of the story they were about to hear.

Memories launched her back in time.

Her legs ached from walking, and Sunny was crying, her ankle swelling. They were both freezing and drenched to the bone. Thunder rumbled as more rain pelted them. Ian had never showed up at the Dairy Mart. How much longer could they walk? Sunny was sobbing . . . Then the sound of a truck's brakes squealed as it rolled to a stop.

Vance cleared his throat, drawing her back to the present.

She tucked a strand of hair back into the tight bun at the nape of her neck. "Anyway, we were cold and wet and a truck came along, so we accepted a ride." A shudder ripped through her. "That's the last thing I remember before I woke up in the hospital."

"You couldn't identify the man driving?" Agent Coulter asked.

"No." Beth struggled for the courage to continue. "For some reason I sensed it was okay to get inside that truck, that there was someone familiar in there." She wiped her clammy palms on her slacks. "But I don't know why."

Ian was watching her, anxiety riddling his face.

"The police report stated that you repeatedly called the coach's name. They thought you were trying to tell them that he was driving," Director Vance said.

"Maybe you asked for him because he was the counselor," Ian suggested.

"I suppose that's possible," Beth said.

"Did you recall anything about where you were kept? Where the man might have been headed?" Peyton asked.

Beth closed her eyes for a moment, but a black void filled her mind. "No. All I remembered was that Sunny had been with me."

Lieutenant Ward from the CSI unit raised his hand. "How about forensics?"

Beth gripped the podium edge. "I'll have copies of the police report and investigation forwarded to each of you. But there wasn't much to go on. They identified mud on my sneakers but found no helpful traces of DNA under my nails or on my body."

"Why would the unsub kill Sunny and release you?" Agent Coulter asked.

Beth's heart pounded. "I have no idea. The police speculated that perhaps I wasn't his type. Now that we know there are others, maybe we can figure out what his type is."

Special Agent Coulter waved a finger. "Do you believe that the coach was responsible for your abduction?"

Beth bit her lip, struggling with her response. "I honestly don't know. Considering the evidence and lack of it, it's possible that he's innocent. The connection with the suicide was incriminating, but some of it was born from gossip that the students started, that and the notes Kelly's mother found where Kelly confessed her undying love for the coach. But the police never proved that he molested Kelly Cousins."

"He pled innocent to the abduction charges?" Agent Hamrick asked.

"Yes. The coach denied having any kind of intimate relationship with Kelly, and he denied kidnapping me. But the gossip had a life of its own. With one teen's suicide and Sunny missing, the parents were up in arms, demanding answers."

"And for someone to pay," Agent Hamrick muttered.

"Did the police investigate Sunny's family?" Agent Coulter asked.

"Unfortunately, both her parents died in a car accident when she was four, and she had no other family."

"What about yours?" Agent Coulter asked.

Beth should have been prepared for the question, but it always pained her. "My mother was killed shortly after she gave birth to me. She was only fifteen at the time. I have no idea who my father was."

"What about the foster father you were running away from?" Agent Coulter asked. "I assume police questioned Otter regarding the abuse and your disappearance."

"Yes, but it was my word against his." Beth fidgeted. "His wife vouched for him in both instances."

"What happened to Otter?" Agent Hamrick asked.

He got what he deserved. "He died ten years ago of liver failure."

Agent Coulter crossed his arms. "How about the girl, May?"

"I don't know," Beth said. "I never saw her again. When I started working with NCMEC, I looked for her name on the list, but no one ever reported her missing."

Dr. Wheeland squared his shoulders. "Do you think she's one of our victims?"

Beth's pulse clamored. "I guess it's possible." Although she prayed May had escaped and found a better life.

She sank into a seat, her legs weak, while Ian explained his connection to her and Sunny and to Coach Gleason. The agents pummeled Ian with questions just as they had her, but their voices faded as she struggled for composure.

She rarely discussed her past, had only confided in a handful of people. But today she'd spilled her guts to a roomful of crime workers, and she'd faced Ian.

With this team of experts working together, she might finally learn the truth.

"Finding the kill spot could provide us valuable insight into the unsub's MO," Ian said.

Guilt nagged at Beth. If she could remember where he'd driven them, where she'd been for those three missing days, she could lead them to that spot.

Then they might get the forensics necessary to find the bastard and stop him from killing again.

Vance dismissed the meeting, and the members of the team dispersed, some stopping to chat.

Beth couldn't get out of the room quickly enough.

Ian caught her at the door. "Beth, Lieutenant Ward said they have a collection of personal items that were recovered with the bodies. He wants to see if you recognize anything."

Her stomach twisted. "Of course."

Beth followed him to a small room with tables where a variety of bagged items lay spread out. One section held a bevy of candles. Another held book bags and backpacks, sneakers, jackets, hair ribbons, purses, CDs, and three stuffed animals.

"We thought these items might be useful in identifying the victims," Lieutenant Ward said as he joined them.

Her gaze settled on a tiny yellow bunny rabbit. It was tattered and soggy, one eye missing, a necklace bearing a best-friend charm around its neck.

Tears blurred Beth's eyes, and she cradled the stuffed animal to her chest. It was the only thing Sunny had left from her family. Her father had given it to her on her fourth birthday, just a few months before he and his wife died.

She'd been so afraid of the dark that she couldn't sleep without the rabbit.

"Beth?" Ian's hand touched her arm.

Beth choked back tears. "It's Sunny's," she whispered.

A second later, she rushed from the room. She made it to the bathroom just in time to run into a stall and drop to her knees before her silent tears turned into a sob.

The anguish in Beth's voice when she'd held that toy rabbit ate at Ian as he stepped back into the hallway.

"Do you really think she's going to be able to handle this?" Dr. Wheeland asked.

"I'm not sure," Ian said, hating to cast doubt on her. "But we need her help." His personal motive bound them together. "Finding her friend and making sure the killer is in prison could give her closure."

Dr. Wheeland pursed his lips. "Or it could tear her completely apart."

Ian would do whatever he could to make it easier. He owed her that much.

"Why do you think the unsub buried these items with the girls?" Ian asked.

The ME shook his head. "Because he didn't want to leave evidence behind?"

"That's a possibility." He indicated the rabbit. "Did you find any DNA?"

"Just the girls'."

"He probably wore gloves," Ian said. "That means he's planning this. The crimes are premeditated, and he's protecting himself."

Dr. Wheeland nodded. "Planning, yes. But do you think he stalks the girls in advance and chooses them for a reason, or does he randomly select them when the opportunity presents itself?"

Ian scratched his head. "Good question. When we learn more about the victims, that'll give us the answer."

That answer could help lead them to the killer.

He told the ME to call when he had more information, then headed down the hall to check on Beth. She was exiting the ladies' room, so he jogged toward her. "Beth, wait."

Her heels clicked as she hurried forward.

"Beth?" He caught her before she reached the exit. The moment he touched her arm, she jerked around, eyes blazing.

Eyes that looked red-rimmed, as if she'd been crying.

"Are you all right?" he asked quietly.

A steely expression replaced the pain. "Yes. I just need some air."

God, she was trying to be tough. But she'd been a victim of the maniac who'd killed more than a dozen adolescents. "I understand seeing Sunny's stuffed animal was difficult. Did it trigger any memories of what happened that night?"

Irritation sharpened her delicate features. "No. And if we're going to work together, you can't constantly be watching me, dissecting my every movement, asking me that question." Her voice grew hard. "If I remember anything, I'll tell you. I don't intend to hold back any gory details either. I'll do whatever I have to do to find this bastard."

With one last tormented gaze, she stormed out the front door.

Regret filled him for not being more sensitive.

Voices echoed down the hall as other team members dispersed. He pushed open the door to catch up with Beth and apologize.

But that unscrupulous reporter Corbin Michaels was rushing toward her.

The parasite had covered the previous serial murders in Graveyard Falls and would do anything for a story.

Beth froze as a camera flashed. Ian rushed to her side just as Michaels fired a question.

"You're working with the task force on the boneyard murders, aren't you, miss? What's your name?"

Beth fidgeted. "Special Agent Beth Fields."

"We're busy, Michaels." Ian took Beth's arm to rescue her.

"Sheriff, there were a dozen bodies found, correct?" Michaels pressed.

Ian silently cursed. Like it or not, he had to deal with the media. "Yes, we've organized a task force. An investigation is underway."

Michaels lifted a brow. "Have you identified the victims?"

"We have identified three of them, but not all. At the moment, we're working to contact the victims' families. Now, Mr. Michaels, step aside. We have work to do."

Together he and Beth hurried down the steps. Beth's legs wobbled slightly, but he kept a firm grip until they reached her car.

Before he could speak, she spun around. "Good God, Ian. What if that man plasters my picture on the news?"

Ian raised a brow in question, then realized her concern. Peyton had recognized her from the facial progression sketch, and he'd known her from the past.

What if the killer recognized her? Would he come after her?

He left the new girl to think about her sins.

Her name was Prissy. So fitting.

Except she wasn't the showy type like her name suggested. She was . . . plain. Homely. Desperate for attention.

Maybe she could be saved.

Her screams echoed off the cavern walls as he eased into the shadows. The lingering scent of the last one's decaying body wafted toward him, clouding the air with an acrid odor. He didn't remember her name.

But the police had found her.

He had to be careful. They were all over the mountains hunting for him.

Excitement stirred as he gazed at the beautiful wall of blood.

Each one was labeled with the giver's name. Each one was noted by date of extraction, blood type, and as he had the time to test them, with genetic markers, including any imperfections in the blood.

One day he would find a way to remove the bad blood and replace it.

Until then he would preserve it and continue his Calling. His destiny had been preordained.

 читатель

As God's humble servant, he had to follow it.

The tarp he'd used to catch the last girl's blood held spatters from the draining. They resembled the outline of a dragonfly.

He hung it on the wall as his inspiration, then mixed a small amount of her blood with his paint.

His hand trembled with anticipation as he dipped the brush into the blood paint and began to create a garden of dragonflies on his canvas.

CHAPTER SEVEN

Beth couldn't escape the reporter fast enough.

Ian ushered her down the steps, staying close to her side as they put distance between themselves and Corbin Michaels.

"Where are you parked?" Ian asked.

"The black Volvo, third row."

He steered her toward it. "I'm sorry about Michaels," Ian said. "He covered the previous serial killer case involving the Butcher. He's persistent."

Beth sucked in a breath. "I created a new identity so the man who abducted me wouldn't be able to track me down."

"It's been years, Beth. If Michaels prints a photo, your kidnapper probably won't recognize you."

"You did and so did Peyton," Beth bit out.

They reached her car, and she removed her keys and pressed the key fob to unlock the car. Two rows over, a ball cap caught her eye. Her skin prickled. Was the killer watching them?

Ian leaned against the side of the vehicle, oblivious to her thoughts. "Peyton only recognized you because of the facial progression software. And because she's trained."

The keys jangled in Beth's hand. "But you knew the moment you laid eyes on me."

"Because I never forgot you." His voice roughened with emotions. "Your face has been imprinted in my mind every day for the past fifteen years."

Beth shifted restlessly. "Because you hated me for your father's conviction."

He shook his head. "No. I hated myself for leaving you in the lurch that night."

Emotions vibrated between them as thick and dark as the storm clouds hovering above. The regret in his voice touched Beth deeply.

"You barely knew me, Ian. I wasn't surprised when you didn't show. I was a loser. I figured you had better things to do."

The wind fluttered, rippling through Ian's hair. Beth had the insane urge to smooth it down. As it was, it gave him a wild and untamed image. He was so damn handsome that she felt a tingle of desire.

"You weren't a loser, Beth. And I'm not making excuses," Ian said. "I told you I'd be there, and I should have come. If I had, you and Sunny wouldn't have gotten in that truck, and she'd be alive."

Beth chewed her bottom lip. Hadn't she thought the same thing a million times? But she couldn't allow Ian to blame himself. "Maybe," she admitted. "But we were runaways, easy targets. I should have tried harder to convince the social worker that Herman Otter was a predator."

"Did you tell the social worker?" Ian asked.

"Yes, but she was so busy she didn't take the time to listen. I was a problem child. She . . . had too many cases to probe into what was going on."

Remorse flickered in Ian's eyes. "I'm sorry, Beth. If I could go back and change things, I would."

Her gaze met his, some emotion she didn't want to think about welling in her chest. "So would I." She hated the crack in her voice.

"But we can't. All we can do is track this bastard down so he doesn't hurt anyone else."

Ian inched closer, making it hard for her to breathe. His masculine scent wafted around her, arousing sensations she hadn't felt before.

The need to lean into someone. To be held by a man.

Although in college she'd dated and slept with one guy, nothing had lasted. It had felt all wrong, impersonal, as if she'd never really connected with any of them.

Trust was not in her vocabulary.

For some crazy reason, though, she sensed she could trust Ian.

"I'm glad you survived," Ian said gruffly.

His comment reminded her of the dark place she'd lived when she'd been released from the hospital. The dark place that beckoned her at night when she was alone.

One of the counselors at the group home had encouraged her to attend therapy and take self-defense classes. She'd also introduced them to a nice little church where the preacher was kind and soft-spoken, the music calming, the people welcoming and personable.

So different from the fundamentalist snake-handling ways at the church Otter had forced them to attend. That man had ranted about hellfire and damnation and convinced Beth she would end up in hell.

Self-deprecation lingered, taunting her that she'd caused Sunny's death. "Who says I survived?"

His expression softened. "You're here. And you're tough, Beth. One of the strongest women I've ever met."

"Everything isn't always what it seems," she murmured.

Compassion filled his expression. Maybe even a sliver of admiration. Or attraction?

The urge to be closer to him made her lean toward him. His gaze fell to her mouth, and fear trampled that urge.

"I have to go," she said, desperate to escape. "I need to get settled in the cabin."

"I can follow you over. Make sure that reporter doesn't bother you."

She shook her head and slid into the car. There was no way she wanted him inside that place with her. She was too vulnerable. She might be tempted to ask him to stay.

And that would be a mistake. Beth didn't depend on anyone but herself.

She had a job to do. She had to focus. "Thanks, but I need to do this alone. Call me if you learn anything else."

"All right." He laid one hand on the door to keep her from shutting it. "If you want to see the place where Sunny was found, let me know. It's been roped off, and a guard is on duty day and night in case the killer returns."

Beth shivered at the thought. But that sight might trigger memories from the past. Memories that would give her answers.

Maybe her abductor's face would finally emerge from the shadows.

Admiration and regret flooded Ian as Beth drove away.

Whether she believed it or not, she was a survivor. A weaker person might have allowed the trauma from her ordeal to stunt her growth as a person. Instead of giving in to despair, she'd channeled her pain into a career to keep other children from suffering abuse and becoming victims of predators. She sought justice for those in need.

Knowing it was dangerous for Beth's picture to go public, Ian strode toward the reporter. "Listen to me, Michaels, our team is aware that the public has a right to know what's happening, but we have to protect the investigation."

Hamrick looked pissed. "We'll give you information on a need-to-know basis. But if you interfere, I'll have you locked up."

Ian reached for the camera. "Give me that picture you took of Agent Fields."

Michaels scoffed. "Why would I do that?"

"Because you want the story," Ian said bluntly. "That means you'll cooperate and refrain from printing pictures of the agents and details of the case unless you clear it with us."

"I won't run it," Michaels said. "But in exchange, I expect an exclusive."

Ian traded a look with Hamrick, then nodded. "Deal."

◆ ◆ ◆

Beth needed time alone.

She felt raw, vulnerable, a feeling she didn't like.

The sun struggled to break through dark clouds, intensifying the gloominess of a town ravaged by the tornado's destruction and the devastation of another horrendous crime.

Memories of Sunny dogged Beth as she turned onto the road that led toward the cabins on the river.

Sunny's pale, thin face as she'd gripped that stuffed bunny haunted her and launched Beth back in time, back to when she was still JJ.

It was raining outside, the wind howling. Sunny cried as the social worker left her with the Otters.

JJ had shut herself off from caring about anyone, hadn't made friends with the other kids in the homes. It hurt too much when she had to say good-bye.

That night, though, as she lay in the dark, huddled beneath the faded bedspread, Sunny's soft whimpers filled the cold room. JJ reminded herself not to care. To stay in her twin bed.

Sunny had to learn to be tough like her or she'd never survive.

A streak of lightning zigzagged through the room and Sunny screamed, a bloodcurdling sound that made JJ cringe.

Herman Otter darted through the door, fists raised as he shook them at Sunny. "Shut up or I'll give you something to cry about."

Sunny huddled under the covers, shaking and burying her face in the pillow. JJ wanted to attack the hateful man. Hit him with something.

But terror forced her to lie still. She'd tried fighting back once and had gotten the shit beat out of her for it.

He whirled on her, his beady eyes shooting a warning to keep her mouth shut.

JJ twisted the covers in her fingers and dropped her head onto the pillow, then froze until he stalked from the room.

When that door closed and another streak of lightning slashed the darkness, JJ could see Sunny shaking under the covers. Her soft cries ripped at JJ, and her rage at Otter forced her from bed.

She crawled in beside Sunny and pulled her next to her, the bunny snug between them.

"I hate him," Sunny whispered between sobs.

"I hate him, too." JJ stroked Sunny's golden hair. Sunny was so thin her bones poked at JJ as she wrapped her tighter into her embrace. "We'll stick together and get through it," she murmured.

Sunny lifted her head, tears streaming. "But I'm not big and strong like you."

JJ rubbed her back. "Don't worry. I'll take care of you. Okay?"

Sunny's chin wobbled but she nodded. Then JJ offered her pinky finger. "Pinky swear we'll be sisters forever."

Sunny joined her tiny pinky finger with JJ's.

From then on, Sunny was JJ's shadow.

The sight of trees ripped from their roots jarred Beth from the memory, and she wiped at the tears she didn't realize she'd been crying.

Tall pines had been cracked in two, branches and limbs broken and scattered along the road, giving the appearance of a war zone. Blue tarps covered roofs that had been shattered by the storm, and the trailer parker had been demolished.

She felt just as ravaged as the town.

Exhausted, she veered onto a side road and headed toward Hemlock Holler.

Remembering the legend of the town, that the cries of three murder victims echoed off the mountain, sent a chill through her.

She could practically hear the cries of the dead girls who'd been left in that graveyard.

Then Sunny's sweet voice whispered through her mind. *"You pinky swore, JJ."*

Beth rubbed the penny necklace.

She hadn't saved Sunny, but she would get justice for her.

She parked on the side of the scenic drop-off near a dark SUV. An older man in a deputy's uniform slid from the vehicle and introduced himself as Clyde Barron. Beth showed him her credentials.

"I retired last year from the county, but under the circumstances I offered to work security till this case is solved."

"Any trouble?" Beth asked.

He shook his head. "Nah. A few locals drove up to see the bone-yard. Just curious I guess. But no one has crossed the barrier."

"Keep us posted if anyone looks suspicious."

He agreed and returned to his SUV while she walked to the edge of the ridge and stared across the land at the flooded valley.

The area had been roped off with crime scene tape.

The wind screeched again. Ghostly images rose from the depths of the muddy water. Something floated along the edge of the embankment.

The hair on the back of her neck prickled, and she shivered. Something shifted in the woods. A tree limb moved. Leaves fluttered down.

Eyes peered through the darkness.

Beth froze, defenses mounting as she searched the thicket of trees.

Someone was out there watching her.

Was it the killer?

♦ ♦ ♦

He ducked behind a tree on the opposite side of the valley, frustrated that his boneyard had been exposed but grateful one grave lay untouched at the top of the hill overlooking the others.

He placed the flowers on top of it and said a prayer.

Leaves rustled to the right. He jerked his head up, senses honed.

Somebody was at the edge, gawking.

A woman.

She didn't belong.

This holler was sacred, a grassy field where he'd laid the girls he'd saved to rest. Hemlock trees thickened the woods, but from the bottom of the holler looking up, on a clear day the clouds looked like angels praying over the land.

Just as he'd prayed for each girl he'd buried.

Prissy's cries rang in his ears. She was just like the others. She'd disobeyed her parents. Turned against them and the Lord.

She was a heathen. She wore short skirts and tight blouses and told him she'd run away because the boy she loved didn't want her.

Whore.

She couldn't help it. It was the bad blood.

He hadn't been able to let her go yet. He felt sorry for her because he couldn't bury her here with the others.

He had to find a new home for his angels.

A ray of sunshine broke through the clouds and slanted light on the figure standing by the boneyard.

She wore black slacks and a black jacket—man clothes. Her hair was dark, pulled back in a tight bun, her mood somber.

One of the Feds. She'd come to the holler to track him down.

Then she titled her face toward the sky, and something clicked in his brain. That dainty nose, heart-shaped face . . .

He raised his binoculars and focused on her profile as she scanned the holler. Not red hair, but dark. Black. Unnatural, as if she dyed it.

Ivory skin, high forehead, those . . . eyes.

They were so blue. So familiar.

Just like . . . JJ's.

The night he'd taken JJ and Sunny to the cave, JJ's eyes had looked at him as if he were a monster. She hadn't understood he'd meant to save her. That he'd been watching her for years.

A memory floated to the surface of his mind as if it had been uprooted just like the bones in the holler. The scars on her neck. On her arms. Burns.

He had to be sure it was her.

He used his binoculars to focus on her slender throat then her wrist.

Good God. It was *her*.

The one he'd let go because she was special.

Jane Jones.

He'd read that she had amnesia. That she didn't remember anything about her abduction or her kidnapper.

No one knew the reason why he'd released her.

No one ever would.

CHAPTER EIGHT

Ian couldn't get Beth—JJ—off his mind as he entered Cocoa's Café. The delicious aromas of buttery biscuits, cinnamon rolls, spicy chili, and apple pie scented the air and made the diner feel homey and as welcoming as Cocoa, the owner.

When she'd first moved here and opened her doors, residents hadn't welcomed her or her business. Apparently her dark-chocolate color had turned them off.

Thankfully she hadn't allowed their attitude to deter her. She'd stepped outside, offering trays of free samples, carrying casseroles and pies to the needy, and soon her friendly spirit and home-cooked food brought them into her café.

Now she was the heart of the town.

When the residents' morale had tanked after the Butcher case, Cocoa had thrown a party to remind people to pull together and rebuild their lives.

She was doing that again now that the tornado and floods had hit. She'd donated meals to those in need and kept a revolving door open for rescue workers and the homeless. She also set a donation jar by the cash register and collected daily.

No one could resist her positive energy and warm smile. Her robust body was in perpetual motion as she raced around the kitchen and popped out to talk to the customers.

A group of teenagers was huddled in a booth sipping malted milk-shakes, talking in hushed voices as if they were nervous.

They *should* be nervous. A killer was targeting girls their age.

Ian's hands knotted into fists as he strode to the bar. He wanted to find the bastard who'd murdered the girls and lock him up. He wanted to find his father and clear his name.

What if doing the first meant he couldn't do the latter?

Dammit, he'd deal with it—that's what he'd do.

"Hey, Sheriff," Cocoa said with a friendly wave of her chubby hand. "I bet you've been working hard and built up an appetite."

Ian glanced around the café, noting the plastic tarp covering one window and part of the ceiling. Repairs were needed, but Cocoa hadn't let it sour her mood.

He leaned over the counter, well aware that curious eyes and ears followed him. "Yeah, we had a task force meeting." He scrubbed his hand through his hair. "Agents and crime investigators will be in town for a while."

Cocoa set a glass of sweet tea in front of him. "If y'all need late-night meals, I'll set something up."

"Thanks." He ordered the special to go—chili, mashed potatoes, and macaroni and cheese.

The door opened, and a man in a white lab coat walked in. Something about the man struck Ian as familiar. "You know him?"

"I know everyone in town." Cocoa laughed and waved to the man as he took a bar stool at the opposite end. "Name's Abram Cain. Anytime there's an emergency, he jumps in to help. He's been driving that blood bank bus around collecting blood for the hospitals. Said he's hit all the churches."

Voices and chairs scraping the floor made him angle his head sideways to scan the room. Someone in this town, perhaps in this room, could be the unsub.

"The town council is having an arts festival to raise money for repairs to businesses," Cocoa said, making small talk. "One of the local artists who lives up in the mountains is gonna donate some of his work."

Ian sipped his drink. He wasn't much into art. "That's generous."

She lowered her voice. "I hear tell he paints religious symbolism, correlations to the wine and blood in the Bible. Jesus shedding his blood to save us from our sins."

Ian kept one ear open to her as he scanned the crowd in case the killer was watching.

A gust of wind swept through the room as Deputy Whitehorse entered and claimed the stool beside him.

"What's our next step?" Deputy Whitehorse asked. "Or should I be asking that Fed since he made it plain he's in charge?"

Ian gripped his tea glass. "Let me worry about him. This is our town. You know more about these hills and the people in it than he does."

The deputy cut him a sideways grin. "We both do."

Ian wasn't about to sit on his ass and let Vance take over. "I'll get Markum to check out the church angle while you comb the mountains for a cabin, chicken house, abandoned outbuilding, any place the unsub could have kept the girls."

"You don't think he killed them in the holler?"

"If he did, the flood and tornado erased the physical evidence." Ian paused. "The unsub probably takes the girls someplace secluded to kill them so no one can hear them scream for help. Let's find that kill spot. Start at the boneyard and fan out from there."

Deputy Whitehorse accepted the coffee Cocoa handed him. "No sweat. I'll organize a team."

Ian thanked him and then yanked out several bills to pay, but Cocoa waved him off. "No bill for the law enforcement officers."

Ian mentally noted the repairs needed and tossed cash on the bar. "You've been generous with your time and restaurant. Take it to help with the cause."

She gave him a smile of thanks and slipped the cash into the donation jar. "There are some families in need. I'll use it for them."

Ian's chest swelled with unaccustomed emotions. His own mother had shoved him away after his father's arrest, yet this kindhearted woman would give the shirt off her back to help a stranger.

Sara Levinson—the mother of a teen killed decades ago in the Thorn Ripper case—approached him, two other women with her. "Sheriff, what in God's name is going on? Have you found out who buried those girls at Hemlock Holler?"

"Will our town ever be safe?" another woman asked.

"We've brought in a task force to investigate," Ian said. "We'll find out who did this."

A white-haired lady wielding a big purse walked up. Good God. It was the former mayor's wife, Jeanette.

"How many have to die before you do?" she asked in a brittle tone.

He didn't know how to answer that. Not when he didn't have a damn clue about who they were looking for.

"So far none of the victims have been from Graveyard Falls," Ian said. "That should give you some comfort."

The women fidgeted as if his observation didn't ease their nerves at all.

Cocoa's fourteen-year-old granddaughter, Vanessa, loped in, her cell phone tucked to her ear as she grabbed a doughnut from the display on the counter. Vanessa was in the same age range as the victims. So were those other teenage girls drinking malts.

An uneasy feeling splintered Ian. Just because none of the victims were from Graveyard Falls didn't mean that the killer wasn't here now, hunting for his next victim among the locals.

It took Beth no time to settle into the cabin. She'd traveled light, bringing only the essentials with her.

Not that she had any froufrou in her life. Easier to pick up and go.

It wasn't safe to stay in any one place for too long anyway. The faceless monster from her nightmares might find her.

Moving didn't bother her. She'd never had a real home. Staying meant attachments. Attachments were something she didn't allow herself.

Although she did keep a wall in her home office featuring the missing children who haunted her.

The not knowing nagged at her, but her grief for them was nothing compared to their families' suffering.

She understood that agony—Sunny was the only family she'd ever known.

Beth spread her own case file across the desk in the cabin. She'd read it a thousand times. She'd read it another thousand times if she had to.

She started with the police report. A uniformed officer had responded to a call from a truck driver who ran long hauls from Atlanta to Tennessee delivering food products.

The trucker's name was Vinny Barlow.

She jotted down his name and phone number.

All these years, she'd never spoken to him or visited the place where he'd found her. She'd been too afraid.

It was time to push past the fear.

Barlow could have retired since then, moved states—the number could be disconnected But she had resources. She'd find him and talk to him herself.

Meanwhile, she read his account:

I was making my run but got sleepy, so I pulled over to a rest stop at the East Ridge exit off I-75. There were a few cars parked in the lot at the other end. Another trucker was asleep in his cab.

When I came out of the john, I heard this noise, thought it was a dog or a cat that someone had dumped. But I walked around the side of the building and saw this bundle against the wall by the snack machine. I went to check it out, and the bundle moved.

It about freaked me out. But I stooped down and checked. It was a girl wrapped in a blanket.

She was delirious, moaning and rubbing at her wrist. She had rope burns on her arms and legs and blood on her clothes, but I didn't see where it was coming from.

I was all shook up. A man and his boy were coming out of the men's room, and I yelled at them to call 911.

The recording of the 911 call had confirmed his story.

She honed in on his description of her—she'd been rubbing her wrist and had rope burns, but her wrists hadn't been cut.

The truth dawned on her.

The blood had belonged to Sunny.

An image flashed behind her eyes.

Blood dripping from Sunny's arms . . .

She tried to reach out to stop it, but she was tied down. The blood kept coming, gushing like a river . . .

She screamed. She had to get loose. Had to save Sunny . . .

A cold sweat broke out all over Beth. She'd been rubbing her wrist because she was trying to tell them that he'd cut Sunny's arms, that they had to hurry to save her.

She flipped to the lawyer's notes on Kelly Cousins, the girl Coach Gleason had been accused of misconduct with. Her wrists had been cut as well.

Had she committed suicide, or had she been one of this unsub's victims?

She closed her eyes, struggling to recall more details of that fatal night with Sunny. She could see Sunny's terrified eyes, see the blood trickling down her arm.

Why couldn't she see the man's face?

All the Dead Girls

Ian had barely talked to his mother the last ten years, not since the day she'd married Bernie. She'd met him at the Holy Waters. A church Ian thought was more of a cult than a place of true worship.

Bernie had brainwashed her into following his fundamentalist beliefs. Fire and brimstone, talking in tongues, snake handling, every sinner was going to hell.

Except for the church parishioners, Bernie kept her isolated. Easier to keep her under his thumb if no one else was around to sway her mind or encourage her to think for herself.

Ian tossed the container from his meal, picked up the office phone, and called his mother. If she hadn't seen the news about Hemlock Holler, Ian wanted to talk to her about it.

The phone rang three times. "Woods residence."

Dammit, Bernie never let her answer. "Bernie, this is Ian. Let me speak to my mother."

A second passed, then Bernie heaved a weary breath. "No, Ian. I don't want her upset."

"I have news she needs to know about," Ian said, determined not to give up. "We found several bodies near Graveyard Falls. We believe the same man who abducted Jane Jones and Sunny Smith killed Sunny, then killed more than a dozen others," Ian said. "I think I can finally prove Dad's innocence."

"Talking to her about that is only going to agitate her," Bernie said, his voice rising.

Every muscle in Ian's body knotted. "Has my father contacted her since that prison flood?"

"No, and if he did, I'd call the police. Now leave us alone."

The phone clicked silent.

Ian cursed. How dare that asswipe deny him a conversation with his mother as if Ian was a criminal himself.

In spite of the way she'd abandoned him, he loved her. Proving his father's innocence would comfort her.

Not that it would bring them back together again. His family had been destroyed the moment those allegations had been made.

His phone buzzed. Damn.

He grabbed it, hoping to hear his mother's voice, but it was another female.

"Ian, it's Beth."

"Yeah?"

"I want to talk to the trucker who found me, and the sheriff who handled the case in Sweetwater."

Headler was sheriff of Sweetwater fifteen years ago when Beth had been abducted. At that time Sweetwater and Graveyard Falls had been in separate counties, but five years ago the lines had been redrawn. Now they fell under the same county, making Sweetwater also Ian's territory.

"Ian?"

"Yes, I'll make the call."

"We should interview Kelly Cousins's parents, too. Now that we know these victims' wrists were cut, we have to consider the fact that Kelly might not have taken her own life."

"But she wasn't buried in the holler or wearing a white dress," Ian said.

"No, but she was holding a white candle and a cross."

Prissy slowly opened her eyes, but it was so dark she couldn't make out where she was.

What had happened to her? Her mind felt fuzzy. Her head hurt. And her stomach . . . She rolled to her side and heaved onto the ground.

The world spun. She tasted dirt and bile. A shudder ripped through her.

A faint memory nagged at her. She'd climbed into a truck.

Someone had drugged her? Or . . . put something over her face?

God, the past few hours were a blur. She'd been at school, excited over being with Blaine . . .

But he was kissing Sari and everyone was making fun of her, chanting, "Pissy Prissy, Pissy Prissy."

She'd been so embarrassed. She'd run . . .

She tried to wipe her tears with her hands, but they were tied behind her back. Her feet were bound, too. And her glasses were missing. She felt exposed without the familiar weight of them on her nose.

Fear clawed at her. Where was she? In some abandoned building? An underground basement? A cave?

How had she gotten here?

The sound of water dripping came from a distant corner. Rain?

Cold air swirled around her. The scent of something rancid. A dead animal?

Music wafted from somewhere nearby. An iPod? A phone? No . . . a man's voice. He was singing, soft, low, some kind of religious hymn about the blood of Jesus.

A door opened, letting in the faintest sliver of light. She couldn't see his face. He was tall, though. And he wore some kind of cloak.

"Please help me," she cried. "I'm afraid of the dark."

He stooped to light a candle by the door, then lifted it in one hand. The flames flickered, but his face remained in the shadows. "Don't worry, I'm here."

Only his voice sounded menacing, not reassuring.

And the shiny glint of a knife flickered against the darkness.

CHAPTER NINE

While Beth waited for Ian, she phoned Peyton. "Can you send me a projected picture of what the most recent victim looked like before decomp set in?"

"The forensic artist is working on it," Peyton said. "Dr. Wheeland thinks her body might have been kept in a freezer, which would have slowed down decomp and messes with time of death."

Hmm. So wherever he kept the girls, he had access to a freezer. It could be a house or someplace with a basement. She shivered at her next thought—possibly a grocery store or an ice cream factory or a meat-packing plant. Hell, even a morgue.

"We did identify two more victims," Peyton continued. "They were from different parts of the state, thirteen and fourteen years old. Dr. Wheeland estimates time of death to be at least fifteen years ago. Agents Hamrick and Coulter are following up with these families."

Beth accessed NCMEC's database and started scrolling through the pictures.

A second passed. "Director Vance wants you to focus on finding out what that sheriff knows."

"He thinks Ian is holding back?"

"Maybe. If he's seen or talked to Coach Gleason, we need to know."

"Right." Although she didn't like being used as a spy, it came with the job. But Ian didn't know any more than he'd told them. Did he?

A knock sounded at the door, and she startled. God, she was a wreck.

She kept her phone to her ear and went to peek out the window. Ian. Relief flooded her. "Okay, but don't forget to send me that artist's sketch."

"ASAP."

Beth ended the call and answered the door.

"You want to visit Sheriff Headler?"

"Absolutely. And the truck driver who found me." He could have been her abductor.

The sound of the wind beating the trees filled the silence as they went to his SUV, and Ian drove to the Headler house. Beth relayed the news that Dr. Wheeland had identified two more victims. "He's working on determining who the latest victim is. I want to talk to the family."

"So do I," Ian said. "If you and Director Vance allow it."

Beth made a low sound in her throat. "Ian, I'm not trying to exclude you."

Ian focused on the road as if he was fighting anger but said nothing until they reached the house.

"Do you remember talking to Sheriff Headler?" Ian asked Beth as they walked up the stone path to the man's front door.

Beth shrugged. "Yes, but things are blurry. The sheriff visited me in the hospital, then questioned me after the coach was arrested and I was placed in the group home."

Ian's jaw tightened. "That home must have been rough."

"It was better than Otter's. It's not like anyone wanted to take in a troubled kid with amnesia."

Ian punched the doorbell, his expression grim.

"You talked to Headler, too, didn't you?" Beth asked.

"Yes. Several times." Frustration and pain edged his voice.

While she'd been struggling with her own nightmares, Ian's had begun when the jury sent his father to prison.

She was beginning to think his conviction was a mistake.

The doorbell chimed a second time as Ian punched it again. Tree frogs croaked and crickets chirped, filling the air with the reminder of spring. Rainwater had collected in pools on the ground, the earth soaked from the flooding. A few shingles had been ripped from the roof, and the shed tilted sideways, but otherwise Headler's property had survived the tornado.

The door opened, and a gray-haired man in a wrinkled plaid shirt and overalls stood frowning at them. "What can I do for you, folks?"

Ian introduced Beth, then himself, his tone abrupt.

"I'm the sheriff of Graveyard Falls," Ian said. "Ian Kimball."

"You were Coach Gleason's kid?"

Ian nodded.

"I heard about all those dead girls you found." He ran a hand through his hair. "Got a mess on your hands."

"Yeah, can we talk?"

Headler hesitated, then led them to a screened back porch.

As they took seats, Headler squinted at Beth. "Agent Fields, you . . . remind me of someone."

"That's because I'm Jane Jones." Beth sorted through her foggy memories. Sheriff Headler had been kind to her during the questioning. Had promised to make the man who kidnapped her go to jail.

Then he'd zeroed in on the coach.

Seeing Headler now had to trigger bad memories for Ian.

The wrinkles around Headler's mouth crinkled. "You've changed, grown up."

"It's been fifteen years," Beth said, steeling herself against his scrutiny. "I work with the FBI and with NCMEC."

He gave a wary nod. "Good for you."

Ian cleared his throat. "You know the reason we're here."

"You think I can help with that graveyard of bones?"

"Can you?" Ian asked.

"I don't see how." Headler folded his work-roughened hands on his belly. "I had no idea corpses were being dumped there. Remember, we were different counties back then."

"Then perhaps you can fill in some blanks for me," Beth said. "What made you so certain Coach Gleason was guilty?"

Headler pulled a pack of chewing tobacco from his pocket, pinched off a bite, and stuffed it in his jaw. "You did. You kept screaming his name like he was the devil incarnate."

Beth clenched her hands, willing more details to resurface.

"You had no physical evidence, no forensics, no eye witness," Ian pointed out.

"We had that truck and Gleason's print." Headler shifted the tobacco in his mouth. "He had no alibi. And all the kids at school were saying he took advantage of Kelly Cousins."

Beth had read the report. Coach Gleason had claimed he and his wife had argued the night of her abduction, and he'd gone for a drive. Alone.

That hadn't helped his case.

Ian clenched his hands. "Sunny Smith was in that river of bones we discovered in the holler."

Headler spit tobacco juice into an empty tin can. "Yeah, I read about that in the paper. I also know your daddy escaped that prison flood. If you're harboring a fugitive, Kimball, you can go to jail."

"I'm not hiding anyone," Ian said brusquely. "But you should have explored other leads."

"I had no other leads." Headler's face reddened with anger.

Beth had expected tension, but it was escalating fast. She started to speak—she had to defuse the situation. But a faint memory flashed back. One from her nightmares.

He shoved her and Sunny into the cold room of the cavern. She tried to fight, but he'd tied her arms behind her back. Sunny whimpered, heaving for a breath. She was tied, too.

He aimed his flashlight toward the far wall. Another girl was there. Tied to metal posts.

Then he forced JJ to her knees . . . She cried out for help. Then she saw blood dripping down the girl's arm.

She looked up at the man; maybe she could strike a bargain.

"Kill me instead of Sunny," she whispered.

His laugh boomed off the cavern walls, cold and evil.

He was going to kill them both.

Ian swallowed hard as the color drained from Beth's face. "Beth?" He reached for her, but she tensed as if she were erecting walls.

"Tell us more, Sheriff Headler," she said in a shaky voice.

The man was watching both him and Beth with snake eyes.

The quicker Ian got what he'd come for, the sooner they could leave.

"Why did you think my father had an inappropriate relationship with Kelly Cousins?" Ian asked.

"One of the boys at school said he saw them together, saw the coach cornering Kelly, said she looked scared. Then her mama found that note. Kelly talked about how much she loved your daddy, that she hoped he left his wife for her."

Ian's lungs squeezed for air. His father never would have done that, or given Kelly that idea. "Did you have that note analyzed to make sure it was her writing?"

"Couldn't. It was typewritten."

Shit. Advances in technology and criminology could do wonders today. "You did log it into evidence, didn't you?"

Headler hooked his thumbs in his overalls. "Yeah. I wasn't incompetent, Kimball."

"We'll have the note analyzed," Beth said as if she'd read his mind. "Where is it? The county office?"

Headler shrugged. "I believe so."

"Did you keep notes on the case?" Ian asked.

Headler worked his tobacco. "Yeah, I think they're here somewhere. Kelly's mother showed us her daughter's diary, too. In it, she talked about seeing the coach, how good he was to her, how much she liked their private time together."

Ian twisted his mouth in thought. "So she had a crush on my dad. A lot of girls did."

"Did she say that he actually molested her?" Beth asked.

"Not in those words." Headler averted his gaze as if he was uncomfortable. "Although the ME said that she wasn't a virgin."

"That doesn't mean she slept with my father," Ian said impatiently.

Beth gently touched Ian's arm to calm him. "I'd like a list of the names of the students you spoke to," Beth said. "I'm also going to request the coach's files from the school."

"You'll have to get a warrant," Headler said.

Beth gave him a tight smile. "We know the law."

Ian crossed his arms. "If Dad's students told him their problems, there might be something in his files proving one of them lied."

"Why would one of them have lied?" Headler asked.

Beth set her cup down. "Teenagers lie all the time. And they get crushes on male role models. Her infatuation with Coach Gleason could have been one-sided."

"If one of the kids had a grudge against my father," Ian said, "he or she could have maligned his character."

"Why would anyone want to hurt the coach?" Headler asked. "Unless he hurt them, which means the accusations against him were true."

Ian's defenses rose. Was this man really that dense? "Did any other female claim impropriety?"

"It's been a long time." Headler scratched his chin. "I'd have to check my notes."

"You were up for reelection around the time of the arrest, weren't you?" Ian asked in a harsh tone.

Headler's nostrils flared. "Yes, but that had nothing to do with how I handled the case."

"Really?" Disbelief rang clear in Ian's tone. "You didn't rush to make an arrest so the people would think you were a hero?"

"Ian." Beth's calm demeanor reminded Ian that if he pissed Headler off, he might not cooperate. But dammit, the man should have explored other possibilities.

Headler pushed himself up from his chair, then rubbed his leg as if it was stiff. "I'll give you a copy of my notes. Then the two of you can get the hell out of my house."

◆ ◆ ◆

Beth tugged her jacket around her as she and Ian hurried to his SUV. The animosity between Ian and the sheriff had been so thick she thought the room would explode with it.

At least Ian had obtained the former sheriff's notes. The file was thinner than she would have expected, but she couldn't wait to read the interviews.

"We should talk to Kelly's parents," Beth said.

Ian started the engine and pulled onto the road. "See if the Cousinses' address is in his notes."

Beth flipped through the folder and located the phone number and address. "They may have moved by now. I'll call."

Ian shook his head. "Let's just stop by. They might not want to talk to us if they get a heads-up first."

"I wouldn't blame them. Dredging up their painful past won't be easy." The strategies she'd learned in the bureau would be helpful. She needed to be compassionate, understanding, tactful with the questions.

"No, but if their daughter didn't commit suicide, they have a right to know."

"We may be jumping to conclusions regarding that," Beth said.

Ian shrugged. "Maybe. But I want to talk to them anyway."

Mixed emotions pummeled Beth. She wanted the truth, but she felt for Ian. Proving his father's innocence was driving him.

What if he discovered his father was a serial killer?

◆ ◆ ◆

Corbin Michaels was tired of being on the fucking short end of the stick. He'd worked his ass off to cover that serial killer case involving Josie DuKane, a complicated shitfest that revolved around the very people working to create a film about the Bride Killer and Thorn Ripper cases. The sheriff and those Feds might argue that Graveyard Falls didn't breed and draw crazies, but he didn't make up these stories—he just reported the facts.

He took another sip of his third high-gravity beer, watching the locals as if he might spot the maniac who'd buried nearly a dozen girls outside of town. Someone that sick should have tattoos of the devil on his head or horns growing from his ears.

Then again, psychopaths often looked normal.

That would make a good slant to his story . . .

The killer might be charming, attractive, at least enough to entice a woman or girl's trust.

Fuck.

He had no idea who this creep was. Neither did the cops.

He set his beer down and grabbed his laptop. He was notorious for recording everything. It used to drive his girlfriend nuts. Then she'd left him for a fucking pissant personal trainer who had abs she said she could eat off.

Who the fuck wanted to eat off a man's chest?

A dark-haired woman walking by reminded him of Beth Fields.

Something about that federal agent seemed familiar. The fact that Kimball didn't want her picture in the paper intrigued him.

He plugged in her name and frowned at the typical run-of-the-mill information that popped up.

No personal information on Beth Fields other than the basics—birth certificate, educational background, documentation of her time studying with the FBI. They seemed almost too . . . pat. Like ones he'd seen when he'd covered that story on WITSEC, the witness protection program.

Victims and witnesses of crimes, and sometimes criminals, often made deals to testify in exchange for a chance at a new life. The U.S. Marshals arranged new identities, jobs, complete lives.

A criminal wouldn't be allowed to join the bureau. But a witness or a victim . . . that was possible.

He tapped his shoe on the floor. What if Beth Fields wasn't really Beth Fields? That would explain the sheriff's insistence upon keeping her picture out of the paper.

Working on a hunch, he pulled up the file on the disappearance of Sunny Smith and JJ Jones. Sunny Smith's body had been found in that sea of bones.

But JJ had survived the abduction. Where was she now?

Seconds later, photographs of Sunny Smith and JJ Jones filled the screen. Sunny had been a blonde doll. JJ—a redhead with freckles and pale skin.

As he zeroed in on the picture, suspicion took hold. The slanted nose, heart-shaped face, those deep blue eyes . . .

He slumped back in his chair as the truth hit him.

Special Agent Beth Fields *was* JJ Jones.

He reached for his beer with a triumphant smile. By God, he had his angle.

He picked up his cell phone and called his editor.

Just wait until his headline ran.

Survivor of Boneyard Killer Returns as FBI
Agent to Track Down Her Abductor.

CHAPTER TEN

Ian punched the couple's address into his GPS and drove back onto the interstate. They lived just a few miles from Headler.

Night was setting in, the skies gloomy, adding a macabre feeling to the land. Although the tornado had swept through, the devastation wasn't as bad as it was in Graveyard Falls. A few trees were down, limbs and debris dotted the roads, and a couple of old outbuildings and barns had been damaged.

The Cousinses lived in a small neighborhood with older brick houses that had probably once been nice but had been ravaged by age.

"I've worked with families who've lost a child. Some of them never recover from the loss," Beth said.

"I can understand that," Ian said.

Beth shifted, her tightly wound bun starting to slip. For a brief second, he glimpsed the sweet, shy young girl she'd been. He'd seen her watching him on the soccer field. Knew she'd had a little bit of a crush on him.

She certainly didn't anymore.

He had the urge to tuck her hair back in place, restore order for her.

Yet at the same time, his body heated. He wanted to tear the strands down, run his hands through the loose ends, and make her lose control in a different way.

The thought of getting involved with her shook him to the core. Ian had never let himself get close to anyone before. Didn't want to get hurt, to lose someone else he cared about.

She absentmindedly rubbed one finger along her wrist. Another scar darkened her arm, making him wonder how she'd gotten it.

The Cousinses' house slipped into view, though, and he put the question on the back burner. They had work to do.

Ian studied the house as he parked. A low lamp burned in the front room, indicating someone was home. A carport held a rusted Impala, and the yard was overgrown, the flowerbeds ragged.

"What do you know about Kelly's suicide?" Ian asked.

"I heard all the rumors, but I didn't know what to believe. Someone said she had emotional problems, that she'd run away before. One of the cheerleaders claimed she'd had oral sex with the coach."

Shock knifed through Ian. "I don't believe that. It sounds like she was needy and wanted attention."

"Maybe so."

"But the parents bought her story and blamed my dad," Ian said bitterly.

Beth surprised him by placing her hand over his. Her skin felt warm, soothing, easing some of the pain.

"The parents were hurting, Ian," she said softly. "They wanted someone to blame besides themselves."

Ian narrowed his eyes. "What do you mean?"

"Working with NCMEC has taught me about family dynamics. More than anything, parents want their children to be happy. When their children have problems, the first question they ask is, 'What did I do wrong?'"

Ian cut the engine. His father had taken the fall for their guilt.

Although if Kelly hadn't committed suicide, that meant she'd been murdered.

◆　◆　◆

Beth hated to dredge up the painful past for the Cousinses, but if Kelly hadn't committed suicide, they deserved to know.

Not that learning she was possibly the victim of a serial killer was any comfort.

Worse, if Kelly was murdered, she might have been the man's first victim, which was significant. First victims were more likely a personal kill than a random one.

Kelly's death was slightly different than the others. There was a suicide note. Her body had been found near a church, not buried in Hemlock Holler. But the cross and candle were common denominators.

The profile taking shape pointed toward an insecure person, one with a strong religious upbringing. One who, in his own twisted mind, thought he was saving these girls.

The killer could have started out with the cross and candle with Kelly, then evolved over the years, adding to his MO with the white gowns.

Chilled, Beth wrapped her sweater around herself and walked up the sidewalk.

Ian knocked. A minute later, feet shuffled and the door opened. A short, pudgy woman with wavy hair streaked with gray looked up at them, the hollow look in her eyes mirroring the emptiness Beth had seen in the eyes of other mothers who'd lost children. Fifteen years might dim the pain, but nothing could completely alleviate the anguish.

"Mrs. Cousins?" Beth said.

Kelly's mother wiped a hand over her tired face. "If you're selling something, I don't want it." She started to close the door, but Ian caught it with one hand.

"We're not selling anything, ma'am. My name is Sheriff Ian Kimball, and this is Special Agent Beth Fields. Please let us come in. It's important."

Wariness flashed in the woman's eyes, but she stepped aside and let them enter. "What do you want?"

"Have you seen the news about the bodies that were recently discovered in Graveyard Falls?" Ian asked.

The woman paled slightly. "Yes. What does that have to do with me?"

Beth gently laid a hand on the woman's arm. "Those bodies were all adolescent girls, all the same age as your daughter when she died."

Mrs. Cousins's frown deepened. "I don't understand."

"Is your husband home?" Beth asked.

Her shoulders sagged. "No. We separated ten years ago."

"Your daughter's death tore you apart?" Beth asked softly.

Anguish shadowed her eyes. "Yes. Now please leave me alone. I've been through enough."

Ian held the door firmly with one hand. "What if we told you that Kelly might not have killed herself?"

"What?" she gasped.

"It's possible that the same man who murdered the girls in the holler may have killed your daughter and made it appear like a suicide," Ian replied.

A choked sound erupted from deep in the woman's throat, and she leaned against the doorjamb. "You mean Coach Gleason didn't just drive Kelly to cut her wrists? He actually cut her himself?"

"That's not what I'm implying," Ian said. "I believe someone else murdered Kelly, then planted suspicion on the coach with phony allegations."

Beth's heart ached for the woman. She hoped Ian wasn't jumping to conclusions. Maybe they should have had more evidence before approaching Mrs. Cousins.

Denial raged in the woman's eyes. "That can't be true. He did it. I know he did."

"How do you know?" Ian asked.

"Sheriff Headler said he did." The woman cinched the belt on her robe tighter. "Besides, I finally made peace with my daughter's death, finally got over my husband leaving, and now you want to stir it up by telling me my little girl was murdered."

Beth patted the woman's shoulder. "Mrs. Cousins, I'm sorry. I realize this is a shock. But we all want the truth. If Coach Gleason didn't hurt Kelly, you want to find out who did, don't you?"

Pain clouded the woman's face. "Of course I do."

Beth squeezed her arm. "Then tell us more about Kelly."

Mrs. Cousins blew her nose on a tissue, then went to the bookshelf and removed a scrapbook. She opened it on the side table, and Beth and Ian watched as she showed them cards Kelly had made as a child, then photographs of her daughter.

"This was Kelly at her dance recital when she was five," the woman said with a sniffle. "All she talked about was being a ballerina one day."

"Did she continue dance lessons?" Ian asked.

Mrs. Cousins shook her head. "She tore a muscle in her calf when she was eleven. After that she never went back." She tapped a picture of Kelly in a canoe with her father when she was a little older, maybe thirteen. "But hormones hit and she became sullen. She used to want to go fishing with her father, but suddenly she didn't want to be with the family anymore. All she talked about was dieting and staying slim so the popular girls would like her."

"That's not uncommon for teenagers," Beth said.

"It was those girls' fault that Kelly was so depressed," Mrs. Cousins said. "They were so mean to her. She just wanted to fit in, to be popular like they were."

"That's when she started seeing the coach for counseling," Beth said.

Mrs. Cousins nodded. "At the time, I thought it would help. But then . . . she became obsessed with him. And when he hurt her, she slunk further and further away."

"What do you mean? How did he hurt her?" Beth asked.

"She was vulnerable," Mrs. Cousins said. "She thought she was in love with the coach. At first he led her on. But later he rejected her."

Beth narrowed her eyes. "He rejected her?"

"He told her she was just a kid. Then he recommended a different counselor. She couldn't stand the thought of that."

She closed the book with a disgusted heave. "The day I heard Coach Gleason escaped prison, I felt like I'd lost her all over again."

Connecting Kelly's case to the boneyard murders was a stretch, but Beth had to know. "My friend Sunny Smith was abducted three months after your daughter died. She was one of the victims found in Hemlock Holler."

"Oh my God," Mrs. Cousins gasped. "Do you think Coach Gleason killed her and those other poor girls?"

Beth shook her head. "I don't think so. There's something else, Mrs. Cousins. I'm JJ, Jane Jones, the girl who was kidnapped with Sunny."

The woman's brows furrowed together. "Then you know who killed her."

"I'm afraid not. I was traumatized and suffered from amnesia," Beth said.

Ian lowered his voice. "The number of victims we found in Graveyard Falls indicates that we're dealing with a serial killer. Coach Gleason doesn't fit that profile, which makes us question his guilt in JJ's kidnapping and the accusations against him regarding Kelly."

Mrs. Cousins turned toward Ian, her eyes widening as recognition dawned. "You . . . Ian is your name? You're his son, that awful man's son, aren't you?"

Ian tensed. "Yes, ma'am, he was my father."

Beth rushed to calm the woman. "Please, we need your help. Was there anyone Kelly was afraid of? Another man who seemed too friendly with her?"

"No, just the coach." Mrs. Cousins flattened a hand over her chest. "That's why you're here. To make me say he wasn't a bad man, but he was. Now get out."

◆ ◆ ◆

Ian stepped back as the woman slammed the door in his face.

Beth called to him as he strode to his SUV, but he ignored her, yanked open the door, and got in.

Beth slipped onto the seat. "Ian, she's been through a lot. It's obvious she's—"

"Grieving." He threw up a hand to halt her. "Believe me, I know she's suffered." He gave her a sideways glance. "So did you."

"We all did," Beth murmured. "Exactly the reason we find the truth."

That was one thing they agreed on.

She opened the folder containing Headler's notes while Ian called the local judge in Graveyard Falls. He explained about the investigation. "I need a warrant for files belonging to Coach Gleason during the time he worked at the high school in Sweetwater." Dammit, he probably should have reviewed them sooner.

"I'll get right on it," the judge said.

Ian thanked him, but his phone was buzzing with another call. "Sheriff Kimball."

"What in God's name is going on?" a man bellowed.

"Who is this?" Ian asked.

"David Cousins. I haven't talked to my wife in three years, and she just called me, hysterical."

Ian gripped the steering wheel with white-knuckled fingers. "I'm sorry—"

The man cut Ian off. "She said you think Kelly was murdered. It's about time someone figured that out. I told everyone that Kelly wouldn't have killed herself."

The photograph of the man and Kelly in the canoe flashed behind Ian's eyes. He'd obviously loved his daughter. "Why do you say that?"

"Because my daughter knew it was wrong," Cousins said sharply. "Committing suicide is a sin in the eyes of the church."

Ian inhaled a deep breath. "Kelly left a note."

"*Someone* left a note to cover up murder," Cousins said. "The note was written on a typewriter. We didn't have one at our house back then."

Ian scrubbed a hand through his hair. "She could have written it at school."

"The coach wrote it," Cousins said. "How could you not know he was a killer?"

Pain ripped through Ian. "Mr. Cousins, if my father did this, I'll find him and lock him up. But if he's innocent, someone else got away scot-free, someone who's murdered several more teenagers since." Ian forced himself to remain professional. "Was there anyone else—another boyfriend, an older man, a neighbor or male relative—who took an interest in her?"

Silence fell as the man's breath rasped out. "No, no one. We raised her right, to attend church, to respect the Lord, to be a good girl." His voice emanated authority. "We had rules, and we made her live by them."

Ian's pulse jumped. Just how did Cousins enforce the rules? "Did you have reason to be concerned that she wasn't following your rules?"

A hesitant pause. Ian could almost hear the turmoil churning in his mind.

"Nothing specific. But she was at that age where she thought she was a grown-up. She started talking back, sneaking out, missing curfew.

Twice I caught a boy in her bedroom. We asked Coach Gleason for help, but that bastard took advantage of her. He played on her vulnerability and made her think he cared about her."

His father had cared about all the kids at school. And the teenage girls had liked him. He was the soccer coach. He talked to them like they were people. He listened to their problems.

"I heard he might have escaped that prison flood," Cousins said. "You'd better hope you find him, because if I do, he won't live to see the inside of a cell."

"I thought you were a religious man, Mr. Cousins."

"I am," Cousins snapped. "The Bible says an eye for an eye."

Then the man hung up on him.

The cold dampness of the cavern soothed the raging heat inflaming him. Here, he could escape. Hide out. Be at peace.

Except the sound of Prissy's crying haunted him.

He clenched the candle in one hand and opened the wooden door. It screeched, announcing his arrival, and she started to scream.

"Please, I'll do anything you want," she cried. "Anything. Let me go and you can have me."

Her sobs increased his agitation, yet his father's voice replayed in his head, calming him. *She's a sinner, son. You can show her the way to salvation.*

He nodded, then slowly walked over to her. She kicked and thrashed against the bindings. "Please," she begged. "I'll do anything."

"Shh," he whispered. "I'll take care of you."

He scooped her into his arms, ignoring the way she fought him as he carried her to the pool of water. The white gown he'd dressed her in made her look angelic in the dim light.

She pleaded for him to let her go, but it was just the demons talking.

He slowly walked into the pool, the warm water swirling around his feet, enveloping him as a ray of light streamed from the center of the tiny opening in the roof of the cavern.

Music from the angels above filled his ears, drowning out the girl's scream as he dipped her below the water. He chanted a Bible verse, praising Jesus for dying for her sins.

She gulped and spit water as he lifted her, and then he carried her back to the blanket he'd spread on the ground.

"No, please," she whimpered.

"Shh, you will soon be free."

Only he hesitated. Maybe he'd read the Bible to her tonight. Give her time to repent.

He retrieved the good book and turned to Genesis.

CHAPTER ELEVEN

Ian's low curse drew Beth's attention from Sheriff Headler's notes. "What's wrong?"

Ian sighed. "That was Mr. Cousins. His wife phoned him about our visit. He claimed he always thought my father murdered Kelly, that he never believed she killed herself."

Beth contemplated his statement. "There are contradictory comments regarding the suicide in the Cousinses' statements. Mrs. Cousins admitted that her daughter had been depressed, that her grades slipped that year. She encouraged Kelly to see the coach for counseling, but Mr. Cousins was vocal against counseling. He insisted his daughter was a good girl, that all she needed was to go to church and pray."

Ian raised a brow. "Something could have been happening at home. Kelly was balking at his strict rules, sneaking out, missing curfew, and bringing boys into her room."

Beth tapped her nails on the file. "There's no suggestion of family problems or that the father was abusive. But if Kelly confided in him, there might be something in Coach Gleason's files about the family."

"Hopefully I'll have the warrant to look at those files soon."

"I'm going with you to the school to interview the teachers," Beth said.

Ian turned onto the highway. "Were you and Kelly friends?"

Beth shook her head. "Are you kidding? I didn't have many friends, Ian."

He gave her a sideways look. "I'm sorry."

She shrugged. She'd been a loner so long she'd accepted it. "It's not your fault. But I can understand if Kelly felt smothered by her father's overbearing attitude. Herman Otter was a snake-handling Christian. He vowed to love God by day, but by night he put aside his vows to his wife to force young girls into his bed." She would have considered him a suspect in these murders, but he was dead.

Beth's head swirled with memories. "Although Herman and Frances didn't keep a clean house and our clothes were ratty, he was fanatical about forcing us to our knees to say prayers at night and attend church. But that wasn't the worst."

Ian swung the vehicle off the road into a diner, cut the engine, and looked at her. "What happened, JJ?"

"Beth." JJ was the scared young girl who'd run away to save herself and gotten her best friend, the girl who'd been a little sister to her, killed.

"Dammit, Beth, tell me."

Beth lifted her chin, the concern in Ian's voice touching her inside. She'd told the task force about Otter, but talking to Ian in private felt too intimate. She felt . . . vulnerable.

Her therapist would encourage her to be honest. She insisted that talking about what had happened would free Beth of the pain and the power it held over her.

But Beth refused to break down in front of Ian. She was a professional.

"Like I said, he thought he was lord of the house. When May was there, she protected me just like I did Sunny after May left."

"How did he take it when May ran away?"

"He flew into a rage," Beth admitted. "Sunny and I locked our-selves in the bedroom so he couldn't get to us that night. Then he beat Frances. He said it was her fault that May got away."

Silence fell between them for a heartbeat. "Were there others before May?"

"I think so, but May didn't talk about them."

"It's hard to imagine his wife standing by and allowing that to hap-pen," Ian said.

Bitterness welled inside Beth. "She seemed relieved. When he had a girl, he left her alone."

"What happened to her?" Ian asked.

Beth shrugged. "After they were questioned about the abuse, she took some pills and killed herself."

"Sick fucks." Ian's dark eyes gleamed with disgust. "When did May run away?"

"A couple of weeks before I did."

"Then he turned his attention toward you?"

"Yes. I heard his wife telling him about my birthday, that he had to wait until then."

"You were about to turn fifteen?" Ian asked.

Beth nodded. "My birthday was the next day. That's why I left that night. Otter was planning the celebration."

Ian's stomach roiled. He'd suspected JJ was being abused, but he'd never imagined Otter's depravity. The gritty details compounded his guilt. She had needed him that night, and he'd failed her.

"You didn't tell my dad? He might have helped."

Beth looked away, stared at the neon light on the diner. "I was too ashamed."

His throat thickened. "You have nothing to be ashamed of."

For a long moment, neither one of them spoke. Ian traced a finger over her hand. She flashed him a weak smile.

That tender moment made emotions well in his throat. It took courage for her to open up.

He wanted to pull her into his arms and hold her. He wanted to tell her how much he admired her. But he didn't dare break the tentative trust they'd just built.

He gestured toward the diner. "Let's grab some dinner. We'll talk more inside."

Beth tucked the files in her shoulder bag, and they climbed from the car. The scent of fried chicken and peach pie drifted toward him as they entered.

Chatter and laughter warmed the room. They slid into a booth, ordered coffee and the day's special. Beth laid the files on the Formica tabletop.

"You asked if this girl May could be among our victims," Ian said. "You could be right."

Beth picked at her food. "I should have told the social worker when she first ran away. But I heard her crying and I knew the reason, so I covered for her."

If the man weren't already dead, Ian would've wrapped his hands around Herman Otter's neck and made him suffer.

"If you can sketch out what May looked like or find a picture of her, it would help."

"I will. And I'll have Peyton compare images of the victims to her." Beth pulled a photograph from Headler's files. "Here's a photo of the Cousins family."

"Does Mr. Cousins seem familiar, Beth? Could he have been the man who picked you and Sunny up?"

Beth shook her head. "I don't know. I . . . don't think so."

"What does Cousins do for a living?" Ian asked.

"He's a traveling salesman," Beth said. "He sells children's toys."

Ian's brows shot up. "He could have lured a kid into his truck with the toys."

"I was almost fifteen," Beth said. "I wouldn't have been lured by a toy."

"Maybe not. But if he had toys with him, you might have sensed he was trustworthy because you thought he had children."

Beth rubbed her temple. "That's possible, I suppose."

"As a traveling salesman, he could have been in Lexington and Chattanooga at the time the other two victims disappeared," Ian continued. "If his wife thought he was working, she wouldn't have been suspicious if he didn't come home those nights."

"I'll have Peyton find out where he was the nights the other two victims went missing."

"I know you're in charge, but I'll take care of it if you want," Ian offered. The day seemed as if it was wearing on Beth—she looked exhausted.

"Thanks. And Ian, we're a team. You were right about locals trusting you. We need you working this case."

Her words soothed the beating to his ego that Vance had given him. "Thanks, I appreciate you saying that."

Beth excused herself to go to the ladies' room, and Ian phoned Peyton. "I need you to run checks on a man named David Cousins."

"Cousins? Wasn't he the father of the girl who killed herself in Sweetwater, the one tied to your father?"

"Yes." He explained about the timing and that Cousins had never been viewed as a person of interest. "I should have files from my father's office tomorrow. That will give us more insight into Kelly Cousins's state of mind."

"If her father had something to do with her death, we'll find it," Peyton assured him. "By the way, Hamrick and Coulter both checked in. The girl from Kentucky, Retha, was a mixed-up kid. Parents were divorced, mother was an alcoholic. Retha suffered from anorexia and had very few friends. Apparently she collapsed at school one day in gym class, and the teacher called Child and Family Services."

"What happened there?" Ian asked.

"They assigned a caseworker and a doctor evaluated her. He discovered the eating disorder, and the mother confirmed."

"Was Retha seeing a counselor?" Ian asked.

"She was supposed to, but she refused. The mother seemed caring when she was sober but let things slip when she was drinking, which was a lot. One morning she was coming off a bender when she found Retha passed out. She rushed her to the hospital. Retha was severely dehydrated." Peyton paused. "A social worker convinced the mother she had to get sober to help her daughter, so she checked herself into rehab. Retha went to a temporary foster home."

"She ran away from there?"

"Afraid so," Peyton said.

Ian sighed. Another troubled girl. Unfortunately, they made easy targets for predators. "Where was the father when she disappeared?"

"Dad worked on an oil rig out of the country for six months at a time."

That eliminated him as a suspect.

"What about the timing?"

"We don't know the exact date she disappeared. Sometime during the first week of November that year."

Dammit, an exact date would help.

"Now for Hilary Trenton. Her mother died in a car accident the year before she went missing, although there were allegations of abuse in the family. The mother reported it twice but backed down from pressing charges. Daughter kept to herself at school, became withdrawn, and started smoking weed."

Ian rubbed his chin. The girls were from two different states, but they both were from troubled homes. "Was there any connection between the two girls? Any way they might have crossed paths?"

"Not that I've found."

He didn't want to consider his father, but he had to in order to clear him. "How about sporting events? Either one of them play soccer?"

Keys clicked in the background. "No."

"How about connecting online?"

"Zilch."

"Was Hilary's father abusive?"

"Allegedly. But he had an alibi for when Hilary disappeared."

Damn, another dead end.

"Ian? I located the truck driver, Vinny Barlow. He still works for that food delivery trucking company. I checked his schedule. He's in Chattanooga."

That might be a lucky break.

Ian waved the waitress over for the check and punched in the number Peyton gave him for Vinny. Through his trucking job, Barlow had the means to have met Retha, Hilary, Sunny, and JJ.

Sometimes, the person who reported a crime turned out to be the perpetrator.

When Beth returned to the table, Ian was ready to go. "Vinny Barlow, the truck driver who found you, is in Chattanooga. Let's go talk to him."

Nerves tingled along Beth's spine, although she was uncertain why. Barlow had never been a suspect in her kidnapping. He had discovered her at that rest area off I-75 at the East Ridge exit near Chattanooga.

Although he could have abducted her, then for some reason decided to let her go, left her at the rest area, and pretended to have found her.

"Are you up for that?" Ian asked.

Beth jammed her hands in the pockets of her jacket. "Yes. By the way, I remembered something about Sunny, the night he killed her."

"What?" he asked, hope tingeing his voice.

"I begged him to kill me instead of Sunny, but he didn't."

Ian shook his head. "You were brave to do that, Beth."

"No, I wasn't. I promised Sunny I'd take care of her and I didn't."

He squeezed her hand. "We will find him and make him pay for what he did."

Beth bit her lip, battling guilt again. Would she ever forgive herself?

It was too dark for her to read the file in the car, so she stuffed it in her bag and glanced out the window at the dismal scenery as Ian veered onto I-75 and headed toward Chattanooga. A light rain began to drizzle, reminding her of the night she and Sunny had run away.

Fog blurred the windshield. Ian slowed, battling the trucks and vehicles clogging the road. Wood chips from a passing truck pinged against the roof of the SUV.

The dispatch officer over the police scanner reported an overturned truck in the northbound lane ahead.

Hopefully it wasn't Barlow.

He might have answers for her.

Ian took the next exit and drove the back roads until they reached the outskirts of the city.

"Where's Barlow exactly?" Beth asked.

"I called when you were in the ladies' room. He had a delivery at a local grocery chain. He agreed to meet us at the rest area where he found you."

Beth gripped the car door. She'd seen photographs of the rest area, but she needed to revisit it.

Yet dread sent a shudder through her as Ian parked. Rain continued to beat down, and the lights of several cars bled through the haze. An eighteen-wheeler was parked along one side, the food delivery truck near the restrooms and snack area.

The glow of a cigarette flickered in the dark, the man smoking it pacing in front of the entrance.

For a second, her surroundings faded, but the sound of rain intensified as the glow of the cigarette grew brighter.

Then darkness swallowed her.

She gasped, lungs straining for air as the scent of blood swirled around her. Light flickered again. Not a cigarette.

Candlelight.

"Fear not the dark or death, love. Death is only the beginning," a voice whispered. "Just follow the light to salvation."

JJ shook her head no, choking out a protest. She tried to get up, but she was tied down, arms and legs bound.

Her gaze latched on to the candle, but a pinging sound made her look to the right. Not the rain this time.

Blood.

A stream of Sunny's crimson life force trickled down her arm and pinged into the vial on the ground below her.

Reverend Wally Benton's lessons on salvation reverberated in JJ's mind. She murmured a prayer for forgiveness for failing Sunny.

Self-hate mushroomed inside JJ. She was a bad girl. No one wanted her or loved her.

How could they?

CHAPTER TWELVE

Ian felt helpless at the torment on Beth's face. Was she in the throes of a memory?

As much as they needed her to recall the details of her abduction, returning to that frightening place would be painful for her. It could be dangerous.

When he'd first attended the police academy, he'd asked questions about amnesia. He'd wanted to know if Beth could have faked it. A specialist in recovering memories had explained that trauma-induced amnesia was usually the mind's way of protecting a person until he or she could handle it.

At fifteen, Beth hadn't been ready.

Was she now?

"Beth?"

She closed her eyes and pressed her hand against her eyelids. He hated the fear on her face.

"Beth, talk to me. What happened?"

She blinked several times. "The candle . . . He lit one because Sunny was afraid of the dark."

"That's odd. It sounds like he cared for her."

Beth chewed her bottom lip. "He acted like he did. He called her *love*."

"*Love*, like a term of endearment?"

Beth nodded again. "He told her not to fear the dark or death, to follow the light to salvation." She gripped Ian's arm. "He thought he was saving her. There's something else," Beth said, an urgency to her tone. "When he cut her wrists, he saved her blood. He caught it in a vial and kept it on his wall with the others."

Good God. "He collected the blood? What for?"

"I don't know yet. But he had a lot of vials."

Ian's stomach knotted. Were there more victims than the ones they'd found in the holler?

Beth rubbed her arms to ward off the chill the memory evoked—the soft, soothing candlelight and the voice murmuring comforting words to Sunny contrasted with the sharp act of slicing her wrist to the bone and watching the blood drain from her.

What was he doing with the blood? Was he some kind of sicko who drank it? Could he be experimenting with it?

Was the blood his trophy?

"Beth?" Ian's voice dragged her from her troubled thoughts.

"He stores their blood in vials," she told Ian. "He has a bookcase of vials against one wall. No, wait, I think it was some kind of refrigerated case." The air grew hot, suffocating. "He was preserving it."

Ian arched a brow. "What wall? Can you see where it is?"

Beth frowned. "There were rooms in the cave. When the door screeched open, I tried to see his face, but it was too dark."

"What else did you see?"

Beth inhaled a deep breath. "Just the candle, a hand lighting it. Then Sunny was screaming . . ." She covered her ears to drown out the sound, but it replayed in her head. She would never forget her friend's pleas to live.

And the soft male voice of her killer acting as if he cared while he took her life.

God help her. She couldn't give in to the fear those memories resurrected. She needed to face them to uncover the truth.

A tap on the window startled Beth. She jerked her head around and bit back a gasp. A burly man with a beard was staring at them through the window.

Ian exhaled sharply, then powered down the window. "Mr. Barlow?"

Barlow shifted the toothpick in the corner of his mouth to the opposite side. "Yeah. You said you wanted to talk. Can we do it now?" He tapped his watch. "I'm on a schedule."

"Sure. Sorry to keep you waiting." Ian gripped Beth's hand. "Are you ready?"

She nodded, although her legs felt weak as she opened the door, and she was relieved at the moment to let Ian lead the questions. She tugged the hood of her jacket over her head, praying her legs held out as she followed Ian and the trucker to the rest area.

They paused by the vending machines and Ian introduced Beth. She'd estimate his age to be midthirties, meaning he'd been around twenty when he'd found her. He had a long jaw, a scar down his right cheek, and a cleft chin.

Barlow lifted his hat and scrutinized her. "It is you. That girl I found here."

Beth tightened the belt of her jacket. "Yes, sir. Thank you for coming."

"I heard you never remembered anything," Barlow said.

"No," Beth said. "Well, at least not until recently. Whoever took me lit a candle and placed it beside the girl he killed." Her voice warbled. "That girl was my friend, Sunny."

He pulled out another cigarette. "I read about her. She was in that holler where they found a bunch of bodies."

"That's correct," Ian interjected. "We were hoping you could fill in the details about the day you found JJ—Beth."

Beth dug her hands in her pocket, her eyes drawn to his cigarette. The scent of smoke had sickened her for years, although she had no idea why.

Had the man who'd abducted her been a smoker?

Ian focused on Barlow as he led them to the spot where he'd found Beth.

Fifteen years ago, Barlow had been in his twenties. Serial killers often struck during their twenties, thirties, and forties.

Barlow blew smoke rings into the air. "I was on a run, just like tonight," he said. "It was late, and I was tired. I was coming off an all-nighter, so I stopped to take a leak and crash for a while. When I came out of the john, I heard a noise, like a sick animal."

"I thought I was unconscious," Beth said.

"You were, but you were moaning." He patted his chest with a crooked finger. "I pushed the bushes apart and saw you curled up on the ground. Your skin was like ice."

"Was anyone else around?" Ian asked.

Barlow scratched his chin as he tossed the cigarette stub to the ground and stomped it out. "Not many folks. Another trucker asleep in his cab. A man and his teenage son came out of the men's room. I yelled at them to call an ambulance. The kid ran for the pay phone to call."

"Did you get the man and his boy's name?" Ian asked.

"No," Barlow said. "It all happened pretty fast. The boy called, and I went to the truck for a blanket."

"How long did it take for the ambulance to arrive?" Ian asked.

"Not long. Five, ten minutes maybe."

Beth inhaled a deep breath. "Did the man and boy stick around?"

Barlow nodded. "Waited until the ambulance got here. Wasn't nothing for them to do then, so they took off."

Ian folded his arms. "What kind of vehicle were they driving?"

Barlow rubbed at his beard. "Geesh. It's been a long time. I don't remember."

"Try," Ian said. "It might be important."

Barlow's jaw went slack. "You think they had something to do with the kidnapping?"

Beth shrugged. "We're considering every possibility. Were they in a car? A truck?"

Barlow shifted on the balls of his feet, then lit another cigarette and took a drag. "Come to think of it, I think it was some kind of pickup. Maybe a Ford. Black."

"So he didn't stick around to talk to the police?" Ian asked.

Barlow shook his head no. "Said he needed to get his son back to his mother or he'd be in trouble."

Damn. After fifteen years, without a name, it would be impossible to track down this other man and his son.

"Glad you got through it, ma'am," Barlow said to Beth. "I had a little one at the time, too, and had nightmares about you for a long time. It was a cold night. If I hadn't found you, no tellin' what would have happened."

"I'm very grateful for what you did," Beth said sincerely.

"Can you walk us through that day?" Ian said. "You found the girl, yelled for the man to call nine-one-one, the boy ran for the pay phone, then what?"

"Like I said, I went to my truck for a blanket. I always keep one in the back in case of a breakdown or if I need to catch some z's."

Ian gestured to the parking lot. "Where were you parked?"

Barlow looked confused about the reason Ian asked, but he pointed to a space three rows down. Then he walked Beth and Ian to his truck.

He lifted the back of the cab and indicated a couple of blankets in the corner. A Bible lay in the midst of the pile.

Ian's gut tightened at the sight.

Stacks of canned and boxed goods filled the back. Boxes and boxes of candles were stacked together, wrapped in heavy plastic, ready to be delivered.

Long white taper candles like the ones they'd found floating with the bones of the dead girls.

◆ ◆ ◆

The glowing candles from that dark place swam in front of Beth's eyes.

She concentrated on the nuances of Barlow's voice, his Southern drawl, the intonation. He seemed kind, like a Good Samaritan, as if finding her had deeply disturbed him.

If she was facing the man who'd abducted her, surely seeing him in person and hearing his voice would trigger her memory. She was stronger now; she could handle it.

"Mr. Barlow, you deliver a lot of candles," Ian said with a sideways look at her.

Barlow shrugged, his expression perplexed. "So? All the grocery stores carry them along with food, birthday cards, and supplies."

True.

Besides, Sheriff Headler had questioned him and checked out his story. They needed something concrete to consider this man a person of interest.

"Is there something else?" Barlow asked as he checked his watch again. "I really need to get on the road. I got one more stop, then it's home to my son."

"I appreciate you coming." Beth offered her hand. "Thank you so much, Mr. Barlow. I owe you my life."

The man slid his beefy hand into hers, then choked up. "I'm just glad they locked up the creep who did that to you."

Beth's hand felt clammy in his, his emotions triggering her own.

Ian broke the awkward silence. "Actually, Mr. Barlow, we're not certain the right man was convicted of her abduction."

Barlow dragged a handkerchief from his pocket and wiped his face. "What are you talking about? I heard he went to prison."

Ian folded his arms. "A man was arrested and convicted, but we have reason to question the validity of that conviction."

"You didn't see anyone else around here that night?" Beth said. "Sometimes killers like to observe when their victims are found."

Sweat trickled down the man's face. "Afraid not, just that man and his kid. I wish I'd gotten his name, but it all happened so fast and I was all shook up."

"Do you think you could describe the man with the boy to a sketch artist?" Beth asked.

Barlow pulled at his beard again. "I . . . God, I don't think so. It was a long time ago, and I was paying more attention to the girl. Boy was playing some kind of video game when I yelled at them to call nine-one-one." He backed away slightly. "Them and that other trucker were the only ones here."

Beth rubbed her temple. "Did you see the driver?"

Barlow shook his head. "Nah, figured he was asleep."

"What kind of truck was it?" Ian asked. "Did it have a company logo on it?"

Barlow wrinkled his nose in thought. "Afraid not. I see so many trucks I didn't pay no mind."

That trucker could be their unsub.

Beth handed him a business card. "If you think of anything, even the smallest detail about the truck or the man and his son, call me. It's important."

Barlow agreed, said good-bye, and hurried toward his truck. Beth studied his profile as he climbed in the cab. He seemed harmless, helpful.

She'd been terrified that night fifteen years ago. Was he the kind of man she would have thought safe enough to accept a ride from?

Ian's dark eyes searched her face. "What do you think?"

"I don't know, Ian. He didn't seem familiar."

"As a truck driver traveling from city to city, he could have picked up girls along the way."

"True. So could the other trucker."

Except they had nothing to go on regarding him.

Ian's cell phone buzzed. Beth crossed the sidewalk to examine the bushes again. She'd read the report—she'd been found wearing the clothes she'd disappeared in.

But her backpack had been missing. Had the unsub kept it for some reason?

Sunny's backpack had never been recovered either. But that stuffed animal had been buried with her.

When Ian turned back to her, his features were strained. "A woman reported her fourteen-year-old daughter as missing—Prissy Carson. Said normally she wouldn't have worried, but Prissy's friend called and said Prissy left school upset, that she didn't meet up with her like she was supposed to do."

Fear crawled through Beth. Prissy Carson was the target age for the unsub.

CHAPTER THIRTEEN

Ian followed the GPS to the Carson residence, a double-wide trailer that somehow had managed to survive the tornado. Although the roof was covered in a tarp, and a tree lay on the ground, partially sawed into logs, indicating it had probably fallen on the roof.

A beagle ran to greet him as he parked, and he patted the dog as Beth climbed from the passenger side. Together they walked up to the door, and he knocked.

A woman dressed in baggy sweats opened the door, a glass of whiskey in one hand. The scent of cigarette smoke swirled around him, and he stepped over a pile of tabloids as he entered. A bald man wearing a wifebeater T-shirt with a sleeve of tattoos stood behind her.

Ian introduced them both. "Ms. Carson?"

"Yes, and this is my boyfriend, Jed Hendricks." He grunted a hello, revealing a gap where a front tooth was missing.

The lecherous look he gave Beth made Ian's skin crawl.

Beth ignored him and directed her attention toward the mother. "Why do you think your daughter is missing? Does she always come straight home from school?"

The ice in the woman's drink clinked as she sipped it. "Sometimes she does, sometimes she doesn't. I'm not always here."

Ian studied the house. Judging from the dirty dishes on the counter, the scent of booze, and the stacks of laundry, the woman was probably drunk half the time.

Or she was passed out by the time her daughter arrived home from school.

Ms. Carson's sweatshirt sleeves rode up to her elbows, exposing bruises. Dammit. The boyfriend was beating her.

"Does your daughter have a cell phone?" Beth asked.

"Hell yeah, she's got her face in it all the time," the boyfriend said. "Girl can't do nothing but talk on it, or play one of them damn games."

"Can I have the number so our lab can trace it?" Beth asked.

Ms. Carson scribbled a number on a pad with a shaky hand, then shoved it toward Beth. "I've been calling for hours, and she don't answer."

"I understand your concern, ma'am. We'll see what we can do," Ian said as Beth stepped aside to make the call.

Ian crossed his arms. "What was different about today, Ms. Carson?"

"What do you mean?" the woman asked in bewilderment.

"Did something happen today or last night to upset her?" He discreetly gestured toward the bruises on her arm. She yanked at the sleeve of her sweatshirt to cover them.

Bastard. Wife beaters were bullies who made women feel as if they'd brought the abuse on themselves.

He'd probably alienated Ms. Carson from her friends just as Bernie had Ian's mother.

The boyfriend shrugged. "How should we know? She comes in and locks herself in her room and don't talk to anyone."

"You said that one of her friends called you," Beth interjected as she returned.

Ms. Carson poured herself another drink. "Yeah, a girl named Vanessa. She said some boy at school hurt her feelings. Prissy can be emotional. You know how teenagers are."

Yes, especially ones from dysfunctional homes.

"She's a tramp," the boyfriend said. "I told you she was, Gail."

Ian chewed the inside of his cheek to control his anger. "We need to talk to Vanessa."

Cocoa's granddaughter was a good kid. She must be worried if she'd called her friend's mother.

He checked the caller ID and found Vanessa's cell number, then called it.

Still, he couldn't rule out a family dispute here. If the boyfriend was beating the mother and Prissy had interfered with his plans or his life with Prissy's mother, he might have done something to get rid of Prissy.

Beth sized up Prissy's mother and boyfriend within seconds of entering the trailer. Sadly, the mother was an alcoholic and desperate enough for male attention to allow him to smack her around.

Where Prissy fit into the picture was anybody's guess. The boyfriend might be abusing her or pressuring her for sex when the mother was passed out. If so, the mother was either oblivious or in deep denial.

The family needed help.

While she was empathetic to the cycle of abuse, her job was to protect the child.

Every second counted.

"Ms. Carson, does your daughter have a computer?" Beth asked.

"Course she does. When her head ain't in her phone, it's on that laptop."

"May I see it?" Beth asked, directing her attention to the mother.

"If you think it'll help find her." Ms. Carson's voice cracked, and Beth squeezed her shoulder.

"It might. Kids are all over social media these days. If she decided to go to a party or meet up with friends, she might have posted it online." Or if a predator had found her through her Facebook page or an online group, they could track him down.

The rock star posters on the wall in Prissy's room contrasted with the pink-and-white gingham curtains that must have been there since she was born. Stuffed animals sat on a faded white wicker bookshelf, mingling with a collection of ceramic frogs, a reminder that Prissy was still a kid.

Beth opened the closet, surprised at the sight of the neatly hung T-shirts and sweaters. Jeans were stacked with precision on a shelf. Perhaps her attempt at order amongst the chaos in her life.

Beth's stomach clenched. She kept her closet neat and organized as well. Her wardrobe consisted of boring suits, plain jackets, jeans, basic black boots, and flats. Her only concession was her underwear—a little wild child beneath the stoic, controlled exterior she displayed to the world.

No one got inside her place. Her head.

Her bed.

God, she was a case for the books.

Ms. Carson cleared her throat. "Prissy's a damn neatnik. Makes hospital corners on her bed. Sweeps her room every night."

Her neatness clashed with her mother's lackadaisical style and probably drove Ms. Carson nuts.

And vice versa.

Beth scanned the room again. A photograph of a skinny teenager with freckles sat on the desk, her big square glasses occupying most of her face.

And probably earning her teasing from classmates. Kids could be so cruel.

"You will find her, won't you?" Ms. Carson asked.

Beth bit back a blunt statement about statistics. "We will."

She just prayed Prissy was alive when they did.

♦ ♦ ♦

Ian mentally crossed his fingers that Peyton could track Prissy Carson's phone. He had a bad feeling in the pit of his stomach.

Grateful that the mother had joined Beth in the bedroom and he had a moment alone with the boyfriend, Ian stepped onto the back porch. The man was chugging a PBR as he puffed on a Camel.

"Mr. Hendricks, where is Prissy's birth father?" The girl could have run off to be with him.

"Dead. Idiot was drag racing."

So much for that.

"I understand it's difficult to talk candidly in front of Prissy's mother, but I sensed you think Prissy is trouble. Do you have any idea where she might be?"

The beefy man leveled him with a cold look. "That girl is fucking weird. One minute she's cleaning like some damn fanatic, then obsessing on that computer, the next crying 'cause she doesn't have friends."

"So she is awkward socially?"

He shrugged. "Listen, I don't mean to be a hard-ass, but she ain't much of a looker. The girl has no tits, wears clunky glasses, and she stutters when she gets nervous."

Ian rolled his hand into a fist to keep from slamming it into the man's jaw.

That wouldn't get him answers. Testing the man might. "Sounds like she's desperate for male attention. Has she ever come on to you?"

The man's eyes flared with surprise, then suspicion, as if he realized Ian's train of thought. "Hell no. I'm not one of those pervs that's into kids."

"I see. Beating up grown women is more your style, huh?"

The man tossed his cigarette on the porch floor and stomped on it. "What I do in my house is my fucking business."

Ian crossed his arms and took an intimidating step toward the man. "Not if it involves abuse or hurting a child. Prissy is a minor."

"Get out of my damn house."

Ian gave him a menacing look. "Prissy's mother called me, mister. I won't give up until I find her daughter." He poked the man in his beefy arm. "And if you touched one hair on her head, I'll lock you in a cell and throw away the key."

◆ ◆ ◆

Beth studied Prissy's computer, analyzing the sites she'd recently visited—one was a teen magazine that offered advice on makeovers and how to attract boys.

Her Facebook page was sad. She had very few friends. She belonged to a science club and a math club, and she liked paranormal fiction, especially zombie stories.

She searched Prissy's posts but couldn't pinpoint whether or not the girl was considering running away.

Her email box was practically empty. Then again, teens didn't email; they texted.

Beth searched further and discovered Prissy had spent hours playing a video game called Deathscape.

She clicked on the icon and scanned the contents. The game enticed the player into a dark world of dragons and monsters, offering various paths to choose from.

Depending on the choice the player made, he or she battled through simulations of real-life dangers and obstacles.

The paths—Road to Temptation, Path to Destruction, Sin Valley, Fun City, Friendship Avenue, the Easy Route, the Loving Hut, Money

Rita Herron

Mountain, Party Town, Freedom Ride, Weed Walk, Flying High . . . the list went on and on.

The game's premise—you couldn't escape death, but each path you chose determined your ultimate destiny. Heaven or hell. Religious undertones were strong, the graphics vivid and frightening. White candles burned like torches. Crosses were everywhere.

Déjà vu struck Beth—some of these scenes seemed hauntingly similar to the cave she'd dreamed about.

She clicked on an icon and found herself plunging into a cavern. It was dark, yet a hot springs pool shimmered at one end. A baptismal pool holding a candle. "Time to cleanse your sins," the voice said in a deep tone. "Repent and wash away the evil."

The ping of dripping water launched her back to the time when she was abducted.

A cold sweat broke out over Beth.

May . . . May was there.

Dead. Her wrists cut. Blood on the floor.

The dripping sound . . . water inside the cave?

Or . . . no. Blood. Blood dripping down Sunny's arms, pinging into the vial.

Sunny's scream as she watched her die.

Then he was coming toward JJ. She cowered against the cold rock, struggling to see his face. Praying she had the strength to fight him.

She crawled sideways, searching for a weapon on the ground. Her hand brushed dirt. Rock. Then something thin. Sharp. Brittle.

A bone.

She jerked back. A skeleton was staring at her. Eyes bulged in the sockets.

JJ tried to scream, but terror choked her voice. Then he yanked her by the hair and dragged her across the floor.

Bones, more bones . . . the sharp, brittle edges jabbed her hands as she clawed for a weapon.

126

God . . .

Sunny was dead now, and she was next.

No one would ever find their bodies here in this cave. No one cared enough to look for them.

◆ ◆ ◆

Tradition meant everything to his family. His father had passed down the family rules, the values, the job they were destined to do.

To be a humble servant.

He'd been groomed for his role since he was a boy.

Find the bad girls and weed them out. Save them from the path to hell they'd already embarked on.

He loved them anyway.

He truly valued his role as the Saver. But things were different from past centuries. Past decades.

Each generation perfected his own technique and style. He had a better way to do things than his father, and his father before him.

His son didn't yet know about the Calling. But one day soon he would.

And he would find his own way to light the girls' way into heaven.

CHAPTER FOURTEEN

"Sheriff, I think you'd better check on that agent. She doesn't look so good."

Ian jerked his head toward the door where Ms. Carson stood. "What happened?"

"I don't know. She was looking at Prissy's computer, and then she grabbed the desk like she was going to pass out."

Ian hurried to the teenager's bedroom. Beth was ashen-faced. He quickly scanned the room, noting the teenage posters, neatly made bed, and closet—nothing in the room that looked suspicious. He'd been half-afraid she'd found Prissy's battered body under the bed or stuffed in the closet.

"Beth?" he said in a hushed voice. "What's wrong?"

She startled, then looked up at him with a glazed blankness.

"Did you find something?" he asked softly.

She shivered. "I felt bones on the ground in the cave."

"Could have been animal bones," Ian suggested.

"I guess that's possible. But I think someone else died there, someone he didn't bury." She pinched the bridge of her nose. "Although if burying them in the holler was part of his ritual, whose bones were those and why did he leave them?"

"Good question." He stroked her arm to warm her. "Don't worry, Beth. We'll find that cave and get to the bottom of this."

"Peyton said that some of the bodies might have been frozen, which would affect the timeline. This cave could be underground or connect to a basement or old building that had a freezer. Or the cave itself could act as a freezer."

"My deputies are on this," Ian said. "If anyone can find that cave, it's them. They know these hills inside and out."

She blinked as if to shake off the shock of what she'd remembered, then nodded. His chest squeezed. Her trust meant more than she could ever imagine.

"There's something else." She gestured to Prissy's computer. "This game," Beth murmured. "It's called Deathscape."

Ian wrinkled his brow. What did a game have to do with finding Prissy Carson?

"Go on."

"Judging from Prissy's social media, she didn't have many friends. But she spent hours playing this game. It takes players down danger-ous paths where they have to make choices that lead them either to redemption or to purgatory. The paths include Road to Redemption, Sinners and Salvation, the Poisonous Apple, Pleasures of the Flesh, Riding Out the Flood, the Parting of the Sea, the Serpent Strikes. It goes on and on."

"A lot of the teen games are violent," Ian said.

"I know, but the religious undertones bother me. I haven't gone through all the levels, but I've looked at the overviews." She paused. "One takes players into a dark world, one with the punishments laid out in the Bible. There's a cave with a hot springs pool where the players participate in a ceremony similar to a baptism. It reminded me of the cave where I was held."

Ian stiffened. "Is there anything on the game to indicate the cave's location?"

"Not that I've found so far." She straightened. "I remember being there, though. My hands and feet were tied. Sunny was begging for her life. Then I heard what I thought was water dripping, but it wasn't water. It was blood dripping into a vial."

"*He* saves the blood," Ian said. "Have you figured out what he does with it?"

Silence filled the air, mingling with the sound of Beth's labored breathing. "No, but it's his trophy. I'm working the element of the blood collection into the profile."

Ian wanted to haul her in his arms and comfort her, but he kept his hands by his side.

"What if there are more bodies, Ian? He could have buried some of them in Hemlock Holler, then left others in that cave. Or in a freezer."

Ian considered her statement. If that was true, they had more victims than they thought. Which would complicate the investigation even more.

Beth lapsed into a pained silence, the remnants of her memory lingering in her troubled eyes.

They confiscated Prissy's computer to take to the lab. Ian phoned Deputy Whitehorse as they left the Carson house.

"I know you've been searching the hills, but have the team hunt for caves near the site of the bones and other remote areas in the mountains near Hemlock Holler." He explained about the freezer and the possibility of an old building that might have one.

Whitehorse grunted. "So that big Fed wants us working on this?"

"I don't care what he wants," Ian said. "You're an expert tracker and have worked these mountains for years with search and rescue. You grew up here—you know where to look."

Whitehorse had always been quiet and kept his thoughts to himself. Some folks had been reluctant to trust him, but the man was honorable and had been dubbed a hero for rescuing a youth group stranded during a freak blizzard last year.

After the recent flood, he'd worked day and night searching for missing locals and reconnecting them with family.

Ian turned onto a narrow road that led to a low-income housing development near the high school. Most of the apartments were run-down, weathered, and in need of repairs. Some had suffered from the tornado with missing shutters and tarps on the roofs while another row stood untouched by the damage.

Like the mystery of why this unsub who seemed merciless had allowed Beth to live.

"This is Cocoa's apartment," Ian said as he parked in front of a unit on the end that had escaped the storm.

Beth vaulted from the vehicle and hurried to the door on a mission. He understood her impatience.

Time meant the difference in saving a life.

He jumped from the seat and followed her. Beth had already knocked, and an older man with gray hair and a beard stood in the doorway.

Ian knew the family, but Beth didn't, so she introduced herself. The man waved them in. "I'm Vanessa's granddaddy, Deon," the man said. "That child's been tore up all afternoon."

"Why does she think something happened to Prissy?" Beth asked.

"Something about a boy, but she didn't get into it." He fiddled with the collar of his plaid shirt as he yelled for Vanessa.

A second later, a dark-haired girl with red-rimmed eyes appeared.

Beth explained that they'd just come from the Carson's house, then squeezed the young girl's hand. "Vanessa, tell us what happened today. Why do you think something bad happened to your friend?"

Vanessa's eyes welled with tears. "I wasn't supposed to tell. She's gonna be mad at me if she comes back."

"Do you think she's going to come back?" Ian asked.

Vanessa's lower lip quivered. "I don't know. The kids were laughing at her at school and she ran. I tried to call her all afternoon and tonight, and she won't answer."

"Why were the kids laughing at her?" Beth asked.

Vanessa's grandfather patted her shoulder. "If she's okay, she can be mad. But if she's not, you'll be glad you talked, honey."

Vanessa wiped at her eyes. "'Cause she was going to, um, you know, meet up with this boy Blaine after school. Blaine's one of the popular kids. She thought it would make her popular."

"You mean if she had sex with him?" Beth asked gently.

Vanessa nodded. Her grandfather's face was grim.

"Then what?" Beth asked.

"He ditched Prissy in front of all his friends. That's why the kids laughed at her." She gulped. "They called her Pissy Prissy. She started crying and ran off."

"What's this boy's full name?" Ian asked in a voice tight with anger.

Vanessa dropped her head forward. "Blaine Emerson."

Beth's phone beeped with a text. She checked it, then gave Ian a troubled look and handed it to him.

A text from Peyton:

Tracked Prissy Carson's cell phone. Somewhere off Route 9. Sending general coordinates.

Route 9 was in the middle of nowhere. And not a good sign. There was no way Prissy could have gotten that far on foot. She had to have caught a ride.

Fear crawled through him.

He had a bad feeling that ride was with the killer.

CHAPTER FIFTEEN

"Please find her," Vanessa cried.

Beth patted the girl's shoulder. "We'll do our best. You can help by making a list of the students you think we should talk to at school."

Vanessa pulled out a school notebook and scribbled down some names.

Ian cleared his throat. "We should go, Beth."

She gave him a quick nod. "Just one more question, Vanessa. Do you know anything about that video game Prissy was playing?"

Vanessa tapped her pencil on the paper. "You mean Deathscape?"

"Yes, do you play it?" Beth asked.

Vanessa shook her head. "Granddaddy won't let me. He says video games are bad. Why?"

"All those paths—the choices. None of them lead to anywhere good."

"Because you can't escape death," Vanessa said matter-of-factly. "That's the game. Some kids like to travel the dangerous paths just like in real life. They say it's a rush to see how close to the edge you can get and come back."

Beth texted Peyton to have her check into the game and its maker.

That cave in the video disturbed her—what if it was modeled after the cave where she'd been held? Although that was a stretch. It would mean the game inventor had something to do with the murders. But fifteen years ago, the game hadn't existed.

Beth took the list of names from Vanessa, and Ian led the way outside. They hurried to the SUV, and Beth jumped in the passenger side.

Dark had set in, the gray sky filled with more storm clouds, the woods bleak with shadows.

Had the unsub kidnapped Prissy and dumped her phone so the police couldn't track her?

Images of the young girl lying helpless in a cold cave with a killer standing over her bombarded Beth. Then Vanessa crying over Prissy's grave . . .

Dear God, she hoped Prissy was alive.

Beth fought a sense of déjà vu as Ian parked at an overlook on a winding section of the mountain. Was the cave where the unsub had held her and killed Sunny nearby?

Was Prissy lying on that stone floor, terrified, freezing, and praying someone would find her alive?

What had her dreams been? Had she dreamed of college, having a big wedding someday? Or maybe she fantasized about a career and traveling?

Tears threatened, but she pulled herself together. Her heart ached for the young girl. She had to save her.

Maybe Prissy's text history would lead them to a suspect.

"If he has Prissy, he might be local as we suspected," Beth said.

Ian gestured toward the sharp ridges above. "You're right. He could live anywhere in these hills and no one would ever know."

Ian handed Beth a flashlight, then aimed his on the ground as they walked along the road's shoulder.

Gravel and dirt crunched beneath Beth's boots. Somewhere in the distance a coyote howled. A smaller animal skittered through the woods.

Beth shined her light in a circle, then along the edge of the road. Ian stepped closer to the embankment, leaned over the rail, and scanned below. Beth paced several feet down the road and then turned around and started back, but something shiny caught her eye on the other side of the rail. Probably trash, a tin can.

She'd check it out. She inched closer to the rail, battling dizziness at the height. The ridges were sharp, steep, and unforgiving with drop-offs over a mile deep. She gripped the rail and let the dizzy spell pass.

When her vision cleared, she maneuvered the flashlight to cover the ground and spotted the object.

A cell phone.

She yanked on plastic gloves, then reached over the rail to dig the phone from the weeds.

"It's over here," Beth shouted. "I've got it."

Ian jogged over to her, his expression grim. "Look, Beth, a few feet down."

Beth's head swirled as she aimed her gaze down the embankment. A backpack lay in the weeds.

Ian climbed over the rail, rocks and dirt skittering as he crept down the side of the hill. Seconds later, he retrieved the backpack and hauled it back up to the road.

Various scenarios raced through Beth's head. Prissy had accepted a ride with someone, realized she was in danger, and then escaped and ran down the embankment.

The unsub had thrown her belongings off, thinking no one would ever find them. Then he took Prissy God knows where.

Or Prissy's dead body lay somewhere in those dark, desolate woods below.

Ian dropped the backpack into the back of his open SUV trunk. He wanted to run the show here, but Vance's order taunted him. He had to answer to Beth.

"You're in charge, Beth. You want to call my deputy and Vance?"

She stiffened. "Forget that Vance said that, Ian. I told you earlier, we're working together as a team. I'll call him while you phone your people."

He nodded, grateful for her concession. She stepped aside to call Vance.

Ian phoned Deputy Whitehorse. "Agent Fields has the Carson girl's computer. We're bringing it to the lab for analysis along with her backpack and phone. We found those in the woods."

"I'll put together a search team and get out there ASAP," Whitehorse said.

"Did you find that cave?" Ian asked.

"I'm afraid not. There was an old abandoned apple house, but that was it," Whitehorse said. "I'm on my way."

"Thanks. We need you."

"The county lab is closer than the federal one," Beth said. "I asked Vance to make some calls so we can work through there."

"He agreed?" Ian asked, surprised.

"Yes. We can't waste time driving back and forth."

She was right.

Beth's shoulders tensed as she examined Prissy's phone.

"Do you see anything?" Ian asked.

Disappointment streaked Beth's eyes. "The last phone call she made was to Vanessa. Last text at two forty-five this afternoon telling Blaine Emerson that she couldn't wait to be with him. She suggested they meet after fifth period, skip their last class, and sneak away."

Ian grimaced. "Poor girl. Did the boy respond?"

"Just with an emoji. Smiley face." Beth sighed. "He was leading her on."

"Punk," Ian muttered in disgust. "I'd like to tear him a new one. At least my father taught me to respect women."

Beth's gaze met his, his comment lingering between them. But Ian didn't retract the words. Coach Gleason had cared about the students.

Once he'd told Ian that he wanted to empower females to stand up for themselves because his own mother had been bullied by her husband.

All the more reason he felt for Prissy's mother and despised her boyfriend. Just as he despised Bernie.

If only Ian could find his father and tell him that he loved him.

◆　◆　◆

Beth saw the wheels turning in Ian's head. More questions about his father—what could she say?

If she remembered the face of her abductor, she could clear him. "I've worked with teens before," Beth said. "It's a vulnerable, stressful age. Everyone's trying to fit in, find their place, break away from their parents. Hormones, insecurities, self-esteem, love—everything is dramatic and life-shattering."

"The humiliating incident with Blaine was probably the trigger. But do you think she ran away to escape her mother and stepfather?" Ian asked.

"Sure, that's possible. If it wasn't for the discovery of those bodies at Hemlock Holler, we wouldn't know Prissy was missing right now. Just like with me and Sunny."

Ian grew quiet, but tension emanated from his every pore. "That's right. No one reported you and Sunny as missing, did they?"

Beth shook her head. "The Otters wouldn't have. They didn't want to get in trouble and lose the money the state designated for us."

Beth's phone dinged, and she checked the text. Director Vance.

`Have identified more victims. Task force meeting at noon tomorrow.`

Beth texted that she and Ian would be there. Hopefully someone on the team had found a lead.

◆　◆　◆

Dammit, Ian wanted to find Prissy Carson and find her alive.

But instincts warned him that was not going to happen.

"There are a few pictures in Prissy's phone. Some at a science fair. Another couple at a blood drive where she volunteered. Then several of her and Vanessa." Beth angled the phone to show Ian. "There are some candids of a teenage boy, probably the jerk who blew her off."

"He might be a punk, but he's only a teenager, Beth. He was just a baby when you and Sunny were taken. He couldn't be responsible for the boneyard victims."

"I know," Beth said. "I can't believe this unsub has gotten away with these crimes for years without any witnesses coming forward."

"He's extremely clever or someone no one would ever suspect."

Like a cop, Ian thought. Or a first responder or rescue worker. Or a . . . father figure? Yet whomever this unsub was, he'd aged fifteen years.

That meant he'd honed his skills, had learned not to leave evidence or to draw attention to himself.

"Let's see what's in the backpack." With latex-covered hands, he unzipped the pockets and catalogued the contents. History, science, and math books. Notebooks full of homework and assignments. A rain slicker. Calculator.

A binder filled with scribblings of her name in various connections to Blaine Emerson. A red scarf. Condoms.

A siren wailed, and seconds later Deputy Whitehorse drove up and parked. Two other SUVs followed, a rescue and search team from the county.

Ian met them and explained the situation. "At this point we aren't sure if the girl was taken or if she ran away. She was upset with her family, and her crush at school humiliated her in front of her classmates.

"She could have hitched a ride with a friend and dumped her stuff to make it appear she's gone for good"—he hesitated—"or she may have climbed into a car with the madman we're looking for, and her only chance at survival is us."

CHAPTER SIXTEEN

"The temperature is dropping," Ian told Whitehorse when he arrived. "We may have an injured fourteen-year-old girl in these woods or down that embankment."

Hayes Weller, a husky guy in his thirties who'd been military trained in recon missions, joined them. He was the leader of the local search and rescue team. He was also an experienced helicopter pilot, lived in town, and ran transports from accidents and smaller hospitals to more critical care units.

Weller made quick introductions and then ordered his volunteer team to work. They brought flashlights, set up larger lights to illuminate the area, and attached ropes harnessing two men to climb down to the bottom of the canyon.

Whitehorse divided the area into grids, assigned each man an area to search, then handed Ian a portable handheld radio so they could keep in touch.

Beth cleared her throat. "I'm going down."

Ian shook his head. "There's no need. That embankment is dangerous."

"I'm trained for this. If she's here and alive, she might need me," Beth argued.

Ian and Whitehorse exchanged concerned looks.

"She's right," Whitehorse said. "A terrified girl might respond better to a female than a bunch of men."

Ian nodded. They were right.

Beth headed into the woods bordering the road, and Ian followed. No way was he going to let her dive in alone.

He used his flashlight to scan for signs of life in the deep pockets of trees covering the ridge. Beth skidded and reached out for a tree limb to break her fall, but he caught her arm.

Her gaze locked with his, the fear in her expression tearing at his gut. She was probably thinking about Prissy, relating to what she might be going through.

But she didn't comment or turn back. She shook off his touch and continued on.

Brush and bramble clawed at Ian's and Beth's arms and legs. Tree branches snapped, showering them with raindrops that clung to the leaves. The moon struggled to break through the storm clouds, but only a thumbnail surfaced.

The wind picked up, howling off the mountain. The temperature had dropped to a cool fifty. The middle of the night would feel more like thirty, and hypothermia could be an issue.

Minutes bled into an hour, then another and another as they combed the woods. The temperature dropped to freezing, and storm clouds moved in.

A low wailing sound came from the right, and Beth halted to listen. Ian gestured to a section thick with fallen branches.

He hadn't lived here at the time of the prison flood, but people still talked about it. It had happened so quickly that no one had been prepared. The river had overflowed, and the dam had broken. Several lost their homes, and although rescue workers had rushed to free the prisoners, they didn't make it in time. The electrical system had failed, and they couldn't get inside.

A cry reverberated in the wind. Either an injured animal or person.

Beth stepped over a tree stump, pushed aside a limb, and abruptly halted. Ian inched up behind her. An injured deer lay in the weeds, blood oozing from its side, its body trembling.

"He's not going to make it," Ian said, hating to see the deer suffer.

Beth stooped and gently brushed her fingers across the animal's jaw. "I'm sorry, buddy, so sorry."

Trees rustled a few feet below. She aimed her flashlight toward it, and he caught sight of something moving. Beth slowly crept closer, careful to be quiet, but as she approached a boulder, a bobcat stalked back and forth.

Beth froze and so did he. Any sudden movement might incite the cat to attack.

Ian lifted his gun and fired at the animal's feet. He screeched and snarled but slowly backed away, the predator's eyes gleaming in the dark.

He didn't want to kill the animal, but if it attacked Beth, he would shoot.

Ian analyzed the animal's behavior. Eyes piercing the darkness, focused on them. Head lifted as if sniffing for their scent.

Static echoed from his walkie-talkie. "Sheriff, what was that?" Whitehorse asked.

He kept his voice low. "A bobcat."

Finally the animal sprinted in the opposite direction, and they began to move again.

Seconds later, Beth's gasp rent the air. He pivoted and saw the reason for her alarm. A garbage bag lay in a clump of weeds. The vile stench of blood and death hit him.

His breath stalled in his chest. Surely to God some maniac hadn't killed Prissy, stuffed her into a garbage bag, and dumped her in the woods.

♦ ♦ ♦

Beth plastered one hand over her heart. Please, dear God, don't let Prissy Carson be in that bag.

Stuffing the body in a garbage bag didn't fit the MO of the man who'd buried the girls at Hemlock Holler.

Although since his burial ground had been uprooted, he might be desperate for another way to dispose of his victims. But that burial ground indicated a ritual. Rituals were important to a serial killer.

Ian's hand touched her shoulder. "I'll check it out," he said in a low voice.

She should prove that she was strong enough to handle the task. But her stomach was roiling. The last thing she wanted was to throw up and contaminate a crime scene.

An object caught her eye, and she shined her light on the brush.

A pair of brown square glasses. Glasses exactly like the ones Prissy wore in one of the photographs at the Carson home.

She pulled on a glove, plucked the pair of glasses from the weeds, and showed them to Ian. "These belong to Prissy."

"Dammit." Ian pulled a baggie from inside his jacket, and Beth slipped them into it.

She stepped aside so Ian could open the garbage bag.

Ian removed his pocketknife and ripped open the bag. The rancid odor of a rotting carcass nearly made him gag.

He forced himself to peek inside and hissed. It was a dead animal, although it was so emaciated he couldn't tell what kind. Probably someone's pet that had died and they didn't want to take the time to bury it. It happened all the time in the mountains.

"Ian?" Beth asked in a raspy voice.

"It's not her," Ian said quickly.

Beth leaned her head down and inhaled several breaths. "Thank God."

She looked so shaken that he pulled her up against him and held her. "It's okay, we won't give up."

She nodded against his chest, although tremors racked her body. For a long heartbeat, he stroked her back, comforting her. "She might still be alive," he whispered.

Thunder clouds boomed above, and rain began to pelt the trees and ground. His radio crackled again.

Beth pulled away, pressing her hair back into place as she did the professional mask she wore to cover her emotions.

"Sheriff, we haven't found anything," Weller said. "I say we give it up for the night. I'll send a team out at first light to search again."

Lightning illuminated the sky, streaking the darkness with its force. Another pop and a tree cracked, sparks flying in all directions.

His gut told him Prissy wasn't here.

"Fine. But first thing in the morning, search again. If she's out here, maybe she discovered a place to hide." Maybe the cave Beth had mentioned.

But finding it in the dark with a storm raging around them was impossible.

Fear sparked in her eyes as she scanned the mountain. "Where does this road lead?"

Ian shrugged. "Up the mountain. There's an old hunting lodge at the top, a few houses scattered around the hills."

A desperate eagerness laced her voice. "We should check them out."

"I have men on it." He took her elbow and gestured for her to start climbing the hill. The rain was starting to pummel them, making the ground slippery, and they had to hold on to tree branches to reach the top.

The rescue team gathered by their vehicles, wet and muddy.

"We found the girl's glasses," Ian said. "No sign of her, though."

"Same here," Weller said.

"Why would he take the time to stop and throw her book bag and glasses away?" Beth asked. "That doesn't fit with his actions to date."

"Maybe he had to pull over for some reason, and the girl tried to escape," Whitehorse suggested. "She could have taken the backpack with her."

"And he caught up with her," Beth said. "That makes sense. We also need to keep in mind that this could be a separate case. The mother's boyfriend was trouble."

"I agree." Ian rubbed his hands through his hair. "I'll ask Markum to verify his alibi."

"We're going to the school in the morning to question the teachers and students while your team searches again," Ian said. "Whitehorse, be sure to cover the old lodge at the top of the mountain."

"There's a 4-H camp there that's shut down," Weller said. "We'll check them out tonight."

Beth climbed in the passenger seat, her shoulders sagging. How could she sleep knowing Prissy was still missing?

Exhaustion pulled at her, but she didn't want to stop looking. There was nothing she could do to help the dead girls except find justice for them.

But if Prissy was alive, they could save her.

The wind howled, slashing rain on the ground, shaking the trees, and pounding the car.

Ian slid into the driver's seat. "The team is coming back in the morning. I'll drive you home."

Tears of frustration threatened to choke Beth, but she swallowed them back. Ian was right. But leaving without finding Prissy felt wrong, like they were giving up. Like they were deserting her.

He started the engine and cranked up the defroster. Beth shivered and tried to tuck her hair back into its neat bun, but loose strands dangled in disarray. She removed the clasp and ran her fingers through it, smoothing out the tangles.

A truck passed, and her vision blurred for a second.

A man's face again. All in shadows . . .

Her abductor?

She blinked and leaned forward to get a better look, but the truck flew past. Then she realized it wasn't a truck. It was an SUV.

Dear God, was she paranoid? Losing her mind? Or could he be here watching them, laughing at the fact that they hadn't caught him yet?

Ian stroked her hand, his gaze dark. Intense. "Are you okay?"

"I won't be okay until we catch him and find Prissy."

"I know," Ian said in a gruff voice.

She feathered her hair over her shoulders again, fighting despair.

Ian's jaw tightened. "Your hair—you always wear it pulled back so tight. It looks good down."

Beth shifted self-consciously. Knotting her hair in a bun had started as a subconscious act to make herself look professional. Less appealing.

Now it had become part of her. With her hair pulled back, she felt in control.

She didn't like *not* feeling that way.

She quickly smoothed the strands into a ponytail and then wound it around and secured it at the base of her neck again. "Thanks, but it doesn't get in the way like this."

Some emotion she couldn't define flashed in Ian's eyes. She averted her gaze, uncomfortable with his scrutiny. For some reason, she sensed he saw through her.

That an attraction was simmering beneath the surface. An attraction she had no time for.

Not with a young girl's life on the line.

He washed the blood from his hands, ignoring Prissy's constant sobs.

He'd butchered a coyote and watched the blood spatter. He'd had the damned thing in the car in a trash bag when he'd picked up the girl. When she'd tried to escape, he'd dumped the animal and chased her.

In his secret room, he scanned the things he'd kept from the others. Backpacks filled with teenage stuff that had no value except to the dreamy-eyed adolescents who lusted after the boys.

JJ's stood out amongst the dusty packs.

A ragged hand-me-down army-green one she must have gotten from a thrift store. He ran his finger along the silly piece of lace she'd tied around the strap, as if she'd thought it made the bag look more feminine.

Probably her attempt to distract the kids her age from seeing its ragged state and making fun of her.

The lace had yellowed, and the fabric was fraying. He didn't know why he'd kept it, but inside it held pages of her diary. The words she'd poured from her soul.

Words of pain and hatred for her foster family. Words of shame for the fact that she had no parents. No one to love her.

Words of yearning for a real home.

But he loved her. And he'd wanted to keep her. He had high hopes for her. Had thought by letting her go she might turn to the Lord and lead others to His kingdom.

He ripped a page from the diary—a passage about wanting to belong—folded it and put it in a plain manila envelope, then headed outside to his truck.

The scent of the coyote's blood lingered on his skin, but it was JJ's scent that tormented him. Fifteen years later and he could smell her sweet innocence as vividly as he had back then.

Dark clouds hovered above, rain beating down just as it had the night he'd found her. He thought of her every time it rained.

She was looking for him now.

A smile curved his mouth. She probably dreamed about him in her sleep.

Knowing she was this close to him made him curious. If he walked up to her, would she know who he was?

Another smile tugged at his lips. He wanted her to know.

Except then she'd turn him in.

And he had more work to do. More souls to save.

More lives to offer up for his own redemption.

He left the cave and wove through the mountain roads, his tires grinding the gravel, then veered down the road to those cabins.

Five minutes later, he scanned the area surrounding the cabin. No cars. She wasn't there.

A smile creased his face as he jumped out, slogged through the rain, and left the journal page tucked inside the screened door.

He wanted JJ to know that he was watching. That he could get to her again if he wanted.

♦ ♦ ♦

The rain slacked off slightly as Ian parked at Beth's cabin and walked her to the porch.

"I live two doors down," Ian said. "If you need anything tonight, call."

Beth patted her jacket where her holster was hidden beneath. "I can take care of myself, Ian."

The fact that she'd been victimized stood between them, a fact he dare not point out. Beth had survived, and she was strong and determined.

She pulled keys from her shoulder bag but came to an abrupt halt at the door.

Ian caught her arm to keep from bumping her. Then he saw what had gotten her attention.

A plain manila envelope was tucked inside the screened door.

His nerves jumped to attention, and he scanned the property. Nothing in the yard except trees. Woods in the back.

Bushes parted. Was someone in those trees? Ian stepped to the side, his senses honed as he searched the perimeter.

Another movement. A body?

No . . . a coyote.

Beth yanked on rubber gloves, then ripped the envelope from the door and tore it open. Her face paled as she searched the contents.

"What is it?"

"A page from my childhood diary," Beth said in a haunted whisper.

"I don't understand."

Her shocked gaze lifted to his. "It was in my backpack the night I was taken."

Ian silently cursed. Her backpack had never been recovered.

Meaning her abductor—Sunny's killer—had kept it all these years.

"He knows where I am, and he wants me to know that," Beth said in a voice oddly strong considering she looked as if her worst nightmare had come true.

Ian gently touched her elbow. She needed his support, but she'd probably bite his head off if he crossed the line and pulled her up against him.

Although that was exactly what he wanted to do.

"I wrote all my thoughts down in that stupid book. I don't know why I took it with me that night," she said in a self-deprecating tone. "I was too ashamed of what was going on in that house to let anyone find out."

Ian choked back a curse. "You have nothing to be ashamed of. That shithead foster father and mother did. And so does the social worker who placed you there."

"She thought he was a God-fearing man," Beth said, her voice faltering.

Ian yanked on gloves, took the envelope from her, and then reached for the page. "Let me send this to the lab. Maybe he left his prints on it."

Beth clutched the page back to her chest. "These are my private thoughts. I don't want anyone to read them."

For a heartbeat, they stared at each other. Ian had no idea what she'd written on that page, but reading it would be a violation of her privacy.

"What if there's some evidence on it?" he asked.

Her hand trembled. "You're right. I'll have the lab analyze it."

He inhaled a calming breath. "Good." He removed his gun from his holster. "Let me check out your place."

"We'll both do it." Beth switched to investigative mode so quickly he didn't know how to respond. She yanked her weapon from her holster and turned the knob.

It was unlocked.

He signaled to let him enter first. As he opened the door, he scanned the interior.

A lamp glowed in the corner.

"Did you leave that light on?" he asked.

Beth nodded, her face strained. He remembered her comment about the unsub lighting a candle to help assuage his victims' fear and wondered if Beth was afraid of the dark.

He paused in the doorway to listen for a noise, a voice, footsteps, anything to indicate someone was inside.

Nothing.

Holding his gun at the ready, he inched inside, instincts alert as he glanced left and right. The kitchen appeared empty. So did the adjoining den.

Only the bathroom and bedroom left.

Beth's breathing rattled as she followed him. He swept the hallway with his eyes, then crept into the hall. Bathroom on the left. He flicked the light on.

Empty.

Beth flipped the switch for the bedroom light. He moved behind her, braced for an attack.

But everything was quiet.

"Do you see anything missing? Out of place?" he whispered against her neck.

Beth gripped the door edge. "That candle by my bed. It wasn't there before."

Dammit to hell, the killer had been inside her house.

CHAPTER SEVENTEEN

Cold fear immobilized Beth. She thought she'd prepared herself for the time she might face her abductor.

She wished to hell he was here. Instead, the sneaky slimeball had left her a reminder of the past to torment her.

Bitterness welled inside her. Years ago, he'd robbed her of what was left of her innocence. Of her peace of mind.

Of the final shreds of her trust.

She didn't intend to let him hurt her again.

"He's getting cocky," Ian said. "That means he'll make a mistake."

Images of the sicko reading her most private thoughts, knowing her pain, made her fury rise. "He kept JJ's diary all this time."

"You mean yours, Beth," Ian said softly. "You changed your name, but you're JJ."

"No, I'm not the same person." Beth balled her hands into fists. "JJ was street smart and tough. But she believed she had a future. Herman Otter only wanted her for the money and what she could do for him, but she'd hoped for a family to love her one day. Beth knows that's not possible."

"You can have all that," Ian said gruffly.

The silence that fell vibrated with emotions. Beth hated herself for exposing her worst fears, her neediness.

Ian laid a hand on her shoulder and forced her to look at him. "Beth, the man who abducted you may have stolen your childhood and your memory, but you're stronger because of it."

She didn't want to be strong. She wanted to be whole again. "I'm damaged," she said, her throat raw with tears she refused to cry. "JJ died that day when she woke up with no memory."

And if Beth didn't remember what had happened to her when she was JJ, she couldn't save Prissy or anyone else.

Then he would win.

◆ ◆ ◆

Ian brushed Beth's cheek as gently as he could with his thumb. It had been a long damn day for both of them. Worse, she'd suffered a shock and needed tenderness.

She jerked her head to the side to pull away, but his fingers trailed along her cheek. "Look at me, Beth. You are not damaged. What happened to you was tragic, but it shaped you into someone who protects others. You help children and families." He rubbed his palm against her cheek, his breath catching when she leaned into him and pressed her hand over his.

Her skin felt soft, warm, tender. The air between them became charged. Intense. Steeped with an attraction that had been building since they'd reconnected.

"You save others because you couldn't save Sunny," he murmured. "Maybe you survived so you could track him down and get justice for what he did."

Beth closed her eyes, a single tear seeping out. "I feel like I left her behind," she whispered. "If I could just see his face . . ."

Her voice faltered, and Ian did what he'd wanted to do since she'd come back into his life. He curved his arms around her. "Shh, it's okay. We have a team looking for him. It's not all on you now, Beth."

Beth tensed at his touch, her breathing shaky. But he didn't release her. He stroked her back, rubbing slow circles between her shoulder blades. More than anything he wanted to assuage her pain. But to do that, he needed to win her trust.

He didn't deserve it, not after he'd let her down fifteen years ago.

But he wanted it anyway.

"You are so much more than what happened to you, Beth. Don't ever let anyone tell you you're not." A strand of her hair brushed his neck, teasing him with its softness and the possibility of what it would feel like to run his fingers through the strands.

To unfasten that clasp and help her forget her inhibitions, her pain.

Her past.

Instead, she needed his friendship. His expertise in finding the man who'd hurt her. So he tucked the strand back into her bun. "You and I are going to make up for what happened back then," he said in a gruff tone.

Then she'd never have to look over her shoulder again.

Beth had blamed herself for so long that Ian's words eased that pain. Although she couldn't completely let go of the guilt, at least she wasn't alone.

Ian wanted to catch this man as much as she did.

The hard planes of his body gave her strength. The steady beating of his heart soothed her nerves. Yet, his touch elicited feelings she hadn't experienced before.

Need. Hunger for a man's love. A closeness that she craved but didn't know how to deal with—she'd never let anyone into her heart.

"I'm calling the crime team to process your place. If the bastard left a strand of hair, we'll find it."

Beth hesitated. A crime team meant more people pawing through her things. In her space.

But she'd do whatever was necessary. This place wasn't her home. It was a rental cabin. She had nothing personal here.

He'd practically challenged her to find him.

And they *would* find him.

Ian rubbed her arms as if he was reluctant to break the contact, but Beth averted her gaze from his probing eyes. She couldn't drop her defenses.

She had to be strong.

When this was over, they'd go their separate ways. Then she'd be alone again.

Her chest squeezed at the thought. But she ignored the twinge of yearning and told him to make the call.

Ian wanted to pull Beth back into his arms, but he restrained himself.

He had no business getting intimate with her.

You were only comforting her.

Yeah, right. It had started out that way, but holding her in his arms made him want more.

He couldn't push her, though. Their past was too complicated. They had answers to find.

That was all that mattered. Solving this case once and for all. Then the families could find closure. Beth would have peace.

Not knowing had stalled his life just as it had Beth's.

Ian phoned Lieutenant Ward, head of the CSU, and explained about the break-in.

Beth resorted to agent mode as well and began opening dresser drawers, checking to see if the unsub had taken anything.

"Anything missing?" he asked.

She shook her head, then stepped into the closet. Her shoes were neatly organized, boring suits hung at even intervals.

More OCD—her way of being in control.

Damn, he wanted to throw away those suits and see her in something sexy.

The thought made him break out in a sweat.

"He left the page from my diary and the candle as a message that he knows where I am," Beth said. "That he's coming back for me."

"I wonder why he kept your diary?"

Beth twisted her mouth in thought. "Maybe because he let me go. He wanted something of mine as a souvenir. He kept blood from the other victims."

Sick creep.

An engine rumbled outside. "That should be CSU," Ian said.

This bastard had the nerve to show up at Beth's place—he might be rattled enough by her presence that he'd gotten sloppy and left evidence behind.

Just one mistake and they could catch him.

Beth walked outside on the back porch as the crime workers dusted the cabin for prints and processed the interior. She should give them the diary page, but she wanted to hold on to it for tonight. Maybe rereading it would trigger some memories.

Rain drizzled from the trees, leaves rustling. Thunder clapped and lightning streaked the mountaintops just like it had that horrible night fifteen years ago.

The religious rituals associated with the crime reminded her of her childhood.

"Reverend Benton says that thunder is God's way of shouting His wrath," Herman Otter used to say.

Once she'd shouted back that God was angry at Herman for being such a pervert. She'd earned a hard slap for her smart mouth.

She touched the narrow scar on her forehead where she'd hit her head on the end table when she'd fallen.

After that, she'd learned to keep her mouth shut.

"I'll find who did this, Sunny, I promise," she whispered to the heavens.

Footsteps made the floor creak, and Ian approached. "They're finished."

She rubbed her arms to ward off the chill. "Good, I'll clean."

Ian caught her arm. "Let me call someone to do that. I'll drive you to a motel."

Beth shook her head. "No way that man is making me run again, Ian. I'm staying here."

Ian's expression darkened. "What if he comes back?"

She patted her gun. "Then I'll be ready."

He squeezed her arms. "You're not going to use yourself as bait. That's too dangerous."

"I'm a trained agent, Ian. I know what I'm doing."

"Do you?" His voice grew rough. "Or do you want revenge so badly that you're not thinking straight? If that's the case, I'll tell Vance that you're emotionally compromised and endangering the case."

Beth seared him with an angry look. "You wouldn't do that."

Ian's chest rose and fell with his breath. "If it means protecting you, I would."

She held her ground. "You're just as close to this case as I am."

They locked stubborn gazes, the heat between them vibrating with turmoil and sexual tension. She'd liked Ian in high school, but now she admired him for his loyalty to the town, for his grit, for the fact that he stood for justice.

Close quarters, danger, uncertainty—it was hard not to want to lean on him.

That's all this crazy attraction was.

But she couldn't give in to it.

She'd vowed to Sunny to find the unsub, and if that meant repressing her emotions until the job was done, she'd damn well do it.

"You're right," Ian admitted. "But I want to keep you safe, Beth. I let you down once. I won't do it again."

His declaration sent a tingle of need through her. She wanted to touch him, hold him, feel his arms around her.

But the fingerprint dust in the house was a reality check.

Cleaning would be cathartic.

Crawling in bed with Ian would be dangerous.

She was walking a tightrope with her emotions already. There was no way she could have a physical relationship with Ian without losing her heart.

"I'm cleaning," she insisted, head held high. "I don't want anyone touching my things." She'd been violated enough already.

Herman Otter used to touch her clothing. Twice she'd found him in her bedroom, running his fingers over her underwear. She'd thrown away everything he'd pawed with those nasty fingers.

"Fine," Ian said. "I'll help."

He followed her inside, and she grabbed cleaning supplies from below the sink. Although it was late and she was exhausted, she was too wired to go to bed.

By the time she finished cleaning, maybe her adrenaline would wane enough for her to fall asleep. Maybe she could erase the image of Herman's paws on her panties.

Maybe the nightmares would leave her alone tonight.

Reverend Jim Benton laid his hands on the girl's chest and spoke in a reverent tone.

"Leviticus 17:11 says, 'For the life of the flesh is in the blood, and I have given it for you on the altar to make atonement for your souls, for it is the blood that makes atonement by the life.'"

A cold chill swept through the dark room, and the girl screamed and thrashed at her bindings.

He continued to pray, using his connection to God to beg for her life. "She walks with the devil now. Take the sin from this girl and free her of the Evil possessing her."

He had watched her in the crowd at the revival. Heard her speak blasphemy under the tent where only sacred words and prayers should be spoken.

Seen the lust in her eyes for the young boys.

Fourteen. The changes in the girl's body could have precipitated her transgressions. All the more reason to exorcise the demons before they possessed her completely.

Just like those girls that sheriff had found in Hemlock Holler. All had been troubled. All veering down the road to drugs, prostitution, and sin.

The girl screamed, her body convulsing, the animal sounds she emitted a sign that her soul had been lost.

He lit a candle and waved the faint light above her, reciting more Bible verses as she fought. Sweat poured down her body and her eyes rolled back in her head.

Then she was quiet.

It was almost two o'clock in the morning by the time Beth retreated into the bedroom. Ian insisted on staying to serve as bodyguard. She'd tossed him a pillow and blanket, and he sacked out on the couch.

Just as he'd suspected, she left the light in the bedroom burning.

His gut clenched at the thought of the nightmares that plagued her. He heard her thrashing around during the night. Twice he went to the door, tempted to go in and wake her.

Or hold her and alleviate her fears.

But he sensed she wouldn't welcome his attention—or him anywhere in her bed.

He was also afraid that once he got in bed with her, he wouldn't want to leave her.

He finally dozed off for a couple of hours but woke at dawn. He rose, dug around in the place for coffee, and brewed a pot. He was about to pour a mug when Beth appeared, dressed in running gear.

She barely gave him a glance, then headed to the door.

"Where are you going?" he asked.

"For my morning run," Beth said as she jammed earbuds in her ears.

"Not without me you're not."

Beth placed her hands on the kitchen counter and stretched. "You can't boss me around, Ian."

He realized he'd sounded demanding, and lowered his tone. As possessive as he felt toward her, he'd never become like Bernie and try to rule her. Or own her. "I'm not, but we both know that the unsub was here last night. He may be watching us now."

Her eyes flickered with unease, making him feel like a heel.

He refused to back down, though. If the unsub thought she could identify him, he might try to kill her to keep her quiet.

Beth desperately needed the run to relieve her stress. Sleeping had been her enemy for years. Having Ian in the house should have made her feel safer.

But he was dangerous to her in a different way.

Last night she'd had the same nightmares of her abduction and that cave where she'd watched the blood drain from her friend's arm. When she'd awakened, she'd wanted to curl up in Ian's arms.

But she'd restrained herself. Then she fell asleep again and dreamed of wild and torrid sex with Ian. Delicious sex like nothing she'd ever experienced.

Sex that felt intimate and wonderful, as if she was tied to the man who gave her pleasure. As if she always would be.

CHAPTER EIGHTEEN

Beth's body was wound tight with need as she waited for Ian to jog two doors down to his cabin and change.

A need she refused to acknowledge or indulge.

Ian appeared wearing running shorts and a T-shirt, making matters worse. His muscles strained the confines of his T-shirt, and his shorts revealed long, muscular thighs and calves that made her mouth water.

Battling temptation, she vaulted outside and took off down the path along the river. Ian followed, and they ran in silence along the trails and through the woods, a three-mile trek. She could have done more, but they needed to get to work.

Whitehorse was already leading Weller's men again in their search for Prissy in the woods.

Every hour she was missing lessened the chances of finding her alive.

They were both sweating and breathing hard when they returned to the cabin. Beth hurried to her room, stripped her clothes, turned on the shower, and climbed beneath the warm spray.

If only she could wash away her guilt and fear, she might be whole again. As whole as a woman like her could get.

By the time she was dressed, her phone buzzed. Director Vance.

Pulse jumping, she pressed Connect. "Agent Fields. Did you get my message about finding Prissy Carson's glasses and backpack?"

"Yes, but that's not the reason for my call. Have you seen the news?" he asked.

Her shoulders tensed and she flipped on the television. "No, why?"

"That reporter knows who you are."

"Oh God." Beth lowered her head into her hands, fear and panic seizing her. "How?"

"I don't know, but the bastard used it as his headline. It's all over the Internet, and the morning news picked it up."

A sick feeling washed over Beth as the news appeared on the screen.

Survivor of Boneyard Killer Returns as FBI Agent to Track Down Her Abductor

A recent photo of her appeared. Then a photo of JJ along with the caption.

"I'm sorry, Beth. I don't know how he found out. We can run something to deny it," Director Vance offered. "But he printed a picture, along with the story of your abduction."

"Thanks for the warning," Beth said, fighting the urge to go home and hide. "But the unsub has already found me. He left a page from the diary he took from me at the cabin last night."

A string of expletives followed. "I want you off the case."

Beth closed her eyes on a sigh. Images of Sunny and May and Prissy and those bones floating in the water tormented her.

There was no way she could quit.

She had to find Prissy.

Get justice for the others. For Sunny.

Lock up this sicko so she wouldn't have to keep running.

◆ ◆ ◆

Ian knew something was wrong the minute Beth entered the kitchen.

"Michaels revealed my identity," she said.

Ian was pissed. "I knew we couldn't trust that scum."

If he could lock up the jerk, he would. But Michaels probably kept a lawyer on retainer and used him every time he crossed the line.

Furious, he punched Michaels's number.

The message machine picked up, so he left a voice mail. "I told you I'd give you an exclusive, but your little stunt just blew that deal. You put Beth Fields in danger. Stay away from her."

Beth gave him a small smile when he hung up. "Thanks, but I doubt it does any good. People like Michaels are out to make a name for themselves. They don't care how they get their information or who they hurt."

Maybe not, but he'd pissed off the wrong guy this time.

"The director wants me off the case," Beth said, irritation in her voice.

He arched a brow. "Are you going back to Knoxville?"

She lifted her chin. "No. I came here to find Sunny's killer, and nothing will stop me."

A smile twitched at the corner of his mouth. He admired her spunk and determination.

A memory tickled his consciousness—back in school. One of the cheerleaders had tripped her in the classroom. JJ had gotten up, brushed herself off, and smiled. But later that day, she'd cornered the girl outside and paid her back by whacking off her hair. The girl had run crying into the bushes like a baby.

"Let's stop by the lab. The sooner they process Prissy's backpack, the sooner we might have a lead."

He nodded, then drove Beth to the county crime lab. Hopefully Peyton would find a lead in Prissy's texts, social media, or computer.

♦ ♦ ♦

A few minutes later, Beth met Ian in the lab hallway. "Let's go, Ian. I have the name of the more recent victim from the boneyard. Lindy Saxton. She lived with her sister in Cleveland, Tennessee. I'll fill you in on the way. I want to talk to her before we visit the school."

They rushed to Ian's SUV and jumped in. Beth fastened her seatbelt as they drove away. "Peyton emailed me the file from the investigation when Lindy went missing."

Ian's jaw twitched. "What does it say?"

"Her parents were dead. Lindy lived with her older sister. They were having a hard time making ends meet. The sister worked as a waitress to pay the bills."

"Maybe one of Lindy's friends saw something," Ian said, a hopeful note to his voice.

Impatience nagged at Beth as they headed toward Cleveland. They needed answers and needed them fast before another girl died.

But traffic was moving slowly on the country road, increasing her agitation.

"What else do you see in the file?" Ian asked.

Beth forced herself to focus. "She had a best friend named Cathy who said Lindy had slipped into a bad funk. Said she'd smoked dope a few times and her sister caught her, and they had it out. Lindy told Cathy she was going to run away to New York and become a model."

"Really? Her friend said she ran away?"

"That's what she thought. Sad, isn't it?" Beth murmured. "The last time Lindy's sister spoke with her they argued."

"Another runaway," Ian said. "It seems that's where our unsub is picking his victims. Girls he finds on the streets."

Beth considered his observation. "That tells us about his victimology, but it doesn't narrow down locations. He's choosing from low-risk victims, but he's all over the Southeast."

Beth skimmed for more information, although the file was slim. The sister had cooperated with the police but had her own problems with drinking.

Thirty minutes later, Ian parked at a duplex near the heart of the small town. The property was overgrown, and a rusted sedan sat in the drive. They climbed out and walked up the sidewalk. Ian knocked on the door, and a young woman's voice called out that she was coming.

When the door opened, a skinny brunette wearing a waitress's uniform stood, hands on her hips as she smacked her gum.

Beth flashed her credentials and introduced herself and Ian. "Are you Terry Saxton?"

"Yes." The young woman's face drained of color. "Oh God, you found Lindy, didn't you?"

Beth gently touched the girl's arm. "I'm afraid so."

Tears blurred Terry's eyes, and she staggered backward inside the apartment. Ian grabbed her arm to steady her just before she collapsed into a rickety wooden chair.

Beth yanked a tissue from her purse and gently eased it into Terry's hand. Losing a sister had to be devastating.

But Terry might know something about the killer that she didn't realize. Beth had to ask questions.

She also wanted to help Terry understand her sister's death wasn't her fault. "I'm so sorry, honey."

The scent of strong coffee and burned bacon filled the air, a stack of dirty dishes were piled in the sink, and bills overflowed from a basket on the counter. Ian discreetly thumbed through them.

"What happened?" Terry cried. "Where has she been?"

Beth did not want to share the details of how Lindy had died. Terry didn't deserve to carry that mental picture for the rest of her life. "We found her body buried outside Graveyard Falls."

Horror widened the girl's eyes. "You mean she was murdered by the Boneyard Killer?"

Beth nodded and rubbed Terry's back. "I'm so sorry."

"It's all my fault," Terry sobbed. "I was supposed to take care of Lindy. I was supposed to be with her, but . . . I had to work, and I was late getting home and tired that night."

The guilt in Terry's voice mirrored Beth's own guilt over Sunny. "It's not your fault, Terry. Your sister knew you loved her."

Huge sniffles followed, and Terry blew her nose. "I did love her, but our folks were killed in a car wreck a year ago, and she was having a hard time, and she was mad all the time." More tears leaked from her eyes.

"I'm sure it wasn't easy on you either. You were grieving and suddenly had a teenager to raise when you were a teen yourself," Beth said. "Do you have other family?"

Terry shook her head, her mop of hair falling in her eyes. "It was just me. I'd just turned eighteen, so I got this waitressing job, and I was trying to take care of us, but the money wasn't enough, and Lindy wanted to have fun, not clip coupons and eat greasy leftovers every night."

Compassion squeezed Beth's chest. The weight on Terry's shoulders had been heavy.

"We had a big fight before I went to the Burger Barn, and when I got home she was gone. I . . . was so tired and had a hard night and figured she went to sleep over at her friend's house, and I crashed."

"Had she done that before? Gone to a friend's and not left a note or called?" Beth asked.

"Yeah, all the time. Usually I'd check on her, but that night I was exhausted and just went to bed. The next morning I tried her friend, but she hadn't seen Lindy or talked to her. And she was just . . . gone."

"So you reported her missing?" Ian asked.

Shame flashed in Terry's eyes. "Not at first. I thought the law might take her away from me, so I spent the morning out looking for her. I drove to all the spots I thought she'd go. The Burger Hut, the high school, that old church where Mama and Daddy used to go. But the preacher said he hadn't seen her."

"Did she pack a bag to take with her?" Beth asked.

Terry gave a weak nod, guilt streaking her face. "Her backpack was gone. She ran away because we'd been fighting." Her chin quivered. "And now she's dead. It should have been me, not her. She was the pretty one, the smart one. I was supposed to help her get to college."

She broke into sobs again, and Beth pulled her in her arms and rocked her while she cried.

"Is there anyone I can call for you?" Beth asked gently.

Terry nodded. "My boyfriend, Liam. His number's in my phone."

Beth gestured to Ian to make the call. There was no way she was going to leave this young woman alone.

While they waited for the boyfriend to arrive, Beth asked to see Lindy's room. Terry stood at the edge as if it was too painful to go inside.

"I haven't changed anything," she said in a choked voice.

Beth nodded and touched a photograph of Lindy and Terry when they were little girls. They were standing in front of a Christmas tree in red-and-white polka-dotted pajamas holding twin dolls. Tears welled in Beth's eyes. Such cute children with their futures ahead of them.

Terry ran to the bathroom, and Beth let her go. The poor girl needed time to grieve.

The doorbell rang, and Ian let Terry's boyfriend in.

Beth ran her hand along Lindy's purple comforter, forming a mental picture of Lindy as she studied her room. Posters of top models and actresses adorned the walls. In her closet, cowboy boots, Western shirts, jeans, and boots remained—an image she wanted to change so she could wear evening gowns and designer shoes.

Beth wiped at a tear that slipped down her cheek.

Lindy would never get the chance to follow her dream.

◆ ◆ ◆

Sympathy for Terry filled Ian as they left Terry with her boyfriend. He'd seen Beth wiping tears from her eyes.

Beth promised to call Terry's boss so she wouldn't lose her job, and Ian assured her that they'd notify her when her sister's body was released so she could arrange a proper burial.

"That girl is going to battle guilt all her life," Beth said as they drove away.

"Then we fight harder to make sure this bastard doesn't escape." He turned onto the main highway. "What's hard to believe is that in all this time, no one saw anything."

Beth worried her bottom lip with her teeth. "Let's look at the profile, Ian. Everything we know so far suggests that the unsub blends into a crowd. He's nondescript, someone people trust. He's probably insecure but seems humble, so he doesn't stand out as a troublemaker. He's methodical enough to hold down a job, but it won't be high profile. He's educated enough to know exactly where to cut the girls' wrists. He chooses low-risk victims. Ones no one will miss or report immediately. Runaways, kids in trouble, ones who won't draw suspicion."

"What if he has access to those subsets because of his job? Maybe he's a social worker or a police officer or . . . a preacher."

"That could fit with the religious aspect," Beth said.

"A man named Reverend Jim Benton runs the Holy Waters Church. I've always thought he was strange, that he's brainwashing people."

"Benton?" Beth's brows furrowed. "The Otters used to take us to revivals led by a preacher named Wally Benton," Beth said. "He was scary, but he'd be in his fifties now."

"This preacher is around our age. They could be related."

Beth shrugged. "I guess it's possible. But if he's murdering girls, it seems someone would have picked up on it and reported him."

Beth massaged her temple. "I'm still stumped over the reason the killer takes the blood. The unsub could be some kind of doctor or research scientist conducting his own experiments. There have been instances of mad scientists using the homeless and prisoners for experimentation."

"Bloodletting was popular once. Some people thought it cured diseases by draining infections."

"Perhaps someone the unsub loved died of a rare blood disorder and he's researching a cure." Beth drummed her fingers on her arm. "His signature involves religious elements—the candles, the cross, the christening gowns. If he sees himself as their savior, maybe he thinks he's draining the evil from them. He was raised with a strict religious background."

"That puts us back to looking at the churches and Benton. If he travels for revivals, he could have been in all of the cities where our victims lived. It could be a connection," Ian said.

Beth nodded. "We'll review it with the task force."

Ian raised his brow again. "I thought Vance wanted you off the case."

"That's not going to happen. We have to find Prissy Carson before she ends up like the others."

Ian contemplated different theories as he drove to the local high school with Beth. Outside the school, the blood bank trailer was parked, a sign on the school marquee announcing that they were collecting blood from the teachers and community for the Red Cross. A man in a white lab coat waved to them.

"Do you know him?" Beth asked.

"I saw him at the diner. Cocoa said his name is Abram."

"Don't you want to donate?" Abram asked.

Beth shook her head and walked on, her face paling slightly. She must have an aversion to having her blood drawn.

They rushed inside to meet the principal, a fortyish woman with a chin-length bob who seemed terrified about the prospect of a killer targeting her students.

She should be nervous.

"I've called an assembly. Follow me." No nonsense, she brushed down her pencil skirt and led them to the auditorium.

The principal strode to the podium and called the assembly to order.

Miss Anderson, the twentysomething school counselor, relayed the news that one of their students, Prissy Carson, was missing. Hushed whispers and chatter rumbled through the room. Fear shadowed faces and eyes.

The counselor soothed the group, then introduced Beth and Ian. "I hope you'll cooperate with the sheriff and this agent. We all want to find Prissy and bring her home."

Ian stepped onto the stage. "We're aware Prissy Carson was upset and she ditched school. At this point we believe she may have been picked up by a stranger and that she could be in danger."

Several students shifted and whispered. A blond boy on the edge of the third row tugged his hat down on his head to cover his eyes.

Blaine Emerson—the boy who'd humiliated Prissy.

"We aren't here to blame anyone." Ian offered the kids a smile to calm them. "If anyone has information regarding her disappearance or has had contact with her, please let us know."

Beth stepped forward. "I want to caution all the young ladies." She paused, giving the group time to absorb the information. Fear permeated the room. "Please be careful and alert. Stay together in pairs if you're walking home. Watch out for suspicious people online. And don't meet or accept a ride from anyone that you don't know well."

Miss Anderson clasped her hands together. "There are a few of you I've already asked to meet me in my office as soon as we're dismissed. I expect you to show up."

Ian liked her directness.

The principal spoke for a minute, then dismissed the assembly.

Ian and Beth followed Miss Anderson to her office, where a handful of kids were waiting. All seemed anxious except the Emerson boy, who stood slouched with his hands in his pockets.

The counselor ordered everyone to sit, then introduced the students.

"I thought no one was in trouble," the Emerson boy said.

"It was just a stupid joke," one of the girls said.

"If she ran off and got hurt, it's not our fault," a brunette said.

Miss Anderson leveled the group with stern looks. "Listen, you guys, you're not in trouble at the moment, although we will address your behavior later. Our priority is to find Prissy Carson before it's too late."

"The sheriff and I would like to speak to each of you in private." Beth gestured for one of the girls to go with Ian. Then she asked Blaine to step into the adjoining room with her.

Ian tried to put the young brunette at ease as they moved to the corridor.

The girl started crying as soon as they were alone. "You think it's our fault that Prissy's missing."

"I'm not here to pass judgment. Just tell me—do you have any idea where she'd go?"

The girl shook her head and wiped at her eyes. "She doesn't have many friends. Just that girl, Vanessa."

Vanessa was the one who'd alerted them to the fact that her friend might be missing. If Prissy hadn't contacted Vanessa, then she was in trouble.

Unless she was hurt.

Or dead.

♦ ♦ ♦

Beth willed herself not to yell at the little jerk for his cruelty to Prissy.

"Blaine, you know what you did to Prissy Carson was hurtful," she said, her voice calm compared to the fury inside her.

"It was just a prank." Blaine folded his arms on the table, his posture defensive.

"Humiliating someone in front of others is not funny," Beth said.

"Listen, lady," Blaine said, "I don't need a lecture from you. I got my own parents."

Beth raised a brow. She wanted to shake the kid, but she had to remain cool. Experience had taught her that reacting to a teen only fueled more animosity. "You think they'd be proud of you for what you did?"

The bravado in his expression faded slightly, and he shrugged nonchalantly. "My dad would understand."

She didn't know about that. Then again, some kids mimicked their parents' behavior. His father could be a sexist creep, too.

But she decided to ignore his comment. "Did you see or talk to Prissy after she ran away from school?"

Blaine set his jaw. "No."

She waited a beat, letting him stew. "She didn't call you?"

He picked at a thread on his shirt. "Hell no."

She extended her hand. "Let me see your phone."

He muttered something nasty but pulled it from his back pocket and slapped it into her hand. Beth searched his texts and calls but found nothing to or from Prissy. There were texts from classmates laughing at what had happened.

Teens could be so cruel to one another. But a lecture would be lost on Blaine. Hopefully, one day, someone would put him in his place.

"Can I go now, lady?" Blaine asked sarcastically.

Beth barely restrained herself from shaking him. "Yes. But don't leave town, *Blaine*."

A tick pulled at his left eye as he left—the jab had hit home.

Ian's phone buzzed just as he finished questioning the last girl. Talking to them was a dead end.

He connected, hoping for good news on something. Maybe a serious lead.

"This is Regina Blythe at the high school in Sweetwater. I was told you requested Coach Gleason's files."

"That's correct. I have a warrant—"

"A warrant won't do any good," she said. "Those files were stolen a few months ago."

Ian gritted his teeth. He'd counted on those files. He needed them, dammit. "Do you have any idea who took them?"

"No, and I don't understood who'd want them. They're fifteen years old."

Ian knew exactly the reason someone would steal them.

They contained information that incriminated the killer.

He mixed the blood with the paint to perfect the right hues for the canvas. Less for the yellow-green, more for the dark red that symbolized her life force and the blood of Jesus.

It was important to use it before it coagulated. He also had the sealant, a varnish, ready to preserve the piece.

He wanted the painting to last forever.

To honor the body of the girl when her soul went to heaven. Hers would rise soon. He could hear the voices of the others singing praises from above. Thanking him.

He would save her just as he had the others.

The families of the ones who'd passed were grieving, though. They didn't understand.

He felt their pain as if it were his own.

Having something of their daughters would assuage their grief. He wished he could tell them that it was their child's blood that filled the canvas when he sent it to them.

But the beautiful painting of the peaceful valley where their daughter found eternal rest would have to do.

He lifted the brush and began to swipe it across the blank canvas. Spring brought the lush green of the grass in its rebirth. The flowers were beginning to bud.

He dipped the end of the brush in the bloodred paint and used it to paint a rose garden where the dragonflies would dance.

He wished he had the time to find a real place like this to bury Prissy. He could plant roses at Hemlock Holler.

Only the cops and federal agents were staking out the area.

He'd have to leave the girl in the cave.

One day soon he'd bring JJ back here, too.

He'd wanted to keep her for himself back then. Tell her the truth about everything. About the reason he'd been watching her.

About the reason he'd taken her.

But that would have to wait.

CHAPTER NINETEEN

The counselor had Blaine and those mean girls in her office. Vanessa ran down the school hallway, tears running down her face. She hated all of them.

They'd humiliated Prissy in front of the school, and they weren't sorry. And that jerk Blaine acted all cocky.

She wished she could do something. Make them pay.

She darted into the bathroom, shut herself in a stall, and cried till she couldn't breathe. Why didn't the teachers stop it? All the bullying and cliques and the pretty girls making fun of the ones who weren't.

"You just haven't reached your time," her grandma Cocoa always said. "You'll shine one day. Just you wait."

She didn't believe that for a second. She was a dork, and she always would be.

She blew her nose and wiped her eyes, but when she came out of the stall, her hair was all frizzed out, her eyes were nearly swollen shut, and her dark skin was splotched.

Grandma Cocoa was wrong. She was one of the misfits. She belonged with girls like Prissy and Carlene, who was a whiz kid on the violin but clammed up when anyone talked to her, and Martha, whose parents had thrown her into a trash can when she was a baby and lived in the group home outside Graveyard Falls.

Boys didn't look at girls like them. Just like they hadn't looked at poor Prissy.

Prissy had been her best friend. And now Prissy was gone . . .

Footsteps and voices echoed outside the bathroom, and she yanked her hoodie over her bushy hair and ducked her head. She didn't want to talk to anyone right now.

Keeping her head cast down so the girls coming in couldn't see her puffy face, she tiptoed past them, trying to be invisible. Hell, she was practically invisible anyway.

Except for the kids who talked racist. They noticed her skin color and asked about her daddy and mama. She wanted to defend her parents and tell those losers that her mama and daddy made her out of love, and her skin was the perfect color, that she was the best of both of them.

But that was a lie, and they would know it.

Heck, everyone in this stupid town knew that her grandma had raised her since she was a baby.

She had no idea who her daddy was, and her mama had cut out a long time ago. If it wasn't for Grandma Cocoa and Granddaddy Deon, she'd have ended up in some foster home or worse—in the trash.

She couldn't stand the thought of going to class now and the other kids laughing at her for breaking down like a baby, so she snuck out the side door.

"Hey, Vanessa."

Out of the corner of her eye, Vanessa spotted Milo Cain leaning against a tree by the breezeway. Milo was about the geekiest boy in school. She'd heard he was a genius, too. That his IQ soared off the charts.

Big clunky glasses, two different-colored eyes, ratty hair. He wore that odd long white coat, too, that made him look like some kind of scientist.

He was into sci-fi and supernatural creatures, and someone said he collected pictures of graveyards.

Hoping he'd give up and go the other way, she kept walking.

Instead, he hurried up beside her, his hands jammed in the pockets of his jacket.

"What was going on in the counselor's office?" Milo asked. "Do the police know who took Prissy?"

Vanessa halted long enough to look at him. He bounced on his boots as if anxious for her answer. "I don't know, I didn't go in. But I'm afraid that bad man has her. You know the one who killed those girls and left them at the holler."

"That'd be awful." Milo's different-colored eyes seemed to drift in opposite directions. Then he focused again.

Shame filled her for being rude to him. It wasn't like she had that many friends.

He gave her a shy smile. "If you're nervous, I'll walk you home after school."

Vanessa sucked in a big breath. Did Milo have a crush on her?

"Thanks, Milo, but I'm fine." But she wasn't fine. She was scared to death.

Milo looked disappointed, but she didn't feel like talking to anyone right now.

She just wanted the police to find Prissy.

Beth rubbed her temple as she walked outside to meet Ian. If she could remember where that damn cave was, they might be able to save Prissy.

"What do you think about that group?" Ian asked.

"Typical teenagers," Beth said. "Scared. Insecure."

"Insecure my ass," Ian muttered sarcastically. "They're spoiled bullies."

Beth veered down the sidewalk. "Yeah, they are. But they're adolescents. They're trying to cover their own awkwardness by putting others down."

She saw Vanessa in the breezeway talking to a boy wearing a white lab coat. Vanessa looked as if she'd been crying.

The boy with Vanessa squeezed her arm. Beth was grateful she had a friend to comfort her. She remembered too well how terrified she'd been for Sunny. And how alone she'd felt.

"Insecure or not, it doesn't make their behavior right," Ian growled.

"I know." Her own childhood memories stung. "You can tell yourself they're wrong, but hateful words and teasing hurts. It damages part of you."

Ian touched her arm. "You aren't damaged, Beth. You have guts."

Doubt brought a dull ache to her chest. She was trying so hard to be strong, but walking back into that school resurrected memories of being teased and not fitting in.

Technology had advanced, but in fifteen years, teenagers hadn't changed one bit.

They passed the blood bank, and Beth's stomach began to churn. An image of Sunny's blood flowing from her arms flashed behind her eyes.

She sprinted down the sidewalk past the trailer.

Ian's chest tightened as Beth rushed down the steps and away from the trailer. But Abram approached him, a concerned expression in his eyes.

"What's going on, Sheriff?"

Ian explained about the missing girl. "Last place she was seen was here. Some students played a cruel joke on her and she ran off."

"Teenagers," the man said with a huff. "I've got one of my own. We go rounds, but I keep him in church. He's a good kid."

Ian nodded in acknowledgement, but his phone buzzed and he connected it as he jogged after Beth. "Sheriff Kimball."

"It's Deputy Markum. I've been reviewing that list of churchgoers and talked to several at the Methodist and Baptist churches. So far nothing, though." He hesitated. "I tried to talk to that reverend at the Holy Waters, but he didn't want to talk. Said he'd pray we find the girl, though, then brushed me off. Said the prayer vigil went so well, he's going to host a revival."

"Maybe I'll drop by." He might get to talk to his mother while there.

He ended the call and found Beth by the car, leaning against it and looking shaken.

"What happened?" he asked as he approached.

She chewed her bottom lip. "I don't know. I'm not usually squeamish about blood. But I've been having flashbacks of the unsub taking Sunny's blood, and I felt dizzy."

Ian's pulse kicked up a notch. "You saw his face?"

Frustration lined her brow. "No. Just a hand holding a knife and then blood dripping down Sunny's arm."

"I'm sorry, Beth." He stepped toward her. He wanted to pull her in his arms and wipe away the anguish in her eyes, but she warned him off with a hand and climbed in the car.

Ian silently cursed, then slid in and started the engine. "You okay?" he asked.

She gave a quick nod, although they both knew she was lying.

Beth was so cold she rubbed at her arms.

For the love of God, where had the unsub taken Prissy?

Ian drove through a drive-in fast-food place and ordered them both coffee. She accepted the cup with a murmured thanks, not trusting her voice to talk as he drove to the morgue for the task force meeting.

When they arrived, Corbin Michaels was waiting on the steps to the hospital.

He shoved a microphone at Beth. "Agent Fields, has the Boneyard Killer contacted you?"

Beth paled, and Ian shoved the mic away. "You mean since you exposed her real identity?"

"I'm just doing my job," Michaels said.

"You put Agent Fields in danger," Ian said.

Beth held up a hand to silence the men. "Mr. Michaels, the only statement I wish to make is to warn the young girls in town to be careful. They should be cautious, travel in pairs, and not accept rides from strangers." She gave him a cold look. "Now, we have work to do, so move out of the way."

Ian took her arm, and they rushed past Michaels into the hospital and to the task force meeting room. The others were waiting. Dr. Wheeland, Peyton, Weller—from search and rescue—and Ian's two deputies.

Beth handed the diary page to Peyton and explained that the unsub had left it for her. "Please be discreet with this," Beth said. "It's personal. I don't want the contents to be leaked, especially to that reporter." Although she'd reread it a dozen times, it had only stirred memories of being lonely and scared. Nothing helpful. No mention that she'd noticed someone watching her or that any strangers had been to the Otter's house.

"I understand," Peyton said softly. "Don't worry. Corbin Michaels won't get any information from me. Maybe the unsub left some DNA on one of the pages."

"Let's hope so. Did CSU find anything at my cabin?"

Peyton gave her a sympathetic smile. "I'm afraid not."

Director Vance made a beeline for Beth. She braced herself for a butt-chewing.

"I thought I told you to go back to Knoxville, Beth. I don't want this guy getting to you."

Ian moved up beside her. "Don't worry, I'll stick with her twenty-four seven."

The director slanted him a wary look. "Why does that not make me feel any better?"

"Please," Beth said. "I can't leave now. My memories are finally returning."

Director Vance jammed his hands into the pockets of his suit jacket. "Then lie low. Let us run things, and I'll keep you posted."

Beth reluctantly nodded, although she had no intention of lying low. Prissy needed her.

Ian sensed Vance's censure from his body language. Beth would never tuck her tail and run.

The best he could do was to protect her.

Director Vance called the group to order. "We need updates from everyone. And let's establish a timeline with the identities of the vics, where they disappeared from, and any evidence we've collected to date."

Peyton tacked photographs of the victims on the magnetic whiteboard and wrote their names below along with dates of their births and hometowns.

Ian studied the names, dates of disappearances, and cities where they went missing.

Billy Lynn Hanover—disappeared 18 years ago from Macon, GA
Sunny Smith (and JJ)—disappeared 15 years ago from Sweetwater, TN
Hayley Pranceton—disappeared 12 years ago from Ringgold, GA
Doris Wyan—disappeared 11 years ago from Calhoun, GA
Drena Cutlit—disappeared 10 years ago from Dalton, GA
Retha Allen—disappeared 4 years ago from Lexington, KY
Hilary Trenton—disappeared 3 years ago from Chattanooga, TN
Lindy Saxton—disappeared 3 weeks ago from Cleveland, TN

A mountain of relief filled Ian. God . . . he'd waited so long to prove his father had been wrongfully convicted.

Those dates were definitive proof of his father's innocence.

He needed to find him and tell him.

Where the hell was he? He had to know that Ian was investigating these murders and that Beth was here. Why hadn't his father contacted him?

"All the victims were between the ages of twelve and fifteen," Wheeland said. "All were either from troubled homes, in foster care, or runaways. Agent Hamrick and Agent Coulter are trying to track down family, teachers, anyone who knew them." Wheeland took a breath. "We believe that Hayley, Drena, and Doris were abducted during the time Coach Gleason was incarcerated."

Ian nodded. "That means my father wasn't the killer."

"Gleason went to prison for nothing," Beth murmured. "And the man who took me and murdered these girls has been out there all along—hunting."

"That's the way it looks, Beth. Now let's focus on the information we have," Director Vance said.

Peyton used pushpins on the wall map to identify the cities the victims had disappeared from.

Beth stood, walked over to the map, and drew a line connecting the cities. "Although the victims are from different cities and states, they're all from the Southeast. Each city runs along I-75."

Ian zeroed in on the route along I-75. The expressway ran through several states, providing a big hunting ground for the unsub. So why had he buried them in Graveyard Falls instead of dumping them in random places along the way?

What was his connection to this town?

Beth stared in horror as the faces of the dead girls burst to life in her mind. All so young and full of life. So vulnerable. So lost. So in need of love.

But they'd ended up being murdered by some sadistic monster.

Not Coach Gleason, though.

Tears of guilt and sorrow burned her throat. That poor man had gone to jail for a crime he hadn't committed. He'd tried to help the teens at school.

Instead he'd suffered and lost his family because of his efforts.

Peyton placed a sketch of another girl on the board. "Our forensic artist used the bones to sketch out an approximation of what this Jane Doe looked like. This is only a likeness, but our artist is pretty good and—"

Peyton's words faded as the girl's face materialized in Beth's mind. Wavy, sandy brown hair to her shoulders. Big, sad green eyes.

Then her voice. *"I'm sorry."*

Beth hadn't understood then.

She understood now.

The girl had been forced to ride with him. He'd used her to lure Beth and Sunny inside the cab.

The girl was May.

A strangled sob caught in her throat and she stood, trembling as the memory rushed back. The sound of May screaming for her life . . .

A wave of nausea rolled through Beth, and she clutched her stomach and ran from the room. The door slamming echoed in her head, as did Ian shouting her name.

She didn't stop.

She was sweating and shaking as she darted into the ladies' room. A second later, she collapsed on her knees in the stall and doubled over. A cry ripped from her gut and sounded like a wild animal as she lost her coffee and the food she'd had earlier.

The face of another girl surfaced. Her name was Willa. Willa had been dead when they'd arrived.

May had admitted she'd been forced to watch Willa die. Three days after he'd abducted May.

When she first ran away, May had lived on the streets. She'd eaten garbage and turned tricks to survive. One man had gotten rough with her, and she'd run.

That night she'd been scared and climbed into the truck with the unsub. He'd given her a bottle of water.

That was all she remembered until she'd woken up in the cave. The place where they all eventually died.

CHAPTER TWENTY

Ian shifted, anxious to go after Beth.

Dr. Wheeland pushed his glasses on the top of his head. "What just happened?"

"Do you want me to check on her?" Peyton asked.

Ian gave a slight shake of his head. "Let's take a break. She'll probably be back by then."

Everyone gathered to get coffee and water. Ian stepped from the room and crossed the hall to the bathroom. He paused and listened.

It was quiet, so he knocked gently. "Beth?"

No answer.

"Beth, it's me, Ian." He eased open the door just a crack. "Are you in here?"

A sniffle echoed from inside the stall. Ian glanced down at the opening and recognized Beth's black flats. Worry knotted his belly.

"Are you okay?"

A heartbeat passed, then shuffling. "Yes, I'll be there in a minute."

He held the door open, hating to intrude but wanting to help. "Is there anything I can do?"

"No, just give me a minute." Another sniffle. "Please."

Ian couldn't stand to think of her alone. She'd already suffered so much. He slipped inside the bathroom and shut the door. "I'm worried about you. What happened?"

Beth's shoes clicked to the floor as she stood, then eased open the door. "I'm sorry. I just remembered the cave again. May is the name of the girl in the sketch. She was in the truck when Sunny and I were picked up."

"She's the reason you thought it was safe to accept the ride?" Ian said.

Beth nodded. "There was another girl named Willa that May told me about. She was dead when we got there. He made May watch him kill Willa. There were others before her. I felt bones on the floor of the cave."

"You said she disappeared a couple of weeks before you left the Otters," Ian said. "How long was she with him?"

"Just a few days. She'd been sleeping on street corners before he picked her up. According to her, he had a pattern. He kept a girl until he found a new one. Then he made the new girl watch the other one die."

"He did it to frighten her into submission," Ian said.

Beth nodded. "May knew what he was going to do to her. To all of us. That's why she told me she was sorry when they picked me up."

Ian released a weary sigh. "How awful, Beth. No wonder you repressed those memories."

A low sob escaped her. "I should have faced them. Then I could have saved these other girls."

Ian soothed her with soft words. "Don't do that, Beth. You were a kid. No one should have suffered what you went through." The turmoil in her eyes ripped at his gut. "Maybe your boss is right. You should leave town, and I'll let you know when we catch this bastard."

"No." She pushed a strand of her tangled hair from her face. It had come loose from the bun and hung in disarray.

She was beautiful. Vulnerable and hurting. But so amazing it nearly robbed his breath. He wanted to change the world for her, show her sunshine and roses and happy places.

The only way to do that was to find the madman who'd hurt her.

Slowly he rubbed her arms. Her face was milky white. "I promise you I'll find him."

Beth squeezed her eyes closed, and he drew her against him. Her body trembled in his arms, and he comforted her with tender strokes, brushing her tear-soaked hair away from her neck.

"I see him everywhere," she whispered against his chest. "I'm sure I'm just paranoid. But I feel like he's watching me."

He probably was. He'd been in her place.

"He won't hurt you," Ian promised.

She rested her head against him for a moment. "I have to remember his face. It's the only way we can stop him."

"We can stop him with good police work," Ian said firmly.

"No, I have to remember. Pieces are starting to come back."

A knock sounded and they both startled.

"Everything all right in there?" Peyton called.

Beth pulled away. "Yes, I'll be right out."

Ian stepped back to give her some space, but he missed the physical contact. "I mean it, Beth, you don't have to keep working this case."

She straightened and walked to the sink, then turned on the water. "I've run from him long enough. If I don't confront him and put him away, I'll always be looking over my shoulder." She offered him a determined smile. "I won't live like that any longer."

As soon as Ian left the restroom, Beth looked in the mirror. She hardly recognized herself. Her skin was colorless, her eyes red and puffy, her hair in a tangled mess.

She quickly smoothed the strands back in place and secured them at the nape of her neck. Her compact was in the meeting room, so she couldn't do anything about her face.

Embarrassment heated her skin, adding some color to her ghostly pallor.

No one in that room cared what she looked like. They were here to solve a case.

And she'd just remembered something that might potentially be helpful.

She took a deep breath and exited the bathroom. Ian stood just inside the conference room door while the others were settling back into their seats.

Ian pushed a cup of coffee into her hand. "Beth?"

"I'll be fine," she said, her tone more curt than she intended. God, she was a mess. But being in his arms had felt too good—she wanted to be back there, where she felt safe.

He studied her for a moment, making her skin prickle with unease. Their connection went back years. He understood her more than anyone else.

She sipped the coffee, grateful for the punch of caffeine, then forced herself to rejoin the others. A hushed quiet fell over the room. Beth ignored the curious looks and slipped into a chair. "I'm sorry I interrupted the meeting, but I remembered something. The girl in the artist's sketch is May. She lived with my foster parents and ran away."

Beth swallowed hard. "The unsub found her and used her to lure me and Sunny into his truck that night. Then he forced us to watch him kill her just as he'd forced her to watch another girl named Willa die."

Hope whispered through the room. She knew they were counting on her, and she hated to let them down.

"Do you know Willa's last name?" Peyton asked.

Beth shook her head. "No, I'm sorry."

Peyton turned to her computer. "I'll see if I can find her."

Beth mentally envisioned the killer's hand as he raised that sharp knife and sliced May's wrist. Did he have a tattoo? Any distinguishing marks?

Candlelight flickered. He murmured something . . . something about saving her. Not to be afraid of the dark or death, that the candle would light the way.

"I've been putting together a profile," she continued. "Because of the number of kills, it seems like he's sadistic, but the religious undertones, the way he leaves the girls with a candle so they're not afraid, and the cross, indicates that he cares about them." She hesitated. "The fact that there is no sexual component also implies that he isn't trying to inflict pain and that he's not a violent person."

"How can you say he's not violent?" Deputy Markum asked.

"It's his pathology. He's not in a rage when he kills the girls. He doesn't torture or beat them or inflict unnecessary pain. Although he cuts their wrists, he does it quickly instead of toying with them. Then he sits with them while they pass."

"You know all that from a profile?" Deputy Markum asked.

Beth gave him a flat look. "I was there when May died."

"What else did you see?" Ian asked.

"The candles glowing. They're part of his ritual, like a ceremony." She tried to piece together more details. "He baptizes the girls in a pool of water, then recites a Bible verse. He comforts them and tells them not to be afraid of death." She paused, in his mindset now. "He believes he's saving the girls and sending them to a better place."

Ian's fingers dug into his thighs as he listened. The details Beth remembered should be helpful, except they needed a description of the man.

"Sunny begged him to let her go," Beth said, her voice laced with the pain of the memory. "I begged him to stop. But it was like he didn't hear me."

"He could be under the influence of drugs," Deputy Whitehorse suggested.

"Or he's psychotic," Dr. Wheeland said.

Peyton gestured to her computer. "According to the interviews Agent Hamrick and Agent Coulter conducted with the families of those victims we've IDed so far, the girls all came from troubled homes."

"We've already established that the victims were troubled kids or runaways," Ian said.

"Yes, but each one mentioned seeking help, spiritual guidance." Peyton held up a finger to make a point. "Retha Allen and Hilary Trenton attended a revival hosted by a traveling preacher."

Ian's pulse jumped. "A traveling preacher?"

"Yes. A man named Reverend Wally Benton."

Beth sighed. "My foster father took Sunny and me to several revivals during the time we lived with him. He and Reverend Benton were friends. Benton was old-school primitive Southern Baptist, a snake handler." Beth rubbed her temple. "But he wouldn't fit the age range of our killer at this point."

Peyton looked up from her laptop. "Wally Benton died—"

"He has a son," Ian finished. "He's the reverend in charge of the Holy Waters Church. And his age fits the profile of the killer."

◆　◆　◆

Beth shuddered as she recalled the sermons Reverend Wally Benton had forced on the people who attended his revivals. If he was dead, he couldn't be their current unsub. She faintly remembered his son. He was a teenager when she was abducted. Could he have started his killing spree back then?

The sound of computer keys tapping echoed through the room. Seconds later, Peyton spoke. "The son, Reverend Jim Benton, is speaking in a small town not too far from here tonight and tomorrow."

"We'll talk to him," Beth said.

Dr. Wheeland stood. "There's one more thing we should discuss." The ME tacked another sketch on the board. "This is one of the Jane Does we haven't identified yet. She was killed approximately thirty years ago."

Beth gasped softly. Thirty years ago . . .

Maybe she had the unsub's age wrong in the profile.

"If this girl was actually his first kill, identifying her is imperative," Beth said. "A serial killer's first kill is usually personal."

"There's another problem," Ian said. "If we're dealing with the same unsub, why did he wait so many years in between victims?"

Uneasy murmurs rumbled through the room.

"He could have been satisfied with the first kill, possibly remorseful," Beth said. "Maybe he married and had a normal life. Then years later something happened to trigger his need to kill again."

"He also could have been incarcerated or in a mental facility," Peyton suggested. "I'll explore that angle."

Ian nodded in agreement. "There's another possibility. He could have killed others during that time lapse and buried them somewhere else."

Beth's chest clenched. She had felt more bones on the floor of the cave.

Good God. Were the bones still there? Or was there another graveyard they hadn't yet uncovered?

CHAPTER
TWENTY-ONE

Beth studied the blank space on the board where there should be a list of suspects. They'd eliminated Ian's father.

Focusing on the Bentons had only stirred more questions—and improbabilities.

"Anything on Gail Carson's husband?" Beth asked.

"He had an alibi the night she went missing," Deputy Whitehorse said.

"As long as we're speculating, we should consider the possibility that we're dealing with more than one killer," Beth said.

Director Vance angled his head toward Ian. "If that's so, the partner could have killed while your father was in prison."

"That's ludicrous," Ian snapped. "For one thing, my father was not a religious fanatic. We attended church, but he wasn't the type to lecture or preach."

Another tense silence. Everyone fidgeted and seemed just as frustrated as Beth.

Herman Otter's face materialized from the bowels of hell to make her draw a sharp breath.

He had been a religious fanatic. Had prayed every night and lit candles on holidays and talked about sin and salvation.

Then forced May into his bed.

Except for the sexual aspect, he fit the profile. But he was dead.

He'd been friends with Reverend Wally Benton, though.

"I'll question Jim Benton," Beth said. "He might know something helpful."

"I told you to sit this out, Beth," Director Vance said. "Hamrick can canvass the church members." Director Vance continued without missing a beat. "Peyton, keep digging for connections between the victims. Dr. Wheeland, see if you can get a solid ID on the body that has been dead thirty years. Agent Fields has a point—that victim might be the key to this mess."

Beth bit her tongue. The elder Reverend Benton had been in his midthirties to forties when Otter had taken her to see him, which meant that if he'd killed victim number one thirty years ago, he would have been a child or in his early teens at the time. Unless he hadn't done it by himself . . .

Now that the elder Benton was dead, his son Jim might be following in his father's footsteps . . .

Beth stood, anxious to leave.

To hell with protocol and sitting this thing out. She wanted to confront Reverend Jim Benton herself. His father had terrified her as a child.

She wouldn't give anyone that kind of power now.

Ian started to follow Beth, but her boss caught his arm before he could leave the room. "I gave Beth orders. Make sure she follows them."

"Why do you think she'll listen to me?" Ian asked.

The director rubbed at his neck. "I don't know, but she seems connected to you because of your past. I don't want her hurt again."

They locked gazes. The man really cared about Beth, in a fatherly kind of way.

"Don't worry. I'll make sure she's safe."

A silent understanding passed between them—they each would do whatever was necessary to protect her.

As Ian left the room, Beth was racing out the door. He hurried to catch up with her. "I'll drive you back to the cabin."

"I'm not going to the cabin," Beth said. "I'm going to see Reverend Jim Benton."

"But—"

"I don't care what Vance said." Beth dashed down the steps, the wind tossing her hair around her face. "I didn't come this far to walk away now."

Ian glanced back at the steps where the director and others were dispersing and made a snap decision.

Beth was not in this alone. He wanted to talk to the man as much as she did. One of his own was missing.

"All right," he said. "I'm in the mood for a sermon tonight."

Beth almost cracked a grin, and Ian's chest squeezed. What would it be like to see that tortured woman smile?

They walked to the car in silence. As Ian drove toward the revival, he passed through the town square. The arts and crafts festival to raise money for those affected by the tornado was in full swing. The sidewalks were crowded, booths lined the streets and filled the park area, and vendors and food trucks had joined in.

He grunted. "Hard to believe that in the midst of the problems the people in this town are facing because of damage from the storm, they have to worry about another killer preying on them at their most vulnerable time."

Beth sighed. "True, but the human spirit is resilient. Just look at the crowd that's turned out for this festival to support each other."

"You're right. Cocoa said an artist who lives in the mountains is donating proceeds from his sales to the town."

They passed several booths selling everything from homemade soaps to spices and herbs to handmade quilts. Someone had tacked posters with a photo of Prissy on street posts asking for help in finding her.

The revival tent was set up on the other side of the park. Ian parked, and they climbed out and walked across the lawn. A sign was posted near the tent announcing sermons at dawn, noon, dusk, and 8 o'clock, with a special praise singing at midnight.

The preacher's voice boomed toward them as they approached. He was lecturing about sin and salvation, sinners and saints, citing Bible verses and pounding his Bible as he paced back and forth on stage.

"You may be lost today, asking yourself where is God in all the horror that's come to this town of yours, but fear not, you are not alone!" he shouted. "If you are that lost person, struggling to find your way, all you have to do is turn to the Lord and ask for His help." He pounded his hand on the Bible. "Take that step and He will lead you into the light."

"He looks like his father," Beth said in a strained voice.

"Did you meet him when you came with the Otters?" Ian asked.

Beth wrinkled her nose in thought. "Yes. He handed out prayer cards and pamphlets listing his father's speaking schedule."

Ian recognized several locals. Bud from the hardware store. Sara Levinson. Myrtle from the supermarket, who always cracked jokes when he bought groceries. Abram Cain from the blood bank.

He scanned the group in search of Bernie and his mother, but he didn't see them.

Cocoa and her granddaughter Vanessa slowly walked up the aisle.

Reverend Benton murmured something to her, then placed a hand on Vanessa's head. "These people are in need of God's love," the reverend said.

Ian shifted uncomfortably as Benton launched into a prayer.

Something about the predatory way Benton looked at Vanessa made Ian's senses come alert.

This man had snowed his mother and dozens of others into following him. He was charismatic. Charming.

Like the serpent that tricked Eve in the Bible.

◆　◆　◆

Beth's heart ached for Vanessa. She was just a teenager, but she looked as if she'd been beaten up by life.

"She's lucky to have her grandparents," Beth said.

"Yeah, she is. Cocoa is the heart of the community. If anyone needs anything, she's there, donating her time and food and love."

Admiration for the woman stirred in Beth.

The preacher said another prayer over Vanessa and Cocoa. Then the group burst into a gospel tune and began clapping. People waved their hands to the music. A woman hurried down the aisle and dropped to her knees in front of the makeshift altar, bowed her head, and prayed. Moved by Benton, others joined her.

"There are some here who want to be saved and others in need of recommitting their lives to the Lord," Benton said. "This Sunday we'll host an old-fashioned baptismal at the river."

Beth waited for the snake handling like the service Otter had taken her to, but she didn't see any sign of snakes. Instead Benton's son relied on his strong voice, which boomed louder and louder as he ranted about sin and temptation.

He slapped the Bible with his hand, then mopped sweat from his face as he gained steam. He strolled down the aisles of the tent, searching and seeking faces, bellowing for the lost ones to testify in front of the crowd.

Religion had its place, and Beth believed in God and prayer. For some reason He had saved her that awful day.

But she didn't believe in terrorizing people with shouts about burning in hell for eternity.

Finally the revival wound down, and the crowd began to disperse. Some of the people were so emotional, crying and shouting that he'd moved them, that they promised to fight sin.

Vanessa and Cocoa wandered through the crowd, Cocoa pausing to speak to everyone she passed. Beth and Ian stopped to talk to the reverend.

"We're investigating the boneyard murders," Beth said. If he'd read the news, he most likely knew her real identity.

And that she'd repressed memories of her abduction.

But he simply smiled at her. "Yes, of course, everyone in the community is upset about them."

Ian cleared his throat. "We're looking for information on anyone who may have known the victims or come in contact with them."

Reverend Benton tugged at his robe. "I'm afraid I didn't know any of the girls personally."

"You didn't meet one of them at a revival?" Ian asked.

"Not that I recall." He gestured toward the crowd. "Mind you, that doesn't mean they didn't attend one of my sermons. As you can see, I don't always get to speak to everyone present."

Beth swallowed hard. "I assume you know who I am?"

His gaze scrutinized her. "I do, but only because of the news. I'm sorry for the ordeal you suffered when you were a young girl. How are you doing?"

Beth's vision blurred. A gospel song about telling it on the mountain played in her head. Herman Otter's hand pushing her forward, pressing hard against her back. His wife, Frances, singing the praises as she aimed an ugly look at Beth as if it was her fault that Herman liked young girls.

Then the preacher's voice, his face . . .

Beth blinked back into focus just as Ian spoke. "Your father was a preacher, and you followed in his footsteps."

"Yes, he taught me to be a God-fearing man. When he passed, I decided to continue his work by spreading the word."

Memories of the revivals Beth had attended flashed back. Wally Benton had been taller than his son, wider jaw, deep-set gray eyes, scar above his right eye.

Herman Otter had taken her and Sunny to his revival service the night before they'd run away.

After the preaching ended, while the Otters were lingering to talk to other followers, she'd snuck away and peeked in one of the tents.

A teenager had been restrained, her body jerking with her screams . . .

Reverend Benton was performing an exorcism.

Bile rose to her throat, and her hand shook.

"Beth?" Ian said softly.

She thought she nodded, but she wasn't sure. Her stomach churning, she excused herself. "I'm sorry. I don't feel well."

The sound of voices and laughter reverberated around her as she turned and ran.

The world blurred and spun, a wave of nausea almost bringing her to her knees. She reached out, clawing for something to hold on to, so dizzy her legs felt like rubber bands.

A few feet away she spotted a wooden building. A ladies' room.

She could make it there. She had to before she passed out.

Another dark wave. The sun moved. The sound of a baby crying. Someone playing a harmonica.

She stumbled forward and reached for the door to the ladies' room, but someone grabbed her from behind and yanked her against the wall.

Then the sharp blade of a knife jabbed her throat.

CHAPTER TWENTY-TWO

Cold fear immobilized Beth. She went stone-still, debating her strategy. Fight him now or look for an opportune moment?

Although if he tried to get her in a car, she would fight.

A woodsy scent hit her, a man's rough beard stubble brushing her cheek as he pressed his mouth to her ear.

"I know who you are," he murmured.

Beth inhaled sharply. "Who are you? What do you want?"

"Just be quiet and do as I say." He tightened his grip, the knife only a fraction of an inch from her neck. If she moved too quickly, he'd slice her carotid artery.

"Just tell me what you want. Take my wallet—"

"This is not about money." He jerked her backward into the shadows of the awning. "Don't you remember me?"

Beth's heart pounded as a memory from long ago stirred. The voice, deep, gruff.

Asking her what was wrong. Encouraging her to talk. Promising to help.

But she'd never accepted his offer of counseling. She hadn't trusted anyone at the time, especially a man.

A shiver rippled through her. "Coach Gleason?"

He nodded against her. "Yes. You ruined my life."

Beth gripped the man's hand at her throat. She had to find some leverage to knock him off guard and get that knife.

"I'm sorry," Beth whispered. "But those girls—"

"I didn't kill anyone," he growled. "Not Kelly Cousins or Sunny or any of the others."

He was pressing her neck so hard he was cutting off her windpipe.

"I know you didn't," Beth whispered.

"You're lying. You're just saying that to get me to release you."

"That's not true. Ian and I have been investigating."

His breath rasped out. "I know. I've been watching."

So she hadn't been paranoid.

Footsteps echoed nearby, and he yanked her up against his body, pressing them both to the concrete wall of the building.

"Don't try anything," he murmured.

"If you didn't kill those girls, you won't hurt me," Beth said in a challenge.

The knife blade scraped her neck. "I have nothing to lose, JJ. Nothing."

◆ ◆ ◆

"We need your help," Ian said in a voice meant to elicit trust from the reverend.

"Whoever killed those girls has a staunch religious background," Ian said. "He's ritualistic." Ian gestured toward the candles lined up at the pulpit. "He sees himself as a god saving sinners."

Reverend Benton's eyes darkened. "You think that's me because I'm a man of the cloth?"

"That's not what I said," Ian said. "Our unsub—"

"Your what?"

"Unknown subject, the killer. His victims are from different cities, so we know he travels. He picks the girls up on the road." Ian watched him for a reaction, but Benton remained cool, so he continued. "The victims feel safe with him, or they wouldn't go with him willingly. Do you know anyone who fits that description?"

"No, I'm afraid I can't help you."

"I'm sure you hear all kinds of confessions in private," Ian said.

"If any such person confessed to me, I'm sworn by the church to keep their confidence." Benton stroked the sash around his neck. "I pray you find this person, Sheriff. I wish I could help you, but I can't. Now, excuse me, I have others who need me."

The reverend headed toward Cocoa and Vanessa. Ian wanted to warn them to be careful, but his gut instinct urged him to find Beth. If she'd remembered the killer's face, they might be able to save Prissy Carson.

He wove through the crowd, searching the people milling around after the revival and the attendees at the arts and crafts festival.

Food trucks were stationed along one end of the park. Country music blared from a stage across the way. A woman carrying baked goods nearly bumped into him, and children laughed at a crafts table where a woman was teaching them how to make paper flowers. A line had formed with people donating blood to the blood bank, and several people had gathered at that artist's booth where he was demonstrating his techniques on canvas.

The wooden building housing the restrooms sat to the left. Beth might be inside.

As he approached, a movement caught his eye. A shadow. There were two people in the corner of the building.

One was Beth. The other—a man.

He moved closer.

The man had a knife to her throat.

Fear hammered inside Ian. He removed his gun from his holster as he moved toward them.

◆ ◆ ◆

Beth remained silent while a group of people walked by. She had to convince Coach Gleason to release her without anyone being harmed.

He tightened his hold around her neck, and she gasped for air. More footsteps. Ian appeared around the corner.

"Don't do it, son," Coach said in a low voice.

Ian aimed his weapon at the coach. "Let her go, Dad."

A slight tremble rippled through Gleason. Beth forced herself to stay calm. "I know you've been through hell, but—"

"I want answers," he growled. "To clear my name. You can do that."

"Then drop the knife," Beth murmured.

His grip on her loosened slightly, and Beth took advantage of the moment and jabbed him in the stomach with her elbow. He grunted, and she stomped on his instep. He'd aged fifteen years and gained weight, but he snatched her arm as she tried to escape.

They rolled and fought for the knife.

Beth kneed him in the groin, then shoved him backward. He lost the knife, then crawled after it.

Ian fired at the ground. "Don't move, Dad."

Beth spun around and pushed to her feet. Coach Gleason froze, a feral gleam in his eyes. "You want to shoot me, Ian, go ahead. But I'm not going back to prison."

"We have to do this the right way," Ian said. "Go through the courts. A girl is missing now—"

"I never laid a hand on any teenage girl."

"What about Kelly Cousins? Were you involved with her?" Beth asked.

The coach barked a sarcastic laugh. "I never touched her," Coach said vehemently. "I swear, Ian. She talked to me about her depression. Perhaps she developed a crush on me, but I wouldn't have let it go anywhere. For God's sake, she was a kid. And I loved your mother."

"Then why run and hide out after the flood?" Ian asked.

"Because I tried to get an appeal and it was denied," he said. "I figured if anyone had to prove my innocence, it was me. I couldn't do that behind bars."

Indecision flickered in Ian's eyes. Beth's heart hurt for him. The coach had been the only father Ian had ever known.

"The only way to clear you is to go back," Beth said.

He shook his head, a wildness in his eyes born of fear and desperation. He'd been wronged by the law and his wife, and suffered God knows what in prison, then had been hiding out in these mountains for years.

She had to make this easy for Ian.

She aimed her gun at the man. "Coach Gleason, you are under arrest. You have the right to remain silent—"

"I won't go back to jail!" He started toward her, and Ian shouted a warning.

"Stop," Beth cried.

But he didn't seem to hear.

He charged her, and Beth reacted on instinct.

She fired a bullet into his chest. The coach grunted, his eyes widening in shock as he pressed his hand to the wound. Blood oozed between his fingers as he dropped to his knees.

Every nerve in Tandy Pooler Benton's body clenched like a fist.

She'd heard that sheriff from podunk Graveyard Falls talking to her husband, Jim. And then that woman, Beth Fields.

She wasn't stupid. She'd read the paper.

That lady was JJ Jones. She'd gone missing fifteen years ago. Supposedly she had no memory of her abductor's face or name.

For now.

What if she remembered?

Tandy had to do everything she could to protect her husband. That was what good wives did.

After all, she'd been on her way to full whoredom before Jim saved her sorry soul.

Not a day went by that he didn't remind her of that, too.

She hated it when he reminded her, but God wanted you to be humble, and she was about as humble as a body could get.

Jim had taken her in when she was a street girl, just a runaway, and he'd prayed over her night and day. Had exorcised the demons from her with his rituals and teachings and lessons—those lessons hurt, but sinners had to be punished.

She rubbed the scars on her arms. They were old, but sometimes she could see the blood dripping from the cuts.

Bloodletting was a practice as old as the hills. It enabled the ill and afflicted to purge themselves of poisonous toxins and the evil within. Snake handling was the best way to weed out the weak. Normally Jim used that at the revivals, but with all the publicity in town over that graveyard of bones, he'd decided to skip it this time.

Jim was the wise one. The chosen one. Just like his daddy.

He'd made her respectable. Married her when she'd thought no nice man would take her for a wife.

Sure, she had to do things for him. Feed his body and sate his fleshly desires. Fulfill his every need.

But that's what a wife was supposed to do.

She couldn't let these damned police mess things up.

Like a good, obedient servant, she'd keep her mouth shut.

The door to the trailer where she and Jim were staying for the revival screeched open, and her husband strode in, wiping at his forehead with a handkerchief. "Did you talk to those cops?" he bellowed.

"No," Tandy said, her insides quivering.

He slid one hand around her wrist and gripped it so hard she winced. "You didn't mention the girls?"

Tandy shook her head vehemently. "No, I swear. I . . . love you, Jim. I know you believe what you're doing is right."

His gray eyes pierced her. "Are you saying you don't think it is?"

Fear crawled through Tandy. "That's not what I mean. You save lives, Jim—I'm grateful to be part of that." The last girl's screams had torn her stomach in knots though. Tandy did her best to drown out the sound.

Nothing kept the screams quiet, though.

But she dared not cross her husband. She knew what would happen if she did.

CHAPTER
TWENTY-THREE

Ian's hand jerked as he lowered his gun and rushed toward his father. He couldn't believe he'd finally found him.

And now he might lose him all over again.

Threatening Beth had been a mistake, though.

Blood gushed from his father's chest. His face was turning gray, his eyes drifting shut. Ian's world blurred.

He heard Beth's voice behind him. She was on the phone. "This is Special Agent Beth Fields. I need an ambulance. A man has been shot." Her voice faded as she recited the address. Ian dragged out a handkerchief to press against his father's wound to slow the bleeding.

People must have heard the gunshot, and a crowd began to gather. Beth took charge, securing the area and asking everyone to stay back. Voices rumbled through the crowd, people shouting questions at once.

"Who is he?"

"What happened?"

"Is he dead?"

"He's going to be all right," Beth said, although she couldn't know that. She was simply trying to appease the crowd.

His father was losing blood too fast. He coughed and tried to speak, but his words came out garbled.

"Someone get some paper towels from the bathroom," Beth ordered.

His father tugged at Ian's arm. "Didn't kill anyone, I swear."

Emotions flooded Ian. A man shoved a handful of paper towels toward him, and Ian pressed them on top of the handkerchief and added pressure.

"I know, Dad, that's what I tried to tell you. Some of the bodies—" His father passed out before Ian could finish.

Beth touched his shoulder, but he jerked away. A siren wailed in the distance, the sound growing louder as the ambulance got closer.

"Dad, hang in there," Ian said. "We're going to get you to the hospital. Then we'll clear your name."

But his father lay limp, unresponsive. An apology flickered in Beth's eyes, but he didn't have time to deal with it.

The ambulance screeched to a stop in the parking lot by the building, and two medics retrieved a stretcher and rushed toward them.

The crowd parted. He waved the medics to his father's side, then stepped away to give them room to check his vitals. They padded the wound with blood stoppers, then lifted him onto the stretcher and rushed back to the ambulance.

Ian followed. "I'm going with you."

The medic started to argue, but Ian flashed his badge. "This man is a wanted criminal. I have to escort him."

More importantly, he wanted to be close by in case his father tried to talk.

Bits and pieces of the past played behind Beth's eyes. The coach promising to help her years ago. Offering to talk to the social worker.

He'd given her a card with his phone number on it and encouraged her to call him.

But she'd been too embarrassed because he'd guessed what was going on in the Otters' house.

May's face flashed again, and Beth struggled to recall that night, to see past her to the driver. But his face was cast in a dark shadow.

Voices jarred her back to reality. The medics were moving with the coach, Ian following.

She ordered the crowd to disperse, then caught Ian just as he was climbing into the ambulance.

"I'll go, too." She reached for the door to join him, but Ian shook his head.

"You've done enough, Beth."

Bitterness darkened his eyes as he shoved the keys to his SUV in her hand. Then he shut the ambulance door in her face.

A second later, the medic started the engine, flipped on the siren, and raced away.

Beth jogged toward Ian's police vehicle, fired up the engine, and followed the ambulance, praying that Coach Gleason didn't die.

Ian would never forgive her if he did.

Ian gripped his father's hand as the ambulance sped toward the hospital. The medics started an IV and oxygen, but his blood pressure was dropping, his pulse weak.

Dammit, he couldn't die.

Not when they had a chance to be father and son again.

The ambulance bounced over a rut in the road, and his father groaned. Ian glanced at the medic. "You think he'll make it?"

The young man shrugged. "He's lost a lot of blood. Depends on internal injuries, if the bullet hit a major artery."

Ian scrubbed a hand through his hair, the scene between his father and Beth bothering him. Would his father have hurt Beth if she hadn't shot him?

The ambulance swerved into the parking lot and squealed to a stop. Beth swung into the ER parking lot behind them and parked.

A flurry of nurses and doctors greeted them at the ER entrance. The medic cited his father's vitals, and the medical staff shouted orders and directions as they ran inside. Chaos ensued as they pushed him into a triage room. Ian tried to go inside with him, but a male nurse blocked his way.

"Sorry, sir, you need to wait outside."

"He's my father," Ian said. "And he's in my custody."

"He's not going anywhere until after surgery," the nurse said. "Let us do our jobs."

Ian bit back a response. He wanted—no, he *needed*—to talk to his father again.

But the nurse pointed toward the waiting room, and Ian had to concede.

Frustration knotted Ian's insides as he walked back to the waiting room. Beth rushed in just as he pulled his phone from his pocket to call his mother.

She had a right to know his dad was alive.

Beth approached him, but the image of her firing that gun into his father's chest made him rush toward the coffee machine.

If she'd remembered who'd abducted her, his father would have been cleared. He wouldn't be a fugitive. And he wouldn't be in a damn hospital fighting for his life.

On some level, he realized he was being irrational, but he couldn't help himself. His family had been destroyed by JJ's case.

The phone rang three, four times. Then a male voice answered. "Woods residence."

"Bernie, it's Ian. I need to speak to Mom."

"She doesn't want to talk to you."

"You mean you don't want her to talk to me."

"It's my job as her husband to protect her," Bernie said.

Ian clenched the phone so hard his fingers went numb. "She doesn't need protection from me. I'm her son, and I'm tired of you coming between us."

"Your mother's found peace in the church," Bernie said. "I'd think you would want that."

"I do, that's the reason I'm calling. I have proof that my father is innocent. She needs to know that."

"Leave her alone, Ian." The phone went dead.

Ian cursed. Ever since his mother had married that holier-than-thou asshole, she'd withdrawn from Ian. Bernie had destroyed her confidence in herself. He wanted control. All along Ian had held hope that proving his father's innocence would help him get her back. But Bernie was still in the way.

Ian shoved some quarters into the coffee machine, waited for it to dispense the coffee, and headed back down the hall. Beth was pacing the waiting room, her expression torn.

She started toward him, then hesitated, chewing on her thumbnail. "Ian—"

"Don't," he said. "I understand you did what you had to do, but you have no idea what it's like to lose your family."

"No, I guess I don't." Hurt flared in her eyes. "Although Sunny was my family. I was supposed to take care of her, Ian, but I got her killed."

Shit. That wasn't what he meant.

One of the nurses appeared. "Sheriff Kimball?"

He faced her, praying she didn't have bad news. "That's me."

"Your father refuses to have the operation until he sees you."

She ushered him through the ER to a room where they'd prepped his father. His father's eyes were closed, his face so gray that Ian was afraid he was too late.

A groan rumbled from his father, and Ian took his hand. "Dad?"

He wheezed for a breath. "Ian?"

Ian swallowed hard. "I'm here."

"Didn't do it," he murmured.

"I know," Ian said, battling fear and annoyance.

"Files . . ." His father's voice cracked. "School files. Answers there."

The stolen ones? "Where are the files?"

"Cabin," he said, gasping for a breath.

"Where?"

"My pocket, a map," his father said. "I was going to give it to JJ. See if she remembered someone."

"You think someone from school kidnapped her and Sunny?" Ian asked.

His father groaned again. "Student," his father said between coughs. "Some troubled kids. One of them had a crush on Kelly. He made up those rumors . . ."

His father's voice faded. Ian wanted the kid's name. "Dad, talk to me. Who was it?"

He patted his father's cheek to wake him, but he'd lapsed into unconsciousness.

Ian glanced at the nurse. "You have his clothes?"

She gestured toward a bag on the floor in the corner. Ian crossed the room and rifled through it. His shirt had been cut off and was soaked in blood. His jeans were old and frayed, but Ian found a scrap of paper in the pocket with a crude map.

"Take care of him," he told the nurse. He squeezed his father's arm. "Fight like hell, Dad. I'll find the truth. Then I'll be back."

He clutched the map in his hand and strode through the ER. Beth met him at the door, questions in her eyes. He didn't have time to hash over what had happened.

If those files gave them the answers they needed, they might save Prissy Carson's life.

◆ ◆ ◆

It was time to say his final good-byes to Prissy Carson. But he couldn't carry her to the holler.

The police and Feds were all over the town, asking questions. Getting close.

He touched the most recent vials of blood he'd collected, memorizing the names.

How many would he have to take to win his own salvation?

The paintings he'd finished with the girls' blood were lined against the wall of his storage room. Their blood decorated the interior of the cavern as well.

A noise sounded from outside the room, then the ping of water dripping. Another sound a second later. Footsteps in the hall of the cavern.

He froze. No one knew about his place but him.

Sweat pooled on his neck. He snuffed out the candle in the corner and flattened himself against the wall.

The door groaned open. The candlelight from the hall flowed inside in tiny glimmers, just enough to allow him to see who'd discovered his secret.

His son's face filled the light. Shock. Disgust. Intrigue. A myriad of emotions in the boy's eyes.

The words of his own father reverberated in his ears. The day his father told him about the Calling.

It was time to pass on the message.

He led his son to the wall of blood and began the story.

CHAPTER TWENTY-FOUR

Ian needed distance between himself and Beth. He understood the reason she'd shot his father. Hell, *he'd* almost pulled the trigger when he'd seen that knife in his father's hands.

But . . . the situation was too damn complicated. His guilt. Hers. The dead girls deserving justice.

All those families needing answers.

Beth's tortured expression made his gut clench. "How is he?"

"They're taking him to surgery." Ian pulled the map from his pocket. "He stole the files from the school. He was going to give them to you."

"What's in the files?" Beth asked.

Ian shrugged. "He said a student made up the story about Kelly and Dad, but he didn't say who. I'm going to get the files."

"Give me the map and I'll go," Beth said.

Ian hesitated. He wanted to stay here and make sure his father survived the surgery. But Prissy Carson's life hung in the balance, and he needed to retrieve the files ASAP.

And Beth wanted the truth as much as or maybe more than he did.

Still, the unsub knew Beth's identity. Knew where she lived. He might be watching her. Following her.

Ian couldn't stand the thought of the sicko hurting her again.

"We'll both go."

"No, Ian," Beth said softly. "You need to be here when your father wakes up."

He shifted, debating what to do. "What happened when we were talking to Reverend Benton?"

Turmoil darkened her eyes. "I remembered one particular revival, the one we went to the night before I ran away. The senior Reverend Benton was preaching. He frightened me. They were handling snakes. Later, I peeked into one of the tents, and he'd restrained this young girl and was performing an exorcism."

"I didn't know people still did that."

"He did. The girl was screaming for help as he chanted and prayed over her. He also talked about bloodletting, said he'd drain the bad blood from her and she'd be healed."

Ian's straightened. "He sliced her wrists?"

"No, her mother was there and stopped them from the bloodletting. I was so terrified I ran. Mr. Otter caught me and threatened to beat me if I told anyone." She hesitated. "Maybe Jim Benton is following in his father's footsteps."

"I'll ask my deputy to tail him," Ian said. "If he's hiding something or has Prissy, maybe we'll catch him in the act."

"Give me the map, and I'll retrieve those files."

Ian licked his dry lips. "Beth—"

She patted her gun. "Trust me to do my job for both of us," Beth said. "I'll keep my eyes open. If he's tailing me, I'll call for backup."

Their fingers brushed as Beth took the map, making her skin tingle.

Ian looked so lost and upset that she wanted to comfort him.

But if his father died, he'd hate her, so she rushed toward the door. The sooner she found the cabin, the sooner she'd have access to those files and what was inside.

The skies had turned a murky gray with rain clouds, and the wind had picked up, tossing leaves and debris across the entrance to the ER. Instinct urged her to look over her shoulder. For years, she'd sensed Coach Gleason had been following her, and she'd been right.

The unsub had been watching her, too.

She climbed into Ian's police SUV and peeled from the parking lot. Although she was new to Graveyard Falls, she'd traveled to the mountains before, and she recognized the general area on the map.

It was slightly north of the falls the town was named after.

Traffic was minimal, night setting in, and she flipped on her lights. The mountains rose around her, lush with newly budding trees, the wind echoing off the sharp ridges. Coyotes, bears, mountain lions, and other wild animals lived in these hills—a perfect place to hide.

A truck passed her on a winding curve, and she sucked in a sharp breath. Crazy driver. It sped on, and she flipped her lights to low beam as she met two other vehicles on another switchback. She slowed, tires grinding on the shoulder as she tried to avoid hitting a sedan that crossed the line.

More storm clouds moved across the sky, obliterating the moon. She passed the turnoff for Hemlock Holler, checked the map, and turned at the point where the rocks were shaped like a bear.

She heard the sound of an engine behind her. A pickup truck on her tail. She hit the gas to move out of the way, but the truck accelerated and slammed into her rear.

Beth jerked forward and braked, but the SUV skidded into a spin. A second later, the truck shifted and backed up, then raced toward her again.

She braced herself for the impact and reached for her gun. She didn't have time to aim. The truck slammed into the driver's door and sent the SUV skidding in the opposite direction toward the embankment.

Beth screamed as the guardrails came at her. God help her—she was going over. Terrified, she flung open her door and threw herself out of the car. The SUV sailed over the side of the mountain and crashed below.

She hit the pavement with her shoulder, and a teeth-jarring pain ripped through her arm.

Gasping for a breath, she rolled to her side, gripped her gun, and took aim.

The truck sat facing her, the lights blinding her. She thought the windows were tinted, but it didn't matter. The headlights were so bright that she had to cover her eyes with her hand. The engine fired up.

Was he coming at her again?

She pulled the trigger. The driver revved the truck engine. Just as she'd feared, he drove straight toward her.

Beth fired again, but the bullet pinged off the pavement. The lights grew closer, the engine roaring. She rolled again and ended up sliding over the mountain ridge.

A boom reverberated through the air. Ian's SUV burst into flames at the bottom of the drop-off.

She screamed and reached for something to hang on to. A limb jutting from the ground. She closed her fingers around it, but it snapped.

Terror seized her. If she lost hold, she'd plummet to her death.

Ian considered calling the director, but the man had ordered Beth to leave the case alone, so he phoned Deputy Markum instead and relayed what had happened. "I'm at the hospital. My father's in surgery."

"I've been watching Benton like you requested. He went home with his wife a while ago. You want me to come to the hospital?"

"No, stay with Benton."

Ian disconnected and went to get another cup of coffee. Through the window by the coffee machine, he watched the sky darken, the wind blowing the trees as if another tornado might be on the horizon.

Fuck. That was the last thing Graveyard Falls needed. They were barely surviving their recent losses and tangling with another lunatic killer.

The seconds ticked by excruciatingly slowly as Ian paced the waiting room. He wanted news, dammit.

For the surgery to be over. For his father to live.

For his mother to act like she gave a damn.

Although as soon as his father went to prison, Bernie Woods had walked into her life and acted like her savior. First he'd been a concerned friend, but soon she'd fallen under some kind of spell when Bernie was around.

And the Reverend Jim Benton—his mother acted as if he were a god.

Could Jim Benton have something to do with these murders? If he was performing exorcisms, had he gone too far?

Although Jim Benton had only been a teenager when JJ and Sunny disappeared.

Something didn't fit.

Ian gripped his coffee, stewing over the information they had. They were missing something.

His father had kept those files for a reason. They held the key.

Anxious to know what was in them, he punched Beth's number. Her phone rang and rang, but no one answered.

CHAPTER
TWENTY-FIVE

Beth's arms trembled as she strained to hold on to the ledge. Her first instinct was to scream for help. But the driver who'd hit her had stopped. Was he going to make sure she was dead?

Gravel crunched. Dirt pelted her face.

He was coming toward her.

Terrified, she glanced down. A small ridge was a few feet below. If she could make it, she could hide beneath the overhang. Then her attacker would think she'd fallen over the ledge.

If she missed, she'd fall hundreds of feet to her death.

Her arms shook with the effort to hang on. The footsteps sounded again. It was now or never.

She whispered a silent prayer, then gauged the distance and width of the ledge and dropped straight down. Thank God her feet hit, but the impact jarred her teeth and her ankle twisted.

Pain ricocheted up her leg as she fell to her knees. Her other foot slid over the edge, and she almost lost her balance and slipped over. She bit back a scream and clawed at the rocky ledge for control.

Heart racing, she crawled beneath the overhang and plastered herself to the wall. She was so dizzy her breathing came out in short pants. She drew her knees up to her chest, wrapped her arms around them, and laid her head on her hands.

The world spun, the past few minutes replaying in her mind. Who had been driving that truck?

Several seconds passed. The air was colder on top of the mountain, the wind sucking at her. Metal popped and glass shattered below. Smoke and fire shot into the air, the blaze leaping as the gas tank exploded.

She covered her head with her hands and forced herself to take deep breaths. Finally her nerves calmed, and the dizziness subsided.

As the fire began to die down, she craned her head, listening for sounds of the driver or his vehicle. Her phone vibrated in her pocket. Grateful it was on silent, she carefully removed it and glanced at the number.

Ian.

She fought the urge to answer. She couldn't give herself away.

She strained to hear above her. The wind picked up. The smoke grew thicker. There was no way she could climb that ledge.

Fear mingled with panic.

Another minute passed, then another. Finally the sound of an engine starting broke the silence.

She gripped her phone and called Ian.

Ian's phone buzzed at the same time the surgeon appeared at the doorway of the waiting room. He glanced at the number. Beth.

He'd call her back. First he had to see if his father had made it.

He rushed to the doorway. "I'm Ian Kimball. How's my dad?"

"We managed to remove the bullet, and he made it through surgery. Thankfully the bullet missed his main artery, but other internal organs were damaged."

Not good.

"Is he going to survive?" Ian asked.

The surgeon gave him a noncommittal look. "The next twenty-four hours will tell. He's lost a lot of blood and has lapsed into a coma."

Ian's chest clenched. "What does that mean?"

The doctor shifted. "His body needs rest and time to recover."

"How long?"

A grave expression tugged at the surgeon's eyes. "It could be hours, could be days."

Ian gave a quick nod. "Do you know who he is?"

"I'm aware that he was shot by a federal agent and that he was handcuffed when he arrived," the doctor said tersely. "But I assure you that that played no part in my surgery."

"I didn't mean to imply that it did." Ian explained about his father's history. "A deputy will guard him twenty-four seven. Please call me if there's any change in his condition. It's important that I speak to him the moment he regains consciousness."

The doctor pushed his surgical cap back on his head. "I'll alert the staff."

Ian shook the man's hand and thanked him again. His phone was buzzing once more. Beth. Maybe she'd found something.

He quickly connected. "It's Ian."

"Help me, Ian," Beth rasped. "I need you."

Fear slammed into Ian. "What's wrong? Where are you?"

"A wreck." Static rattled over the line, the wind howling in the background. "On a mountain ledge."

He raced toward the door. "What? Jesus, Beth, what happened?"

"A truck ran me off the road." More static.

"Where?"

"On the way to the cabin," she said over the noise.

Panic set in. "I'll be there as soon as possible. Are you hurt?"

More static. He shook his phone. He couldn't hear a damn thing. God. What if she'd lost consciousness?

A siren wailed from an incoming ambulance outside. Tires squealed as another car roared up behind it. A group of people were leaving, one woman crying on a man's shoulder.

He glanced at the parking lot and realized Beth had his SUV.

Fuck.

He ran back to the nurses' station. "I need an ambulance. A federal agent had an accident on the mountain."

She picked up the phone and consulted with someone. A minute later, two medics appeared.

"What's the address?" one of them asked.

Dammit, he'd given Beth the map. But he knew the general area. He'd look for signs of an accident. "I'm not sure, but I can take you there."

◆ ◆ ◆

Beth clenched her phone with clammy hands.

Déjà vu struck her. She'd had that feeling of helplessness before, a feeling of despair.

When she'd been restrained by the man who'd killed Sunny.

She hugged the wall of the mountain, her gaze scanning the valley below. Thick trees climbed the hills, their limbs bared.

The fire from the SUV lit the night. A patch of evergreens caught her eye. Then a rock formation that reminded her of a cross.

Dear God, she recognized that place.

Images swirled behind her eyes. Kneeling before that cross. Being baptized in the springs nearby. No, not nearby.

In the cave behind those rocks.

The rocks were a natural formation. Tiny crystals hung from the ceiling inside that sparkled and resembled angels.

His deep voice reverberated in her ears. He'd picked the place because it was sacred. He claimed he was the chosen one.

Chill bumps cascaded up her arms and neck.

The cave where he'd held her, where he'd bled Sunny and the other girls to death—she remembered.

Her heart jumped to her throat. If she could lead Ian there, they might find evidence to determine the unsub's identity and save Prissy.

A siren wailed, signaling its approach. She eased an inch away from the wall, then twisted to look upward. An engine rumbled. Gravel crunched.

Footsteps.

She held her breath. The driver could have come back. The wind rustled the trees. Metal popped from below, and smoke clouded her eyes.

"Beth!" Ian's voice carried in the wind. "Beth, are you down there?"

Relief surged through her, and she released the breath she'd been holding. "Yes! I'm on the ledge!"

"How the hell did you get there?" Ian asked.

"I jumped when the car started over the edge."

A dizzy spell assaulted her as she looked down. Smoke billowed from his SUV, a fiery blaze curling upward.

She clung to the rock, shaky and terrified she might slip. "I can't climb up," she yelled.

"Hang on," Ian shouted. "Let me get a rope."

Beth heaved a sigh of relief. When they got her up, she'd tell Ian about the cave.

Prissy Carson might be there now.

Cold fear consumed Ian. How in the world had Beth landed on that ridge and not plunged to her death? His car had nosedived into the rocks below and was smoldering, a total loss.

Beth would have been, too, if she hadn't jumped.

Shit.

He ran back to the medics. "Do you have some strong rope I can use?"

One of the medics jogged to the ambulance and returned with a thick rope. The other medic shined a flashlight to illuminate the area, then helped Ian secure the rope to a boulder. Ian tied it around his waist and climbed down the ledge.

Beth was plastered against the rocky wall, trembling. He steadied himself and inched to her.

She fell against his chest, and he couldn't help himself. He cradled her against his body and rocked her in his arms.

CHAPTER
TWENTY-SIX

Beth hated herself for being weak, but she couldn't bring herself to pull away. Ian's arms felt warm and solid, comforting, strong.

For a brief second, she felt safe. As if her past wasn't about to catch up with her.

She'd been running from it all her life.

Hiding behind a new identity. Trying to save other girls to compensate for not saving Sunny.

"Beth?"

Ian's gruff voice shook her back to reality. She'd shot Ian's father, and he was in the hospital fighting for his life. She didn't know if he'd survived the surgery.

But Ian had just saved her life anyway.

She inhaled a deep breath and removed herself from his embrace. "I'm sorry."

Ian brushed her hair from her cheek. "Are you hurt?"

"No, just shaken."

"Then let's get you off this ledge."

She caught his arm as he began to loosen the rope. "Ian, what about your father?"

"He's in a coma." He slid the rope around her waist and tied it securely. "The medics are going to pull you up. Hang on tight."

"I . . . don't know if I can do it," she whispered. "I hate heights."

Ian cupped her face between his hands. "You can do anything, Beth. You're the bravest woman I've ever met. Just don't look down." He gave her a deep kiss on the lips, and thoughts of the ledge faded.

He yelled for the medics. She took a deep breath, gripped the rope, and began to climb the ledge as the medics hauled her up.

Her legs and arms were shaking by the time she reached the top and the men helped her over the edge. She fell onto the ground panting, still reeling from that kiss.

One of the medics untied the rope and threw it down to Ian. Beth brushed dirt from her face and clothes as she watched them help Ian climb to the top.

His breathing rasped out as he untied himself and crawled to her. "Are you okay?"

She nodded. The medic checked her vitals, but she refused to go to the hospital. "Ian, I remembered something. We need to go."

She signed a waiver for the medics just as CSU and Deputy Whitehorse arrived. The deputy was going to oversee the investigators and then hitch a ride back with the CSU. Whitehorse turned his keys over to Ian.

She and Ian hurried to his police car.

They had to find that cave.

Hopefully they'd find Prissy there.

Alive.

◆ ◆ ◆

Beth's statement spiked Ian's adrenaline, giving him hope they'd find the sick bastard who'd murdered the girls.

The unsub had let Beth go free once. But today he'd returned to kill her.

Why? Because he was afraid she'd remembered his face?

"Where's this cave?" Ian asked.

Beth tried to smooth her hair into some kind of order. "Behind those rocks to the east. The rock formation is unique. It's a natural formation that resembles a cross."

Ian veered onto the highway. "Did you see the person or vehicle that hit you?"

"No. His lights were so bright they blinded me. But it was a truck."

Ian steered the car onto the highway, then headed around the mountain. "What about the make and model? Color?"

Beth massaged her temple. "Black, maybe."

"That's good," Ian said. "Anything else? Was it a short bed? Long bed?"

"I couldn't tell," Beth said. "When he hit me, he must have damaged his own vehicle. I'll text Peyton and ask her to search for a black pickup being serviced for body damage and to look in the system for locals who might drive a black truck."

He maneuvered a series of switchbacks, alert for the truck in case the driver returned.

Beth finished the text, then pointed to a V in the road. "It's that way."

Ian maneuvered the turn easily, his gut tightening.

They had to hurry.

Anxiety gnawed at Beth. Soon she would be at the cave, back to that torture chamber where she'd been held like an animal, forced to beg for her life.

The sedan bounced over ruts in the dirt as Ian plowed along. The road that led into the woods was barely a road, more like a path that had been cut by a tractor.

She closed her eyes and tried to recall how the unsub had brought her and Sunny here.

She'd been unconscious. But she faintly remembered the rumble of an engine.

She'd stirred a few times, only to be slammed against the truck wall by the impact of a pothole. Then her head had spun and she'd passed out again.

Ian suddenly came to a halt. Tires ground the gravel.

Beth stared into the dark forest. Night creatures howled and an owl hooted. Leaves rustled.

"The road ends here." Ian laid his hands on the steering wheel, frustration lining his face. "What do we do now?"

Beth climbed from the car. The wind chilled her, or maybe being close to the cave where Sunny had died was making her cold from the inside out.

The sound of water rippling over rocks broke the night. The river was close by. They needed to follow it.

She paused, another memory surfacing. Water dripping in the cave. The pool where he'd baptized them.

It was some kind of springs the creek fed into.

She pivoted toward the sound. "This way. We have to hike in."

"He carried you in on foot?"

Beth rubbed her temple again, snippets of the past returning in jarring bits. "He had some kind of wagon or board in the back of the truck. He used it to haul us." She swallowed. "I remember being tied to it. Trying to claw my way to reach Sunny."

Ian retrieved two flashlights from the sedan and handed her one. Determined, she forged ahead, using the flashlight to shine a path.

Their boots made crunching sounds on the dry leaves. A mountain lion growled somewhere in the distance. Other forest creatures darted through the weeds and brambles as if they thought she and Ian were hunting them.

A buck hesitated in the sliver of light from her flashlight and looked up at her, startled. She knew how the animal felt. Trapped. Always watching for a predator.

Using the trees and brush to camouflage their true colors just as she hid behind her job and gun.

It was the only place she'd ever felt safe.

Except she'd felt safe in Ian's arms earlier. Safe and cared for.

He was just doing his job, she reminded herself as she stepped over a broken tree limb. Other branches had been flung down and shattered in the tornado.

She lost her way for a second, confused. Which way to go?

The dark sucked her in. The scent of marshy earth. The ripple of the water. The stench of . . . blood.

She pivoted toward the sound of the water. Follow the stream and it would lead them to the baptismal pool.

Follow the scent of blood that had permeated her soul for years and it would lead her to the evil one who'd destroyed her life.

Ian checked his watch. They'd been hiking for twenty minutes.

He hoped to hell Beth was right about this place. Occasionally she stopped and scanned the area as if she was lost.

Maybe she was—lost in the traumatic memories of her abduction and her friend's murder.

She stumbled over a tree root, and he caught her arm. She might have hurt her ankle, but it hadn't slowed her down. Once she'd heard that rippling water from the river and the creek, she'd taken off, shoving brush and branches aside as she followed the sound.

Ian imagined her at fifteen, how terrified she'd been.

They broke through a small clearing, and he stopped behind Beth, giving her space and time to think. Her eyes were dark with pain, haunted with the reality of what they might find, but she shifted to the left and led the way.

She was the strongest, most courageous woman he'd ever met.

A deer ran past, then another. So much beauty in the midst of the dark, thick foliage. So much danger for a girl alone with no one to guide her through life.

Beth came to a halt again. He inched closer to her, senses alert.

A cold breeze ruffled the leaves and brought with it the strong smell of earth.

And death.

Beth pointed to the cluster of rocks that resembled a cross.

He surveyed the area surrounding the rocks. More trees. A small clearing. A pool of water fed by the creek to the right.

He clenched his hands. This was the spot she'd talked about. Where the bastard had baptized the girls before he slit their wrists.

"He forced us to kneel before the cross while he prayed over us," Beth said in a low whisper. "He said he was chosen to save us from a life of sin."

Ian muttered a curse. He'd never understood psycho freaks who used religion as a justification to kill.

She started ahead, and he caught her arm and gestured for her to stay behind him. She might outrank him, but revisiting the place where she'd been held and seen her friend die was traumatic. He wanted to protect her. "Let me go in first."

A myriad of emotions glittered in her eyes. Indecision, fear, resignation, determination.

Then a long-suffering sigh and a nod.

He eased forward, careful to keep his senses honed. So far, he didn't detect anyone around. No wagon or board the unsub used to haul anyone in.

Maybe Beth was wrong. He might have used this cave long ago but found a new spot.

Behind Ian, Beth's breathing brushed his neck. Choppy and uneven, it cut through the air, a reminder of her personal stake in this mess.

She gestured to a cluster of branches and limbs stacked in front of stone. He crossed to it, yanked the branches and limbs away, and tossed them into a pile.

A door was underneath.

Beth's pain-filled gasp made him tense. He removed his gun and held it at the ready as he eased open the wooden door built into the opening. Had this once been some kind of mine?

The interior was so dark that he blinked to clear his vision. The rancid scent of death was overpowering. He yanked a handkerchief from his pocket and pressed it over his mouth, then motioned for Beth to stay outside.

She shook her head no, determination hardening her expression.

He handed her the handkerchief and then directed the beam of light around the interior and listened. No sounds of anyone inside. No footsteps or voices. No one crying out for help.

Slowly he crept deeper into the cave. A hundred feet in he spotted another door.

He pushed it open, gun braced and ready to fire.

Beth gasped again. Ian pulled her to him to hide her from the grisly sight.

They were too late.

Prissy Carson was lying on the ground, tied and bound, her body still. Her eyes wide open in death.

CHAPTER TWENTY-SEVEN

Beth stared at Prissy Carson in horror.

Just like the girls they'd found in the holler, she was dressed in a sheer white cotton dress that resembled a christening gown.

Bitterness blended with anger and guilt, and Beth broke down. The sobs that came from her were ripped from her soul.

This was so unfair. Prissy was so young. She should be alive, talking to her friends, planning her first school dance.

Ian's curse reminded her that she wasn't alone, and she swiped at her tears. Ian slowly knelt beside the girl and pressed two fingers to Prissy's neck, checking for a pulse, although it was obvious she was dead. The candle in Prissy's hand had burned down, the wax clumping on her fingers. Blood spatter dotted the floor.

"She's in rigor," Ian said, "but she hasn't been dead long."

Self-hate hit Beth like a sledgehammer. If she'd been able to lead her FBI team and the police to this place sooner, they would have saved Prissy's life.

An hour, maybe even minutes, could have made a difference.

She shined her flashlight across the interior of the cave, sickened at the swirls of blood on the wall. Religious symbols covered the stone, a cross, angels, a Bible verse.

Ian's voice startled her. "Yes, Lieutenant Ward, send another crime team. We found the kill spot. Hopefully he left DNA somewhere in here."

Ian gave him the coordinates, ended the call, and then examined the girl's face for injuries. "Except for the fatal slash of her wrist, it doesn't look like he tortured her or hurt her."

"The mental torture was enough," Beth said in disgust. Another memory rose from the grave of her mind. *He dipped his fingers into Sunny's blood and painted the outline of an angel on the wall.*

"He used the girls' blood to paint the symbols on the wall," Beth said. "It's part of his ritual."

"I thought you said he collects their blood in a vial."

Beth nodded. "He does both." Another image flashed behind her eyes. The blood-spattered cloth he'd placed below the bodies. "He studies the blood spatter," she said. "It intrigues him. He paints an image based on what he sees in the spatter."

Beth snapped back into agent mode and took pictures of the symbols.

Using both hands, Ian pressed the wall, pushing along a portion that was cracked. The wall began to move—a door in the cave.

What was on the other side?

Beth's statement about the killer studying the blood spatter ran through Ian's mind as he stepped inside the room. The walls were covered in blood.

Blood from his victims.

A natural hot spring pool gurgled in the center.

"He uses that pool to baptize the girls," Beth said in a distant voice, as if she were drowning in the past.

"I thought he did that outside," Ian said.

Beth wrinkled her nose. "Maybe he uses both. The outside one in pretty weather, this one when it's cold or snowy."

"He baptized them here, then carried them to the holler to bury them," Ian said.

Beth nodded. "Since we discovered his burial ground, he left Prissy here. That has to be bothering him." Beth snapped more pictures of the gruesome scene. "He doesn't know we found this place yet. He might return."

Yeah, with another victim.

Beth heaved a weary sound. "I'll have to let the director know we found Prissy and this place. We should station someone here to watch the cave."

"I'll do it." Ian made the call but there was no answer, so he left a voice mail for the director. "CSU is on its way. Since this was his private kill spot, there's a good chance the unsub left fingerprints or forensics."

Beth examined the cross around the girl's neck, then the cross on the wall. "There's something about his art that seems familiar."

"You saw him painting the symbols when he held you?" Ian asked.

Beth worried her bottom lip with her teeth. "Yes, but I've also seen similar paintings somewhere else."

Ian froze, his brain working. He'd seen a painting that reminded him of this bloody artwork, too. Where was it?

His phone buzzed with a text. Ward and his team had arrived. "I'm going to meet Ward."

"I'll wait here." Guilt and grief clouded her eyes. "I don't want to leave Prissy alone."

He understood. He hated to leave her, too, but they needed to work fast.

"I'll be back soon." He strode through the cave and out the door, grateful for the fresh air. The sooner they processed this place, the sooner they might find DNA and stop this maniac.

The smell of blood was fresh in his mind as he backtracked through the woods.

Twigs snapped. Leaves rustled. A wild animal howled. The wind picked up and hurled a tree branch to the ground.

He pivoted, the hair on the back of his neck prickling. Prissy's body hadn't been that cold. What if the unsub had been nearby when they arrived?

He shouldn't have left Beth alone.

◆ ◆ ◆

The cave walls closed in around Beth.

Remembering that she was a trained agent, she fought the temptation to run her fingers over some of the religious symbols painted on the wall.

She needed to protect the evidence.

The sound of Sunny's cries reverberated off the walls. Then Prissy's.

She sank down beside Prissy, her heart aching as she imagined how terrified the teenager must have been.

"I'm so sorry, honey," Beth whispered. "We tried to find you in time. But we failed."

Defeat and anger weighed on her.

The gurgling of the pool water carried her back years. Desperate to see the killer's face, she closed her eyes and allowed the emotions and memories to flow through her.

Sunny was curled up beside her, crying. She looked so tiny and weak. JJ had to take care of her. Had to find a way out for both of them.

She swept her gaze across the cave, but it was so dark she couldn't see. Just a tiny sliver of light seeping through a crack in the rock wall.

"I'm scared," Sunny whispered.

So was she, but she had to be brave. Her hands and feet were bound, so she scooted as close as she could to Sunny and rubbed her arm with both hands. "Shh, I'll get us out of here. I promise."

"He's gonna kill us," Sunny whispered.

JJ shook her head. "No, I'll get help."

"How?" Sunny said on a sob. "We don't know where we are."

Tears pricked at JJ's eyes, but she blinked them back, then tried to untie the knot at her wrist with her teeth.

Sunny was right. If they did find a way out of this dungeon, she had no idea where they were. Caves were in the mountains.

No telling how many miles they were from a town or a road.

Worse, bears and snakes and other wild animals roamed the hills. But if she could find the river, she could follow it.

Clunk. Clunk. Clunk.

Footsteps pounding the rocky floor.

Then shuffling.

And voices.

Voices?

Not just the man's. Another voice. Not quite as deep. Male. But . . . younger?

Someone was with him.

"Son, we are the chosen ones. This is our Calling."

Cold fear enveloped JJ. He was coming back for her and Sunny. And he had a helper.

A scream lodged in her throat. Maybe the other one would save them.

She swallowed a cry and yanked at the ropes binding her wrists. But she couldn't get the knot to budge.

"Give me your hands," JJ whispered. If she could untie Sunny, Sunny could untie her. Then she'd find something in the cave to use as a weapon.

Sunny was shaking as she lifted her hands. JJ tugged at the ends.

The man's voice drifted through the doorway. "They cannot help who they are. The sin is in their blood just as it was in hers."

Who were they talking about?

"I'll find a cure," the younger man said.

"There is no cure," the older man murmured. "Only forgiveness through Jesus."

Fear choked JJ. The memory of Reverend Benton's rantings screamed through her mind. He was always singing about the blood of Jesus.

The door squeaked as it opened. The big hulking figure appeared, drenched in the shadows. Then another figure, smaller, thinner, also in the dark.

JJ ripped at the rope with her fingernails, desperate. But the bigger figure loped toward her and Sunny. Sunny screamed, and Beth tried to cover her with her body.

He yanked her off Sunny and pushed JJ so hard she fell back against the rocky wall. Pain shot through her skull, and the world spun.

"Please let her go. Take me instead. She's so little." The man ignored her and dragged Sunny across the floor. JJ crawled after him and clawed at his ankle. "Let her go!"

He kicked backward and slammed his foot into her face. Blood gushed from her nose.

The room went completely dark.

Beth jerked from the memory just as a footstep creaked. She peered around the cave. Something moved. A man.

"You remember me, JJ?"

Beth's pulse quickened. The whisper of a breath puffed in the air. She tried to see him, but he knocked the flashlight on the ground, and it went out.

She scrambled to retrieve it, but he kicked it away.

She froze and reached for her weapon.

"JJ . . ."

The voice . . . it cut through the silence. Deep. Cold. Not a memory—*he* was here.

"Yes, show me your face."

A dark chuckle boomeranged off the cold walls.

Beth pivoted toward the source and fired the gun. She missed, and the bullet pinged off the wall. She blinked to see where he'd gone, then suddenly he was on her.

A second later, the world turned upside down, and she slipped into the dark.

◆ ◆ ◆

The sound of the gunshot triggered Ian's worst fear.

He might have lost Beth.

"What the hell was that?" Lieutenant Ward asked.

Ian gestured toward the path through the woods. "Beth, she's back at the cave." Dammit, he'd had a bad feeling before he met up with the crime team.

He took off running, not bothering to wait for the two crime scene investigators climbing from their vehicle.

"We're right behind you!" Ward shouted.

Ian drew his weapon and shoved at the branches and weeds, using his flashlight to guide him toward the cave.

Something moved to the right.

He paused, then spotted a deer. Dammit.

He picked up his pace, racing past fallen branches and listening for more gunfire, but he stayed alert in case he was running into a trap.

Finally, he reached the clearing. Then the cross-shaped rock formation. Brush moved to the right of the entrance.

Was Beth inside, or did he have her?

Ward raced up behind him.

"Check the cave for Beth," Ian said. "I saw someone in the woods. I'm going after him."

Fear shot through him, and he ran past the cave toward the bushes.

He gripped his gun, ready to shoot as he charged forward. A tree limb moved. More footsteps ahead.

Then a figure disappeared through the trees. "Stop, police!"

But the figure didn't slow.

Ian picked up his pace and fired, then heard a grunt. The figure veered to the left. He dashed forward and released another shot. Tree limbs shook, and leaves scattered as the bushes parted.

Dammit, the perp was getting away.

Ian pushed through the bushes, then ran through a cluster of pines and searched the forest. The figure had disappeared again.

But Beth was lying against a rock, unmoving.

CHAPTER
TWENTY-EIGHT

Ian quickly knelt and checked Beth's pulse. She was so still, her face pale, and blood matted her hair. He checked for a gunshot wound, but it looked as if she'd hit her head on a rock.

"Beth, honey, talk to me." He leaned closer to her, listening for a breath. Seconds ticked by.

Finally her chest rose and fell.

Relief surged through him.

A voice broke the quiet. "Sheriff?"

Ian pivoted slightly to see Lieutenant Ward approaching.

"Call an ambulance," Ian said. "And stay with her. I'm going after him."

"Medics are on the way," Ward said.

Ian reluctantly left Beth with the CSU and sprinted into the woods. He was so close to catching this SOB, he couldn't waste a second.

Bushes parted as he wove through them. Tree limbs snapped and popped. He cursed as he nearly stumbled over a rotting tree stump. The scent of a dead animal assaulted him. A mauled creature in the bushes.

Ahead the forest sounds grew quiet. Wind shrieked through the pines, and another animal wailed. The sound of the river rushed over rocks.

He pivoted toward it, shining his light in a wide arc as he searched for the unsub. Something moved to the left.

His gun at the ready, Ian braced for an attack.

A mountain lion growled on a cliff above, its eyes glowing in the dark. For a moment, Ian sensed it was staring straight at him, daring him to charge.

The forest became eerily quiet.

No voices. No footsteps. No trees parting or twigs breaking.

Then a snake hissed behind him.

Ian cursed, spun around, and saw the rattler in the weeds, a reminder that dangers lurked everywhere in these mountains and came in all forms.

"Fuck you," he muttered to the snake. He fired at the snake, then heard the mountain lion trot away.

But there was no sign of the unsub.

Where the hell had he gone? How had he escaped?

He strode a few more feet. The sound of a motor rumbled in the air. A boat.

Shit. The unsub had come via boat, parked along the river, and then carried his victims inside the cave.

He checked his phone for reception, then phoned Whitehorse. "Prissy Carson is dead. We found her body in a cave in the mountains. We need a chopper to comb the area along the river heading due east from the coordinates I'm texting you."

"They won't be able to find anything this late," Deputy Whitehorse said.

"Then tell them at first light to get on it. I want to know where every house, trailer, RV, or campsite is. And I want every one of them searched."

"Copy that," Deputy Whitehorse said.

"I also need you to make the notification of death to the mother."

A tense silence stretched between them. Death notifications were the worst part of a cop's job.

Whitehorse had been forced to tell his own sister when their mother had been murdered three years ago.

But his deputy didn't argue. "Yes, sir."

Ian thanked him, then called Markum and explained about the attack. "Where's Benton?"

"I don't know. He must have slipped out the back."

Dammit.

"Find him, Markum."

He hung up with a curse. Heart racing, he headed back toward Beth and the cave. Sweat trickled down his neck as he jogged through the woods. The stench of that dead animal assaulted him again, but it was the sight of Beth lying unconscious that made his stomach clench.

He'd promised her justice.

If he failed her a second time, he might as well turn in his badge.

Beth was falling into a deep dark hole.

She flailed her arms in search of something to hold on to, but her fingers connected with empty air.

Sunny's screams boomeranged off the cave walls. The metallic scent of blood swirled around her.

The faces of the other dead girls floated by her, skeletal hands reaching out, pleading for her to save them.

Prissy—her shocked eyes begged for mercy. She'd wanted to live.

Beth hit the hard ground. Then the earth split and sucked her deeper under the surface. More skeletons sailed at her, pummeling her as the grave swallowed her.

"Beth, honey, wake up. Tell me you're all right."

That voice . . . It was familiar.

Almost as familiar as the face of the man hovering above her with the knife.

She screamed, kicked, and pushed at him as he came closer. Then the prick of the knife. Her own blood seeping out.

Blood dripped onto the bones beneath her, the bones he'd made into a bed.

"Beth, can you hear me?"

Yes, and she wanted to go back to him. Escape this grave of horror.

But she needed to stay here, too. There was some reason . . . What was it?

His face.

She searched the shadows. She needed to see his eyes. Needed to know what he looked like.

The shadow moved. Another inch closer. Then the second figure, smaller.

"We have to let her go, Father."

She gasped. That other person . . . He was her age.

Dear God, she'd seen him before. Somewhere at school.

Who was he?

♦ ♦ ♦

Worry knotted Ian's stomach as he rode in the ambulance with Beth. He'd left Lieutenant Ward the police car and convinced the medics that he needed to be at Beth's side in case she regained consciousness and could identify her attacker.

"What happened?" the medic in back asked.

"She's an FBI agent working the boneyard murders. We were investigating and someone attacked her." He lifted her hand in his and squeezed it, hoping for a reaction, but Beth didn't respond. "I'm going to take samples of the blood on her face and scrape beneath her nails in case her attacker left DNA."

The medic agreed and watched as Ian examined her hands and face and collected the samples. He found an errant hair strand that looked a lighter shade of brown than Beth's and bagged it to send to the lab.

The siren wailed, lights flashing, as they careened into the hospital. Beth hadn't stirred—but she was alive.

The medics jumped out and rushed into the ER entrance with Beth. A nurse met them, and the information exchange began.

"BP is low and thready, heart rate steady. Head injury . . ."

Their words blurred in his mind as he followed them inside and they rushed her to a triage room.

Beth opened her eyes and blinked at the bright lights. Machines and voices hummed around her. The scent of antiseptic and medicine permeated her nostrils.

"She's back with us," a female voice said. "Hello there, Agent Fields. You're in the hospital."

Beth blinked again, confused as she stared into a pair of green eyes. A nurse.

She tried to speak, but her throat was so dry she had to swallow twice to make her voice work. "What happened?"

"The sheriff who brought you in said you were attacked."

The last few hours rushed back. She was in the cave where Sunny had died. She hadn't wanted to leave Prissy Carson alone. Then someone had snuck in . . .

A male figure in a white coat joined the nurse. "Glad to see you've regained consciousness. You have a few stitches in your head and a slight concussion. You'll probably have a headache for a couple of days, but the MRI was clean."

Beth shoved at the sheet covering her. "I have to go. I'm working a case."

The doctor put out a hand to stop her from climbing from the bed. "You're not going anywhere tonight, Agent Fields."

"I'll get the sheriff." The nurse's footsteps padded slowly as she left.

The room spun, and Beth sank back against the pillow. God help her, she needed to find this bastard.

"We want to keep you overnight for observation," the doctor said.

The door swung open, and Ian appeared, his jaw set tight, his dark eyes pinning her in place. "Beth?"

"I'm fine," she murmured, although frustration and a feeling of helplessness brought tears to her eyes. She blinked them away. She was an agent, not some weak victim.

Not anymore.

Except the maniac who'd killed her friend had ambushed her. Because she'd let her emotions get the best of her.

It wouldn't happen again.

Ian paused by her bed and looked up at the doctor. "Is she going to be all right?"

"A light concussion, a few stitches, but the MRI was clean. She should be fine to go home in the morning."

"I want to leave now," Beth said, pushing herself up to a sitting position. "We have to find him before he hurts someone else."

Ian squeezed her hand. "We will, Beth, but you're not going anywhere. You need rest."

She gripped the edge of the bed with white-knuckled fists. "I should have stopped him a long time ago. I have to do it now."

The doctor cleared his throat. "We'll leave you two to talk."

The doctor and nurse left the room, and Beth twisted the sheets between her fingers. "I can't believe I let him escape."

Ian offered her a sympathetic smile. "You didn't let him get away, Beth. He assaulted you. Judging from your broken nails, I have a feeling you put up a fight."

Her heart fluttered. "You got DNA?"

"I scraped under your nails and sent it to the lab." He stroked a strand of hair from her forehead, his hand so tender that tears threatened again. "Because you fought, we might be able to ID him."

Beth's head throbbed relentlessly. She closed her eyes, but the attack had stirred memories to life as if it were happening all over again.

"I remembered something, Ian. When I was abducted—he wasn't alone."

Ian's eyes narrowed. "What?"

"There were two of them," Beth whispered. "A father and a son." She reached for Ian's hand and clung to it. "I think I knew the boy. I'm almost certain he attended high school with us."

Two killers could explain how there were so many dead girls over the years and the time span between some of the kills.

Also, one killer could provide a diversion while the other lured the victim into a trap. The girls trusted the teenager because he was near their age.

The religious aspects pointed toward Reverend Wally Benton as a person of interest. If he'd killed Sunny, had his son Jim been there to watch? Or to assist?

"If one of the killers attended our school, maybe there's something about him in my father's files. That's the reason my father wanted to give them to you."

Beth nodded. "We have to get them."

Ian gently pressed her back onto the bed. "I'll go."

"But Ian—"

"Listen, Beth, the crime team is processing the cave, Deputy Whitehorse is notifying Prissy's mother of her death, and you just gave us a clue." He stroked her cheek with the pad of his thumb. "I'll bring the files here. If you're up to it, we'll study them together."

He'd track down a yearbook of the students that year as well.

If Beth saw the boy's photograph, maybe she'd finally recognize him and put a name to their killer.

◆ ◆ ◆

He guided the boat to the edge of the creek, his adrenaline churning. He'd had JJ in his hands. A few more minutes and he could have escaped with her.

He knew she wanted answers. She didn't understand why he'd let her go and killed her friend.

He wanted to tell her.

He'd kept his secret long enough.

But it had been a close call in the woods. Too close. The sheriff had almost caught him.

Had JJ seen his face this time? Would she remember him after all these years?

His son sat looking at his hands, mesmerized by the blood staining his fingers. For so long he'd studied the blood. Kept it and researched the elements.

He wanted to know what made some blood bad and others untainted by evil.

So far he hadn't found the answer.

But he wouldn't give up.

If he did, *they* would have died for nothing.

His son made a low sound in his throat. He'd worried the boy wouldn't accept the Calling, that he had his own plans and would defy his destiny.

His anxiety dissipated as a smile creased the boy's face.

"You have someone in mind, don't you, son? Someone who needs saving?"

The boy nodded.

And everything was as it should be.

CHAPTER
TWENTY-NINE

Something was wrong.

Vanessa heard Grandma Cocoa on the phone. "That's awful. Yes, I'll tell her."

Vanessa pressed her hand over her mouth and started to shake. It was bad news. It had to be about Prissy.

She stepped into the kitchen. Grandma Cocoa was leaning on the counter clutching her chest. She gasped for a breath and then dropped the phone.

"Grandma?"

"Vanessa, baby . . ." Grandma Cocoa swayed and staggered to a chair.

Terrified, Vanessa ran over to help her. "What's wrong, Grandma?"

Sweat beaded on her grandma's face. "Baby, they found Prissy."

Tears pricked at Vanessa's eyes. For Grandma to look this bad, the news must be awful.

"I'm sorry, honey," her grandma wheezed.

All the Dead Girls

Tears blurred Vanessa's eyes. She wanted to scream no and hit something. Prissy couldn't be dead. She was her age. Just a kid.

They were supposed to be best friends forever. Be college roommates. Bridesmaids in each other's weddings.

Grandma Cocoa's eyes turned glassy. More sweat drenched her face. She made a pained sound and toppled from the chair.

"Grandma!" Vanessa dropped down beside her. But Grandma Cocoa didn't move. Was she breathing?

Cold terror choked Vanessa.

She'd lost her best friend. She couldn't lose her grandma.

Vanessa shook her shoulder. "Grandma!"

Nothing.

Fear seized her. She had to do something. Get help.

Vanessa ran for her grandma's phone. Her hands shook as she pressed 911. "Please help," she cried. "My grandma passed out. She's on the floor . . ."

"Where are you, honey?" the 911 operator asked.

Vanessa spit out their address between sobs.

"I'll have someone stand guard by your room while I retrieve those files," Ian said.

"That's not necessary, Ian." Beth clenched the sheet between her fingers. "He won't take a chance by coming here, not with all the staff around."

Ian wasn't so sure. But they were short on manpower. "I'll alert security not to allow anyone in your room."

"Thanks." Beth closed her eyes as if she couldn't keep them open any longer.

Ian stroked her forehead. She needed rest. And the nurses would be monitoring her for the concussion.

247

He hesitated, though. She could have been killed tonight. Lost forever. All because he'd left her in the cave alone.

But if he didn't find this unsub, the maniac would come back for her. Beth thought there were two of them . . . that complicated the case more.

His fingers brushed her hair again, and need heated his blood. Unable to resist, he pressed a kiss to her forehead. "Get some rest, Beth. I'll be back. I promise."

Her eyelids fluttered open for a moment, and their gazes locked. A spark of attraction he didn't want to feel ignited in his gut.

Her eyes flared with recognition as if she felt it, too.

Or maybe he'd imagined it. She was half-asleep and injured.

Fool. How could Beth feel anything for him after he'd let her down fifteen years ago?

That brutal reminder sent him toward the door. He stepped into the hall and explained to the nurse that he had to leave.

She promised they'd keep a close eye on Beth, and he hurried to see his father.

Dammit, his father looked exactly as he'd left him.

Ashen-faced and comatose. What if he never regained consciousness?

Machines beeped, blending with Ian's footsteps. He laid a hand on his father's arm. "Dad, I'm working hard to find the man who killed those girls. Beth finally remembered something—she says it's a father-and-son team." Emotions thickened his throat. Once he and this man had been a team.

He wanted that again.

"I'm going after those files, and we'll prove your innocence." Although nothing could replace the fifteen years of his life his father had lost.

He stood for another few minutes talking quietly, hoping that his father would hear his voice and that hope would help him heal.

"Fight, Dad, fight," Ian said. Then he squeezed his father's hand and left.

Just as he headed out the ER door, a car screeched up behind an ambulance. Cocoa's husband, Deon, and Vanessa jumped out. Both looked terrified. Vanessa was crying.

Ian jogged toward them. "What happened?"

Cocoa's husband wiped at his sweaty forehead. "Cocoa heard the Carson girl was dead, and she collapsed."

Vanessa sobbed against her grandfather while the medics unloaded Cocoa.

Emotions flooded Ian. Cocoa was like a mother to everyone in Graveyard Falls, including him. She had to be all right.

The town needed her.

◆　◆　◆

Tandy Pooler Benton buried herself deep in the covers of the bed she shared with her husband, cringing as the door to her house creaked open.

He'd slipped out earlier, but he was home now.

Her son's voice drifted through the door, and Tandy's heart broke. Her husband insisted it was time their son followed in his footsteps.

Tandy disagreed, but her opinions didn't matter.

The light flickered on in the living room, sending a faint stream beneath the door.

Footsteps pounded as he walked across their living room floor, and the low hum of the gospel tune he sang echoed through the eaves of the old house.

She shivered at the sound.

He'd been at it again. Saving another lost soul. Exorcising the demons.

At first she questioned his interest in the young girls at the revivals. She'd suspected he had a physical thing for them, that his own sin was lusting for the innocent.

But he staunchly denied it.

Not that she approved of how he handled bringing them to salvation, but she was his wife, and he was her master.

She had to obey.

Questioning him was a sin in itself.

More footsteps, then the light flicked off in the living room. Tandy closed her eyes tightly, struggling to control her breathing.

Some nights after the girls, he came home all wired and demanding she service him like a wife was supposed to. Those nights he branched into dirty stuff that had shocked her in the beginning. Painful sex that left her hurting and wishing she'd never married.

Other times, he was so wrung out that he fell into bed and slept like the dead.

Those were the nights she prayed for.

The sound of his zipper rasping rent the air. Buttons unsnapping on his shirt. His pants sliding down.

She'd long ago memorized every nuance of her husband's routine.

She continued to pretend sleep, her eyes closed, forcing her breathing to remain steady as he hung each garment up neatly. He slipped into the bathroom, and she prayed with all her might that he'd leave her alone tonight.

The water turned on in the bathroom. The toilet flushed. The door opened again.

Footsteps shuffled as he approached the bed. Instead of climbing in on his side, though, he stopped and stared down at her.

Tears burned the backs of her eyelids, but she didn't dare move.

His breathing rasped out, uneven and filling her with dread. He reached out and slid his hand around her neck.

A sob caught in her throat, but she swallowed it. If she fought him or told him she was tired, she'd get the sermon again, and the punishment.

"It was a rough night," he murmured as he crawled on top of her. "She was a fighter, but I saved her in the end."

Tandy choked back a cry of protest and spread her legs.

◆ ◆ ◆

Ian kept alert as he drove into the mountains. Anxiety thrummed through him as he passed the burial site where they'd first found the bodies.

The scent of the blood from the cave lingered on his skin.

Had the unsub already chosen another victim?

Anger forced him to punch the accelerator. He couldn't waste time.

He took the curve on two wheels, tires screeching, then sped up the gravel road. Three miles down he veered onto a narrow dirt road that led deeper into the hills. Thunder boomed and a streak of lightning zigzagged across the dark sky.

The clouds opened up, and rain pounded the roof of the SUV, making him slow. He turned the wipers to full speed, tires grinding over gravel and mud.

How had his father found this place?

His father had been living on the run, probably hiding in caves and bushes and wherever he could. No telling what he'd eaten or how he'd survived.

The GPS indicated Ian had arrived, and he slowed as a run-down shanty appeared. Ian pulled off the side and parked in front of the rotting structure.

He scanned the area but saw nothing. No cars or signs that anyone was here.

He yanked his jacket hood up over his head, pulled his weapon, and held it at the ready as he climbed out. He scanned the perimeter as he rushed up the rickety steps and peeked through the broken, muddy windows.

No lights inside. He leaned his head to the door and listened. All was quiet.

He jiggled the door, and it swung open. He stepped inside and raked his hand along the wall to find a light switch, but when he flipped it, nothing happened. Using his flashlight, he crossed the room, the wood floors bowing beneath his weight. No lights in the kitchen either.

Of course there wouldn't be. His father had been a criminal on the run. He hadn't any way to pay for electricity.

Ian swung the flashlight in a wide arc and spotted a couple of tin cans that had held food, a ratty couch covered with a threadbare blanket, and a scarred wooden table.

He checked the kitchen drawers in search of the files. Nothing but rusted flatware, mice droppings, and a can opener.

Anger at the conditions his father had been forced to live in hit him again. But he didn't have time to dwell on it.

Where had his father stored those files?

He waved the flashlight across the room again. A cardboard box sat on the bookshelf, so he hauled it down. A yearbook was also tucked inside with the files.

He thumbed through the folders, noting the names of dozens of students.

Beth could help him read through them faster.

He searched the rest of the tiny cabin, his heart aching when he found a photograph of Coach and Ian's mother on the nightstand.

All those years, his father must have felt so alone. Must have felt betrayed.

His phone buzzed as he hurried to his vehicle with the box. Peyton. He quickly connected.

"Sheriff, I tried to call Beth, but she isn't answering. Director Vance said she's in the hospital."

"She had an accident, but thankfully she didn't suffer any serious injuries," Ian said.

"Good. I was worried about her."

So was he. "Her boss is upset with her, isn't he?"

"That's putting it lightly, but you two did good work." Peyton hesitated. "I may have found something helpful."

Hope spiked in Ian's chest. "What?"

"When you sent me pictures of that art on the cave walls, it seemed familiar."

"I thought so, but I couldn't place it."

"I did some digging," Peyton said. "The symbols and style are very similar to paintings done by an artist local to Graveyard Falls."

A memory tickled Ian's consciousness. "Good God, I know who you're talking about. I saw him at the festival in town."

"That's not all," Peyton said. "When I reviewed the notes Agent Hamrick and Agent Coulter took when they interviewed the victims' families, at least three of them mentioned they'd received a painting after their loved one went missing."

"A painting? You mean one with religious symbolism?"

"Yes. The note that accompanied the painting indicated it was a gift from a churchgoer who wanted to offer comfort."

"Who sent the paintings?"

"They were anonymous, but I've called Agent Hamrick and Agent Coulter and asked them to follow up. I'm also securing photos of the local artist's work for comparison."

Ian pressed the accelerator. "You think the unsub sent the victims' families a painting?"

"I don't know," Peyton said. "But that artist in Graveyard Falls has a technique that sets his work apart from others."

"What are you talking about?"

"He mixes human blood with the paint he uses in his pieces."

CHAPTER THIRTY

Had the killer used his victims' blood in his artwork and then sent it to the families?

Ian's mind raced. What kind of demented person did that?

"I'll talk to the artist," Ian told Peyton. Although it was the middle of the night, and he needed a warrant. "If there's anything to it, I'll let Director Vance know."

Ian hung up, then phoned the local judge and requested a warrant.

"Do you have probable cause?" the judge asked.

"More than a dozen girls have been murdered, Judge. The killer collects the girls' blood after he drains it. This artist uses human blood in paintings he sends to the victims' families." He hoped he was making his point. "Do you want to give the unsub time to add another victim to the list?"

A big weighted sigh. "Of course not. I'll issue the warrant."

Ian ended the call, then phoned Deputy Whitehorse and explained the latest development.

"I'm still at the cave with CSU. It's going to take hours, maybe even days to process the place."

"I trust Lieutenant Ward to oversee it."

"You want me to pick up the artist for questioning?" Whitehorse asked.

"Let's wait until we get the warrant. If we tip him off, he might run. Stake out his place. If he makes a move to kidnap another girl, we might catch him in the act."

Ian disconnected and swung into the hospital parking lot.

He carried the box of files into the hospital with him. Although the staff was watching Beth, he needed to see her in person.

He passed through the waiting room. Vanessa was hunched in a chair, looking despondent. Her grandfather was snoring in a chair beside her. A few locals he recognized from the café had arrived to offer comfort, another reminder of how the people in Graveyard Falls supported one another.

His heart went out to Vanessa. First she'd lost her best friend, and now her grandmother was ill.

She looked up at him with tear-stained eyes as he approached.

"How's Cocoa?" Ian asked.

Vanessa gulped. "She had a mild heart attack, but the doctor said she'll be okay."

"That's good news," Ian said.

Vanessa shrugged, unconvinced. He'd heard that her mother had abandoned her, and his heart gave another pang. She reminded him of Beth at that age. She tried to be tough, but she'd already suffered a lifetime of loss in the few years she'd been in this world.

He ruffled her hair. "Hang in there, Vanessa. Cocoa will be back bossing everyone around in no time."

A tiny crack of a smile gave him hope that Vanessa would be okay. But the sadness returned to her eyes a moment later. "Did you find the man who killed Prissy?"

His gut pinched. Not a question any fourteen-year-old should have to ask.

"Not yet, but we're getting close." He indicated the files. "I'd better get back to it."

Vanessa dropped her head back against the vinyl sofa as Ian hurried to Beth's room. He relieved the security guard, then entered the room, lightening his step. He didn't want to disturb her.

But he had to touch her.

Her skin felt warmer than it had before, a good sign. Her breathing was steady. He stroked her cheek with the pad of his thumb.

"We might finally have a lead, Beth. I promise I won't stop until we catch this guy."

Except Beth had said there were two—a father and son.

Reverend Jim Benton and his father? He texted Peyton to dig up all she could on both the Bentons and the artist and his family.

Ralph Lewis was his name.

Ian settled in the corner of the room. His father had kept a file on each student he'd counseled, complete with notes on their conversations.

A file labeled Jane Jones stirred his curiosity. His father had made notations regarding his concern over her foster father.

Emotions thickened his throat. So his father *had* been trying to help her.

He turned his focus to the remaining files.

His pulse jumped when he discovered one for Ralph Lewis. Funny, but he didn't remember the guy. Not that he'd paid much attention to his younger classmates, and Lewis was a year younger.

He flipped open the folder and skimmed. Lewis had been a good student, quiet, but antisocial. He was not athletic, but he excelled at science. He was creative and enjoyed painting.

Religious symbols filled the pages, along with drawings of angels. There were also macabre sketches of graveyards and bones.

Ian bounced his leg up and down, his mind working. According to his father's notes, Lewis was obsessed with blood.

At fifteen, he was experimenting with combining it with paint as an art medium.

Lewis's mother had died when Ralph was an infant, leaving him to be raised by a single father, Hugh.

Ian rubbed his temple. If they were dealing with a father-son team, Lewis's father might have murdered some of the girls. Then Ralph started killing as a teenager.

If Ralph was in the truck that night, Beth might have felt it was safe to take a ride with him because she knew him from school.

Ian searched the notes for more information on Lewis's father. Hugh Lewis was a truck driver who made deliveries up and down the Southeast.

Another notation indicated that Ralph and his father also followed the teachings of the Holy Waters—Benton's church.

Ian shifted. They had to be connected.

Morning sunlight spilled through the hospital room, rousing Beth from the nightmarish images of bones and ghosts. Claw-like broken pieces of skeletons had flown past her along with skulls and hollow empty eyes begging for help.

Blood swirled and sprayed the air and her face as if the bodies had exploded and their blood had erupted like a volcano.

Her head ached as she opened her eyes. It took her a few seconds to realize she'd been dreaming. It had seemed so real.

She glanced around the room. Ian had fallen asleep in the chair in the corner. His head was lolled to the side, his lips parted, his breathing puffing out as if he was exhausted.

A box of files sat in front of him, one clenched in his hand.

He looked big and awkward and uncomfortable.

And so sexy that her heart fluttered.

He'd probably worked all night while he guarded her to make sure she was safe.

All that after she'd shot his father.

She tossed the sheet aside and swung her legs over the edge of the bed. She had to get back to work.

A dizzy spell swept over her, and she gripped the bed with clammy hands to steady herself.

"What the hell are you doing?"

Ian's gruff voice made her jerk her head up. His tone had been harsh, but worry darkened his sleep-ridden eyes.

"I need to get out of here." She indicated the file box. "Did you find something?"

Ian scrubbed a hand over his face. His five o'clock shadow was morphing into heavy beard stubble this morning.

He must be totally worn out.

He stood and coaxed her to sit back. "I think so. Peyton phoned last night. That local artist who does the religious paintings is from Sweetwater. He went to school with us. His name is Ralph Lewis."

Beth tried to recall his face.

Ian waved the folder in his hands. "He saw my father for counseling. He was obsessed with blood as a teenager, and he uses blood in his paintings." His voice rose a notch. "According to Agents Hamrick and Coulter, three of the victims' families received a painting with religious symbols similar to his work after their daughters disappeared. I'm getting a warrant to pick up Lewis and search his house, car, and studio."

"My God, Ian, you think the paintings he sent the families contained their daughters' blood?"

Ian grimaced. "We'll know once the paintings are tested."

Beth had seen the vials of blood. Seen a figure mixing blood with paint.

The pieces fit.

"Ralph's father was a trucker, Beth. He serviced the same route our killer did."

"The father-and-son team," Beth whispered.

Ian flipped the file to a photograph. "This is a picture of Ralph Lewis as a teenager. Do you recognize him?"

♦　♦　♦

Anxiety knotted Beth's shoulders. An hour ago she was berating herself for not having the courage to identify her kidnapper years ago. Yet the thought of finally looking into his face triggered her old fears.

Time to get over that.

She reached for the file. Ian moved up beside the bed, his presence oddly comforting and disconcerting at the same time.

"This is him. Ralph Lewis. He was fifteen at the time."

The high school picture launched her back in time.

Ralph was skinny with frizzy reddish-brown hair and large ears.

"Does he look familiar?" Ian asked.

Beth focused on the details of the teenager's face. A long crooked nose, muddy brown eyes. His face was tilted away from the camera as if he was shy or didn't want his picture taken.

He looked as harmless as a puppy.

Could he have possibly been devious enough to lure May and then her and Sunny into that truck so his father could kill her?

"In school, he liked art and was a science geek," Ian said. "Maybe you had a class with him?"

"I didn't take art. But he was in my biology class." An image of him dissecting the frog surfaced. "He enjoyed dissecting animals. He always wanted to do the cutting. He liked to watch the animals' guts spill out. And he talked about how the blood spray made artistic patterns."

♦　♦　♦

Ian's phone buzzed just as he picked up the warrants for the Lewis house and property.

He sent Peyton a text.

`Need address for Lewis's father. Also a photo of what he looks like now and what he looked like at the time of JJ Jones and Sunny Smith's abduction.`

She responded.

`Copy that.`

Ian stood. "I'm going to question Lewis."

Beth tugged at the hospital gown. "I'll go with you. Get my clothes."

Ian shook his head. "No, you need to rest."

Beth pushed to her feet. "You and I have worked this case far too long for me to lie in bed when it goes down."

"I can handle it, Beth."

"I know that, but I need to do this."

The pain and determination in her voice ripped at Ian. How could he deny her when he'd do the same thing?

"All right, but only if the doctor releases you. And if you start feeling dizzy or weak, you have to let me know."

Beth agreed, although he had no doubt that she'd fight through whatever discomfort she felt in order to lock up this unsub.

It was his job to protect her.

He buzzed for the nurse and left the room for Beth to get dressed.

Fifteen minutes later, Ian climbed the winding highway and turned onto a dirt road that went uphill to the top of a ridge. Beth sucked in a breath.

"Are you sure you're up to this?" he asked.

She wiped a bead of perspiration from her forehead. "I wouldn't miss it for anything."

"I sent Deputy Whitehorse to run surveillance on him last night."

Branches and weeds scraped the sides of the SUV. Thick trees and hemlocks shrouded the light, making it appear dark and shadowy.

The SUV chugged over the ruts, slinging gravel as he maneuvered the sharp right turn.

Ian passed Whitehorse where he'd parked in the woods and motioned for him to follow him to the house. Deputy Vance might be pissed that he'd taken initiative and brought Beth here, but if he and Beth and Whitehorse solved this case, the director would get over it.

A battered pickup truck was parked beneath a makeshift garage. Ian expected to see a canoe, but he didn't find one. Of course it could be in the back somewhere, or Lewis could have left it tied at the riverbank.

The cabin looked small until he realized a covered walkway connected it to another space, which was probably the man's studio.

Ian turned to Beth. "You look like hell, Beth. You must be sore from the accident. Wait here. Deputy Whitehorse and I'll check out the house."

"I'm going, too."

The look on her face indicated arguing was pointless. "Do you have your weapon, or did you turn it in?"

"No way I'd give it up. Vance knows I need it for protection." She reached for her holster. "Let's go."

A second later, the three of them headed toward the house together.

Ian pointed toward the rear of the cabin. "Deputy, cover the back in case he tries to run."

Whitehorse nodded and crept to the right to guard the back. Ian gestured for Beth to stay behind him, then held his gun at the ready as they inched up the porch steps.

Ian glanced through the windows. Simple furnishings. Rustic. Leather furniture. A round oak table.

He didn't see Lewis.

Was he in his studio?

Ian raised his hand, knocked, and waited. Beth eased to the left and checked the other window.

"His bedroom," she mouthed.

He motioned toward the adjoining section, and they eased down the walkway until they reached the door. Beth knocked this time, and he raised his gun, braced to fire if the man was armed.

Footsteps could be heard inside.

"Ralph Lewis, open up." He pounded the door again. "It's Sheriff Kimball and Special Agent Fields from the FBI."

Footsteps again. More hurried. The wind whistled, sending a tree branch banging against the window of the building.

The door opened, and Ralph Lewis rubbed a hand over his apron. An apron streaked with blood.

CHAPTER THIRTY-ONE

A memory struck Beth as she stared at the blood on Ralph Lewis's shirt.

Ralph in biology class dissecting the frog, then the pig. The odd smile on his face as he studied the blood on his fingers. Then he'd drawn a design of the spatter on a piece of notebook paper.

It had chilled her to the bone.

She scrutinized his features, hoping to put his face at the cave as he killed Sunny.

"What's this about, Sheriff?" Lewis asked.

"The boneyard murders." Ian lifted the envelope in his hand. "We have warrants to search the premises and your vehicle."

Lewis's eyes widened in shock. "What are you talking about? I haven't done anything wrong."

"You sent gifts to the victims' families, didn't you?"

He shook his head. "No, why would you think that?"

"Some of the families received paintings that are similar to your style," Ian said curtly.

A nervous tic started at the corner of the man's mouth. "You mean someone is copying my work?"

Ian shouldered his way into the house and gestured for Deputy Whitehorse to begin the search.

Beth struggled to recall details of her abduction. How the man's voice sounded. Was it gruff? Deep? High pitched? Did he have an accent? And what about the boy?

Canvasses lined the wall. There were macabre renditions of bones and the graveyard along with several paintings of a garden with angels overlooking lush fields of grass, red roses, tulips, lilies, and violets.

One featured a rose garden with dark reds and shades of pink. The same shades as the paint on Lewis's apron.

Her heart thumped wildly. Was it painted with blood?

More specifically, Prissy Carson's blood?

Ian's gut instincts nagged at him. Ralph Lewis did not look tough. His body was soft, his face colorless, his voice weak.

Beth said the Boneyard Killer was probably someone who appeared nonthreatening.

The pieces fit.

Ralph Lewis's father was a truck driver. He belonged to the Holy Waters Church. Ralph had been troubled as a teen, painted scenes of bones and graveyards, and his paintings focused on religious symbols.

He also used blood in his artwork.

Although the painting on the canvas wasn't creepy at all—it was almost ethereal.

Ian hadn't seen the paintings the families received. Did Lewis create something beautiful from the girls' blood as some kind of symbol to imply that he'd sent the girls to a better place?

"What do you think you're going to find in here?" Lewis chased after Beth, then moved in front of her as she reached a hand toward the paintings. "Don't touch it. The paint isn't dry yet!"

"Mr. Lewis, take a seat and let us do our jobs," Ian said as Beth disappeared into another room.

"This is crazy," Lewis protested. "Why would you think I had something to do with a murder?"

Ian gestured at the man's stained shirt. "You have blood on you?"

Lewis glanced down at his shirt. "Yes. It's mixed with paint. It's one medium I use. But it's my blood, not someone else's."

Ian's brow lifted. "Really? So I won't find DNA from any of the victims in the paint?"

"No." The man shook his head vehemently.

Beth returned, her gloved hand holding a vial of blood.

"There's a refrigerator in back with dozens of these stored inside," Beth said.

"It's all mine. I've been saving it for months." Lewis wiped his hand on his apron. "It's what makes my work unique. I literally put myself into every piece. It's my signature."

Ian's gaze met Beth's. Serial killers had signatures.

"Call Ward to collect them and have them tested," Ian said.

"You can't take my blood," Lewis snapped. "I need it for my work. I have a showing in two weeks!"

Beth used a calm tone. "If you're innocent, Mr. Lewis, let us run a couple of tests to exclude you as a suspect. I'll make certain your work isn't damaged."

Lewis staggered backward. "I'm calling a lawyer."

Ian gestured to the phone.

Guilty men needed lawyers.

Beth had hoped for details to rush back when she faced Sunny's killer, but that hadn't happened.

Lieutenant Ward arrived with his team to process the house and collect the blood vials. Agents Hamrick and Coulter were transporting the art from the victims' families to the lab for comparison.

One CSI concentrated on Lewis's computer, studying his history and social media sites. Two others went to the main house to search.

If they found references to the cave or pictures the man had taken of the victims, it would help cement the case.

A confession would be better, but she didn't expect one, not unless they discovered concrete evidence to use to coerce him.

Like the murder weapon. Or something that led to that cave. Or—the victims' blood.

Footsteps clattered and Lieutenant Ward appeared, his expression grim. "There's something you should see." Ian gestured to Whitehorse to watch Lewis.

"Did you find the murder weapon?" Beth asked.

"No," Ward replied. "But look at this." With gloved hands, he picked up a black book and opened it.

Lewis had assembled a list of prayers along with photos of his artwork. The last page in the book held several pictures of the boneyard.

Ward had also found more paintings—before and after of the graveyard at Hemlock Holler. Before the tornado had struck, green grass and wildflowers dotted the holler. Another painting depicted the eerie way it looked with the graves uprooted. Bones jutted through the dirt and floated in the floodwater, the thin white gowns shimmering in the moonlight.

The third painting was disturbing in a different way. He'd painted a graveyard in the holler, but this time the mounds of dirt held headstones with names on them.

Retha Allen. Hilary Trenton. Sunny Smith.

There were more graves scattered throughout, several unnamed.

Were they for future victims?

Frustration filled Ian. Those damn paintings were graphic and disturbing, but they hadn't found any definitive proof that Lewis was the unsub.

He'd counted on the man keeping pictures of the victims, some kind of journal describing the kills, articles about the missing girls or about Sunny and Beth. A painting of the cave.

None of that was here.

The blood vials might be the key. He needed to hold the man until the tests were run. He didn't want to chance giving Lewis time to escape—or to grab another victim.

"Ralph Lewis, you are under arrest." He yanked the man's arms behind him and handcuffed him.

"You can't do this," Lewis said, his voice filled with panic.

"I can and I am." Ian pushed him toward the door, reciting his rights as they walked.

Whitehorse appeared, his jaw set. "You want me to take him in?"

"Yes," Ian said. "Agent Fields and I are going to track down his father. By the time we return, maybe he'll be ready to talk."

Or they'd have the proof they needed for an indictment.

"Let me know as soon as the lab analyzes the forensics from the cave and whatever you find here," Ian told Ward.

Ward agreed, and Ian turned to Beth. "You look exhausted. Do you want me to drive you back to your cabin to rest?"

"No," Beth said as she headed to the door. "I need to see the elder Mr. Lewis. Maybe I'll recognize his voice or remember him."

She laid her head against the seat and fell asleep as he drove. Ian's heart squeezed at the strain on her beautiful face. She needed to be at home tucked in bed, safe and sound away from the monsters who had robbed years of her life.

Instead she was charging ahead full speed.

Affection for her mushroomed inside his chest. Today, with her hair in a ponytail, she looked so much like the young girl he'd known from school that he wanted to give her back that time.

If he could rewind the clock, he'd insist his father let him take the car.

All of their lives would have been different if he had.

Ian veered onto a road that led into the countryside, then swerved onto a narrower road and passed Reverend Jim Benton's church. Beside the Holy Waters, a cluster of homes had been built for followers to create a tight community.

Reverend Jim Benton and his wife lived in the parsonage.

Ian found the address for Lewis's father, pulled into the drive, and parked. A black pickup sat near the side of the house, the truck bed covered in a tarp.

Hadn't a black pickup run Beth off the road?

Ian's skin prickled. What if Hugh Lewis was working with his son Ralph, and he'd taken another victim? He could have hidden her in that truck bed.

Beth roused and looked up at him, her eyes cloudy with sleep.

"We're at Hugh Lewis's." Ian gestured toward the truck bed and pulled his gun. Beth's eyes widened in understanding.

Then she removed her weapon and slid from the vehicle.

CHAPTER THIRTY-TWO

Ian paused as he neared the pickup to listen for signs that someone was under the tarp.

Animals skittered in the woods, and a dog barked from one of the neighboring houses. But nothing from the truck.

A noise came from the left, and he jerked his head around, expecting to see Hugh Lewis.

But it was only a trash can lid rolling across the yard.

He motioned for Beth to keep an eye on the door. She signaled in understanding, and he tugged at the edge of the tarp covering the back of the truck.

He held his breath as he peeled it back. The heavy plastic rattled, but no one was inside.

A girl's backpack lay at the edge of the truck bed, a pink jacket wadded up in the corner.

He pulled on gloves and picked up the bag, then examined the contents.

If Lewis had kidnapped another girl, this bag might belong to her.

◆ ◆ ◆

Beth edged her way to the truck, relieved to see it was empty. Ralph Lewis was in custody—maybe they could lock his father up as well before anyone else was hurt.

She examined the front bumper and sides in search of dents or paint damage. A few scratches here and there, but nothing definitive indicating that this was the truck that had hit her.

The front door of the house opened, and a heavyset man in overalls lumbered onto the porch. His face was round and craggy, his white hair shaggy, and a full beard covered his chin and hung to his chest. He adjusted a pair of wire-rimmed glasses on his nose. "What are you two doing on my property?"

Beth's gaze swept over the man in search of a weapon, but he didn't appear to be armed. "I'm Special Agent Beth Fields with the FBI, and this is Sheriff Kimball from Graveyard Falls."

The gold cross dangling on a chain around his neck glinted. But it was chunkier than the ones they'd found with the victims.

"What you doing snooping around my truck?" Lewis growled.

Ian lifted the backpack and jacket. "Who do these belong to?"

Lewis strode down the steps, limping on his left foot. "I reckon it belongs to one of the kids in the neighborhood."

"Why is it in your truck?" Beth asked.

Lewis ran his fingers through his beard. "Sometimes the church borrows my truck to haul the kids to the farm to help gather crops."

"The children ride in the back of the truck?" Beth asked.

"Sure do. But listen, lady," Lewis said, "it's not on a main road. I grew up riding in my daddy's truck and I turned out okay."

Beth bit back a retort as Ian took a step toward the house. "We'd like to come inside."

Lewis covered his mouth on a cough. "Wait just a dad-gum minute. What is this about?"

Ian folded his arms. "We have your son in custody, Mr. Lewis. We have reason to believe he may have kidnapped and killed the girls we found in Hemlock Holler."

Lewis jumped back as if Ian had physically punched him.

"Are you crazy?" He coughed again. "My son may be strange, but he wouldn't hurt a fly."

"Are you sure about that?" Beth said.

"Of course I am."

"Then you won't mind if we look around," Beth said.

His eyes darted back and forth between them. "Go ahead. You won't find anything that incriminates Ralph."

Beth motioned for Ian to start the search. "Go on. I want to talk to Mr. Lewis for a minute." She needed to study him, his voice, force the memories to return.

Was Hugh Lewis the man who'd given her and Sunny that ride?

Ian scanned the street before he entered Hugh Lewis's house. This entire neighborhood was built around that damn cultist church.

His mother and Bernard lived three houses down from the reverend.

Maybe he should drop in on her when he was finished and tell her his father was innocent.

First things first. Find evidence to back up an arrest.

His gaze swept across the interior of the small house. A crucifix hung above the fireplace. Paintings of Jesus, the last supper, and angels decorated the wall.

A Bible lay open on a small table surrounded by white taper candles, the same type found with the bodies.

Ian read the verse. Romans 3:25. "God presented Christ as a sacrifice of atonement, through the shedding of his blood—to be received by faith."

Did Lewis believe the girls should shed their blood as a sacrifice to atone for their sins?

He combed the kitchen in search of the murder weapon—the knife that the man used to kill the girls. He found a set of kitchen knives, but they were dull and there was no evidence of blood on them.

The ME said the murder weapon was a hunting knife, but Ian didn't find one anywhere.

More religious symbols covered the walls. Two bedrooms held similar artwork. Men's clothes filled the closet, and another Bible lay on the nightstand beside the bed, open to Genesis and the story of Adam and Eve.

Nothing incriminating in the room or bathroom.

An antique iron bed covered in a rustic quilt. A pungent odor assaulted him, and he yanked down the covers.

Blood.

He snapped a picture and then opened the closet door. Three boxes of candles were stacked inside along with an ancient trunk.

Fear slithered through him. That trunk was big enough to hold a body.

Ian slowly lifted the latch.

Relief filled him—no body inside.

But the contents were interesting. Two girls' backpacks. A stuffed bear that looked ragged, as if it had been well loved. A purple headband. A tattered girls' gown.

His jaw tightened.

Had these things belonged to the victims?

Snippets of being tied in that cave trickled through Beth's mind. The voice—no, two voices. One deeper than the other. One with more of a Southern drawl.

Beth decided to take the direct approach. "Mr. Lewis, do you remember me?"

His bushy eyebrows climbed his forehead. "Should I?"

"Think back fifteen years."

His mouth grew pinched. "Fifteen years ago?"

Was he stalling by answering her question with a question? "Yes. Two girls were kidnapped in Sweetwater that year. A girl named JJ Jones and another, Sunny Smith."

Recognition dawned in his eyes. "I saw the story on the news. They found one of the girls, but seems like she lost her memory."

"That's right, JJ was found traumatized but alive," Beth said. "Sunny Smith turned up in that graveyard of bones."

A frown deepened the lines around his eyes. "That's terrible. But I don't see what it has to do with me."

Ian appeared, holding a purple headband. Finding a teenage girl's belongings in the man's house was a bad sign. Something was wrong.

Guilt streaked the older man's eyes. "That's not what you think it is."

"It's not a girl's headband?" Ian asked bluntly.

"Where did you get it?" Beth asked.

The man clawed through his beard again. One of his fingers had been cut off. "A girl at church must have left it in the truck."

"Why did you keep it?" Disgusting scenarios bombarded Beth. Had he kept other items from the victims in addition to the blood? Or was the blood his son's version of a trophy?

Lewis averted his gaze. "Just hadn't got around to returning it."

"What about the blood on those sheets?" Ian asked.

Lewis muttered a low sound. "I want to call a lawyer."

Ian grunted. "You're going to need one."

The interrogation at the jail dragged on. Ian vacillated between frustration that they hadn't found sufficient evidence to prove the Lewis men were guilty and hope that the crime lab would.

Hugh Lewis, the father, called a lawyer he knew through the church, a man named Bill Huffstead. He showed up to represent both father and son.

Ian and Beth pressed them for a confession. Both staunchly denied the kidnapping and murder charges.

The son had no alibi for the night Prissy Carson died but insisted he'd been alone in his studio painting. The father claimed he'd attended a revival service led by Reverend Benton.

"Hugh Lewis has explained the presence of the items in his house and truck," Mr. Huffstead said. "Unless you have evidence you haven't disclosed, you need to release these men."

Ian shook his head. "As you know, they have to be arraigned first. Then we'll see about bail." By then, hopefully he'd have the forensics he needed to make the charges stick—and the judge would deny bail.

Then the residents of Graveyard Falls would be safe again and his father's name cleared.

The senior Lewis leaned over and whispered something in his lawyer's ear. Huffstead nodded. "Reverend Benton will confirm Hugh Lewis's alibi."

"How do we know Benton won't lie to cover for him?" Beth asked.

"For God's sake, he's a man of the cloth," Huffstead said irritably.

"The unsub we've been looking for is a religious fanatic who believes he's saving the girls he murders," Ian pointed out. "Ralph Lewis and his paintings fit that description."

Huffstead rapped his knuckles on the table. "Sheriff, get me a list of the times and dates of death for each victim." He gave the Lewis men a reassuring look. "They're looking for a serial killer. When we get those dates, you can figure out where you were during the times of death and provide your alibis."

He laid his business card on the table. "Meanwhile, Sheriff, Agent Fields, my clients are not to be interrogated without my presence. Do you understand?"

Ian folded his arms. "Yes. But know this, when I get the proof I need, they're both going down."

"*If* you get proof," Huffstead said, his tone challenging.

The man insisted on accompanying his clients to the cells alongside Ian, then left.

Deputy Whitehorse had stayed at the Lewis residence while the crime team processed it. Ian called Markum and asked him to canvass the people in Benton's neighborhood with photos of the items they'd found. He wanted to know if those items belonged to church members or to kidnap victims.

Fatigue lined Beth's face. He couldn't remember the last time they'd eaten. And neither had had any decent sleep since the bones were found.

"Come on, I'll drive you back to the cabin."

More storm clouds rolled in as they went to his SUV. Ten minutes later Ian drove by the diner and picked up two specials.

As soon as Beth stepped inside her cabin, she removed her coat. "I have to get a shower, Ian. I feel grungy from the hospital."

"I'll put the food in the oven to stay warm and run to my cabin and grab a shower, too."

Beth disappeared into the bathroom, and the shower kicked on. An image of Beth standing naked beneath the spray of water teased his mind.

He wanted to join her. Hold her. Make sure she was safe.

Put a smile on her face and love her until she cried out his name in pleasure.

His chest clenched. Dammit. She'd been injured and was exhausted. He had to control his libido.

Beth needed rest, not for him to make an advance.

But he couldn't shake her image from his mind as he hurried to his cabin and undressed.

Vanessa huddled on the park bench behind the school. She'd been here for hours, sitting and thinking and crying and wishing that her best friend was alive and that her grandma Cocoa was well.

She couldn't go back to her house, not without her grandma there. In her mind, she could see Grandma Cocoa falling over at the table, hear her strangled breath.

She'd been so scared . . .

Those doctors said Grandma Cocoa was going to make it, but Vanessa didn't know what to believe. She wanted to stay by her grandma's side until she woke up, but Granddaddy Deon wouldn't let her. He could be a hard-ass sometimes. Always talking about praying and doing what God wanted and being a good girl and forgiveness.

He'd forced her to go to school, but she hadn't been able to stay there either.

Not with everyone talking about Prissy's murder.

That stupid boy Blaine that Prissy liked—he was the reason Prissy was dead. Someone ought to make him pay.

Granddaddy would say that was wrong. That she shouldn't hate or want revenge.

But Vanessa figured she must be a hateful person or her own mama wouldn't have left her.

She swiped at her eyes again. She'd cried so much her face was puffy, and her nose was sore from blowing it.

Leaves rustled from the woods, and she peered through the trees. The buses and cars had left hours ago, but the baseball team had a late practice on the field. Blaine was strutting around, laughing like he was some big shot. Prissy's death hadn't fazed him. Selfish prick.

A shadow caught her eye, and she stiffened. She didn't want to talk to anyone. She just wanted to be alone.

"What are you doing here, Vanessa?"

She heard footsteps behind her. Before she could turn to see who it was, he shoved a dark bag over her head.

She tried to scream, but a cold hand covered her mouth and drowned out the sound.

CHAPTER
THIRTY-THREE

Beth's body ached from the assault the night before, but the warm water felt heavenly.

It would feel more blissful if Ian joined her. She closed her eyes as she ran the soapy loofa over her skin. Her body tingled as she imagined Ian's fingers replacing the loofa.

She wanted him.

Beside her in bed. On top of her. Touching her. Loving her. Making her feel alive.

And safe.

Not just safe, though—wanted. Hopeful. As if she might actually have a future and not be a prisoner of her past.

Not that she was totally inexperienced. In college she'd fooled around, but it hadn't meant anything. She'd begun to think she was stunted, that she couldn't feel those giddy sexual feelings people talked about because of what had happened to her.

But Ian had awakened sensations and desires she'd never anticipated.

Desires she wanted to act on.

She rinsed off, climbed out, and pulled on a long-sleeved T-shirt and jeans, then left her hair loose to dry. She was suddenly starving.

And looking forward to seeing Ian.

By the time she emerged from the bathroom, Ian stood in her kitchen looking freshly shaven and showered in clean clothes. His broad shoulders stretched the fabric of his button-down shirt, and his jeans hung low on his muscular hips.

Working with a partner, especially Ian, stirred something inside her that had been dead for a long time. Actually, something that had never thrived because she'd been too afraid to trust anyone. Too afraid to give herself to a man—at least emotionally.

"It's just beef stew, but it's hot," Ian said as he set the food on the counter.

"It smells delicious. Do you want a beer?" Beth asked as she pulled a bottle of white wine from the fridge. She rolled her neck. "After a night like last night and today, I could use a drink."

"A beer would be great." He filled their bowls, and they carried them and the drinks to the table.

She'd expected it to be awkward, but he must have been as exhausted and hungry as she was, because he took a sip of his beer and dug in.

She cleaned her bowl in minutes, then sat back and sipped the wine. "How's your dad?"

His dark gaze rose to meet hers. "In a coma. Time will tell."

Guilt once again mushroomed inside her. "I'm so sorry, Ian. I . . . it's my fault he went to jail. My fault he's in the hospital." Much to her chagrin, tears filled her eyes. "Those girls—Prissy, the others—if I'd remembered sooner, they'd be alive. And you and your family might be together."

Ian had spent half his life being angry with Beth and the world for the upheaval to his family. His father's arrest had driven him to become a cop, to focus on solving crimes. It had also made him bitter.

He was tired of being alone. And blaming the world.

Especially Beth.

Good God, she'd been a victim in the worst kind of way. Thrown away by her mother. Forced into a system that hadn't taken care of her. Abused by the people who should have protected her.

Then she'd witnessed her best friend's murder.

It was time for both of them to let go and live again.

Beth pushed the heels of her hands against her eyes as if embarrassed by her display of emotions.

Ian couldn't restrain himself any longer. He walked around the table and gently pulled her to stand. "Beth, none of this was your fault."

"I shot your father," she said in a tortured whisper.

"He held a knife to your throat. I would have done the same thing if he hadn't released you."

Her eyes searched his. "But he was driven by desperation. He never would have gone to prison if it wasn't for me."

Ian traced a finger along her jaw. "No, Beth, he wouldn't have gone to jail if a serial killer hadn't kidnapped you and Sunny. If he hadn't had files that incriminated the real killer, files he probably didn't realize he had at the time that could prove his innocence."

"He was a good man and suffered for it," Beth said, her voice cracking.

"That's true. You were innocent, too, and you suffered just as much. All the more reason we put this bastard, or this team of killers, away." Ian drew her to him. She felt small and fragile and so damn womanly that his body hardened, desire replacing the need to comfort.

"I don't understand why the unsub let me go. I need to ask the Lewises that tomorrow."

"Think about it, Beth. If his goal was to save sinners, maybe he decided you weren't a sinner. You were unselfish, you offered your life to save your friend. Maybe he realized that you deserved to live."

Understanding dawned in Beth's eyes, and the pain diminished slightly. "I never thought about that. But it doesn't make it right. It's like he's playing God."

Ian leaned closer to her, their noses brushing. "No, it's not right. But like you said in the profile, he thinks he's saving the girls." He stroked her cheek. "We'll get him. We're close. I feel it."

She lifted her hands to rest them on his arms. Their gazes locked. Heat simmered between them. Desire flamed as if someone had lit a match, and he lowered his head and closed his mouth over hers.

Her lips met his, and he tasted sweetness and hunger and a need that rivaled his own.

The flame grew hotter as he deepened the kiss, and she moved her body against him. Her breasts brushed his chest, and when her nipples beaded beneath the thin shirt, he realized she wasn't wearing a bra.

Lust shot through his groin, and he trailed kisses along her neck and throat, eager to taste every inch of her.

♦ ♦ ♦

Beth's body hummed with pleasure as Ian slid his hand beneath her T-shirt. Her nipple beaded as his fingers stroked her sensitive nub, and she raked her hands over his back, urging him closer.

He deepened the kiss, teasing and exploring, and she met his tongue thrust for thrust.

A little voice inside her head warned her that making love to Ian was not a good idea. But her body ignored that voice. She ached for more of his hands and his mouth.

He lowered his mouth and kissed her neck, nipping at her earlobe, and then he tugged her nipple into his mouth and suckled her.

Titillating sensations rippled through her. Ian groaned and raked his hand over her hip. Beth clung to him, savoring the passion in his touch as his fingers danced across her skin.

She wanted more. Wanted to be skin to skin, naked in his arms.

She coaxed him to the bedroom, yanking at his shirt as they kissed again. He lifted her T-shirt over her head, and cool air brushed her skin. Then his hands and mouth brushed her belly and breasts, inflaming her with desire.

Hunger and need sparked to life as he eased her down on the bed, and she gave in to the moment and tugged at his belt.

He yanked at her jeans at the same time.

His hands were big but tender, his body hard yet giving as they stripped each other's clothes and he crawled above her.

He gently stroked her hair from her cheek and searched her face. "Beth?"

The hunger in his tone matched her own and made her body throb for his.

"I want you," she whispered.

He teased her neck with his mouth. "I want you, too."

The fire between them ignited, and he trailed his fingers over her skin again, loving both of her breasts. He tugged one taut nipple into his mouth, and she groaned and threaded her hands in his hair. He teased her other nipple with his fingers, his body moving against hers, and she stroked his calf with her foot.

Instead of joining her, he trailed kisses down her abdomen until he found her sweet spot and ran his tongue along her tender folds. She cried out his name and tugged at his arms, lifting her hips in invitation.

He took a second to roll on a condom, then nudged her legs apart and stroked her thighs with his sex. It was thick and long and throbbed against her. She moved against him, savoring the erotic sensations of his body melding with hers, sweet bliss filling her as he thrust inside her.

Ian's body ached with the need for release, but he wanted to prolong the pleasure. For himself. And for Beth.

She'd been hurt so much. He'd do anything to keep her from being hurt again.

He thrust deeper, her low moan of pleasure nearly driving him over the edge. He held on, though, determined to enjoy every minute of the ride.

Her skin was soft, her touches sensual, her kisses so erotic that she was ruining him for another woman.

She clawed at his back, gripping him tighter as he filled her, then pulled out and thrust inside her again. Passion built, sensations spiraled, and her whisper of need coaxed him into a frenetic rhythm that drove everything from his mind but making love to her.

She met him thrust for thrust, his cock plunging deeper and deeper until she whispered his name and her body spasmed around his. She clutched his hips, driving him to move faster and faster, until he couldn't hold back any longer.

He groaned as he came inside her.

Beth clung to him and he held her tightly, the past fading as the possibility of a future replaced the pain.

Tandy tiptoed to the office door at the church where her husband had called a meeting of the deacons and elders.

Something serious was going down, but as usual she was in the dark. The men in the church believed God meant for them to be the leaders. Women were subservient. Put on earth to serve their husbands.

She tried to remember a time when she'd had a mind of her own and hadn't been afraid to speak it.

It was years ago, before she'd joined the church and taken her vows.

Sometimes she missed that woman with the brains and the spunk.

But that wasn't who she was now. As her mama used to say—you make your bed, Tandy girl, you lie in it.

Voices rumbled inside the room. Earlier Jim had received a call from Hugh Lewis. That call had done something to her husband—he'd gone ashen-faced and reached for a drink.

Jim only took to the whiskey after he'd saved one of the girls.

He said the savings drained him and that he needed sustenance, either in booze or in sex.

She was grateful the nights he chose the whiskey.

Jim's voice boomed through the doorway, and she leaned against it and listened.

"The sheriff and that FBI agent have arrested Hugh Lewis and his son for the boneyard murders."

Shocked responses followed.

"What are we going to do?" one of the deacons asked.

"Do they have evidence?" another man asked.

Tandy gripped her stomach, trying to tamp down the bile.

"I don't know what they have, but Lewis knows to keep his mouth shut about what we're doing here," Jim said. "No one speaks to the police about it, do you understand?"

Fear slithered through Tandy. Jim and the other men claimed they were doing God's will.

She didn't agree. Every time she heard the girls crying and screaming, she wanted to intervene.

She wanted to tell.

But telling would mean she'd be punished. It wouldn't stop them. Nothing would.

◆ ◆ ◆

Beth curled into Ian's arms, warm and sated, and already craving more.

Exhaustion tugged at her limbs, but her mind relived each delicious second Ian had touched her.

He stroked her arm with his fingers, a gentle soothing motion that finally relaxed her into sleep.

She dreamed she was standing in a green field of wildflowers with butterflies fluttering around while she and Ian exchanged wedding vows. The breeze ruffled his hair, making him look sexier than a man had a right to be. But it was the love in his eyes that warmed her body and soul.

The sound of a phone buzzing jarred her from sleep.

Beth opened her eyes, disoriented. She wasn't in a field of flowers. And she was cold.

She raked her hand across the bed, but it was empty.

Damn. The dream . . . was just a dream.

Ian's deep voice echoed from the bathroom. She slipped from bed, pulled on her bathrobe, and went to the door. It was the middle of the night.

"Listen, Deon, have you tried her friends?" Ian asked.

"What's wrong?" Beth whispered.

Ian motioned for her to hang on. "How about the hospital?" A pause. "She's not there. Okay, I'll get my men looking for her right away," Ian said. "Call me if you hear from her or think of someplace she might have gone."

He ended the call, worry flashing in his eyes. "That was Vanessa's grandfather. Vanessa is missing."

CHAPTER
THIRTY-FOUR

Beth fidgeted with the belt to her robe. "Are you sure she's missing?"

A muscle ticked in Ian's jaw. He grabbed his shirt and yanked it on. "She wanted to stay at the hospital with Cocoa, but he thought it would be best if she went to school. He assumed she came home from school and fell asleep last night. But when he went home to change, her bed hadn't been slept in."

Beth's pulse clamored. The poor young girl had suffered heartache over Prissy, and then she'd nearly lost her grandmother.

"She's scared," Beth said, thinking out loud. "Her grandparents are all she has. Did he check with her friends?"

"Yeah, the few she has." Ian pulled on his jeans and zipped them.

Beth couldn't tear her gaze from the masculine movement. Just a short time ago, she'd been lying naked in his arms. She wanted to go back to that blissful place.

Not to think about another missing teenager.

But she couldn't ignore the facts. So she quickly dressed. "Ian, what if she didn't just run off? What if we're wrong about the Lewises and the unsubs are out there? They could have Vanessa."

Fear slashed Ian's face.

"I'll issue an APB for her and get my deputy to search around town." He dropped a quick kiss on her cheek. "Stay here and rest."

Beth pressed one hand to his jaw. "There's no way I could sleep knowing Vanessa is out there alone and scared." Or in the hands of a madman.

Ian gave a quick nod, his expression worried. Then he ran his hand down her backside. "I'm sorry. I wanted to go back to bed with you and wake up with you in the morning."

A small smile tugged at the corner of her mouth. "Good, I was afraid you'd have regrets."

"I think I'm supposed to say that to you."

"Don't bother," Beth said softly. "It was too good to regret it."

She could have sworn his cheeks flushed, but his phone buzzed again and he snatched it up. Knowing they had to look for Vanessa, she hurried into the bathroom and washed her face.

Her cheeks looked pink from their lovemaking, her lips swollen from his kisses.

Making love to Ian again had to wait. She grabbed her gun and holster.

Vanessa was in trouble. She needed them.

They'd failed Prissy Carson.

They couldn't let Vanessa down.

◆ ◆ ◆

Ian gripped the phone with clammy hands. "It's Kimball."

"This is Peyton. I figured Beth might be resting, but you'd want results from forensics as soon as I got them."

"What do you have?"

"I ran a few of Lewis's blood vials and the blood was his. The blood from the paintings Agents Hamrick and Coulter collected matches our vics. Lewis's fingerprints are not anywhere on the paintings either."

Ian chewed over that information. "So Lewis didn't send the paintings to the families?"

"Not unless he has another studio or blood collection that we don't know about."

"He said using his blood was his signature. Was any of his blood in the paintings the families received?"

"Not that the lab found."

"What about the blood on Ralph Lewis's shirt?"

"His own."

Shit. "Did you find anything on those items confiscated from Hugh Lewis's truck?"

"They belonged to three teenagers who attend Benton's church. Your deputies verified it when they canvassed the parishioners." Peyton paused. "All three girls are alive and accounted for. Although all three have been admitted to the ER over the past year."

"What for?"

"One was dehydration, another of a snake bite. The third had bruises on her body as well." Peyton made a sound of disgust. "All three also bore scars from rope burns on their wrists and ankles. Because of that, the doctors notified social services."

"Something's going on in that church community." Ian jangled his keys as Beth pulled on her jacket and indicated she was ready to go.

"Sounds like it," Peyton agreed. "But the girls were taken for medical care by family members."

So the families did care about the girls. Maybe that's why they'd survived.

"You think you could be wrong about the Lewis men?" Peyton asked.

Ian didn't want to be wrong. He wanted this damn case closed. But he had to keep his mind open to the possibility that although the Lewises might be involved in something questionable, they weren't the unsubs.

Which meant the killer—rather, killers—remained on the loose. And one or both of them might have Vanessa.

By six in the morning Deputy Whitehorse had commandeered Weller to organize a search party for Vanessa. Half the town had shown up to search.

Beth's emotions ping-ponged between fear that they had the wrong men in custody and hope that Vanessa was simply upset and hiding out with a friend.

By eight, she and Ian drove to the school to meet with the school principal and counselor.

"I talked to Vanessa's grandfather," the counselor said. "We made an announcement asking anyone who may have talked to or seen Vanessa to come to my office."

"What about that kid Blaine Emerson?" Beth said. "Do you think he'd do something to her?"

Miss Anderson shrugged. "Blaine and his friends are snarky, but he's never been violent before. I talked to him after you left the other day, and he assured me he had no idea what happened to Prissy. He even seemed remorseful about what he'd done."

He should be. "Tell us about Vanessa," Beth said. "Her grandfather mentioned that she didn't have many friends."

"She's shy," the counselor said. "Her only real friend was Prissy. Although I saw a junior, Milo, talking to her."

"Milo?" Beth asked.

"Milo Cain. He's a loner, too. A genius with computers. He's seriously into gaming. He relates more to technology and science than to the other students."

He was the kid wearing the white coat she and Ian had seen at school the day they'd questioned students about Prissy.

"Can you ask him to come to the office?" Ian asked.

She nodded, then checked her computer for his class schedule. "I can't. He's absent today. Father called and said he has the flu."

"Did Vanessa discuss personal problems with you?" Beth asked.

The young woman fidgeted. "You know I can't divulge our private conversations."

"Does that mean you were counseling her?" Ian asked.

Indecision played across the woman's face. "I tried to convince her to join a teen support group, but she wasn't interested."

Ian cleared his throat. "We saw her grandmother and Vanessa talking to Reverend Benton at the revival. Did she ever talk about that?"

A wary look crossed her face. "I probably shouldn't divulge this, but Vanessa said the preacher suggested performing an exorcism to purge the demon trying to possess Vanessa's soul."

Beth went rigid. "The demon?"

"That's what she said." Miss Anderson rolled her eyes. "I planned to talk to her grandmother about it, but Vanessa didn't want me to."

Beth's throat thickened with revulsion. She'd seen the senior Benton performing an exorcism, and it had terrified her.

Was Reverend Benton killing the girls he deemed had failed to be purged of the demons?

Every second that passed increased Ian's anxiety as he drove toward the reverend's house. He relayed the information Peyton had passed along.

"You think we have the wrong men in jail?" Beth asked.

Ian grunted. "I don't know. But we can't take any chances."

Her soft sigh reminded him of the passionate night they'd shared. He wanted her again.

His heartbeat stuttered. He'd never felt such a strong connection to a woman before.

Was it his guilt over what had happened to her, or could there be something else? Was he . . . falling in love with Beth?

An image of the two of them—living together, sharing a house, building a family—teased him. He'd never imagined having a family of his own.

Not . . . since he'd lost his own years ago.

He swung onto the street leading to the church and the parsonage.

A young man and his wife were walking their dog, but she kept her head bent down almost as if she feared the man.

He'd seen his mother display similar behavior.

His stomach clenched into a knot. Just what was going on in this church community? *Was* his mother afraid of Bernard?

He pulled into Benton's drive and parked behind a black Cadillac. Beth opened the door and climbed out, her movements agitated. They rushed up to the door, and he rang the doorbell.

Seconds later, the door opened. Reverend Benton's wife, Tandy, stood on the other side, her arms wrapped around her waist. Dark circles beneath her eyes suggested she hadn't slept much the night before, and her chin quivered as if she wanted to say something but was too afraid.

"We need to speak to your husband," Ian said. "Is he here?"

She jiggled her foot. "What do you need to see him about?"

"We just want to talk to him," Beth said calmly.

Benton's wife lifted a shaky finger and pointed toward a door in the hallway that appeared to lead to a basement. "He won't like it if you go down there."

Ian gave her a cold look. He didn't give a fuck what the man liked.

Beth gently touched her arm. "Mrs. Benton, is there something you'd like to tell us?"

She fidgeted with the wooden cross around her neck. The details of the design were identical to the one his mother wore. Wooden, carved with flowers.

They'd also found crosses with the bodies. Except they were simple gold ones.

Mrs. Benton cast her head down and murmured a no.

Ian strode past her, adrenaline kicking in.

Just as he reached for the doorknob, a scream filled the air.

Beth's eyes widened in alarm, and she slid her gun from the holster. He yanked the door open and raced down the steps.

CHAPTER THIRTY-FIVE

Gun drawn, Beth followed Ian down the steps.

A low light hung from an overhead chain, centered over a table where a young girl lay tied to posts.

Beth's breath caught.

Not Vanessa.

"Please, stop!" the girl cried. "I'm not bad. You can't do this to me!"

"Move away from her," Beth said between gritted teeth.

Ian inched up behind Beth. Out of the corner of her eye, the shiny metal of his gun glinted. "You heard what she said, Reverend," Ian growled.

A woman and man stood to the side, the woman crying in the man's arms as they watched. Had to be the teenager's parents.

The girl jerked at the thick ropes. Her wrists and ankles were raw from fighting to free herself. "Help me, please, help me."

Reverend Benton lifted his hands in surrender, his face stone cold. "You have no right to come into my house with a gun."

Beth's heart hardened. "And you have no right to tie this girl down and torture her."

"I'm not torturing her," Benton said. "And I have every right. I am the spiritual leader of our church and am sanctioned to oversee my parishioners."

Beth rushed to the girl and began to untie her wrists. The girl was sobbing openly, her body shaking, her eyes glazed and unfocused.

Ian addressed the parents. "How can you stand by and watch this man terrorize your child and do nothing?"

"Our daughter is out of control," the father said, a mixture of anger and fear streaking his face. "Reverend Benton knows how to handle adolescents like her."

Beth wanted to slap the creep, but she shot him a venomous look instead as she desperately worked to free the girl.

The teenager's eyes rolled back in her head, and then her body went limp. Beth felt for a pulse. Low and thready but she had one. She punched 911 and asked for an ambulance. "Hurry. We have a teenage girl, unconscious."

"What did you do to her?" Ian barked.

The reverend exchanged questioning looks with the couple. "I was simply performing an exorcism."

"An exorcism?" Beth said shrilly. "This girl is dehydrated. Did you drug her?"

"Everything I did was in the name of the Lord," Benton said. "She was possessed by the devil. I was helping rid her of the demons so we could save her soul."

"We would never let him hurt her," the girl's mother cried.

"He *was* hurting her," Ian snarled. "I'm charging all of you with child endangerment and abuse."

A siren wailed, and Beth rushed up the steps to meet the ambulance. Benton's wife was huddled by the door, as if she had no idea what to do.

Beth bypassed her, greeted the paramedics, and showed them where to go.

A mixture of sympathy and anger warred inside Beth, but she tempered her tone. "You knew what he was doing and stood by and did nothing?"

The woman dropped her head forward, her body trembling. "He was the master, the prophet," she said in a shaky voice. "It's my job as his wife to obey."

Beth fought rage at the man who'd browbeaten her into thinking like that, into not allowing her to be her own person. "I know you're frightened, but it's also your job as a human to protect children. Yet by doing nothing, you endangered that young girl's life."

The woman gave a humble nod but didn't look up. Mrs. Benton exhibited classic signs of spousal abuse. Even if it wasn't physical, Benton had obviously brainwashed her into thinking she was subservient to him.

No telling what he might have done to her if she'd called the police.

"One question," Beth said quietly. "The Boneyard Killer has murdered over a dozen girls. Is your husband the man we're looking for?"

Finally Mrs. Benton lifted her head. An icy chill swept over Beth at the desolate expression in her eyes. "I don't know," she said in a low voice. "I honestly don't know."

Reverend Jim Benton staunchly denied taking Vanessa. "Yes, I spoke with her and her grandmother at the revival. Vanessa was depressed over her friend's death, and I suggested counseling."

Ian paced the small interrogation room in the back of the jail, determined to get to the truth. Beth watched, her demeanor calm, although he sensed she was seething with rage at the man.

"Just as you were counseling that girl in your basement?" Ian asked.

"I was doing God's will, saving these young girls' souls so they could have a future devoted to helping others and fighting sin. I didn't feel Vanessa was possessed, just grieving."

He'd already spoken with the girl's parents and they'd backed him up. Benton's wife refused to talk further.

Ian claimed the chair across from the reverend, his hands planted firmly, his face inches from the preacher's. "Listen to me, if you stashed Vanessa someplace and planned to go back to her, tell me now. Saving her life could go a long way toward lessening your sentence."

Although with multiple murders on the table, he was looking at death row.

"I'm a man of the cloth. I have told you the truth." Contempt flared in Benton's eyes. "Badgering me won't change my answer."

"Because you're a bully," Beth said with derision. "You bully the women in the church and teach the men to do the same."

"God made men to be the leaders," Reverend Benton said with a feral gleam in his eyes. "It is His will." He folded his hands in prayer fashion. "But I will pray for Vanessa and her grandmother. I'll also pray that you find the person responsible for these heinous murders."

Ian barely resisted punching the man as Benton bowed his head and launched into a prayer.

Dammit, they were getting nowhere.

Frustrated, he locked the man in a cell, and he and Beth drove back to the church neighborhood.

They spent half the afternoon questioning neighbors and church members.

When he reached his mother's house, he paused, his nerves on edge. He hadn't seen her in so long that emotions crowded his throat.

He had a job to do, and by God, Vanessa's life depended on him doing it.

"Stay by the car and keep an eye out for anything suspicious," Ian told Beth. "I need to talk to my mother alone."

Beth squeezed his arm.

Ian squared his shoulders and walked to the door. He knocked, surveying the property for Bernie. Thankfully he didn't see him, and the man's car wasn't in the drive.

Everyone they'd talked to in the neighborhood had sung Reverend Benton's praises. A pattern had emerged, though—the wives remained silent, obedient, in the shadow of their husbands.

It was surreal, as if he'd walked into another time.

When no one answered, he pounded on the door. He didn't intend to let his mother ignore him. If Bernie was home and tried to stop him from talking to her, he'd find some reason to haul the bastard in.

Dark clouds rolled across the sky, obscuring the sun and making the wind feel colder than it should be. Footsteps clattered inside, and then someone pushed the front curtain aside and peeked out.

His patience was about gone. "It's me, Mother—open the door. Please."

The curtains slid back into place. More footsteps. Finally the door opened a crack.

His mother's face appeared, although she looked gaunt. Her cheeks were sunken, eyes dark, skin sallow.

"Mother?"

"Go away, Ian. My husband doesn't want you here."

She sounded terrified. "What about you, Mother? Don't you want to see your own son?"

She bit down on her lip, regret mingling with fear on her face. "We have nothing to talk about."

"Yes we do. You're my mother and I love you." She started to shut the door, but he caught it with his hand. "Are you all right? Are you ill?"

"I'm fine," she said in a meek voice.

What was she hiding? Bruises? Was the man beating her?

Ian wedged his foot into the doorway and pushed it open. "We need to talk. What has he done to you?"

His mother lifted a frail hand to her cheek and then brushed at her hair, which she'd let grow long. It was graying, and she'd secured it with a scarf. "He takes care of me, Ian. Now say what you came to say and leave before he returns."

Ian inhaled sharply. "Dad is innocent, Mother."

She shook her head, her expression tired. "We've been through this—"

"No, I mean he's innocent. I have proof. But he's in the hospital now, in a coma."

She fidgeted with her scarf but said nothing.

"I believe Reverend Jim Benton may be involved in the boneyard murders and Jane Jones's kidnapping," Ian said gruffly. "Crime workers are searching Benton's house now for evidence."

His mother gaped at him in shock. "You're wrong. He's a good man."

"He had a girl tied in his basement," Ian said. "They've taken her to the hospital."

"He . . . saves souls over there," his mother said.

"You knew about the exorcisms? You condone his behavior?" he asked, incredulous.

She gave a small shrug. "It's part of our church culture. God wants Reverend Benton to save teenage girls before they become lost as adolescents."

Ian ground his molars. "The killer we're looking for believes he's saving the girls' souls, Mother."

Panic flickered in her eyes for a brief second before she masked it. "Leave, Ian. Please, just let me be in peace."

Sadness flooded Ian. His mother was broken. He should have realized that sooner. His father's arrest and trial had taken its toll and made her weak enough to succumb first to Bernie and now to this preacher who'd swept in like some savior.

They'd stolen what was left of the fight in her—not that she'd had much. She'd given up on his father too easily.

But she was his mother, and he loved her. He'd do whatever he could to save her from this cult and the man who'd dragged her into it.

♦ ♦ ♦

The afternoon passed in a dreary blur. Rain set in, compounding the search efforts.

Vanessa wasn't at the cave or any other place they'd checked.

A despondent feeling swept over Beth. They'd failed Prissy. What if they didn't find Vanessa in time?

The crime team found more girls' clothing and items in Benton's basement. Ian called a meeting of the church community, and parents identified their daughters' personal items.

They didn't belong to any of the victims buried at Hemlock Holler.

She rolled her hands into fists. How archaic a group to punish the females for the sins of the world.

The child abuse and endangerment charges would stick, although they had no proof that Benton was a killer. He'd already consulted with a lawyer.

Michaels had gotten wind of the arrests, had gone to the sheriff's office, and was running with a story about church corruption.

Ian had actually given Michaels that angle to distract him while they continued the search for Vanessa.

As evening fell again, desperation clawed at her.

Vanessa's grandfather called, frantic. The poor man was distraught and wanted his granddaughter back. He wanted answers.

Answers they didn't have.

♦ ♦ ♦

Vanessa stirred, her shoulders and body aching. She blinked, trying to orient herself. Grandma Cocoa was in the hospital. Her grandpa had dropped her off at school.

She hadn't stayed, though. She'd run to the bench at the park behind the school and cried her heart out. Then she'd heard a noise.

She tried to move, but her hands were tied behind her back and her feet were bound at the ankles.

Fear choked her.

Someone had put a bag over her head. Then she was smothering and then . . . then she'd passed out.

She glanced around the dark room—it was a room, wasn't it?

It was so freaking cold. The sound of water dripping made her shiver.

Something smelled bad. A dead animal?

She remembered the story on the news. The story about Prissy being killed and those other bodies in the holler, and she gagged.

Was she going to end up like that?

Nausea cramped her stomach. Her mouth was so dry she could barely swallow. Something tickled her leg. A spider! She shook it off with a squeal.

"Help! Someone please help me!"

Her voice boomeranged back as if she was in a tunnel.

Tears slid down her cheeks. They'd said Grandma Cocoa was going to be okay. But what would happen if Grandma came to and found out Vanessa was missing?

She struggled with the ropes behind her back, determined to pull them free, but they wouldn't budge. Desperate, she raked her hand over the floor to search for a knife or a piece of broken glass or a sharp rock. Something to cut the ropes.

She didn't want to end up like Prissy.

Footsteps sounded in the dark. The whisper of a voice. A door screeched open, letting in a tiny sliver of light.

"Shh, don't cry, Vanessa."

She froze in shock at the voice. She knew him.

She'd trusted him.

But he was going to kill her just like he had Prissy.

CHAPTER
THIRTY-SIX

There was no way Beth could sit in the cabin and do nothing. She paced the task force meeting room while Ian talked to Vanessa's grandfather.

She checked the boards noting the details, dates, times of deaths, locations of victims' homes.

The identity of the girl who'd died thirty years ago was still unknown. Could she be the key to the unsub's identity—rather, the unsubs' identities?

She studied Reverend Benton's photo along with his father's picture. Reverend Wally Benton was familiar and set her nerves on edge, but it wasn't his face in that truck, was it?

Next she examined the photos of Ralph Lewis and his father, Hugh.

She'd healed a lot in fifteen years, and she wasn't that terrified child anymore. She had been trained as an agent.

So why couldn't she see her abductor's face? If he was one of these men on the wall, why didn't she recognize him?

She'd looked into Reverend Jim Benton's eyes earlier, but nothing had clicked into place.

Because none of these men were guilty?

She spread Coach Gleason's files on the conference table and sorted through them, quickly skimming the names.

Ralph Lewis had attended school with her, Sunny, and Ian. But if he wasn't the killer, and the reverend wasn't, then they were missing something.

She flipped through Sheriff Headler's notes. He'd asked the students about her and Sunny.

He'd also questioned students about Kelly Cousins.

Something that looked like coffee had spilled on the page, blurring the writing, and she couldn't read the interview. She phoned Headler. "Who suggested that Kelly Cousins and Coach Gleason were having an illicit relationship?"

"Several of the students," Sheriff Headler said.

"Does anyone specifically stick out in your mind?"

"It was a long time ago, Agent Fields."

"I'm aware of that, but this is important. Think, dammit."

A tense pause. Then a low breath. "Well, one kid was insistent. He seemed disgusted by the whole thing."

"What do you mean?"

"He said the coach shouldn't be looking at young girls, talked about how sinful it was, that someone needed to save them from men like him."

Chill bumps skated up her arms. "What was his name?"

"Some religious name, something like . . . Abel—no, Cain. Last name was Cain. Abram was his first name."

The name Cain struck a bell. She'd seen it somewhere.

Beth checked the notes on the students they'd interviewed at Graveyard Falls. The boy who'd dissed Prissy, Blaine Emerson. The other students who'd been a party to that nasty prank and others who'd witnessed it. No Abel or Abram.

But the counselor had mentioned a boy named Milo Cain.

Milo was the boy in the white coat she'd seen talking to Vanessa. What if he was related to Abram Cain?

Did Milo know where Vanessa was?

She thanked the sheriff, retrieved the yearbook from her high school, and searched for a photo of Abram.

The moment she saw his face, the room spun into a dizzying blur.

Ian tried to calm Vanessa's grandfather, but the man was pacing the hospital waiting room.

Unfortunately, Deon had reason to worry.

"Cocoa is awake, asking for me and Vanessa." His age-spotted hand shook as he pulled at his chin. "If I tell her Vanessa's missing, she might have another heart attack."

Ian swallowed hard. The man was right. He wished to hell he had good news. "Tell her she's with a friend. That she didn't sleep last night and you insisted she rest."

The man sucked in a breath. "Cocoa and I been married nearly forty years. I've never lied to her before."

"We'll find Vanessa," Ian said, although he hated to make promises he might not deliver on. But maybe Beth would find something they'd missed. She'd insisted on returning to the task force room and reviewing all their notes.

"I pray you're right." Vanessa's grandfather's shoulders were slumped, though, the worry radiating from him a palpable force.

Ian gave the man's shoulder a pat. "I'll keep you posted. Let me talk to Beth and see if there are any new developments."

Deon headed back to Cocoa, and Ian hurried to the morgue to meet Beth.

When he entered the task force meeting room, Beth was leaning over the table, one hand rubbing her forehead. The concussion must be worse than he thought.

He rushed to her. "Beth, are you okay?"

A glazed expression muddied her face.

"What's wrong?" he asked.

Beth blinked several times, then seemed to regain her focus. "I've been studying Headler's files as well as your father's." She picked up the yearbook from the floor. "The last name of one of the students Headler interviewed rang a bell. A guy named Cain."

Ian narrowed his eyes. "Cain—that's the blood bank guy's last name."

She nodded and flipped the yearbook to show him a photo. "That's him, Abram Cain. He went to school with us, too."

"I didn't realize he attended our school."

"Abram first pointed the finger at Coach Gleason. Headler said the teen was upset about Kelly Cousins and implied that Coach was being inappropriate with her. He's the reason the sheriff focused on your dad as a suspect." She hesitated. "When I saw him that day at the school, I felt panicky. I thought the blood was the trigger. But when I saw his photo in the yearbook, the same thing happened."

"You think Abram Cain framed Dad because he had something to do with Kelly Cousins's death?" Ian asked.

"Maybe." Beth rubbed her temple again. "There's more, Ian. He used to live next door to the Otters. His father was a trucker and a follower of the Holy Waters Church."

Her words made him stiffen. A trucker, another Benton follower. And he knew the Otters.

Too many coincidences. "So he could have known what was going on at the Otters' house?"

Beth nodded. "If we're dealing with a father-son team, Abram's father could have killed the girl who died thirty years ago. Then he kept on killing. Maybe Abram watched or . . . helped him with Kelly. Now he's the one supposedly saving the girls."

"My God, you think this has gone back generations?"

"It's possible." Beth released a pent-up breath. "There's another connection. Abram Cain has a son named Milo. He's the boy Vanessa was talking to when we were at the school."

The timing was right. Vanessa would have trusted Milo. He could have lured her to go with him.

And if his father was the Boneyard Killer, she'd walked into a trap.

Director Vance had been pinging Beth all day. He was furious she hadn't followed orders.

She decided to hold off responding until she had something concrete to tell him.

"Do you remember Abram's face from the cave?" Ian asked.

"Yes. He was in the truck with May." Now that she remembered his face, more and more details were sifting through her consciousness. He'd read Bible stories to her and Sunny the first night—had read passages about evil and redemption.

Ian gripped his phone. "I'll call and get a warrant."

Beth threw her purse over her shoulder. "Let's go. I have Abram Cain's address. He lives in the same neighborhood as Benton."

As they left they picked up the warrant. Ten minutes later, Ian sped into Cain's neighborhood. He parked at a gray wood house a few houses from his mother's. The driveway was empty, suggesting no one was home.

They pulled their weapons, jumped out, and approached the house. Beth scanned the surrounding area and spotted an outbuilding with a padded lock.

Were the Cains holding Vanessa inside?

If so, how had they managed to do so without a neighbor either seeing or hearing what was going on?

Ian retrieved a crowbar from the back of his SUV and jogged toward the building. Beth stood watch in case the Cains returned while he pried the door open.

Ian shined a flashlight across the dark interior. Shelves lined the walls, but they were empty. So was the room.

If something had been here, Cain had moved it.

Beth crossed the room, searching for anything that might indicate what Cain had stored inside, but the room had been cleaned out and smelled of bleach.

"Let's check the house." Ian strode out the door, and Beth followed.

The Cains had probably seen the police canvassing the neighborhood, gotten spooked, and run.

They hurried toward the house anyway.

Ian scanned the kitchen as he entered, listening for any signs indicating someone was inside.

The kitchen appeared spotless and smelled like Pine-Sol and bleach, just as the outbuilding had.

Either Abram Cain was their unsub and had cleaned to get rid of evidence, or he was OCD about cleanliness.

The fact that he'd lived next door to Beth as a teen and that he'd created suspicion about Ian's father was too coincidental to ignore.

Abram's infatuation with collecting blood from the victims fit with his job at the blood bank. Working at the blood bank also fit with the profile of the unsub believing he was saving people.

Beth had seen images of blood vials in her memories.

Ian opened the cabinet doors and refrigerator in search of the vials but found only dishes and a neatly organized refrigerator holding basic food items.

Beth searched the pantry. Canned goods. No blood. "Clear."

Shoulders knotted, Ian moved to the den. A staircase led to the second floor. Beth gestured that she was going up. He spotted a door in the hallway and pointed to it. A basement would be a good place to hide a girl—or a body.

He turned the doorknob, then stuck his head inside and paused to listen.

Nothing but the windows rattling from the wind.

He shined the flashlight along the stairs and inched down them, gun at the ready in case Abram or his son was hiding out, but the basement was empty as well.

He climbed the steps and heard Beth calling his name. Hope surfaced as he jogged to the second floor. He found Beth in a room he assumed was Milo's—sci-fi posters adorned the walls along with disturbing drawings of supernatural creatures and monsters.

Beth was sitting at the boy's desk, her expression haunted. He scanned the room for blood. "Did you find something?"

"Maybe. Look at these." She pivoted to show him the computer screen. "It's that Deathscape game that all the teens are playing," Beth said. "It was all over Prissy's computer."

Beth clicked a few keys, and an avatar of a young girl encountered several doors, each labeled with a temptation. The theme appeared to be sin and punishment for those sins.

"Milo didn't just play this game," Beth said. "Remember the counselor said he was a genius. He invented it."

◆ ◆ ◆

He gestured toward the young girl who lay on the floor, her eyes wide as she studied him. "She is a sinner, son. It is your time."

"But Father, I am saving her in my own way."

Impatience blended with the need to make this as quick and painless as possible. He did not enjoy the suffering. But sinners had to be punished.

"I understand your need to reinvent our methods," he said. "That is the reason I study the blood. One day I'll figure out a way to purge the bad blood and replace it with untainted blood. But for now, we follow tradition."

He placed the knife in his son's hands. The young girl fought and tugged at her bindings, her sob for help bouncing off the walls of his cavern.

Only no one knew where she was . . .

She could scream at the top of her lungs and no one would hear.

CHAPTER
THIRTY-SEVEN

Milo Cain had designed Deathscape, and he was only a teenager—a scary indicator of his future.

He fit the profile. He was awkward in social situations, didn't have many friends, was raised with strict beliefs under the umbrella of the Holy Waters Church. And he was detail-oriented.

Had he invented his own method of researching potential victims? Was his father grooming him to become a serial killer?

"If we're right and the Cains are responsible," Ian said, "we need to find them fast." He called Peyton for information on what kind of vehicle the father drove, then had her issue a BOLO.

Beth seemed entranced by the game. "The punishments for sin in the game are horrific, each taken from the Bible. Stoning, brick and mortar, floods, snakes, plagues."

"Is there a clue to where he's taking the victims in the game?" Ian asked.

Beth tapped the keyboard. "I'm looking."

"Okay, I'll search the rest of the house."

Ian rummaged through Milo's closet and found another book of graphic sketches. The boy was a meticulous artist, his renditions of Biblical figures, demons, and the devil disturbing.

Ian searched for a key to another house or storage building—nothing. Dammit. The clock was ticking.

In Abram's room, he found work uniforms and casual clothing, but nothing with blood on it. A bookcase was filled with medical journals and research articles on blood disorders.

He discovered a shoebox and opened it, hoping to find a trophy. A stack of envelopes was tucked inside.

He quickly thumbed through them and noted the return addresses. They were from medical schools across the country.

All rejections, dating back ten years.

Ian clutched the box in one hand and went to tell Beth. "Abram Cain wanted to attend med school. He was hoping to find a cure for mental illness through blood, but he was repeatedly rejected."

Beth frowned. "That may be the reason he started keeping the girls' blood, so he could study it."

"What about the artwork the unsub sends the victims?"

"Maybe his way of giving them back part of their daughters." She gestured to the copy of the game in her hand. "I think he took some of the blood vials to a place he could use as a lab. In the video game, there's a sterile underground building."

Ian's mind raced. "The cave we found was far from sterile."

"I know, but this is the son's version. Since we exposed the cave, maybe he took Vanessa to the lab." Beth continued to view the game. "Ian, call Peyton and find out if there's an old abandoned laboratory in the mountains near here or outside Knoxville."

Ian tapped his boot up and down on the floor while he made the call. He quickly told her what they needed, then heard keys tapping as Peyton ran a search.

"Actually, a research company was housed not far from Knoxville, but the company went belly-up," Peyton said. "I'm sending you the GPS coordinates for its location."

"Thanks." Seconds later, with the location in hand, he and Beth rushed to his SUV.

His phone buzzed.

Peyton again.

He quickly connected. "Yeah."

"Ian, we have blood work results from the cave. We may have DNA from the killer."

Her voice sounded odd. Something was wrong. "Who does it belong to?"

A tense pause. "The blood matched someone in our system."

He veered around a curve. "Who it is, dammit?"

"Actually, there are two familial matches. One is to the Cain man. Abram. His father's blood is not in the system. Abram's father actually died a while back."

"You said two. Who else?"

A deep sigh. "I probably should tell Beth this first, but I don't know what to make of it. That's why I called you."

What the hell? "Just spill it, Peyton."

Peyton sighed. "It was a familial match to Beth—I mean to JJ Jones."

Beth struggled to tamp down her panic as Ian flew around the mountain and then onto the highway toward Knoxville. As he hung up the phone, he gave her an odd look.

"What is it?" she asked.

A muscle ticked in his jaw. "We'll talk about it later."

"No, tell me now," Beth said. "Is it Vanessa? Did they find her?"

If Vanessa died, she'd never forgive herself.

"No."

Beth grabbed his arm. "What's wrong, Ian?"

He swung to the left and careened around another car.

"Ian, please talk to me," Beth said softly.

He exhaled, his look dark. "Peyton has results on DNA and blood from the cave, blood they think belongs to the unsub."

"That's good news," Beth said. "Is it Abram Cain's?"

"There is a familial match to him," Ian said through gritted teeth.

"Then we can use it against him," Beth said. "This is evidence we needed."

"There was also a familial match to someone else. Someone in our system."

Beth twisted her hands together. "Who?"

Tense seconds passed. She thought he wasn't going to answer. When he did, Ian's voice grew low. "To you, Beth. The familial match is to you."

Shock waves rolled through Beth. "What are you talking about? There's got to be a mistake."

Ian's sharp look cut her to the bone. "Forensics don't lie, Beth. People do."

Hurt engulfed Beth. "You think I'm lying?"

"I didn't say that," Ian snapped. "But it's odd that the killer turns out to be related to you, yet you forgot his face."

"Because I was traumatized," Beth said. "I told you, I don't have any family. My mother gave me away when I was an infant. I never even knew my father's name."

◆ ◆ ◆

"Maybe you didn't know," Ian said, torn by the hurt in her voice. "But he could have found you. He could have moved next door to Otter to watch you."

Beth wrapped her arms around herself as if she might fall apart. "You can't think that I knew or that I'd cover for him," she said in a strained tone.

He didn't know what to think. "Maybe he told you when he abducted you and you repressed that memory." He gripped the steering wheel as a truck barreled around them. He careened around the turn on two wheels. "We'll discuss it later."

He pointed to a white van ahead and the top of a steel building that looked as if it had been built underground. The plant had been some kind of solar-related project.

Had Cain been using it to conduct his own science experiments with blood?

♦ ♦ ♦

Beth fought hurt and confusion as she and Ian crept up to the building. Ian couldn't possibly think she'd lied or kept the truth from him.

But what if he was right? What if the man had confessed he was her father? The shock of learning her own parent was a killer could have been enough for her to block out his face and repress details of the abduction.

She searched her mind again, but all she remembered was the Bible verses and prayers and preaching. Nothing about being related to the man who'd killed Sunny.

She needed answers. Abram Cain might have them.

Were he and Milo here?

An eerie quiet hovered over the property. Did Cain have surveillance cameras? Would he see them approaching?

"Ready?" Ian mouthed.

She nodded.

Ian pointed toward the right to a cluster of bushes and the door to the underground lab.

Beth followed his lead and provided backup as he eased open the door, and they inched down the steps. It took a moment to adjust to the dark. It was cold. Clammy.

They heard a voice from somewhere deep in the place. Chills cascaded down Beth's neck.

Vanessa.

Crying.

Begging for her life.

Ian paused, listening as well. His gaze met hers, and she gestured to go ahead. She followed, each second that passed torturous.

By the time they reached the end of the hallway, Beth could hardly breathe. Memories of being trapped in the cave threatened to immobilize her.

She didn't realize Ian had gone so far ahead until someone grabbed her from behind and shoved a knife to her neck.

Ian froze. Footsteps behind him, then Beth's low gasp boomeranged off the walls.

Shit. He'd moved too quickly. Left her behind.

Cain or his son had her.

It was Ian's fault.

He spun around, aiming his gun at the place he thought they'd be, but they were gone.

Ian took off at a dead run.

He nearly passed the corridor to the right. But Beth was dragging her feet, making noise.

The direction of the sound launched him forward. He reached the end of the corridor and peered to the left, then the right.

Dear God.

He could hardly believe his eyes.

Vanessa was tied to a metal gurney with her arms extended over a plastic tarp meant to catch excess blood. Cain hadn't bothered to gag her. He must have thought no one would hear her cries for help.

A low voice bellowed below Vanessa's screams. Beth pleading for the man to listen to her as he shoved her down beside Vanessa.

Jesus, God. The sick fuck was going to make her watch—just as he'd forced Beth to witness him slay Sunny.

Ian remained immobile, assessing the situation. He needed to take the man off guard.

Milo was kneeling beside Vanessa, his hand holding hers, as if to comfort her.

Abram Cain pressed a hand on top of Beth's head. "I shouldn't have let you go. I should have ended it like Father said."

"What are you talking about?" Beth said, her voice much calmer than Ian would have expected.

"You were to be my first," Abram said. "I messed up with Kelly. I slit her wrist to drain the bad blood from her, but then I panicked and wrote that suicide note. I should have buried her with the ones Father saved."

"You killed Kelly Cousins?" Beth asked.

He nodded, eyes wild. "She was a sinner. She threw herself at the coach like some two-bit whore."

"Then you came after me and Sunny," Beth said. "Why?"

"Father killed your mother because she enticed him into sin. She gave you away thinking she was protecting you, but he tracked you down. He watched you for years, hoping you wouldn't become one of the whores. But he saw the way Otter looked at you and figured you were already lost."

"He knew what was going on in the Otter house?" Beth said.

"Yes. He watched to see what you would do. Then you ran." His voice cracked. "Father was proud that you resisted. And when you got in the truck with us, I thought we might bond. I finally had a sister."

Beth's face turned ashen.

Ian moved closer. Abram truly believed what he was saying. Which made him even more dangerous.

"You watched him kill other girls and did nothing," Beth said in a steely voice.

"It is our calling," Abram said. "We must save the sinners." A hysterical laugh followed. "I wanted to add to our legacy by studying blood and finding a cure for the evil."

"Prissy wasn't evil, and neither is Vanessa." Beth's labored breathing rattled in the air. "Let her go like you let me go."

"That was a mistake. You came back to hunt me and now *my* son. It has to end."

Ian gripped his weapon as the shiny metal of Abram's knife glinted in the dark.

It was going to end all right.

But Vanessa and Beth wouldn't be the ones to die.

The idea that she might be related to this man sickened Beth and spiked her anger.

He'd stolen so much from her already. She wouldn't let him take anything else.

She had to save Vanessa.

Maybe the boy could be redeemed after all, and she could save two lives.

"Did your son help you murder Prissy?" she asked.

Abram tightened his grip around her neck. The knife pricked her skin. Blood seeped down her throat.

"He has his own ways of saving souls, but he's being indoctrinated tonight. Vanessa will be his first. Of course I must baptize her before the bloodletting."

"Why did you bury the girls in the holler?" Beth asked.

"Because my grandfather—our grandfather—is buried at the top of the hill," he murmured against her ear. "I wanted him to watch over them."

He was crazy.

A shadow moved in the corner. *Ian.*

She didn't hesitate. She jabbed her elbow in the man's side, then stomped on his foot, spun around, and grabbed the knife. He grunted in pain, but he was strong and they fought for the knife.

"Dad!" Milo vaulted toward them.

His voice distracted Abram just long enough for her to knock the knife from the man's hand. Rage flared in his eyes, and he lunged toward her, his hands bared as he closed them around her neck.

A gunshot blasted the air.

Beth tried to catch her breath, but he dragged her down with him. Blood soaked her chest as she collapsed onto the floor.

CHAPTER THIRTY-EIGHT

Ian's heart stopped.

Beth was down and bleeding. Cain was on top of her.

"Get him off me!" Beth shouted.

Her voice jerked Ian from his shock.

Vanessa was screaming, and Milo was running for his father, shouting, "Dad," over and over again.

Afraid Milo was armed, Ian frisked him, then handcuffed him to a metal pipe.

By the time he reached Beth, she'd rolled Cain to the ground and pushed to her feet.

Blood soaked her blouse. "Beth?"

"I'm not hit. It's Cain's blood."

Thank God.

"Help. Get me loose!" Vanessa cried.

Beth ran to her and untied her while Ian knelt to check Cain's pulse. He was alive.

The sound of Vanessa's sobs bounced off the walls as he called for an ambulance.

◆ ◆ ◆

The next few hours were chaos as the paramedics arrived to examine Vanessa and transport Abram to the hospital. The bullet had pierced his abdomen, but the man should live.

Ian hoped he did. He wanted Abram to spend years suffering in prison for what he'd done.

The CSU arrived along with Director Vance to process the lab. They found a collection of the victims' blood vials, neatly labeled and alphabetized.

Another room held paintings that he'd done using the girls' blood. Although he had sent some of the paintings to a few victims' families, he obviously hadn't known where other victims' parents lived because they were runaways living on the streets.

"Abram's father is dead," Director Vance told them. "Peyton found a reference to his death in the obituaries."

"I know, he told me," Beth said.

Director Vance gave Beth a sympathetic look. "The young girl they found who'd been dead thirty years was your mother, Beth."

"Abram's father—my father—killed her," Beth said in a raspy voice. "Apparently my mother gave me away to protect me from him. I guess she loved me after all."

The medics loaded a nearly unconscious Abram Cain onto a stretcher and started toward the ambulance.

"Please let me talk to him," Milo said.

Ian didn't know what to make of the kid yet. He was scary weird. He escorted Milo over to his father but stayed close enough to listen.

"Dad," Milo murmured. "I'm sorry."

Abram Cain had the nerve to smile. Then he lowered his voice to a whisper. "I know you won't let me down, son."

The sinister look Milo and his father exchanged made Ian's blood turn to ice.

◆ ◆ ◆

Beth spent the next week overseeing the indictment of Abram Cain for multiple homicides. Reverend Benton also faced charges of abuse and child endangerment, and Beth was trying to make charges of accomplice to murder fit.

Apparently Abram and Benton were cousins.

Benton had known what Cain was doing all along.

The family believed they were destined to save young women from the streets, each in their own way. It had started generations ago. Some of the bones she'd felt in that cave belonged to her great-grandfather's victims.

The Feds and Ian's deputies continued to search for other victims and another burial spot. So far, Abram refused to tell them anything. Beth had initiated comparing Milo's DNA to the remains from the boneyard to determine if *his* mother was among the victims.

Abram admitted that he and his father were the ones Vinny Barlow had seen at the rest stop when they dumped JJ in the bushes. When the trucker had found her so quickly and spotted them, they'd pretended to be passersby and had called 911.

Beth rubbed her forehead where another headache pulsed. She couldn't believe she shared the same blood as these men.

Or that Ian had doubted her, had thought for a second that she would have protected them.

She packed the last of her clothes to drive back to Knoxville. She needed time to forgive herself for repressing memories that could have saved a dozen lives.

Agent Hamrick's wife, Josie DuKane, who'd written stories of the other serial murders in Graveyard Falls, had reached out to her. Beth was giving Josie the exclusive story with the inside scoop.

Michaels was furious, but his story on the church corruption had earned him enough attention to temporarily placate him.

Ian had called her multiple times. He'd left messages saying that the reverend's wife had spilled her guts about the mistreatment of the women in the church.

He was doing everything in his power to get his mother away from the cult and her husband—who also faced charges of child endangerment because he'd presided over many of the exorcisms.

Agent Coulter's wife, Mona, a counselor, had volunteered to work with Ian's mother and the other women in the church to help them heal and rebuild their lives.

Graveyard Falls could finally go back to normal again.

As if it had ever been normal.

At least Vanessa was home safe, and her grandmother Cocoa was recovering.

Beth stroked the penny on the chain around her neck. She'd found a beautiful cemetery called Memorial Gardens and had given Sunny a proper burial. When she'd placed the jar of pennies inside the casket, the sunshine had popped through the clouds.

She had a feeling it was Sunny smiling down at her from heaven.

Beth shoved her suitcase into the back of her car. She'd come to Graveyard Falls to find Sunny's killer, and she'd achieved that.

Too bad she'd fallen in love with Ian.

Her family had destroyed his.

How could he ever forgive her for that?

Beth was leaving town today.

Ian wanted her to stay. But he had no right to ask.

She'd insisted on following Abram Cain to prison and interrogating him herself. There were holes that needed to be filled in. Questions about the time lapse between her mother's death and the recent victims buried in the holler.

Answers about how many others Abram's father had killed and where their bodies were. They might never know.

The bones Beth had felt on the cave floor belonged to some of them.

Now, Ian held his mother's arm as they entered the hospital. His father was in a coma, but hopefully hearing her voice would bring him out of it. At least he'd made progress. The doctors had weaned his father off the ventilator, which was a good sign. He was breathing on his own.

"I did this to him," his mother said, her voice breaking.

"No, Mom, you didn't," Ian said. "Sheriff Headler dropped the ball by not investigating properly. But Dad is free now, and his name is clear. Hopefully, he can have some kind of future when he wakes up." He squeezed her arm. "Maybe you can, too."

She nodded weakly, her eyes downcast.

A low moan rumbled from the bed, and Ian jerked his head toward his father. He was awake and looking at them.

"I must be in heaven," his father said. "You're both here."

His mother burst into tears, rushed toward his father, and stopped by the bed. "I'm so sorry I didn't believe you, that I deserted you."

His father looked up at him with tears in his eyes. "Thank you, son, for finding the truth."

Ian's gut pinched. "I always believed in you, Dad."

His father reached out his hand to his mother. Emotions swelled in Ian's throat as they hugged. Maybe the two of them would reconcile, and then he'd have his family back again.

But what about Beth?

He wanted her in his life. But what would his family think? There were old hurts, maybe bitterness between his father and Beth.

"Dad, about Beth—I mean JJ. She shot you."

"I brought that on myself." His father's voice cracked. "I was desperate and out of control. I was wrong to pull that knife. Please tell her I'm sorry."

Ian squeezed his father's hand. "I have to talk to her, Dad."

His father nodded. Then Ian left the room. If his father could forgive his mother and Beth, maybe Beth could forgive him.

♦ ♦ ♦

Beth thought being alone would help her heal. Had thought locking up Sunny's killer would make the nightmares go away.

But she was lonelier than ever.

Because she'd tasted what it was like to be loved.

Worse, she'd learned that she'd been bred by a serial killer, that her brother was also a murderer. Who knew if her nephew could be saved?

Director Vance had ordered her to take a leave of absence to heal.

This time, she'd agreed.

She dressed in her running clothes, keeping alert as always as she rode the elevator down to the lobby and scanned the building. Old habits died hard.

Knoxville was teeming with life, with city noises and traffic and people. So different from the small town of Graveyard Falls.

At least here she was anonymous.

Did she still want to be anonymous? To have no one to answer to or come home to at night? No one to love her or hold her or whisper sweet nothings in the dark?

Don't be foolish. Ian didn't love you. If he had, he wouldn't have let you go.

Traffic buzzed by as she clipped her phone to her belt and adjusted her earbuds to listen to her music. A few early morning joggers were already out, people heading to work. She turned to run her usual route toward the river.

It felt good to be outside again, to breathe fresh air, to know that Sunny could rest in peace.

As she'd done a dozen times this past week, she reviewed her conversations with Abram Cain in her head. She'd spent hours interrogating him, probing for answers about the victims and his father.

Her father—his name was Carl.

Such a normal name for such a twisted killer.

She'd also been starved for more information about her mother.

Her name was Mary. She'd grown up in Kentucky but had a rough home life and had run away. Carl met Mary at a truck stop coffee shop. Mary had been young and vulnerable and had thought traveling with him across the country would be exciting.

The fun had ended when she became pregnant. Carl's father did not approve.

Beth jogged past the park, but suddenly the hairs on the back of her neck prickled.

Instincts alert, she glanced over her shoulder but didn't see anyone.

A brittle laugh escaped her. Maybe she would never stop looking for trouble. It was a hazard of her job.

Her job—God. Did she want to go back?

With every case, she was inundated with the vile ugliness of some humans. Just as with her own birth father.

Each generation of the ones who believed in the Calling had developed his own MO, adding to the legacy. Abram had been infatuated with blood and paintings and decided the families should have something of their daughters to keep.

Milo's generation was obsessed with video games and technology, so he'd developed Deathscape.

If Milo wasn't healed, what would the next generation think of?

No . . . he had to be saved. She'd been in touch with counselors who'd gotten him placed in a residential mental health therapy program.

The wind whistled around her as she jogged by the river. Unease pricked at her again.

Irritated, she spun around, braced to fight.

Ian nearly ran into her.

She gaped at him in shock. Was there a problem with the arrest?

He gently gripped her arms. "Beth?"

She searched his face. "What are you doing here?"

"Trying to catch up with you." He was breathing hard, but the wind ruffled his hair and made him look sexier than ever. Or maybe she just missed him that much. She'd never imagined how much love could hurt.

A heartbeat stretched into a full minute, the past a bleakness that hung between them. There had been lies and pain and nightmares and so many deaths.

She didn't want to focus on death anymore.

But panic tapped at her nerve endings. "Is something wrong? Did Abram escape?"

His gaze locked with hers, the bitterness in his eyes when she'd first seen him at the task force gone. "No, he's locked away tight. I just had to see you."

Hope warred with worry. They had things to settle. "Ian, I had no idea about my father."

He cupped her face between his hands, making her heart stutter. "I know. I never thought you did. I was just upset that day. I don't know why I reacted like that."

"We were both afraid for Vanessa," Beth said.

"And I was terrified for you," Ian admitted.

The air between them became charged. People rushed by and traffic noises surrounded them, but Beth felt like they were in their own cocoon.

"I love you," Ian said gruffly. "I love you and I miss you, and I want you in my life."

Beth's heart soared with a happiness she'd never known. Did she really deserve this? Love?

Ian dropped to his knees in front of her and dug something from his pocket. Her eyes widened at the sight of the velvet box.

"Ian?"

His mouth tugged into a smile, but his hand was trembling as he opened the box.

A heart-shaped diamond glittered back.

"I've never given my heart to anyone, Beth. I'm giving it to you." He took her hand in his. His skin felt warm, callused but soft at the same time.

"Will you marry me?"

Shock made her voice quiver. "You want to marry me? After all that's happened?" She bit her lip. "After my family destroyed yours? After I shot your father?"

His chuckle rumbled, deep and full of affection. "Yeah, after all that."

She couldn't believe it. "I told you, I'm damaged, Ian. Evil runs in my blood."

"Evil is not in your blood," Ian said firmly. "You fight evil every day. That means you have a good heart." He pulled her to him and slipped off the band holding her hair into a ponytail, freeing her hair. Gently he ran his fingers through it.

Freeing the strands seemed to free her reservations as well.

His fingers, his smile, the gleam of desire in his eyes warmed Beth inside.

"I'm so damned proud of you," he said gruffly. "And I'm so in love with you that I can't sleep at night."

"I'm in love with you, too." Beth blinked back tears as she pressed her hand over her chest. "This heart has belonged to you since I was fifteen."

A tender smile flickered in Ian's eyes, need and hunger mingling. "I love you, Beth. I've missed you."

"I missed you, too."

He squeezed her hand. "So are you going to answer me? Will you be my wife?"

A tear seeped from her eye as she whispered yes.

Ian slid the ring on her finger, then cupped her face between his hands and kissed her with all the love in his heart.

Beth poured herself into the kiss. The bleakness she'd felt for years faded away as love and hope budded in her heart.

She'd never settled anywhere. Never had a real home.

The sun beamed down on her, sparkling off a shiny penny on the ground, and Sunny's whisper of approval tickled her ear. Sunny wanted Beth to fulfill her dreams for the both of them.

And she would.

She was going to make a family with Ian.

ACKNOWLEDGMENTS

Thanks to my wonderful editor Mallory Braus for her attention to detail and for pushing me to make my characters better! Also to the Montlake team for great covers and marketing—and for letting me write the twisted stories I want to write!

As always, a special thanks to writer friends Stephanie Bond and Jennifer St. Giles for always being there to talk murder over martinis.

And last but not least, thanks to my three children and hubby for not committing me to the loony bin when they hear me talking to myself—there are no words for how much I love you!

ABOUT THE AUTHOR

USA Today bestselling author Rita Herron fell in love with books at the ripe old age of eight, when she read her first Trixie Belden mystery. Twenty years ago, she traded her job as a kindergarten teacher for one as a writer and now has more than ninety romance novels to her credit. She loves penning dark romantic suspense tales, especially those set in small Southern towns. She has received multiple awards, including a Career Achievement Award from *RT Book Reviews* for her work in Series Romantic Suspense, and she is listed on RWA's Honor Roll. Her novels have also received rave reviews and appear regularly on PW's bestseller list. Rita is a native of Atlanta, Georgia, and a proud mother and grandmother.

Photo © 2008 Marie Williams